DETROIT SHUFFLE

Also by D. E. Johnson

The Detroit Electric Scheme
Motor City Shakedown
Detroit Breakdown

DETROIT SHUFFLE

D. E. Johnson

Minotaur Books ❧ New York

For the oppressed and the brave few who battle to free them

This is a work of fiction. All of the characters, organizations, and events portrayed in this novel are either products of the author's imagination or are used fictitiously.

DETROIT SHUFFLE. Copyright © 2013 by Daniel Johnson. All rights reserved. Printed in the United States of America. For information, address St. Martin's Press, 175 Fifth Avenue, New York, N.Y. 10010.

www.minotaurbooks.com

LIBRARY OF CONGRESS CATALOGING-IN-PUBLICATION DATA

Johnson, D. E. (Dan E.)
    Detroit shuffle / D. E. Johnson.—First U.S. Edition.
      p. cm
    ISBN 978-1-250-00676-9 (hardcover)
    ISBN 978-1-250-03648-3 (e-book)
    1. Murder—Investigation—Fiction.   2. Automobile industry and trade—Fiction.   3. Detroit (Mich.)—Fiction.   I. Title.
   PS3610.O328D48 2013
   813'.6—dc23
                                                              2013013935

Minotaur books may be purchased for educational, business, or promotional use. For information on bulk purchases, please contact Macmillan Corporate and Premium Sales Department at 1-800-221-7945, extension 5442, or write specialmarkets@macmillan.com.

First Edition: September 2013

10 9 8 7 6 5 4 3 2 1

ACKNOWLEDGMENTS

Thanks to my early readers: Shelly Johnson, Nicole Cybulski, Grace Shryock, Hannah Johnson, and Yvonne Cooper. They deserve special credit, as I present them with a moving target. The story they start reading seldom has much relationship to what they read at the end.

Likewise, thanks to the members of the West Michigan Writers Workshop for the nagging, carping, and complaining otherwise known as criticism, without which my books would be pale imitations of themselves. I have learned over the years that a good critique group is a precious commodity, and one that I am very lucky to possess.

Thank you to Daniela Rapp, my amazing editor at Minotaur Books, who is always able to cut through the clutter and deliver the evaluation I need to hear. Also, to Alex Glass for his advice and assistance, as well as his belief in me and my vision.

Thanks again to the fine folks at the Benson Ford Research Center at the Henry Ford Museum, the Detroit Historical Museum, the National Automotive History Collection, and the Detroit Public Library.

A big thank you to bookstore owners and employees for all that you do. Hang in there! Thanks as well to all at our public libraries. I have met many of you over the past three years, and you have been nothing but supportive and helpful.

A special thank you to Jack Beatty, the owner of a pair of beautiful Detroit Electric automobiles, for letting me take a spin in one of those beauties, as well as helping out with some of my events.

All mistakes are mine.

CHAPTER ONE

Monday, October 14, 1912

The man in the gray suit slipped behind a marble pillar and appeared again on the other side. His face was shaded by the brim of his fedora, but his eyes seemed to linger on the policemen. Unlike the two thousand other people who filled the convention hall at Wayne Gardens, he didn't even glance at Elizabeth, who stood at the lectern onstage. Behind her, a dozen women sat in front of a burgundy velvet curtain, beneath a large canvas banner that read: MICHIGAN EQUAL SUFFRAGE ASSOCIATION ELECTION RALLY: SPONSORED BY THE DETROIT SUFFRAGE CLUB. Elizabeth held her arms out to her sides, gesturing for the crowd to quiet.

I watched the man from across the hall. I knew he wasn't a policeman. Detective Riordan had set up the security for this event. All the cops were in uniform. The only thing extraordinary about the man was his manner, furtive and nervous. I shook my head. He didn't belong here. The men around me generally fell into one of three classes: portly husbands of rich women, men young enough to still believe they could make a difference, or stereotypical Socialists—emaciated, extravagantly bearded, a crazed cast to their eyes.

Still, I tried to dismiss him. He couldn't be a serious danger. The police had searched everyone coming into the hall this afternoon after the Detroit Suffrage Club had received unspecified threats from some anarchist group.

I turned my attention to Elizabeth, bathed in the spotlight. Most women would have been made harsh by the glare, but Elizabeth's beauty shone so true it put the light to shame. She wore a tight gray skirt and white shirtwaist, an outfit that she would have thought utilitarian and therefore perfect for this audience, but I'm sure she dazzled the rest as she did me.

I felt the weight of the little box in my coat pocket with the diamond ring seated in a silk bed. I was hoping for an opportunity to take her out after the donor party tonight, though she hadn't been encouraging. I'd barely had five minutes with her since I'd gotten out of the hospital, but she had at least invited me to the party. That was a start, though I'd have to share her with a score of other people. We'd planned to go to the flickers the last two weeks, but she'd canceled both times. She said she'd make it this week for sure. I hoped she was right.

Elizabeth leaned down to the microphone and shouted, "It is time for us!"

The crowd roared back their agreement. The noise set my head to ringing, and the pain behind my eyes, which hadn't abated in nearly two months, ratcheted up a notch.

I was just tall enough to be able to look over the sea of hats before me. A black derby or homburg poked up in spots, but most of the chapeaux were in muted colors—pale blues, greens, yellows, lavenders. Though the fashion had gone to narrow-brimmed hats, wealthy women still tended to favor brims that extended as much as a yard wide, and they were standing so close together that their hats touched those of their neighbors, which created the extraordinary effect of a field of massive flowers laid out before me, an effect magnified by the heavy flowery perfume favored by this set that permeated the hall.

Eyes shining, Elizabeth leaned down to the microphone. "We have waited for our time for one hundred and thirty-six years. We have waited, and watched men drive this country to near ruin. Allowed them to make our decisions for us. To brutalize us. To use us and cast us aside as if we were chattel." She paused and glared fiercely at her audience. Her voice raw with emotion, she shouted, "Will we continue to allow men that power?"

"No!" the crowd bellowed back to her.

"The tide of time is with us now!"

Again, the crowd roared. I looked for the man in the gray suit. It took me a moment to find him, as he had moved closer to the stage. I could see none of his features. Now I saw his hand snake up inside his coat and rest there for a moment, as if he were reassuring himself that his gun was still in his shoulder holster.

Oh, Lord. I stood on tiptoes and turned in a circle, looking for Detective Riordan or one of the cops. None were in sight. Of course, for all I knew the man in the gray suit was fingering his Bible or some Socialist manifesto, but . . . I had to be sure.

I began working my way around to the front of the stage, but it was slow going. The Convention Center at Wayne Gardens was packed to the rafters for the event. These people had arrived early to claim spaces at the front and were only very grudgingly giving way for me to pass.

I glanced at Elizabeth as she began speaking again. "Before we hear from Miss Addams and Miss Pankhurst—Sylvia," Elizabeth added, glancing back at the young lady with a smile, "I'd like to introduce one of the great leaders of the woman suffrage movement, who in 1884 helped found the Michigan Equal Suffrage Association, and has given loyal service to its cause ever since. As president, she led the drive that culminated four years ago in a decisive first step—women who pay taxes winning the vote on tax and bond issues—and is now leading us in our fight for real equality. Please join me in welcoming the president of MESA, Mrs. Clara Arthur!" Clapping, Elizabeth stepped back from the lectern and waited for Mrs. Arthur to take her place.

I squeezed between a pair of matrons, tipping my derby and shouting, "Excuse me," so as to be heard over the tumult. Both women gave me withering glances. One reached out and swatted me in the side with her purse. The bag slammed into my burned right hand, and the glove did little to cushion the sharp edge of the bag from striking the inflamed nerves. Swallowing the comment that came to mind, I winced and pushed on.

Mrs. Arthur's powerful voice boomed out over the crowd. "We have an extraordinary opportunity before us!" She paused and continued more quietly, though with no less passion. "But we have only three weeks to persuade those not yet persuaded. We must use that time—all of that time—to exert our will. This is not only a question of the vote. It is a question of a fundamental right of human beings. The right to have a say in our lives. The right to stand shoulder to shoulder with men as equals!"

The crowd responded as one, shouting and surging forward, knocking me off balance and nearly to the floor. My eyes focused again on the spot I'd seen the man. Now he was gone, lost in the sea of hats. I kept moving, zigzagging through the crowd toward the other side of the stage, craning my neck to catch a glimpse of him. There—a hundred feet from me and perhaps fifty feet from the stairway that led backstage.

No one stood guard at the base of the steps.

A policeman was supposed to be there. Detective Riordan had posted men at all the stage entrances. I checked when I arrived. Then again, Riordan's man was a Detroit cop. Was he on someone else's payroll?

I spun again, searching in vain for a policeman. Now I started shoving and shouldering my way toward the steps, shouting, "Coming through! Watch out!"

The crowd quieted again, and Mrs. Arthur got back to it. "You all know the story of Jane Addams and Hull House. Miss Addams, a tireless supporter of our cause, will tell us of her discussions with Colonel Roosevelt and his Progressive Party staff."

The man in the gray suit bobbed in and out of my view as he moved toward the stairway. When he reached it, he turned back once before disappearing up into the darkness. I had narrowed the gap between us to thirty feet, but he was free of the crowd while I still waded through the mass of people.

"Sylvia Pankhurst," Mrs. Arthur continued, "is the daughter of Emmeline and sister of Christabel Pankhurst, two of the other courageous leaders in the British suffrage movement. She has been jailed twice for her actions, sent to the miserable Holloway Prison, where she suffered through months of hunger, thirst, and sleep strikes to bring attention to the plight of English women."

I burst out of the crowd at the stairway and ran up the steps two at a time. At the top, I whirled around, trying to get my bearings in the backstage gloom. A bright band of light glowed around the edge of the curtain, where half a dozen people stood in a pack, trying to see the stage. The man in the gray suit was not among them.

Mrs. Arthur's voice blared on, drilling a hole behind my eyes. I ran around the back of the stage, passing a few men, though none was the one for whom I was looking.

There. The opposite side of the stage. He stood alone, illuminated by a single narrow beam of light that angled across his chest. I ran toward him. Fifty feet away. Dark metal glinted—a pistol. He raised it and aimed down the barrel, concentration so complete he didn't see me streaking at him from the side.

"No!" I shouted and dove at him, batting at the pistol with my hand just as he pulled the trigger. The report blasted my ears. I fell to the floor, pulling the hot gun barrel down with me. I wrenched it from his grip and rolled, then braced myself, reversed the gun, and aimed it at the man.

Except that all I saw before me was shadows. He had already disappeared into the darkness.

Now I heard pandemonium out in the hall—people screaming, shouting, a stampede.

I climbed to my feet, with my bad hand against the side of my head, which felt like it would explode.

"Drop it!" a man shouted. "Now!"

I turned. A Detroit policeman stood ten feet away, his pistol aimed at my face.

When Detective Riordan scowled, the scar that ran from the left corner of his mouth nearly to his ear bulged into a fat burgundy earthworm. I tried to meet his eyes. "Are you out of your mind?" he demanded.

"I'm telling you, it was the other man! Why would I start a riot?"

By the time order had been restored, most of the attendees had fled. Elizabeth and Mrs. Arthur canceled the remainder of the rally. Fortunately the bullet hit no one, and the resulting rush for the doors caused only a few minor injuries, though a number of people had been taken away in ambulances.

Now, half an hour later, the ringing in my ears had decreased to a high-pitched hum. We were jammed in a little office tucked behind the stage. I sat on a wooden chair against the side wall, squeezed between a pair of old filing cabinets. I wore the tinted wire-rimmed glasses

Dr. Miller had given me for light sensitivity, but the bright light in the room still found its way inside, burning into my brain. The room was stifling, and the space tight. Riordan stood across from me, staring down, fedora cocked over his brow. Behind him, the walls were covered in old playbills.

He held up the pistol I had stripped from the grasp of the gunman. "This is your gun."

"It's not. Do you know how many Colt .32s there are in Detroit?"

"Will?" Through the ringing in my ears, Elizabeth's voice called out to me. She cautiously advanced into the office. Mrs. Arthur and Miss Addams stood behind her. "Will, what did you do?"

"I saved someone's life is what I did. There was a man with a gun, and I ran after him. I grabbed the gun just as . . ."

Elizabeth and Detective Riordan had locked eyes. He gave one short shake of his head.

My face got hot. "Why in the hell would you think I'd shoot a gun backstage? I'm no assassin. Anyway, I'm on your side. I *believe* in universal suffrage."

Elizabeth knelt down in front of me. "I know, Will. But you're also . . . confused sometimes."

"It's nothing to do with that. I remember this clearly."

She squeezed my knee. "It could be from the radium."

Only a few months before, the administrator at Eloise Hospital, Wayne County's huge insane asylum, had tried to erase my memory with a massive bombardment of radium to my head. I still had nearly constant headaches, light sensitivity, and gaps in my memory, but right now, even though my head pounded, my mind was crystal clear.

"If I'm so confused," I shot at Riordan, "how did I manage to get backstage? You had a man guarding all the stage entrances, did you not?"

"We did," he said.

"Ladies," a man behind them said. "We need to get you somewhere safe." He stepped into the room. He wore a gray suit, no hat. He looked like a tough, big—six feet, two hundred pounds.

I looked at Elizabeth. "Who's this?"

"Name's Warren Brennan," he said. "With the William J. Burns International Detective Agency."

Gray suit, I thought. I tried to piece him together with what I remembered of the man with the gun. I tried without success to picture his face. He had always been in the shadows. Brennan wore a bushy bottlebrush mustache, with small features in a no-nonsense blocky face. The man with the gun was smaller. Wasn't he? Still, it wouldn't hurt to ask. "Where were you when the gun was fired?"

He gave me a dismissive smile and turned back to Elizabeth. "Miss Hume?"

"Will, don't be silly. Mr. Brennan is protecting us."

"Where was he?"

"I was onstage," Brennan said, "with my eyes on the crowd. I didn't think it would be necessary to watch my client's friends." He shot a glance at Riordan. "I didn't think I had to keep a man everywhere you were supposed to have one, either."

"I'm sorry, Mr. Brennan," Elizabeth said. "All right. We should go, ladies." She turned back to Detective Riordan. "You're not going to arrest Will, are you?"

He took a little longer to answer than I was comfortable with. "No. It was an accident."

"An accident?" I said. "My God! Why don't you believe me?" The headache was rapidly becoming a drill bit cutting into my brain.

"Detective," Brennan said, "I have to get the ladies out of here. We obviously can't rely on the DPD's security."

Riordan shot him a warning glance but said nothing.

"Mr. Brennan," Elizabeth said, "I'm sure they did their best."

"Sorry, miss," he said, with no apology in his voice. "But—I'm sure the detective here will agree with me that the Detroit Police Department is one of the most corrupt in the country. You hired us for a reason. So, could we go now?"

Riordan glared at him. "Mr. Brennan, you are treading on thin ice."

Brennan shook his head. "What I'd like to know is what happened to your man, Detective. He was supposed to be guarding the stairway. If he had been there, this man would never have gotten onstage."

Riordan's ice blue eyes gave Brennan nothing. "I'm looking into that."

Brennan glared back at Riordan. "Are you on the take too, or is it just your man?"

A little smile snuck onto Detective Riordan's face. "I'll give you that one, Mr. Brennan. The next time you impugn my character you and I are going to spend a little time together—and you're not going to like it."

I was hoping Brennan didn't take him up on it. Detective Riordan looked sick and weak—hollowed cheeks, sunken eyes, pale complexion. He didn't look like he'd recovered from the injuries he suffered while he and Elizabeth were trying to find a murderer a few months back. Three of his ribs had been broken, and one of them punctured his spleen. I didn't think he'd be able to take a body punch.

"Fair enough," Brennan said. "We'll see what your bosses think." He threw open the door, strode out without closing it behind him, and began herding the women away.

Elizabeth stopped at the door. "Will, wait for me, will you? We're just going to talk for a few minutes."

I nodded. She left with Brennan and the ladies.

I looked back at Riordan. "Do you know Brennan?"

"Yeah. He headed up the Wabash-alderman case for Burns last summer."

William Burns, otherwise known as "America's Sherlock Holmes," had blown apart a bribery ring in Detroit's city government involving the confiscation of real estate for the expansion of the Wabash railroad terminal. One of Burns's men, posing as a representative of the railroad, had elicited the demands for tribute, which were transmitted from a sound collector to a machine called a Dictograph that recorded the conversations. The case terminated with the arrests of nine alderman. At the moment, Burns's name was solid gold in this city.

"Oh, you were involved in that?" I asked.

"No, but I think they railroaded those aldermen. Tom Glinnan asked me to look into it for him."

Glinnan was the secretary of the council and, prior to being arrested for accepting a thousand-dollar bribe, had been a leading mayoral candidate. Now he was just hoping to stay out of jail.

"He's what?" I asked. "A friend?"

"Of sorts," Riordan said.

"You think the Burnsies cheated somehow?"

"Tom says they planted the thousand dollars in his pocket. I don't know that he's past looking the other way for a bribe, though. The whole thing just stunk."

"To get back to today," I said. "Do you know the cop? The one who left his post?"

He shook his head. "No. Brennan was probably right about him. He claimed he ate some bad oysters and had to run to the toilet. The odds are good he's lying."

"Listen, you need to protect these women. Someone is trying to kill them. Even if you don't believe me, you know what a divisive issue this is. And you have to admit there are a lot of crackpots out there."

"They've received threatening letters at the office. Someone threw a rock through the window last week."

"Any idea who?"

"No.

"What was the threat?"

Shaking his head, he said, "That's confidential information."

"You can't tell *me*? Why?"

"Because I can't trust you in your current condition. Who knows who wrote those letters?"

"As in . . . I might have?"

He nodded.

"What the hell are you talking about? Why would I threaten Elizabeth?"

"People who've gone through what you have get confused. Sometimes they try to reenact the situation that brought them success before. You've had to save Elizabeth. Maybe you're re-creating that situation."

My heart thumped faster. Blood rushed to my face. "So I threaten her, come backstage and shoot my gun, then claim I was fighting with a nonexistent attempted murderer."

He shrugged.

I spat out a laugh. "Is this your theory?"

With his wolf eyes still locked on mine, he slowly shook his head. "But I have to guard against all threats just the same."

Goddamn you! My eyes focused on his nose. The first disorienting punch to the nose, double him over with a shot to the solar plexus, kick him in the face, stomp him into the floor.

Watching me from the corner of his eye, Riordan said, "Now tell me about your gunman. What did the man look like?"

"If you think it's me, what's the sense?"

"I told you—I guard against all threats."

I should do it, I thought. Take this son of a bitch to the floor, take out my frustrations. It wasn't like he hadn't done it to me before. But . . . *Elizabeth.* I had to remember, this was all for Elizabeth. "I couldn't see his face. Frankly, I mostly remember the gun, but my impression was that he was smaller than you or Brennan—more my size. He had dark hair. Gray suit."

He pointed at my head and then my chest. I caught his point. I also had brown hair and wore a gray suit. "Oh, good one, Dr. Freud," I said. "It's my subconscious trying to get me caught."

After watching me another moment, Riordan said, "Anything else you remember?"

I shrugged.

"Not very helpful."

"I saw him at a distance and then I saw him in the dark." I stood. "Can I go now?"

Riordan put his hand on my shoulder. He seemed to tower over me in the little room. His six feet in height had me by four inches, but his ramrod-straight posture and ever-present gray fedora made him seem like an even taller man. "Listen, Will, I know you've been through a lot, but you've got to stay away from the campaign. You're not helping."

"You have to be kidding me! I kept that man from shooting—"

"Elizabeth needs to get through this election." He spoke over the top of me. "Let her do that. That's a remarkable young lady you have there. Saved my life."

I nodded, thinking again about the ring in my coat pocket.

I was waiting for Elizabeth in the convention center's lobby when people suddenly began shouting and screaming in the backstage area.

He's still here! I drew my gun and ran down the hall. When I burst through the door, searching for the man with the gun, all I saw was Elizabeth and her companions with their arms around each other. Many were crying.

"Don't worry," an older man said loudly. "He's a bull moose. He'll be fine."

"He was shot in the chest, James," a woman said through her tears.

I pulled up next to Elizabeth, who was embracing a woman I didn't know, and took her arm. My eyes still scanning the room, I said, "Where is the gunman?"

She stepped back and turned to me. Her eyes floated in tears. "President Roosevelt was shot, Will," she said, her voice strangled. "In Milwaukee. He's still alive, at least he was half an hour ago. We just got the wire." She burst out crying. "They shot the Colonel."

CHAPTER TWO

I walked next to Elizabeth as she hurried from the convention center into the cold night. Warren Brennan strode out in front of us, his eyes scanning the horizon. In the bright lights of the convention center and the streetlamps in front, I could see programs from the rally scattered across the lawn and Jefferson Avenue. Their covers flapped up and down in the frigid wind like the wings of dying seagulls. Across from us, the Detroit River flowed, its depths so dark and solid as to appear impenetrable. The air was heavy and wet, and smelled of more rain to come.

"Elizabeth, he was trying to kill one of you."

"Will . . ." She didn't continue.

"This could have been a coordinated attack. It can't be a coincidence it happened at the same time the Colonel got shot."

She kept walking.

"Someone could have been killed." *I should be the hero here.*

She stopped and faced me, hands on hips. "I'm trying, Will. I'm really trying. I love you, you know that."

"Yes."

She reached up and caressed the side of my head. "I won't abandon you. . . . but you have to know that your brain was damaged. You aren't thinking clearly."

"Miss?" Brennan had rounded back and stood next to her. "You shouldn't be out in the open like this."

"Yes, all right, Mr. Brennan. I'm coming."

I touched her arm. "I know what I saw."

"There were dozens of people backstage. None of them—except for you—saw a gunman. Doesn't that seem improbable?"

"No, it seems like negligence on the part of the police and Mr. Brennan there."

She sighed. "Don't you think it could have been one of your fits?"

"No, I remember it perfectly."

"Do you remember disappearing from the hospital?"

"That was almost three weeks ago. I'm fine now." I had lost nearly an entire day, during which I had vanished from the hospital. I turned up at the Bethune Street police station, asking for Detective Riordan. It wasn't the only—or most recent—example, but it was the only one with which she was familiar. "Elizabeth, that man was trying to kill one of you."

"Miss Hume?" Brennan said. "I must insist."

"Yes, yes." Elizabeth gestured for me to walk with her, and we followed Brennan toward her car. "Then where did he go, Will? The police and the Burns men searched the entire backstage area. No one was there who wasn't supposed to be."

"Then you need to investigate all the people who were supposed to be there."

"Will, they were all supporters. If they're trying to kill us, we should just stop now. Listen, honey. Go home and rest. We'll talk later—at the party. It's too late to cancel that."

"Elizabeth, I'm fine. I can't believe you're taking this attitude with me."

She stopped. Her head tilted back. From behind her, I couldn't see whether her eyes were open and she was looking at the gray sky or, more likely, her eyes were closed and she was focused on the storm clouds within. Turning back to me, she said, "I love you, Will. I'm just worried about you. And we were so close to winning this vote, but now . . ."

"Would you prefer I stay home tonight?"

Her eyes closed for a moment, then popped back open, and she put on a smile. "No, honey." She leaned in and kissed my cheek. "Come."

I nodded, and Elizabeth hurried over to her automobile. I stayed where I was and watched her go, the ring a lead weight in my pocket.

I pulled to the curb in front of my apartment building, a faux castle in miniature, gray granite exterior with towers and turrets, lit by flood lamps on the outside. Most of the apartments throughout its three floors were well-lit. Other than this building, the neighborhood was filled with large three-story Victorians, mostly redbrick single-family homes, though a few housed apartment dwellers.

I threw open the door and walked into the carpeted interior. The lobby had been remodeled while I was performing my investigation at Eloise Hospital a few months ago, and it now matched the exterior, with marble floor and scrolled ceiling, velvet-covered chairs and sofas, and a doorman. The landlord had then immediately increased everyone's rent by ten dollars a month.

I threw open the door and walked inside.

"Good evening, Mr. Anderson."

"Hello, Frank," I replied.

Frank, the night man, stood behind the walnut desk. He was a chunky youth perhaps twenty years old with a round face and a nervous yawning grin that put me in mind of a hippopotamus. In his stiff blue uniform with gold piping and a matching brimless hat, he looked like he belonged in the circus. With a big smile on his face, he said, "No mail for you today, sir."

"Thank you, Frank." The day man, William, seemed competent, but Frank was a little slow on the uptake. So far, I hadn't had a problem with him, and I hoped that continued.

Upstairs, I threw my coat on the sofa and jerked all four of my daggers from the target on the wall. Taking dead aim at the center of the board, I flung the first one. It spun through the air, clattered off the target, and fell to the floor. Soon its three companions joined it in similar positions. I was rusty, I knew that, but this was ridiculous. I picked up the knives, walked behind the sofa again, and took aim.

As I darted around the room, I thought about the would-be assassin. I found knife throwing to be beneficial to my concentration. I needed it at the moment. A man had tried to shoot one of the ladies. He could have been aiming at any of them; at the angle from which I came, all I could tell was he was aiming at someone onstage—Elizabeth, Mrs. Arthur, Miss Pankhurst, or Miss Addams. I wondered, could the assailant have been partners with whoever shot Colonel Roosevelt? If so, Jane Addams would almost certainly have been the target. She was perhaps the best-known woman in the country and without a doubt the most polarizing. Not only that, she famously seconded Roosevelt's nomination for president at the Progressive Party convention last summer. The connection was obvious. Perhaps more assassination attempts had been made as well.

I fell into an easy rhythm—step, spin, fire. Once I found that rhythm, I thought less and less about the knives or the target, and I hit the center again and again.

Elizabeth seemed the least likely target for an assassin. She wasn't well known, nor was she prominent in the state's prosuffrage machine. Sylvia Pankhurst wasn't much different. Her family was famous—some would say infamous—in England for the action they took in support of suffrage, but that was a long way from here. Mrs. Arthur was well known in Michigan, but not someone whose death would send a shock across the country.

No, the target had to have been Miss Addams. She probably hadn't been told an assassin had made it backstage, only that some fool had fired a gun, hoping to trick people into believing him a hero. I'd warn her tonight. She would be going back to Chicago after the party, which I thought—I hoped—might end the danger to Elizabeth. I certainly wouldn't wish harm to Miss Addams, but I'd be happy to see her leave town. Just in case I was wrong, I would watch Elizabeth carefully. In ten days' time, the Suffrage Club was having its last big rally, and she would be the featured speaker. She would be vulnerable before then, but if the assassin was trying to kill her *and* was interested in creating a spectacle, it would surely be when he struck again.

I thrust all four knives into the board and flopped down on the sofa. When I did, the box in my coat pocket dug into my side. I leaned over, pulled it out, and threw it on the coffee table, from which I snatched up a *Horseless Age* magazine I'd just gotten in the mail. I glanced at the pictures, but my mind and my eyes kept returning to the little cherry-wood box.

After my return from Eloise Hospital, I'd spent almost two weeks in Grace Hospital, recovering from the radium "therapy" to which Dr. Beckwith had subjected me. He was getting his, though. According to the newspapers, compulsive dictation was his undoing. He recorded all his important notes onto wire reels. The police had missed the machine in their initial search of the premises, because the device was located next to his secretary's desk in the outer office. She clearly hadn't been a fan of Dr. Beckwith, as she phoned the district attorney after Beckwith had been released without charges being filed.

I didn't know what he said on the wires. I only knew that the prosecutor's office was certain they would win convictions on multiple charges, including conspiracy to commit murder, attempted murder, and acting as an accessory to murder after the fact. Adding insult to injury, his medical license was also in the process of being revoked.

Elizabeth stopped by only three times in the two weeks I was at Grace. Each time she told me excitedly about her work with the Detroit Suffrage Club and said she'd come back the next day—if she could. My head hurt so much I didn't really mind her absence. I spent most of the time sleeping. By the end of the two weeks I was feeling better, though still nothing approaching well. (I find it irritating that saying you feel "better" is most often interpreted as meaning the pain or disease is gone, which then requires you to explain your meaning in gruesome detail. What *I* mean by better is that the constant pain in my head had lessened to a tolerable level, with the occasional migraine splitting my skull.)

What I couldn't understand, and neither could the doctors, was my fits. The first week in the hospital was a blur, with random remembered moments. The doctors said I acted lucidly, and they could never tell what I would remember and what I would not. At least half of that week is lost to me.

The gaps continued, though with less frequency and generally shorter duration. I say generally as a few of these fits lasted a long while. There was the incident at Riordan's station—a twelve-hour loss. Six days ago, I had found myself outside the Toledo, Ohio, train station, with no memory whatever of the previous day. When I was lucid, I seemed, at least to myself, to be in complete control of my faculties. Of course, no one else could expect that of me, never knowing if I was in one of my states.

Until this, my momentum with Elizabeth seemed unstoppable. God knows I had made up, to the extent I ever could, for what I'd done to her. In the last two years, I'd gotten her off drugs, saved her life, and cleared her brother of murder charges.

It had been time to ask her, again, to marry me. The first time I'd nearly destroyed both of us. This time I had intended to make no mistakes.

So much for plans.

I picked up the box and opened it. The half-carat diamond glistened from within the platinum setting. It was the same diamond—my grandmother's—I'd given Elizabeth before, though this time in a new hand-wrought filigree setting, with diamond-studded flowers on the shoulders. I'd spent three hundred dollars, but I thought it worth the price. I know she felt attached to the diamond because of its heritage, but a new setting meant a new beginning for our lives together.

I closed the box and set it on the side table. Dare I show up at the party? Perhaps I'd come late. Elizabeth was embarrassed by me, but surely after she thought about it she would realize I'd done nothing wrong. I'd go—late—but I would wait until she was alone to approach her. Hopefully she would have had time to think, and she would believe that someone other than me had caused the riot. I thought she would understand, but I wasn't so confident that I would risk a public scene.

The engagement ring would stay home. Proposing on the night our candidate was shot would be in very poor taste.

Truth be told, after today, I wouldn't have brought it anyway.

Fat raindrops splatted onto my derby, and I cursed myself for not bringing an umbrella. I pulled my overcoat tightly around me, but its wool absorbed the rain like a sponge, making me colder rather than warmer. I stood staring at the Hotel Cadillac from the grassy divider in the middle of Washington Boulevard. My eyes drifted up to the windows of the ballroom on the top floor, where the party was being held.

The Cadillac had been here forever but still was one of the nicest hotels in the city. I was thinking it was probably a lot more pleasant right now on the inside than it was on the outside. I had to decide what to do.

The rain had been falling steadily for the past hour, thin white lines zipping past a backdrop of electric lights. Cars sped past behind me; in front of me they swerved to miss a bright red Abbott-Detroit limousine double-parked in front, and their tires sprayed a fine mist into my face. Every few minutes, I heard a passerby shout to someone, "TR got shot," or "They shot the Colonel!" Half a dozen people I didn't know had told me. Word was spreading rapidly, but no one seemed to know what had happened or how he was doing.

For the tenth time, I decided to go in and face Elizabeth. This time, when a small break in the traffic appeared, I actually did. I darted across the street and ran to the entrance. The doorman held the door for me, and I skipped past him into the lobby and across the marble floor, feeling the warmth of the place work its way into me. The elevator operator, in his crisp red uniform, brought me up to the sixth floor.

The door opened, and I was welcomed by the muted sound of a crowd and a chamber ensemble. The ballroom was just down the red-carpeted hall, where in front of the closed doors stood a queue of a dozen people and a pair of men in tuxedos. Warren Brennan, the Burns man from this afternoon, checked the invitation of each guest. The other, a slightly less-big fellow with acne-scarred cheeks, searched the men and the handbags of the ladies. He fidgeted in a way that suggested his trousers were not fitting well in the seat. I guessed the tuxedo was not the preferred choice of either of the men.

After checking my soggy overcoat and derby, I queued up. I decided to save my sociability for the party itself and didn't try to engage the people before or behind me in conversation. Each time the door opened, the buzz of a crowd and music swelled, quieting again when the door closed. Finally, it was my turn. I handed Brennan my invitation and opened my coat for the other man.

Brennan scrutinized the invitation, nudged his partner, and spoke quietly into his ear. The man gave a nod and slipped through the door, closing it behind him.

"Just one moment, sir," Brennan said.

"What's the problem?" I asked.

"Routine check is all, nothing to be concerned about."

I tapped my foot on the marble, shot my cuffs, and tried to quell the anger rising in me. He was doing his job. He likely thought I was insane and a danger to the people inside.

After a minute, the other man returned and nodded to Brennan. He handed my invitation back to me. "Thank you, sir. If you would just allow my colleague to search you, you can go right in."

The acne-scarred man searched me and stood aside. I walked into the ballroom, dimly lit by six huge crystal chandeliers, where at least two hundred people milled about. In the corner, a chamber quintet played Mozart. I scanned the room for Elizabeth. The regal Mrs. Arthur and Miss Addams, a severe-looking woman stooped from a childhood illness, stood to the side between a pair of eight-foot-high potted palms, leaning in to speak to each other. Elizabeth and Sylvia Pankhurst stood with their backs to me, speaking to a man and woman of perhaps fifty years of age, behind whom stood a pair of much younger and much larger men.

I walked over to Miss Addams, noticing a big man in a cheap suit hurrying to intercept me. More security. I held my hands out to the sides and said, "I just want to speak with Miss Addams for a moment." He held a hand in front of him to stop me and glanced at her.

She was now looking at me. I thought I saw recognition in her eyes "Yes?" she asked.

I greeted Mrs. Arthur, whom I had met previously, and then turned to Miss Addams and introduced myself.

"What can I do for you, young man?" she asked.

I outlined to her my theory of the coordinated assassinations. As I did, she seemed to listen, but when I finished, she thanked me and turned back to Mrs. Arthur without comment. She hadn't believed a word I said. I was apparently a known lunatic.

Feeling a complete idiot, I drifted over toward Elizabeth's group and stood at one of the small tables about ten feet away so I wouldn't interrupt their conversation. The older man, a short, portly fellow with wavy gray hair, a trimmed handlebar mustache, and a very red nose, was holding court, speaking between puffs on his pipe. He wore a perfectly tailored black silk tuxedo. The men standing behind him gave off the air of bodyguards or perhaps simple thugs. Both were large. One was young and blond, Nordic, with a long face, tall and rangy, the other swarthy, older, with dark hair, thicker through the middle. It was impossible to imagine them being in the same social circle as the couple.

The musicians stopped playing just as I came into listening range. The older man was still speaking. ". . . are not on different sides, ladies." He spoke with a strong Irish brogue. "The MLA supports family. How can we support family if we don't put that same belief in supporting women? Right, my dear?" He looked at the woman, presumably his wife, a matronly lady of ample girth squeezed into a violet silk dress designed for someone thirty years younger and thirty pounds lighter.

She nodded and said he was absolutely right. The man glanced at the younger men behind him, and they burst out in agreement, with the requisite number of sincere nods and hear-hears.

While they did, the man knocked out the ashes from his pipe onto a plate, popped the lid off a small red and white tin of Old English tobacco, and dug his pipe into it. "I hope you catch whoever fired that gun this evening," he said. "Startled me so much I nearly fell to the floor."

"I'm surprised you came," Elizabeth said.

"Wouldn't have missed it. Although now that I think of it, we all missed hearing Miss Addams and Miss Pankhurst"—he nodded to her and smiled—"because of some incompetent."

"It was an accident," Elizabeth said.

"Ah, well." He started in with a harangue regarding the cowardice causing the major political parties to shy away from the universal suffrage movement.

Elizabeth and Sylvia listened to the man blather on with obvious skepticism, mouths tight, arms folded. With Miss Pankhurst's doe eyes, rosebud mouth, and straight brown hair parted in the middle and pulled back from her face, she appeared an ingenue, but I knew the truth was far from that. She was a tough-minded member of Britain's leading suffragette family, and though her stance on methodology was less extreme than that of her mother and older sister, she had dedicated her life to "the Cause" and would brook no nonsense.

Elizabeth smiled. "Perhaps the association would like to make a donation to the Detroit Suffrage Club, Mr. Murphy. Our supporters have been generous, but we certainly would not refuse a show of support from you."

Detroit Shuffle | 21

As he packed his pipe, he said, "That is precisely why I'm here, Miss Hume." He plopped the stem of the pipe into his mouth, reached into the inside pocket of his jacket, and pulled out his wallet, from which he extracted an oversized green check and held it out to Elizabeth. "With our compliments and best wishes."

Elizabeth took the check, glanced at it, and met his eyes again. "Most generous, Mr. Murphy."

He took the pipe from his mouth and used it to gesture toward her, smiling what I thought he believed to be his most sincere smile. "I only wish we could do more, Miss Hume. The Michigan Liquor Association believes in equality for all, regardless of race, creed, religion, or gender."

Elizabeth looked around the room. "Would you mind telling that to the *Free Press* reporter? He's around here somewhere."

Murphy bit the end of the pipe's stem and turned to the side. The Nordic man hurried to pull out his lighter and held it over the pipe while Murphy puffed away like a steam engine. With the pipe lit, he glanced at the bowl with a look of distaste before pulling his watch from his pocket and glancing at it. "I'd love to, but I must get my wife home. My press man is around here somewhere. He'll speak with the reporters." He gave Elizabeth an intimate smile. "You should come see our new offices one of these days. We're in the Dime Savings Bank Building." He nodded toward the door, and the men, one lighting a cigarette, the other a cigar, preceded the older couple as they filed away from Elizabeth and Sylvia.

"How impressive," Elizabeth said as they walked away.

I left my perch and walked up to the ladies. Her forehead furrowed, Elizabeth folded the check in two and opened her purse. Sylvia nodded and smiled at me. "Hello, Will."

"Good evening, Sylvia, Elizabeth."

Elizabeth tucked the check into her bag, gave me a quick hug, and let me buss her on the cheek.

"You'd better cash that one fast," Sylvia said in an amused tone. Her accent was upper-crust, though with a touch of the semi-Scottish brogue of northern England. "I can't imagine his members know he gave you that check."

She was watching the man and his retinue, which had stopped to speak with another man. Something about the new man was familiar, though it was too dark for me to place him, not that I cared anyway. I was here for Elizabeth.

Frowning, Elizabeth said, "A thousand dollars. I don't understand. They have fought us from the start."

"Who was he?" I asked.

"Andrew Murphy," Elizabeth replied. "The director of the Michigan Liquor Association."

"He's the leader of the 'wets,' and he's giving you money?"

"One of them, anyway." She looked off toward the doors. "Strange."

"Perhaps the antiprohibition camp sees they can't stop suffrage," I said, "and they want to win some influence."

"Perhaps." Elizabeth turned back to Sylvia and explained. "Across the state, we've distanced ourselves from the Woman's Christian Temperance Union and the Anti-Saloon League, to try to keep prohibition off the minds of voters, but we haven't been nearly successful enough to receive donations from an association whose sole purpose is to get people to drink more." Her perfectly plump lips turned down in a scowl. "We should speak with Mrs. Arthur."

Sylvia nodded. "Yes, indeed."

"I'm sorry, Will," Elizabeth said. "Would you excuse us for a few minutes?"

"Sure. Before you go, have you heard anything further about Colonel Roosevelt?"

"He went on with the speech. Can you imagine? They say he had a bullet lodged in his chest, and he went on with the speech. I just don't understand why someone would . . ." She lapsed into silence.

"If he went on with the speech, he must be all right."

"The reports say the doctors are very concerned." She shook her head and pointed to the table in the center of the room with a lavish display of foods. "Why don't you get yourself something to eat. I'll be back as soon as I can."

"Of course," I said. "Take your time."

She smiled at me, one of those compassionate smiles one might give to a sick child, before joining arms with Sylvia and crossing the room to Mrs. Arthur and Miss Adams.

Had I not been starving, I would have left immediately. As it was, I grabbed a glass of cider and moseyed over to the food table, where

I picked up a plate and loaded it with crackers and cheese and oysters. I made short work of that and returned to the table to pick at the salmon, or what was left of it, a little pink flesh clinging to the bones between the tail and the very surprised-looking head.

Elizabeth returned. "Mrs. Arthur has been called out of town. We need to have a chat before she goes."

"I hope it's nothing serious."

"No, I don't think so. Will you wait for me?"

Agh. "How long do you think you'll be?"

"Half an hour? Surely no more than an hour."

"All right," I said. "Go on ahead."

"Thanks, Will. I appreciate you being so understanding."

She left to join the other ladies. I picked a little more at the food table, trying to decide what to do. As the camp loony, I had no interest in starting up a conversation only to see the amused look when I introduced myself.

I decided to stay at the food table. When all else fails, eat.

CHAPTER THREE

W ill?" a man behind me said in surprise. "Will Anderson?"
I turned and took him in. It was the man with whom Andrew Murphy had stopped to talk. He was grinning at me, wide-eyed, waiting for me to make the connection. I had no idea. As when I'd noticed him before, something was familiar, but—

"David," he said, pointing at his chest. "David Sanford."

Even with his name supplied, it took a moment. *Davey Sanford.* "Of course," I said. "Hello, Davey. It's been, what . . . since high school?"

"Junior year," he said, looking relieved that I had finally recognized him. "And, please, David. It's not Davey anymore."

"Sure. Sorry." As I recalled, his parents had moved to Detroit at the beginning of high school. We'd never been friends, but he had been well-to-do and did all right for himself socially until his family moved again before our senior year. I took stock of him. I thought of him as being smaller than me and was surprised to see we were about the same height. He had been a good-looking lad, and eight years hadn't changed that. He wore his dark hair parted in the middle, pomaded to the sides, and he had a pair of thick black mustaches with the barest of twists at the ends. He was tall, handsome in a dandyish way, and looked fit.

"How have you been?" he asked.

"Quite well. And you?" I wasn't about to go into it with a man I hadn't seen in the better part of a decade and didn't really know then.

"Fit as a fiddle." He was still grinning. "It's bully to see you. I wondered if you were still in town. I've only just got back."

"Oh? Where've you been?"

"New York, Chicago, San Francisco, and those are just the highlights. I've been seeing the country one job at a time."

"What do you do?"

"Public relations." His grin got wider. "Make other people look good. You must be a supporter, then?"

"Supporter?"

"Of universal suffrage, of course! I think it's the most important issue in the country."

"Oh, right," I said. "I'm a supporter. Although, truth be told, I probably wouldn't be here tonight without ulterior motives."

"Oh? And what might those be?"

"Do you know Elizabeth Hume?"

"I know who she is, of course I do. I've never had the pleasure, however. Wait, now that I think about it, weren't the two of you courting way back when?"

"Yes." I was surprised he remembered. We'd barely known one another. Of course, when a young man saw Elizabeth, she became seared into his memory for life.

The chamber group started playing again—Bach? I couldn't remember.

"Listen." David raised his voice to be heard over the music. "I'm here for work, but I've got that taken care of. Would you like to go downstairs and have a drink? I'd really love to catch up on where your life has taken you."

"Well . . ." This fellow came on like a hurricane. Friendly sort, much friendlier than I was used to. "Sure. Why not. I'm just waiting for Elizabeth anyway."

We walked to the door, and I stopped in front of Brennan, who was still on duty. "Would you ask Miss Hume to get word to me when they finish? I'll be downstairs in the bar."

"Yes, sir," he answered. Complete professionalism.

"Thank you." We got our coats and caught the elevator to the first floor. On the way, the operator said, "Awful about Roosevelt."

"Terrible," David said.

"It sounds like he's going to be all right, though," I said. "The doctors are hopeful."

We discussed his prospects until we reached the first floor. The operator pulled open the gate and said, "Floor number one."

I pressed a quarter into his palm, and David and I walked across the lobby to the hotel bar. As we approached, the soft sound of a piano became clearer. The bar was dark, with muted lights over the tables and booths. The piano sat in a back corner, the sound unobtrusive because of the player's light touch. Perhaps half the seats at the bar were occupied, and a scattering of people sat around the room. That group included a few women, which, while they didn't look particularly scandalous, made me wonder about their employment. It was unusual, though not unheard-of these days, to see a respectable woman inside a drinking establishment. In a hotel saloon, however, even a posh hotel saloon, certain assumptions would be made.

We stood at the bar and waited to be served. I breathed in the smell of alcohol and tried not to enjoy it. Above the liquor bottles against the wall were the obligatory print of *Custer's Last Stand* and a painting of a naked woman, entitled, as they always seemed to be, *Venus*. I suppose the classical reference made it socially acceptable for men to look at a naked woman. I suppose I'd have looked regardless of the title.

I glanced over at David. "You said you were here for work. Who's your employer?"

He reached inside his coat and came out with a business card, which he handed to me.

I read it. "Michigan Liquor Association?"

He grinned again. "Can you believe I got that old so-and-so Murphy to give money to the movement?"

"You did that?"

His answer was an even wider grin.

"Well, you were always persuasive, I do remember that. How did you manage to talk him into it?"

"I just pointed out—about a dozen different ways—that he needs to maintain some influence, no matter what happens."

"Good luck with that. If the amendment passes, he's going to need all the help he can get."

Grinning again. "Yes, it's splendid, isn't it?" Clearly not a loyal employee.

We ordered drinks—he a Jameson's neat, and I a Vernor's ginger ale on the rocks. When we'd gotten them, we sat at one of the tables, the only light a candle inside a red glass holder. The flame danced, suffusing our surroundings with a glow like embers.

We each took a sip of our drinks. The sweet soda bubbled down my throat with its little burn, the closest feeling I'd found to drinking liquor. "How long have you worked for Murphy?" I asked.

"Just started, really. About a month. I'm only contracted until November fifth."

"Election day."

"Exactly," he said.

"What then?"

"I find my next adventure." He glanced down at my hands. "Why don't you take off your gloves?"

"Oh, I had an accident." Holding up my right hand, I said, "I got an acid burn on this one. People always ask questions if I wear only one."

"Oh." He looked curiously at my hand. "Sorry."

I'd finally gotten to the point that my right hand functioned, so long as I used it for tasks that required little dexterity. I didn't need to ask others for help and didn't stand out nearly as much as I had.

He took another drink and pulled a pipe from his side coat pocket. "Isn't it about time for you and Miss Hume to tie the knot?" he asked in a teasing tone. "It's been, what? An eight-year courtship?"

"Not exactly," I said. "We've had a few ups and downs."

"You're happy now, though?"

"Yes. We are."

"Bully. Simply bully." He tapped the pipe upside down against the ashtray and blew through the stem to clear it. "She must be extremely busy," he said. "It's a wonder she can find any time to spend with you." He pulled a tin of Old English from his coat, identical to the one Murphy had, and started to pack his pipe.

"You have no idea," I said. "I'll be happy when the election is over."

"It must especially be strange with all those bodyguards."

I laughed. "Well, it doesn't help with intimacy, that's for certain."

Smiling, he bit the end of his pipe, struck a match, and held it over the bowl while he sucked in the smoke. In seconds the tobacco glowed like the light thrown off by the candle. "Can you ever be alone?"

"Not really. There's always someone in the wings. Ah." I waved off the problem. "There's only three weeks left. She'll be finished then." I wondered if she and I would also be finished.

"The bodyguards are even at her house?"

"Unfortunately."

A memory of David flooded in. He had talked a group of boys from school, including me, into a late-night trip to the haunted mansion on Zug Island. Ghost research, he called it. David's little brother, who couldn't have been more than twelve, tagged along with him. We all thought he was too young until he started scaring the pants off the rest of us. Among other things, the kid had jumped off a ten-foot-high concrete wall, screaming like a banshee, onto my friend Michael Courtney, who burst into tears. Michael never lived it down. That kid was a lunatic.

"How's your little brother?" I asked. *Dead? In prison? Heading a labor union?* "What was his name? Eli?"

"Yes, that's him. He's fine, last I heard. Moved out to New Mexico to mine gold." He sipped his drink. The smoke from his pipe wafted up to my nose, and I inhaled deeply of the smoke, which had a sweet undertone, like cherries. I missed smoking.

We ran out of things to say at the same time. We looked at each other and then the table.

I glanced up at him again. "Perhaps my father might have need of a press man." I took a drink of my soda. "I could ask him if you'd like."

"Why, that is so kind of you," he said. "But I'm not sure where I'll want to go next. Could I let you know?"

"Of course." I pulled my business card holder from my coat and fished out a card for him. "Just give me a call or stop on by."

He took the card and glanced at the front. "Detroit Electric! That must be exciting."

I laughed. "You'd think so, wouldn't you? I work in engineering. It's not that thrilling."

"You must have some inside stories of the automobile industry."

"Well . . . I suppose I do." I told him about setting a—short-lived—world record by reaching 211.3 miles on a single charge of an electric car, and the 1,000-mile endurance tour Mr. Bacon and I had made.

David was glued to me, hanging on every word. When I finished, I said, "That was a couple of years ago. Now I just try to figure out how to make one little piece work with another or how to stamp out a part or something else equally boring." I shook my head. "I picked the wrong career."

"We're young. You've plenty of time to make your life what you want it to be."

"I wish I had your attitude," I said.

"You just have to want to, Will. That's the secret." He looked at his wristwatch and finished his drink. "I hate to say this, but I've got a news release to write. The exciting life of a press man, you know. It was simply bully running into you tonight, Will, simply bully. Maybe we could get together again. What do you say?"

"Well, sure." He was a handful, but why not? I could use a friend, even if he ended up being a long-distance one.

We stood and shook hands. David slipped into his overcoat. "Listen," he said, "I've got to be down at Wayne Pavilion tomorrow night. Could we meet there? Say, eight o'clock? I'd love to hear more of your stories. I'll buy the drinks."

"I . . . I'll have to see if Elizabeth has anything scheduled for me, but let's plan on it. She's likely got eighteen meetings and six meals with donors, which will squeeze me out." I picked up his card and looked at it. "If I can't, is it all right if I phone you at this number?"

"Perfect. Good night, Will." Smiling and shaking his head, he walked away, repeating, "Bully. Simply bully."

He was an enthusiastic one, all right.

After he left, I took a seat at the bar and looked again at his card. He'd gotten the MLA to support the suffrage amendment. That was a confidence job worthy of the greats.

I tucked his card into my breast pocket. We'd have a drink together, perhaps see each other another time before his contract ran out and he headed for ports unknown. From there, perhaps a letter back and forth, ending quickly when we realized we still didn't know one another very well. He was here, he would soon be gone, and I was certain we would have forgotten each other within the year.

I ordered another Vernor's, nursed that for half an hour, and had another. I passed some time discussing baseball with a couple of fellows who were in from Cleveland on business. Our conversation was more pleasant for them than me, as the Naps had regularly thumped the Tigers this year and were likely to do the same next year as well.

The music mesmerized me. I didn't know what the man was playing, but it sounded improvised, variations on a theme, tickled so softy on the keys I thought it might have been my imagination. I had just looked at my watch—11:30—when a tan-capped bellman entered the saloon, calling quietly, "Mr. Anderson. Message for Mr. Anderson."

Raising a gloved hand, I said, "I'm Anderson." Finally. Word from Elizabeth.

He hurried in and handed me an envelope. I gave him a dime from my change on the bar, slit the envelope, and pulled out its contents—a single sheet of hotel stationery. I flipped open the note, expecting to read that Elizabeth would not be able to see me tonight. Instead, I read this, written in a flowing feminine script:

> *Will,*
> *I must talk to you. The election is fixed, and Miss Hume is in danger.*
> *I have no one else to turn to. Room 534. Now! Talk to no one!!*

It was unsigned.

My first response was to laugh. Was this Elizabeth's joke? I looked more carefully at the handwriting. It didn't look like Elizabeth's. Perhaps she had someone else write it for her. But would she joke about the election being fixed or herself being in danger? Unlikely.

Then who in hell could have written this?

My mind was blank. My involvement in this election was peripheral at best. I was just trying—and failing—to support Elizabeth. I believe in universal suffrage, but I wasn't the one leading the charge.

I mentally flipped through the calling cards of the people who might want me dead: the Gianolla gang, any living remnants of the Adamo gang, the Teamsters. They all wanted to kill me at one point, but I hadn't heard from any of them for a number of months now. None seemed like the type to delay gratification. I didn't think I needed to worry about them. Besides, other than the people upstairs, no one knew I was here. Unless . . .

I glanced around as surreptitiously as I could. No one seemed to be paying attention to me. I left my change on the bar, picked up my over-coat, and walked to the front desk, wondering if they would tell me who was registered in that room.

When I caught the attention of the young man behind the desk, I said, "I was speaking with a gentleman here earlier today about busi-ness, and I seem to have lost his card. I've forgotten his last name. He sort of mumbled it out, and I'll never be able to get in touch with him without that."

"Yes, sir?" He was a fresh-faced lad, maybe twenty, with red hair and a gap between his teeth.

"I do remember, though, that he is staying in room 534. Could you please tell me the name of the guest in that room?"

He looked doubtful.

"Please?" I said. "My boss is going to kill me. This is a big contract. If I don't come in tomorrow morning with the name, I'll be out of a job."

He gave me a nod and a knowing grin. He knew that kind of boss as well. We wage earners had to stick together. He glanced around to be sure no one was paying attention, opened up the register, and ran his finger down the page until he came to 534. Leaning in to me, he whispered, "Murphy."

"Andrew Murphy," I said.

He nodded.

"Yes, that's it." I thanked him, hiding my confusion. I walked toward the elevator, deep in thought. How would Murphy even know who I was? Setting aside for a moment the confusion as to why he'd be concerned about the amendment, I couldn't understand why he'd be contacting me.

I returned to the bank of elevators, rode one up to the fifth floor, and followed the signs to room 534. I stood outside for a moment, evaluating the risk. There seemed little. While I knew nothing about Murphy, he obviously knew about my connection with Elizabeth and was using me to communicate with her. I'd play along.

I knocked on the door. A few seconds later, the door opened a crack and someone looked out—a woman? She closed the door, threw off the chain, and opened it.

"Come in," she whispered. "Come in."

I stood in the hall, dumbfounded. Before me stood a woman who had played a part in the murder of the best man I ever knew. A woman I had wanted to kill for two years.

"Hurry, Will." She ducked her head out into the hall, glancing back and forth, and took hold of my arm. "Please. I can't be seen with you."

Still stupefied, I stepped into the room with her.

Even though two years had passed since I'd seen her last, there was no doubt.

It was Sapphira Xanakis.

CHAPTER FOUR

I grabbed hold of Sapphira's arms and shook her. "I ought to kill you here and now."

"P-please, close the door, close the door," she stammered, her voice shot through with panic.

I stalked into the room, glanced around, looked under the bed. We were alone. "Why shouldn't I just haul you off to the police station?"

To my surprise, she started crying. "You should. It would be the kindest thing for me."

I wasn't falling for her nonsense. I grabbed her and shook her again. "Stop that. Now tell me what you have to say."

"Please! Let me close the door. Mr. Murphy will kill me."

Murphy? I'd listen. Releasing her, I said, "Turn around. I'm not going to search you, but I need to know you have no weapons."

Sapphira turned slowly, and I took her in. Her sheer robe and nightgown left her nowhere to hide a hatpin, much less a gun or knife. I'd been attracted to her before, and for good reason. Even though she had lost a great deal of weight, much more than would be healthy, she was still beautiful. Her hair, long and black, hung in ringlets cascading down her shoulders; her large eyes were nearly as dark as her hair; her high cheekbones were flushed pink with rouge; her full lips glistened with bright red lipstick; her body, barely covered by a mint green silk robe over a white nightgown, still hinted at the voluptuousness she had previously possessed.

And she left me cold.

I felt no attraction to this Greek viper. John Cooper's accomplice and mistress. A prostitute. A sophisticated, well-dressed beauty. She had lured me here, but this wasn't the kind of place one would choose for a murder. She was up to no good, of that I had no doubt—but what? I thought to drag her in to the police and let them sort her out, but if she knew of some plot to hurt Elizabeth, I had to get it out of her.

I closed the door, turned, and folded my arms over my chest. "If you've got something to say, say it now."

"Will, I am so sorry."

"I don't care."

"John used me. I had no choice."

"We all have choices, Sapphira."

"You do not understand."

"Stop wasting my time. If you have something to say to me, say it. Then I'll bring you in to the police."

"I belong to Andrew Murphy," she said.

"You're his whore?"

She winced. "I work in his office and . . ." She hung her head. "I am his mistress."

"Why would I care?"

"Because he is fixing the election."

I gave her a measured stare. "Andrew Murphy of the Michigan Liquor Association?"

"Yes."

"Your note said Elizabeth was in danger. How?"

"Mr. Murphy paid men to stop the rallies. There was talk of bombs."

"Who is he paying?"

"I do not know."

"Then what help are you?"

She grabbed my arm. "Please, Will. Talk to Roger. He knows more than I do."

"Roger?"

"Roger Flikklund. He is—was—Mr. Murphy's accountant." She shook her head. "He is very afraid."

"Because?"

"He took something that belongs to Mr. Murphy. He said it was proof of a fix. Talk to him, Will. Please. For Miss Hume's sake." She pulled a folded piece of paper from her bag and handed it to me. "This is where he is hiding. He is expecting you."

"I'm not going to some strange man's home in the middle of the night."

"Tomorrow, then."

"I've got to work tomorrow."

She shook her head in frustration. "Do you want Miss Hume hurt?"

"Of course I don't."

"Then see him."

I stuffed the paper in my pocket. "Why did you contact me?"

She looked back at me for a moment before saying, "I have to live with myself. You have no reason to believe me. I will not ask for forgiveness, because I cannot be forgiven. I do what I have to. Go ahead, call the police. Have me arrested. If you do, I will not fight you." She stepped up closer to me and tilted her head back to look into my eyes. Tears streamed down her cheeks. "I just want a chance. I don't want to be a . . . I hate my life." She balled up her fist and held it tightly against her chest. "I want to be free. I want to live like an American."

I reckoned it a safe bet to believe absolutely nothing she said. Still, if this Flikklund fellow had something of Murphy's, it might be helpful. I'd think about it, but I wouldn't tell her. No sense giving her confederate a warning. "You work in the MLA office?"

"Yes."

"So that Murphy can justify to his wife why you are around?"

"I can type," she said mildly, "but . . . yes."

"Maybe I'll come down and see if you really do."

"No, please. Mr. Murphy will kill me if he finds out I am talking to you. Now you must leave. He will be here as soon as he puts his wife to bed. Please, Will. Talk to Roger."

"Who is Murphy working with?"

"I have not seen anyone. I have only heard some of Mr. Murphy's telephone calls and talks with his guards."

I couldn't tell if she was lying. Her words rang of truth.

"Please, Will," she said. "You must leave."

"Sapphira, if you are lying to me, you won't live through the week."

"I am telling the truth."

I walked out into the hall. The door closed, and the chain clanked against it as she slid it into place. I headed for the elevators, thinking. She'd completely fooled me two years ago, but at the time I was a drunk wallowing in self-pity. Now I was clearheaded, though for how long was anyone's guess. Could she be telling the truth? This could all be a plot to extract revenge against me for killing her lover, but it seemed she was going a long way around to get to that location. A knife to the liver would have been much more elegant.

No. I could see no angle for her in telling me this.

I'd go see Mr. Flikklund and hear him out. And I would be well armed.

I returned to the bar in the lobby and waited another hour before going up to the sixth floor to find the ballroom empty. I wondered if Brennan had even given Elizabeth my message. I supposed she could have tried the saloon while I was up in Sapphira's room.

Wow, would she be angry to hear those words. I planned on keeping that to myself.

I pulled up in front of Elizabeth's house at a quarter to three in the morning. I was not looking forward to her reaction to me ringing the bell at this hour, but I didn't feel I could let this wait. If I wanted to keep my job, I had to be at work at 7:00 A.M. As to the part about wanting to keep my job, it was not my priority. However, keeping a roof over my head was, and I had no other ideas on how to accomplish that. My father was unlikely to become soft enough in the head to give me an allowance at this point in either of our lives.

I switched off the car and hurried up the sidewalk and steps to the door. The house was dark and still. I knocked softly four times, waited, and tried again. Were I able to wake Elizabeth without rousing the houseful of lunatics who now resided here, I would be a happy man. Elizabeth's brother, Robert, slept as lightly as a gnat, and Francis Beckwith didn't strike me as a sound sleeper either. The two of them used to wander the tunnels of Eloise Hospital by night when they couldn't sleep. Now it was the Hume residence that was haunted by lunatics, though perhaps I should call them "schizophrenics," a much less loaded term, to my way of thinking. They weren't crazy, exactly. Their minds worked more or less rationally, but somehow the connections were different in their brains, which not only gave them odd thoughts and obsessions, it made them mercurial. Francis would be calm one moment, spitting mad the next. Robert's moods turned from placidity to crying jags. They were visibly different from normal people as well. Both men moved like automatons, and they abhorred the touch of others.

A curtain twitched. A ghostly face appeared in the window—Robert Hume. He stared at me blankly, then he was gone. Only a few short weeks ago, no one, including Elizabeth, had publicly acknowledged Robert as her older brother—he was considered a "cousin"—and no one would ever have expected that he and Francis Beckwith would seek refuge at the Humes' home.

Dr. Beckwith, the Eloise administrator, was in jail, so Francis, nineteen years old, had to live apart from his father for the first time in his life. He and Robert were temporarily living with the Humes, though exactly what "temporarily" meant was in question. Elizabeth and Bridie Kelly, the young woman I viewed as the savior of the family, were serving as the men's de facto guardians. Elizabeth had hired Bridie a few months earlier to watch over her mother, who had been besieged by ever-increasing bouts of dementia.

Inside the house, footsteps sounded, coming closer. Alberts, the old gentleman who was the Humes' butler and chauffeur and Elizabeth's surrogate father figure, switched on the outdoor light and peered out at me, then opened the door and let me in.

"Good evening," he whispered. Always the gentleman.

"I need to speak with Elizabeth. It's urgent."

Robert lurked in the hallway, half in sight, a thin wraith in a white nightshirt. I didn't see Francis, which I hoped meant he was still sleeping.

A voice spoke, only inches from my left ear. "Hello, John Doe."

I jumped. "My God, Francis, if you keep sneaking up on people like that, someone's going to shoot you."

Francis, wearing a black tricorner hat with white piping, looked at me over the wire frames of his eyeglasses. "I was not sneaking. That is an unfair accusation."

When I was masquerading as an amnesia patient at Eloise Hospital, they called me "John Doe." That was how Francis learned my name, and I was finding it very difficult to change his mind. He was built like a rail, with brown hair and a face that matched his build—long and thin. His most notable physical characteristic was that he showed no emotion, other than when he was angry; then he showed plenty. Otherwise, his face was as flat as his words, no smiles, no frowns, no sign of enthusiasm.

"Do not call me Francis," he said. "My name is Edward."

"Edward?" I repeated. "What?"

"Edward Teach," Francis said with an enigmatic smile.

"You're Blackbeard now?"

The corner of his mouth twitched. "Some may call me that."

He had a scrub of nearly blond whiskers on his chin and cheeks. It surprised me that the Humes weren't paying more attention to his personal grooming. I saw now that he wore a crimson sash tied around his waist. A belt over his nightshirt. Very chic.

I looked back to Alberts for help. He only raised his eyebrows. "Would you get Elizabeth for me?" I asked him. "I need to speak with her—privately."

He bent slightly from the waist, which, when done by Alberts, felt like the deepest of bows in a European court. "I'll see what I can do, sir." He took a step backward, then pivoted and headed up the staircase.

"Do you realize it is almost three o'clock in the morning?" Francis asked. His wiry hair tufted up at all angles.

"I do," I replied.

Robert peeked out from the doorway and said in a meek voice, "Elizabeth needs her sleep."

"I need my sleep," Francis said. "I am helping the Detroit Suffrage Club win the election."

"Me, too," Robert whispered.

"That's great," I said. "You're working with Elizabeth?"

"Yes," Francis said. "You should leave."

I told him I would take only a minute of her time. With a pair of guardians like this, she could become a modern Sleeping Beauty.

Fortunately, I had Alberts on my side, because Elizabeth appeared at the top of the steps a moment later, tying her yellow bathrobe around her, and he started trying to herd the boys off to bed.

Elizabeth yawned. "Oh, Will. I was hoping to see you after the party."

"Yes. I, uh, well, I was detained. I need to speak with you on a most urgent matter."

"Fine. Go to the den. I'll be there in a moment."

"Blackbeard could make John Doe walk the plank," Francis said hopefully. "That way you could sleep."

"No, you boys run off to bed," she said. "You shouldn't be up now either."

Alberts rousted Robert and Francis and sent them off to bed. I retreated to the den, turned on one of the lamps, and sat on the burgundy sofa in the sitting area. When I looked around, it occurred to me that the boys must have spent some time in here recently. The Gainsborough reproduction had been swung out on its hinges, exposing the wall safe behind it, and the bookshelf that served as the entryway for Judge Hume's secret room was tilted open.

No one but Elizabeth's father had known of the room's existence, and the secret had died with him two years ago. A few months back, the Humes' maid had discovered the room by accidentally triggering the door mechanism. She'd alerted Elizabeth, who searched the room and found records of her father's involvement in illegal activities. She'd also found a great deal of cash. She never told me what information the documents contained or how much money she'd found. Though I was curious, I was not gauche enough to ask. The matter ended when she burned the papers and donated the money to charity.

My reverie abruptly halted when I heard Elizabeth padding down the hallway. I stood and walked toward the door. She came to me, and we kissed, and my anxiety melted away.

"How are you doing?" she whispered.

"I'm fine." So long as she questioned my sanity, I would give no other answer. "Did you hear anything else about the Colonel?"

Shaking her head, she sat on the sofa and took my hand, pulling me down next to her. She leaned against me, snuggling in close.

"What do you think this means for the election?" I asked.

"Neither Taft nor Wilson has the courage to support suffrage." She yawned. "If Colonel Roosevelt . . . dies, the Progressives will have no chance—suffrage will have no chance."

"What if he stays in the race?"

"He and Taft will split the Republicans, which will leave us with Wilson. I hoped at least that Roosevelt would bring Progressive Party voters out, perhaps win some of the lesser offices."

"This will rally the troops," I said. "You'll see a bigger show of support for your cause."

"I don't know." She worried at the belt of her bathrobe. "Perhaps. If the amendment doesn't pass in this election, it's hard to see when it will have a chance again."

"It will pass, Elizabeth. You've said so yourself. The support is overwhelming."

She yawned again. "I hope you're right."

I glanced down at her. The lamp cast a soft white glow on her face, hiding half of it in shadows like a Rembrandt portrait. Above us, bedsprings creaked and quieted. Rain pattered against the windows. Elizabeth breathed deeply, and her shoulder and arm moved ever so slightly against me as she did. I wanted to freeze this moment of calm and intimacy, our first such moment since Eloise Hospital.

I didn't want to ruin it, but I hadn't come here for this. "I've had . . . an interesting night."

"How so?"

"I don't know if this is true, but I was told tonight that the Michigan Liquor Association is scheming to fix the election and disrupt suffrage rallies by any means possible. I think the man I disarmed tonight was part of it."

Her breath expelled from her mouth in a whoosh. She sat back heavily against the sofa and turned so she could look at me full on.

"Andrew Murphy," I said, "the man from the party, is allegedly behind the whole thing."

Her eyes narrowed, and she shook her head. "Then why would he give us money?"

"His new press man claims to have talked him into it, so they would have a chance to maintain influence."

"I wish him good luck with that," she said sarcastically. "Why would the press man have told you about the scheme?"

"Well, no, that wasn't him. I was contacted tonight at the hotel while I was waiting for you."

"By who?"

"Frankly, I'd rather not say."

"You won't share his identity with me? Will? Really?"

I could see I was going to have to spill the beans—beans that would have a decidedly rotten taste for Elizabeth. "First of all, let me say that I plan to investigate the information I was given before I take it completely seriously. I just don't want to risk you being hurt."

"Who was it?"

I took a deep breath. "Sapphira Xanakis."

Elizabeth's eyes opened wide, and she leaned forward. She was silent, though I could see her outrage building. Finally she burst out with, "Are you out of your mind?"

"Just forget about her. I'll chase down the lead she—"

"She tried to kill us, Will! Both of us. Have you forgotten that already?"

"No, but—"

"But nothing. Phone Detective Riordan in the morning and tell him what corner she's working so he can pick her up."

"Elizabeth, that's not fair."

"No? She's a prostitute, isn't she?"

"She was, yes."

"And now—what? She's a lady of honesty and virtue?"

"She claims to be working for Murphy. Listen, I know how ridiculous this sounds. I'm not taking her word for anything. I'm going to check it out and see if there's any validity to what she's saying. I just wanted to warn you immediately, so you could take precautions."

Elizabeth stared down at the coffee table in front of her for a moment, thinking. Glancing up at me again, she said, "How have your headaches been?"

"Better."

"And how is work?"

"It's . . . all right. They've got us working on a big presentation we're making to the bosses on Thursday. I'm just hoping they leave me out of it." I looked at the grandfather clock against the wall and coughed out a laugh, realizing the amount of sleep I was going to get. "I have to be there in less than four hours."

She took my hand. "I love you. You know that, don't you?"

"I—yes."

"Get some sleep. Leave this alone."

"Elizabeth, I don't—"

"I need you to let me do this, Will. Think about it. What are we supposed to do, cancel the rallies?" I started to reply, but she cut me off. "I know you mean the best, Will—really, I do—but we have professionals to do this work. Give me the information, and I'll have one of the Burns men look into it."

She was right. Of course she was. I walked over to the desk and took a note card from the drawer, copied Flikklund's name and address, and handed it to Elizabeth. "This is the man who is supposed to have information about the election fixing. She said he worked for the MLA until he was fired."

Elizabeth took the card, set it on the table, and stood. "Thank you for being sensible. We will look into it. Now, would you like to sleep here? I'm sure we've got a bed made up somewhere."

"No, thank you. I'll have to be home soon to change anyway."

She walked me out of the den and down the hallway. The boys were nowhere in sight, and I imagined Alberts tucking them both in bed, a ridiculous thought. "We're still on for Thursday night, aren't we?" she asked. "For the flickers?"

"Yes. Maybe we could have dinner first?"

"That would be nice. We'll have to see how my schedule works out, though."

"Should I plan on picking you up here or at your office?"

"I expect I'll still be at the office. Let's plan on six. I'll sneak out the back if I have to. I don't want to miss this installment."

What Happened to Mary was a national sensation—for women. The serial had opened to great fanfare last summer, and the publicity only increased every month with each new episode. This was the first time a flicker had been serialized, with the story being laid out, twelve minutes at a time, every month for a year, while also being told in the

Ladies World magazine. I'd become mildly interested, though of course spending time with Elizabeth was the primary attraction.

"Oh, and don't forget," she said. "Church Sunday morning with my mother and the boys. I am definitely going to need your help."

That I *had* forgotten. Church was not the priority to me that it was to her. In fact, since I'd moved from my parents' home, I'd only gone when specifically invited by them or Elizabeth. She wouldn't be able to handle all three of them if her mother was having one of her spells or Francis was in one of his moods. If both happened, she and I wouldn't be enough.

"I'll be here."

"Good. By eight thirty. Last time you made us late."

"Then it's a darn good thing you have your own pew. Otherwise we might have had to give up on the service altogether." *Which would have been nice.*

"It's embarrassing for my mother, Will. She likes things just right."

"I know. I'm sorry. Any chance of seeing you before Thursday?"

"Sorry, I don't think so. Meetings, dinners, more meetings—the usual. I'll be glad when this is over." At the door, Elizabeth stood on tiptoe and kissed me. "Now get some sleep," she said. "I'll be fine."

CHAPTER FIVE

Tuesday, October 15, 1912

A t seven o'clock, I put on the tinted glasses Dr. Miller had given me and stumbled out into the bright morning to my Torpedo, which was fortunately still parked against the curb. My brain barely acknowledged the trip to the Detroit Electric Automobile Company, other than when I was stopped by traffic at Woodward and Grand Boulevard. The men at the streetcar stop milled about, with a great wailing and gnashing of teeth:

"They should've lynched the son of a bitch!" one man shouted.

"No, the Colonel oughtta've shot him down like the dog he is."

Then I heard another man utter the always popular refrain, "What has this country come to?"

It wasn't an unreasonable question. McKinley—shot to death by an anarchist. His successor, Roosevelt—nearly killed last night. Taft, the incumbent, was the only one immune, and that was only because the anarchists considered him so ineffectual they didn't care enough to shoot him.

Finally I was able to get through the intersection. Even with the dark brown lenses, my eyes did not want to open. The car splashed through the puddles and crashed into potholes hidden by still more puddles on the cobblestone streets. It was nearly half past by the time I pulled to the curb on Clay Avenue in front of the factory. Five minutes later, I ran through the door into the Mechanical Engineering office.

My boss, Mr. Hanley, a stout man with a wispy blond beard, was standing at the desk of one of my colleagues when I entered the room. He glanced at the wall clock and then cocked his head at me. Gesturing at my face, he said, "Did you catch a dose?"

"What?" His question made no sense.

"The sunglasses. Got yourself a case of the syph?"

"Oh." I took off the glasses and tucked them in my breast pocket. "No. Just headaches."

He looked skeptical but didn't comment further. People his age wouldn't consider tinted glasses for fear they would be thought to be suffering from syphilis, which was in fact why Dr. Miller had them lying around his office. Wearing sunglasses was getting less unusual, though, among healthy younger people since Florence Lawrence, the Biograph girl, had taken to wearing them to hide her familiar face from adoring fans. I liked wearing them. I thought they gave me a mysterious air. However, that was not at all useful at the office.

None of the other men made eye contact with me as I squeezed past to my desk. Like most of the other professional offices at the factory, this was a large white room with desks lined up in rows, in our case twelve desks in rows of six. Mine was in the back corner, which suited me just fine. Hanley's throne was at the head of the room in an enclosed office. His desk faced us, and he spent more time watching us through the window than doing anything else. I didn't really know anyone, as I'd been here only a few weeks, and that over a period of months. I had the impression the other men didn't care for me, which could have been for a number of reasons. I was the son of the owner; I didn't show up for weeks and still didn't get fired; I was a lousy engineer; I had a less than sparkling personality.

A *Detroit Free Press* lay folded on the desk of the man in front of me. As I passed him, I asked if he would mind me looking at it. He glanced up, gave me a distracted nod, and returned to his work. I unfolded the paper. These words were splashed across the top of the page in thick black ink:

ROOSEVELT SHOT BY ANARCHIST

I sat at my desk and read the article. The Colonel had been shot in the breast at point-blank range with a .32. The assassin was an avowed anarchist, a European immigrant named John Schrank. Fortunately for the Colonel, the bullet had to plow through his metal spectacle case and fifty folded pages of manuscript in his coat pocket, which slowed it down enough to keep him alive. Then he went on and spoke for an hour before collapsing. *The Bull Moose.* The bullet was still in his chest, and he'd been taken to Chicago for surgery. The outcome was in doubt.

I took a quick scan of headlines but saw no other attempted assassinations, only a tongue-in-cheek article about a "Suffrage staffer" accidentally firing a gun last night, ending the Detroit Suffrage Club's second-to-last major rally, under the headline RALLY PANIC, SIX INJURED. The good news—I wasn't named.

Back to Roosevelt. Anarchists didn't seem too particular as to whom they shot, but was Jane Addams a worthy second potting, rather than Wilson or Taft, who were bound to have been stumping last night, too, or even a senator or congressman? However, no one else at the rally made nearly as much sense as Miss Addams, which left me with troubling possibilities—that the two events were completely unrelated or only peripherally connected. And, of course, there was the third possibility—that I was off my rocker.

I'd already taken too much time with this. I tapped the paper against the fellow's back, and he reached over his shoulder to take it. Now I opened my briefcase and pulled out the file on our new design. It was bold, unprecedented—and, I thought, stupid. In two days, we'd see if my father agreed with me. In the meantime, I had to become familiar with what I was already thinking of as "Hanley's Folly."

As the day went on, my thoughts kept returning to what Sapphira had told me. Elizabeth did not want to hear of a threat, and I feared that she and her Burns allies would not give the matter the attention it deserved.

As soon as I could leave, I would go see Mr. Flikklund.

Hanley left at four, and I waited ten minutes before following him out. What he didn't know wouldn't hurt me. Ten minutes later, I turned from Sanders onto Dumfries, a street of blinding white. The houses were whitewashed, the lawns ivory with hints of dead weeds poking through the dust. Only portions of roofs and the electric poles gave contrast, and those only above fifteen feet. The Detroit Salt Mining Company lay two hundred feet behind the house, surrounded by a tall fence constructed of wire shaped into small squares. The creaky conveyor carried huge chunks of salt from the depths of the 1,200-foot-deep mine and spewed them into an open train car. Even this far away the noise was deafening—bangs, slams, thuds.

A hundred-foot-tall white cloud drifted east toward the river and, fortunately, away from me. The yard of the mine was completely white, needing only a snowman to appear a ready-made winter scene.

The rest of the area, however, wasn't so well disguised. It lay in the lowlands that flowed on a dusty white trail from the River Rouge on the east through a mucky swamp to the west. I'm sure at one time this space would have been green and filled with birdsong, the clicks and whirs of insects, and the croaks of frogs. Now the ground was covered with a poisonous white coating. I'd been to the Atlantic Ocean, and it had taken me a while to get used to the odor—salt, seaweed, life and death. The air here smelled somewhat similar, but no odor survived except the dry tang of salt—not even death. For acres around, everything had been dead so long it left no olfactory evidence.

A cheery place to hide, indeed.

The address was for a small, rectangular, one-story house with a flat roof at the dead end of Dumfries. Along with what I assumed to be white paint on the clapboard siding, the flat roof gave the building the most appropriate appearance of a gigantic salt block. I pulled the Torpedo onto the shoulder and shut it off. No hint of life showed inside the house, with dark curtains pulled tight.

Pulling the Colt .32 from my shoulder holster, I checked the load, cocked the gun, and clicked on the safety. Rather than returning it to the holster, I put the Colt in the left side pocket of my overcoat, so I could hold it on whoever answered the door without drawing suspicion.

Most of the houses here had dozens of lines of recent footprints in the salt crust leading to and from their doors. Not Flikklund's. Four sets of footprints led to the front door—two toward the house, the other two away. Either two people had been here or one man, Flikklund, presumably, had come, left, and returned. The footprints looked similar, if not identical.

Crunching across the front yard, I hurried to the door and pressed the buzzer. It was stuck, glued by the salt, and didn't ring. I pounded on the door with the heel of my right hand, so that I could keep my left on the grip of the Colt. With the first knock, pain blazed through my hand, so I waited, hoping for a response. After perhaps thirty seconds, I knocked again.

The curtain to my right twitched. After waiting another fifteen seconds, I started pounding on the door. Either this idiot would receive me or I would forget this whole thing here and now.

I heard the snap of a dead bolt unlocking. The door opened a crack, stopped by the snap of a heavy chain. "Stop it, stop it," a man whispered. I couldn't see him in the dark of the house. "They'll hear you."

"Who?"

"What's your name?"

"Will Anderson. Are you—"

"Prove it."

I pulled my identification from my wallet and slipped the card between his fingers. His hand withdrew, and, after a moment, he slipped the chain off the door and opened it halfway. "Get inside! Quickly!"

Keeping my eyes on him, I slipped into the dark house and plucked the card from his hand. The man was heavyset, more stocky than overweight, with thin reddish blond hair parted in the middle. Without the use of pomade, his hair lay lank across his forehead. He had a small mouth, a sharp chin, and little blue eyes that looked like marbles. He wore a white shirt and a pair of brown tweed trousers held up by red suspenders. His eyes darted back and forth across the lawn, at my car, the house across the street. He took a quick glance up above the entryway, and then he slammed the door, turned the dead bolt, and hung the chain again on the hook.

"Down here. Quickly, now!" He bustled into the kitchen and down the stairs to the cellar. At the bottom he turned the key on the gas lamp on the wall, and the room lit with a yellow glow. The floor was packed black earth. Bedsheets hung at odd angles from the floor joists above, nailed in place, creating a maze of shadows.

Flikklund barreled through the sheets, heading for the back wall. I followed, slower and more cautiously. When I pushed aside the last sheet, I saw him already seated in a wooden chair in the far back corner, sandbags piled in a four-foot-high semicircle around him. A shotgun rested against the wall. He made no move toward it.

"You're Roger Flikklund?"

His mouth was opening and closing as if he were rehearsing a speech, but nothing came out.

"You *are* Flikklund, right?"

"Yes," he finally said. "Right you are."

I looked around us. "Why are you hiding down here?"

He leaned in toward me and whispered, "He wants me dead."

"Who does?"

"Andrew Murphy."

"Why would he want to kill you?"

Leaning in even further, he spoke under his breath. "Millions of dollars are at stake with this suffrage amendment. I hold its fate in my hands."

Delusions of grandeur. Not a promising start. My head, which had been pounding all on its own, stepped up the pace a bit. "Perhaps you should tell me what's happened. From the beginning."

"Yes, quite right. The beginning." He took a handkerchief from his shirt pocket and mopped his forehead. "I'm the MLA's accountant. Murphy is trying—" Stopping abruptly, Flikklund shouted, "Damn! Damn the bells!" He shook his head to clear it and continued his story, now speaking louder. "He is trying to fix the election." Flikklund covered his ears with his hands and pressed tightly. "My head hurts all the time, Mr. Anderson. Do you have any aspirin?"

"Sorry, no."

He sat back in the chair and let his hands drop to his sides. He looked bone weary. I thought about leaving. Before I could, Flikklund said, "Tell me this—what would happen if you could keep the rich folk from voting in this election?" He paused, waiting for me to answer.

I wasn't quick enough.

"The wealthy are conservative Protestants. What do they want more than anything?"

"Prohibition, I suppose."

"Exactly!" Flikklund shouted. "The last census showed almost ninety percent of Detroiters were immigrants. Most of them are from where?"

I hadn't come here for a lecture but thought to humor him—for now. "Germany, Ireland, Greece, Italy. Eastern and Southern Europe."

"Right." He started ticking off points on his fingers. "Germans—brewers and drinkers. Irishmen, Greeks, Italians, Southern Europeans—Roman Catholic drinkers and distillers. Eastern Europeans—Jews and Eastern Orthodox drinkers. They all drink. Therefore, they fear prohibition, and, consequently, they don't want women voting."

"It all comes down to prohibition?"

He nodded, his eyes wide.

"So the immigrants will vote against the amendment and the rich people will vote for it. It'll lose here, but the outstate voters are going to carry this one. Everybody knows the suffrage amendment's going to pass."

"If all the votes are counted." He sat back in his chair.

"They won't be?"

He shook his head. "The fix is in."

"How do you know that?"

"I have the evidence."

"Show it to me."

His head cocked to the side. His eyes narrowed, and he held up a hand, gesturing for me to be quiet. I waited him out, and perhaps ten seconds later, he said, "There! Right there! Did you hear it? Did you?"

"No." I hadn't heard a sound, but it did give me a moment to recognize that my head was really starting to pound again. "I'm not sure what you're talking about."

"The bells," he whispered, his eyes unfocused now. "They ring all the time. I don't know if . . ."

"What?" I prompted him.

He looked at me again, and I would have sworn he was lucid. "If they're trying to drive me crazy."

I was getting less optimistic by the second that he would have useful information for me. "Mr. Flikklund, what is Murphy doing?"

"He's . . . he's fixing . . . I have evidence."

"Please show it to me."

Flikklund's eyes closed.

"Mr. Flikklund?"

He gave a little jump and opened his eyes, startled. "Yes? Yes?"

"What is your relationship with Sapphira Xanakis?"

His eyes lowered, and an inward-looking smile crept onto his face. "Helen. Helen is her name."

"I don't understand."

"Sapphira is the name she was forced to use when she came here."

"All right, then. What's your relationship with Helen?"

"She is one of Murphy's secretaries."

"Where does she live?"

"Dalzelle."

"Dalzelle Street? Over by Navin Field?"

His eyes slid shut again.

"Mr. Flikklund? Does she live on Dalzelle Street?"

His eyes opened, suddenly focusing on something behind me, widening in fear. I spun and pulled the Colt from my pocket, but all I saw was sheets.

"No," Flikklund called. "I didn't. I swear. Please, Mr. Murphy."

My head pounded, worse than it had for a week. I was having a hard time concentrating. "There's no one here but us," I said.

"He's . . . he's right . . . you see him, don't you?" Flikklund's face had an expression of abject terror.

"We're the only people here, Mr. Flikklund," I said. "Now what about that evidence?"

His eyes closed again, and he slumped in his chair. When he started snoring, I decided it was time to abandon this charade. The man was having extreme delusions and hallucinations. There was no way to tell what was real and what was fantasy manufactured by a sick mind. I saw myself to the door, walked back across the crusted yard to my car, and started the drive downtown.

On the way, doubt began to tug at me. The man was crazy, that much was certain. But did that mean his information was wrong?

I still had two hours before I was to meet David, so I thought perhaps I could speak with Elizabeth, tell her of my suspicions. My head spun. Someone was trying to kill at least one of the leaders of the suffrage movement, but I was the only one to believe that. Murphy gave money to the suffrage club, yet a man—a crazy man—who worked for him was certain he was fixing the election.

Could it be true? Flikklund was nuts, but that didn't make the would-be assassin I'd disarmed any less real. If Flikklund was right and Murphy was behind the one, he could also be behind the other. The consequences for ignoring the possibility were too strong to just let it drop. I would pump David for information. He'd been there only a month, but perhaps that was long enough to learn something of their plans. It was clear he felt no loyalty to Murphy. Perhaps he would talk.

At an intersection I sat back and stared out the windscreen. David Sanford might just be the man to help me bring down Andrew Murphy. Tonight, I would find out.

CHAPTER SIX

I drove straight to the Detroit Suffrage Club's headquarters on the chance I might get ten minutes of Elizabeth's time to fill her in on what I'd learned. Parking, as usual, was a mess, and I had to leave the Torpedo on Congress and walk the remaining four blocks.

The sky was clear and blue, which, while I appreciated the relative warmth, was less beneficial to me than it had been previously. I wore the tinted glasses, but the sun still shot its beams into my brain, ratcheting up my headache.

Warren Brennan stood outside the storefront at the corner of Cass and Lafayette, wearing a black derby and the Burnsies' trademark black duster, for all the world a desperado highwayman, an effect I'm certain they intended. A cigarette dangled from his lips, and his arms hung loosely at his sides. He saw me when I was still in front of the post office and eyed me the rest of my way down the nearly empty sidewalk.

I stopped in front of him. "I need to see Miss Hume."

"I'll see what I can do, sir. Wait here." He flipped his cigarette onto the street and disappeared inside the building, locking the door behind him.

One thing about the Burns men, I thought. *No matter what they think of you, they act like professionals.* He put me in mind of Alberts. You'd never know if he hated you. It was hard enough to tell when he liked you.

When Brennan returned, he showed me in. "The boardroom is down the hall." He pointed. "Last door on the left."

"Thanks." I walked inside the building to a cacophony of voices. The lobby was packed with desks of all sizes and materials, all of them strewn with papers, and all of them occupied by a man or woman speaking into a telephone. I couldn't imagine how they heard the callers over the top of each other. That there were enough Detroit residents with telephones to make such a contingent necessary was surprising, but that, I supposed, was another piece of evidence of the progressive nature of the city. Smelling sweat, soap, and cigarettes, I skirted the desks, walked down the hall, and knocked on the door.

The acne-scarred man opened it and stood aside, letting me pass. Elizabeth sat on the other side of the three wooden tables that had been joined together to form a boardroom table of sorts. Four other women and three men sat around it, only one other that I recognized—Sylvia Pankhurst, who sat next to Elizabeth.

"Elizabeth?" I said. "May I speak with you a moment, please?"

"Certainly." She walked around the table and out of the room.

I closed the door behind us and followed her a few feet down the hall. She whirled around. "Did you tell the police about that woman?"

"No. She's not going anywhere, though."

She didn't reply, instead just stared into my eyes. It wasn't quite a glare, but not far off.

"I spoke with a man who works—worked—as the MLA's accountant. He was a little strange, but I think there's something to what he said. He claims to have evidence that they are fixing the election. I couldn't get it out of him, though."

"Talk to Detective Riordan."

"I will. I'm going to keep looking into it, too. I'm having drinks tonight at eight at Wayne Pavilion with Murphy's press secretary. I'll see what I can find out from him."

Elizabeth nodded, looked down. "You shouldn't go alone. If you really believe Murphy is involved in some kind of fraud, you could be walking into a trap."

"No, I'm not worried about that. It turns out I knew him. An old acquaintance by the name of David Sanford."

"David Sanford?" Recognition?

"Do you know him?"

"Oh, well, no, probably a different man. My father had a . . . well, a onetime friend by that name."

"This David Sanford went to school with me for a couple of years."

"Different man. This one was my father's age. Now, Will, about tonight. Would you agree with me that you would be better safe than sorry?"

The headache just wasn't going away. "I'll be fine."

She took a step closer. "All right, honey. Be careful."

"Don't worry." We kissed. "Say, have you heard anything else about the Colonel?"

"They say the surgery went well," she said. "The doctors think he'll make a quick recovery." She pushed the conference room door open. "I've got to get back. Before you go, you should say hello to Robert and Francis. They'd like that."

"Sure. Where are they?"

"My office." Pointing behind me, she said, "Three doors down," and ducked back into her meeting.

I walked down to the indicated door and knocked. After a moment, Francis said, "We're very busy in here right now."

"It's Wi John Doe. I just want to say hello."

Francis opened the door a foot and stood against it, looking out at me from under the tricorner hat. I could just see Robert sitting at a table on the left side of the office.

"Hello," Francis said, and then he closed the door in my face.

I dropped my car at the Detroit Electric garage and caught a streetcar to the Wayne Hotel. From there I walked down Third Street toward the river, along the redbrick wall that stretched for a block on the side of the Michigan Central Station. To my left, in front of Wayne Pavilion, the *City of Detroit III* pushed back from the dock with a long blast of the horn. Flood lamps lit snatches of the dark roiling water, swollen by the recent rains. The buffeting wind was wet and heavy, biting through my overcoat. I'd gotten here half an hour early. At seven thirty it was dark.

The massive steamer angled out into the river in slow motion. The sidewheel churned the water, and the engines roared, yet the ship barely moved. A few passengers stood on deck, overcoats pulled tightly around them, but most were snugged in the warm interior, probably well into their cups by now, readying themselves for a nightlong party after which they would be deposited, exhausted and hungover, in Cleveland or Buffalo or somewhere equally uninteresting.

I hopped down from the car and hurried across the street in the wake of noise from the ship. It was so loud, the engines, the horn, the churning water, that I felt deaf. People walked past, any noise their shoes made on the pavement swallowed in the roar. Flags flapped and fluttered silently, and I knew of the passing of a streetcar two streets behind me on Jefferson only from the vibration of the cobblestones beneath my feet.

The pavilion was a long, low structure alongside the river, contiguous to the convention center—Wayne Gardens—and separated by Front Street from the Wayne Hotel and the mineral bathhouse. I threw open the door and walked into the pavilion, which, while having disgorged much of its contents into the *City of Detroit*, held the better part of another ship-full of passengers. Perhaps a hundred people sat at the round white tables, and dozens more milled about. Most of the men had a drink in their hand, and I saw the same with a few women.

The window panels facing the river, which opened like garage doors in the summer, were all bolted shut, but even with the body heat of all the people here it was decidedly chilly, unlike the saloons or restaurants inside the hotel. Once David got here, I'd talk him into going someplace warm.

I wandered through the people, my gloved hands in the pockets of my overcoat, looking for David. Seeing no sign of him, I sat at an empty table near the back and, while I watched the doors, marveled at the number of people who were here to take an overnight steamer trip.

The owners of the Wayne had recently added the bathhouse in their fight to maintain relevancy, but I thought it a moot point. They had already lost their battle to force the Michigan Central Railway to expand the main station across the street, which, the railway owners claimed, did not have sufficient space to build the structure. Seemed odd to me, given that the station already stretched two blocks along Jefferson and then all the way down Third to the river.

The new station was being constructed in Corktown, which I guessed to be another piece of political profiteering. Someone who owned property nearby had likely paid a pretty penny to see their real estate increase in value tenfold or more. When the new station opened next year and passengers lost the confluence of rail and shipping at Third and Jefferson, I wondered what would happen to the Wayne. Their business was strong, but, just as we were seeing in the electric automobile business, adaptation to change was crucial, and at the rate things were changing these days, an ability to read tea leaves was nearly mandatory.

After a few minutes at the table, I maneuvered through the crowd and walked outside again, heading down the walkway that separated the building from the water. Now that the steamer was well down the river, it was quiet again—or at least quiet for Detroit, with a hum of activity like a gigantic beehive. Only a few people were about, and they were walking quickly in one direction or the other, bound for somewhere warm. I pulled my watch from my pocket and glanced at it— 8:15. Given that David had specified the pavilion, he'd likely be entering from either the Front Street or Third Street entrance, though it was possible he'd use the overhead walkway from the hotel. There was no way for me to watch all three. I'd wait inside.

I had just grabbed hold of the door handle when I heard a shout.

"Hey! Stop—" The voice cut off abruptly, like a switch being flipped. It sounded like . . . could it have been David?

I ran around the building toward the sound, which came from the back of the rail station, by the walkway along the river. Two men tussled under a streetlamp. A big man had hold of the other and clubbed him across the face. The dull smack was loud enough for me to hear, even a hundred yards away. The smaller man—David?—staggered and backed away toward the river. "Help!" he shouted. "Will?"

Any doubt I'd had about his identity was gone now.

The larger man advanced, the object he'd used as a club—a pistol— pointed at David's face.

"Hey!" I shouted, racing across the street. I pulled my Colt and fired it into the air. "Stop!"

The attacker's head spun toward me and then back to David. The brim of the big man's derby shadowed his face. David stumbled back, almost to the water, holding his arms up in front of him. "N-no, please, don't—"

The pistol flashed, the report echoed. David tumbled backward over the edge. After a beat, he splashed into the river.

"No!" I shouted, sprinting toward them. I took a shot at the big man, but he bolted away into the train yard without another look my way. Ducking between a pair of train cars, he disappeared. At the water's edge, I stopped and frantically scanned the river for David, looking around the rowboats moored along the edge.

There! Floating facedown, just ahead of me. I ran toward him, preparing myself to jump in, keeping my eyes on the dark form in the water, now lit by the streetlamps along the river. Churned by the roiling water, he rolled over, and again. I stopped, aghast.

The bullet had torn through David's nose and taken a huge circle around it.

I stopped, watching David's lifeless body sail downriver, and then spun and raced after the killer. When I reached the spot where he had ducked into the train yard, I leapt over the couplers between the cars and landed in the gravel on the other side. I looked both ways, and, seeing no one, ran away from the station, away from the lights. He could very well have hidden in a car, but I thought it unlikely, given that police would soon swarm this area. No. He had to escape—fast.

I raced along, crashing through the gravel, to the end of the train. There, I spun in a circle, looking for any sign of the man. A movement—a man in a derby running up the street, heading into the city, his long dark coat fanning out behind him like a cape. He had to be a hundred yards ahead of me. I flashed to my first look at the killer. The size was right. The clothing? . . . I'd thought he'd been wearing a short coat.

After a moment of hesitation, I hopped over the tracks and raced after the fleeing man, over Jefferson and up Brooklyn, running down the middle of the street to avoid the crowds on the sidewalks, dodging wagons and automobiles. He was out of sight and then back in view. By the time he raced around the corner on Porter, he was slowing, and I had cut the distance between us in half.

When I hit Porter, I saw him slip behind the second house on the left. I followed, though now I slowed, gun at the ready. I came around the back of the house. Nothing. I ran around the other side to the front again. Nothing. I ran through the backyards, out onto Abbott, thinking he might have doubled back. No one was on the street or sidewalks.

I turned around and ran back to Porter—and saw the man just before he disappeared up Brooklyn again. I tore off in pursuit. I was exhausted, but thankfully so was he. I gave it everything I had. Now I was only twenty yards behind him. I raised the gun. "Stop or . . ." I gasped for air. "I'll shoot!"

He cut left up Michigan Avenue, knocking over a woman on the corner, scattering a pile of chairs in front of a restaurant. I dodged the woman and jumped over the chairs. He cut left again, down an alley. I sprinted ahead and turned the corner.

A garbage can smashed into my head and chest, knocking me to the muddy ground. The gun flew from my hand. My momentum spun the man backward, against the wall, and his head hit the bricks with a hollow *thwack*. He fell heavily to the ground and landed facedown in the mud. I dove for my gun and came up with it, ready to shoot, but the man wasn't moving.

Hurting everywhere, I pushed myself to my feet, stumbled over to him, and grabbed hold of his coat. I flipped him over and stared in disbelief.

It was the Burns man—Warren Brennan.

I slapped Brennan across the face to try to wake him, harder than necessary. A yellow pathway of light from a streetlamp angled into the dark alley, ending over his senseless body.

Why would Brennan have shot David? Could he be on Murphy's payroll?

His head jerked to the side, like a delayed reaction to the slap. He turned his head left and right, trying to figure out where he was. When he saw me, he pawed at the inside of his coat but found his switchblade missing. It was in my pocket. He started scrambling to his feet. I pointed my gun at him. "Let's go."

He stood on wobbly legs, holding his head. "Was it you chasing me?"

I felt my eyes narrow. "Of course it was." I shoved him toward the mouth of the alley.

He stumbled forward a few steps, caught his balance, and turned back to me. "Why?"

I laughed at him. "That's your defense? You don't know why I chased you?"

"A man shot at me, and I ran. I ain't proud of it, but I've locked up powerful people in this town, and I'm not carrying a gun."

"Why did you kill David?"

He looked up at me sharply, and the movement made him wince. "What the hell are you talking about?"

"You shot David Sanford. I saw you."

He shook his head. "First of all, in case you're deaf, I don't have a gun with me. Second, I don't even know who David Sanford is."

This was ridiculous. I shoved him ahead again. "You could have tossed the gun anywhere along the way. It was you. I saw you. Now move. Back to the pavilion."

Still wobbly, he walked out of the alley and turned right onto Michigan Avenue. "I don't know what you're talking about."

I jammed the gun barrel into his back and pushed him forward. "It's no coincidence that you're here. If it wasn't you, then what the hell are you doing here?"

He moved faster. "Miss Hume assigned me to watch you tonight—to make sure you didn't get hurt."

"So you expect me to believe you were running from a man shooting at you?" I stuck the gun in my coat's side pocket, keeping the barrel aimed at Brennan.

He didn't reply, just rubbed his neck and, with occasional shoves from me to speed him up, walked to the corner, down Brooklyn, and over the railroad tracks to the Wayne Pavilion.

Half a dozen men stood on the sidewalk, peering into the train yard, their breath chuffing out in white clouds. Two were policemen in blue wool uniforms, over which they wore short blue coats. Typical of Detroit cops, they were overweight but big through the shoulders and arms, likely in good enough shape to beat someone to death if they put their minds to it—assuming the victim didn't have enough money to make it worthwhile to blackmail him. One of them looked near fifty; the other was a red-faced kid of no more than twenty.

"Did you find the body?" I called.

"That's him," an old man in a gray wool overcoat said, pointing toward me. "He's the one was shootin'."

"Give me the gun, bub." The older cop held his hand out to me. "Now."

I took my gun from my pocket and handed it to him butt first. "This is the man you're looking for. He killed the man in the river."

"What are you talking about?" The older cop checked the safety before pocketing the gun.

"You haven't found the body yet, then," I said. "I shot in the air"—I didn't think admitting firing at Brennan would be in my best interest—"after this man pistol-whipped and shot David Sanford."

The cop looked around at the other men. "Any of you see somebody get shot?"

None of them had.

I glanced at the old man who had identified me. "You saw me shoot, but you didn't see him"—I pointed at Brennan—"kill the smaller man?"

"Didn't see nobody else," he said. "You shot at the trains."

He'd only seen the second shot.

"Listen," I said to the cop. "A man was shot point blank in the face about fifteen minutes ago. He fell into the river. You have to get people out looking for the body."

The cop watched me carefully. "Either of you got any other weapons?"

I handed him my knife as well as Brennan's. The Burnsy held his coat open and said nothing. The cop slipped the knives into his coat pocket.

"The body will wash up somewhere." I pointed at Brennan. "When it does, remember, I caught him running away from here."

Brennan pulled out his badge. "I'm with the Burns Detective Agency." Nodding toward me, he said, "This man shot at me and took me prisoner at gunpoint. He's insane and needs to be locked up."

The older cop nodded to the younger man, who spun me around and slapped handcuffs on my wrists.

"W-wait," I sputtered. "Brennan shot David Sanford. I saw him."

"We don't know no David Sanford." The younger cop began marching me toward the train station, his hand on my shoulder.

"Listen to me," I said. "He shot a man!"

"All I know's you shot a gun in city limits and threatened a man at gunpoint. You're going to jail."

I turned as much as I could toward the older cop. "Find the body!" I shouted. "It's there, downriver." Face hot, anger swelling in me, I twisted harder and nearly broke the younger man's grip. "You're going to pay for this, Brennan, you son of a bitch!"

CHAPTER SEVEN

Detective Riordan sauntered up with a guard and looked in at me, head cocked, a sardonic smile on his face. Even then, I thought he looked worse than I felt. He was thin and looked exhausted. Taking in the other four men in my cell, who lay sleeping on the benches, he said, "Comfortable?"

I jumped to my feet and met him at the bars. "No, I'm not comfortable. Get me out of here."

"You're shooting guns within the city limits and taking a man hostage at gunpoint? What's this all about?"

"Get me out of here, and I'll tell you."

"I think you ought to tell me anyway." He pulled a cigar from his pocket, bit off the end, and lit it with his lighter, puffing away until he was obscured by a cloud of noxious smoke.

"I saw Warren Brennan—the Burnsy—kill David Sanford." When Riordan's eyebrows arched, I added, "David is—was—the press secretary for Andrew Murphy, the director of the Michigan Liquor Association. Brennan just about blew his head off."

His eyebrows arched further. "You saw this?"

"Yes."

"Nobody else saw anything other than you shooting your gun and coming back with Brennan in tow. Nobody's reported a shooting victim, or anyone else, for that matter, in the river."

"I saw Brennan beating David, but I was too far away to stop him. I fired my gun into the air to warn him off; Brennan shot David, who fell into the river. When I saw he was dead, I chased Brennan and caught him. That's what happened. I'll bet Brennan is involved in the conspiracy."

Riordan cocked his head. "Eh?"

"To defeat the amendment. Murphy must have gotten wind that David was talking. He had Brennan shut him up. He has to be involved somehow."

He nodded to the guard. "Open 'er up." While the guard unlocked and opened the door, Riordan looked back at me. "For some reason, Brennan decided not to press charges on the forced imprisonment. The desk sergeant—at my request—has already lost the paperwork on the gunfire."

"Thanks. Listen, that body is going to turn up, and you'll see. He was shot from a foot away."

We walked out together, down the hall and into the lobby of the big police station.

"Can I have my gun and knife?" I asked.

"I think the patrolman still has them," he said. "I'll work on it. Tell me what you think is going on."

I moved him to an empty corner of the lobby, and told him about my talk with David and a little about Roger Flikklund, though only the parts that sounded sane, and then added my concerns about Elizabeth's safety.

But what about Flikklund's safety?

"Could you get your hands on a car right away?" I asked. "Maybe we should go see Flikklund."

"It's a little late for a social call, isn't it?"

"It just occurred to me that he might not be crazy."

"Crazy?"

"Humor me," I said. "It's not far. Over by the salt mine."

Riordan studied me for a moment. "Might be interesting." He looked toward the back hallway and said, "Give me a minute." He disappeared into the back. When he returned a minute later he was jingling a pair of car keys in his hand. "Let's go."

We walked side by side to the garage at the end of the block. He stuck the key into the ignition of a black Chalmers runabout and started it, and then we climbed in. I gave him Flikklund's address on Dumfries. While Riordan drove, I filled him in on my meeting with the man the previous day.

"He sounds crazy to me," Riordan said.

"Flikklund said he had evidence of this conspiracy. It's worth talking to him."

Riordan shot me a glance. "He'd better be more convincing than you've been on that shooting tonight. Have you considered that maybe Brennan and everyone else is right? No one got shot. Brennan was there to protect you. You scared him off when you shot the gun, he ran, and you caught up and knocked him out."

"I know what I saw."

"Well, we'll see if Mr. Flikklund can enlighten us." Riordan drove over by the salt mine and stopped in front of the house on Dumfries. The yards and houses glowed, like on one of those snowy nights when, even cloudless, the sky seems to be lit from the earth.

Flikklund's house was dark and still. Riordan grabbed a big, heavy flashlight, and we climbed out of the car and crunched over the front yard. I couldn't be sure in the dark, but it looked like another set of footprints had been trodden into the salt crust alongside the ones I'd left when I last was here.

Riordan had noticed them as well. "Don't step on any of those prints."

I was already steering clear of them. "One advantage Flikklund has," I said, listening to the sharp crunch of salt under our feet, "is that no one could sneak up on him." I realized the salt conveyor was silent now. "At night, anyway."

"Not unless he was deaf."

"Or he was hearing ringing in his ears," I muttered. "Shit."

Riordan slammed his fist against the door, in the same fashion I had heard in my apartment—from the other side of the door. It was a much less frightening sound from this side. "Detroit police! Open up!"

He waited a few seconds and repeated the action. Still no response. He tried the door—locked. "Let's check the back."

We started around the front of the house. A set of footprints most definitely preceded us to the rear. I didn't remember seeing tracks that went around the side of the house on my previous visit. We walked outside of them to the back door, where the other set of prints stopped.

On the step the salt was scattered, as if someone had moved around a bit while waiting at the door.

Riordan, avoiding the footprints, knocked and shouted again. This door hung a bit crooked in the frame and rattled back and forth when he knocked. He looked back to me. "I don't expect anyone's home."

I raised my foot and kicked the door just to the side of the knob. It sprang open, slammed against the wall, and rebounded. "What do you know?" I said. "It's open. We may as well go in."

Shaking his head, Riordan scowled at me but pulled his gun and strode inside. I did the same, calling, "Roger! It's me, Will Anderson! We talked the other day! Roger, are you here?"

No response.

"Last I saw, he was down here." I started for the cellar stairway. My headache, which I hadn't thought about since before David was killed, began throbbing again.

"No. I go first." Riordan switched on the flashlight and ran the beam over the stairway and down to the landing. "Mr. Flikklund?" He started down the stairs. I followed. About halfway down, he grabbed hold of the rail, wobbly, and stopped. "Does your head hurt?"

"My head always hurts," I said.

"Worse than before we came in?"

"Yes."

"Was Flikklund hallucinating?"

"How do you know that?"

He switched off the flashlight. "Get the hell out of here! Now! It's gas!"

"Mother Mary," Riordan said. "What were you thinking?"

We sat in the car in the dark, waiting for the fire department. "I don't know," I said. I couldn't imagine how I hadn't put two and two together.

"Every schoolchild knows the symptoms of gas poisoning."

"I know." It seemed that every week the newspapers reported another family dying from the odorless, colorless coal gas leaking from their lines. When the house didn't explode from sparks igniting the gas, as could easily have happened from Riordan's flashlight, the residents of the home would be asphyxiated. Generally, the symptoms progressed from

headaches and nausea to delusions and hallucinations and, shortly there-
after, death. I didn't know for certain if Roger Flikklund lay dead in his
bunker in the cellar, but I had no reason to believe otherwise.

When the fire truck, the standard messy amalgamation of water
tank, hoses, axes, and other tools, finally arrived, Riordan climbed out
of the car, and I followed. The first man off the truck walked up to him.
"This the joint?" he asked, gazing at Flikklund's hideout.

Riordan nodded. "Mind the footprints. Those are evidence."

The fireman squinted at him. "In a suicide? Who cares?"

"Who said it was a suicide?"

"Gas poisoning. What else would it be?"

"Just keep off the footprints, or you're going to have my footprint up
your ass."

That seemed to impress the fireman, and he got the other men working. They shut off the gas, sledgehammered the lock off the coal chute
and threw it open, and opened all the doors and windows. In half an
hour they were gone, leaving Riordan and me waiting for the house to
air out so we could search it.

We returned to the relative warmth of the police car, and Riordan
tipped his fedora over his brow and told me to wake him when it was
fully light. I felt obliged to follow his orders, given that I had nearly led
him to his death.

I heard men beginning to arrive at the salt mine around six, and the
conveyor started up a little before seven. The sun peeked over the trees
an hour later, changing the unearthly white glow of the ground to a soft
orange. The desolate landscape warmed with the color, and I thought of
looking over Lake Huron early on a winter morning, seeing the sun rise,
sparking the ice floes to pinks and oranges. The endless grind and squeals
of the conveyor, and the boom of the salt blocks into the train car,
quickly put an end to that vision.

When I judged it to be light enough, I roused Riordan, and we
walked back up to the house. On the way I put on the dark glasses.
Without turning his head, Riordan said, "Syph?"

"No. Headaches," I replied.

At least he had the manners to drop it. He squatted next to the line
of footprints. In the light, they looked useless to me. Given the hard
crust of salt over the ground, the shoes hadn't been molded in the

prints, as they would have been in snow. These were amorphous ovals, now surrounded by dozens more, which had cracked the edges of the original prints.

Riordan studied them nonetheless. "Useless," he finally said. Straightening, he continued toward the house. "As I recall, you and I had a discussion about shoe sizes a couple of years ago."

"Yeah, thanks for bringing that up." Back in 1910, Riordan had beaten me senseless over his suspicion that I killed a man. Given that I had tracked that man's blood around my father's factory, shoe size played a part in his suspicions, though, of course, I hadn't killed the man—or anyone, at that time. Since then, while the bodies piled up, I had initiated a long and painful quest to win Detective Riordan's trust. I thought I'd finally gotten there.

I followed Riordan's big frame into the house. He stood just inside the door for a few minutes, waiting for symptoms to manifest themselves. When he was satisfied, he turned to me and handed me the flashlight. "Go on down," he said with a big smile—always disconcerting because his scar carried the smile to his left ear, like the leering grin of a macabre jack-o'-lantern. I had learned to identify Riordan's sincere and happy smiles, which were none too freely given. This was not one of those. "I'll come down in a few minutes," he added. "Don't touch anything."

Clear enough. I was to play the role of canary. I stared at him a moment longer. "You'll come down for me if the gas is still there, right?"

"Probably," he replied. He wasn't smiling.

I slipped the tinted glasses into my pocket, turned on the flashlight, and started down the steps. Breathing deeply, I descended to the dark of the cellar, waiting for feelings of nausea or an increase in my headache, which was simmering but not boiling over at the moment. The sheets fluttered and rippled in my wake. I pushed through them to the back corner of the cellar, to the bunker Flikklund had built from sandbags.

He was not sitting on the chair on which I'd left him, and I had a moment of hope. As I got closer, though, I saw a dark shape on the floor. The sour smell of vomit wafted up to my nose. Flikklund lay curled on his side, reddish hair fallen over his forehead, eyes glassy, bits of food pasted to the lower side of his mouth by stomach fluids. I hadn't known this man, but I could have saved him, and for that I was filled with sorrow. He was a good enough man to risk his life to stand on his principles, and he died for it.

"Detective Riordan," I called. "He's here."

Riordan's footsteps pounded down the stairs and then became soft thuds on the dirt floor. His hands batted the sheets to the sides with soft whumps, and then he was at my side.

I held the beam of light on Flikklund's face. "What do you think? He died from gas, and his actions were consistent with gas poisoning. He had evidence of the conspiracy, and he could very well have been murdered."

"He may have been," Riordan said. "Or it may have been an accident. Happens all the time."

"This ought to be enough evidence to get your department investigating. Elizabeth was going to give this address to Warren Brennan to have him investigate Flikklund. Brennan might have killed him."

"What?" He squinted at me and shook his head. "I'm telling you, since you went to Eloise, your mind doesn't work right."

"There's nothing wrong with my thinking. Flikklund worked for Andrew Murphy, as did David Sanford. Both were murdered. Everything points to the MLA."

The sardonic smile reappeared. "You want us to investigate Murphy? He's on Mayor Thompson's side, and the noses of the department brass are so far up Thompson's behind they can smell what he had for lunch. They don't bite the hand that feeds them."

"What about those aldermen who were arrested in the Wabash scandal?"

"Did you just fall off the turnip truck?"

"What?" That didn't even make sense.

"You think they were the ones in power?" Riordan asked.

"Of course they were."

"Take Tom Glinnan, for example. 'Honest Tom,' they used to call him."

"Yeah? So?"

"He was running against Mayor Thompson in this election."

"Oh. Right."

"The powers-that-be want to stay the powers-that-be."

I laughed and kicked at the dirt floor, thinking, *As it was in the beginning, is now, and ever shall be.*

CHAPTER EIGHT

Wednesday, October 16, 1912

We were looking through the cabinets in the kitchen when Detective Riordan asked, "You said he lived elsewhere, correct?"

I answered without thinking. "I think so. Sapphira said he was hiding here."

When Riordan didn't respond, I turned around. He was staring at me, eyes narrowed, concentration deadly.

"What?" I asked.

"Sapphira Xanakis?" His voice was soft, but it carried the weight of the world.

Perhaps it was sleep deprivation, but I hadn't thought about the implications of mentioning her to Detective Riordan. "Yes."

"She's in town?"

"Well . . . yes, but let me explain."

"The Sapphira Xanakis who was John Cooper's accomplice in the murders of Elizabeth's father and Wesley McRae? The Sapphira Xanakis who helped Cooper nearly kill Elizabeth?"

"And me. Yes, but she's not—"

"First of all, I don't hold nearly killing *you* against anyone. The whole thing was your fault. Second"—he put his hands on his hips and squared himself to me—"are you out of your goddamn mind?"

"You don't understand."

"Where the hell is she?"

Detective Riordan didn't normally curse. I knew I was straying into dangerous territory, but he was making me angry now. "I'm not saying."

"What?" His face was turning red.

"You heard me. Flikklund was murdered. I wouldn't even have known about him without her. Somewhere in this house there's evidence of the conspiracy against suffrage."

"We don't know anyone was murdered. Even if he was, we don't know that *she* didn't do it. Sometimes . . ." He looked away, shook his head, and took a deep breath. "You've got to think, boy. Why would she help you?"

I stared at him for a long moment. "Redemption."

A laugh burst past his closed lips. "Redemption." Sarcasm dripped off the word.

"It's something I understand, Detective. God help me, I think I believe her."

He looked up at the ceiling. I thought he might be counting to ten before replying. Finally he said, "I think you're past the help of the Almighty."

I just stared back at him.

"Look. If you want to have your way with her, get done with it and bring her to me. In that order, if you want her sometime in the next twenty years."

It was my turn to shake my head. "Don't you believe in redemption, Detective? Can't people change?"

"No. A person is who a person is. Find me a reformed thief and give him a chance to steal and not get caught, it's done. Find me a *reformed* murderer such as Miss Xanakis, give her a motive—like revenge on the people responsible for killing her lover—and what looks like a sure escape, she'll slit your throat in a second."

"You are one cynical son of a bitch."

"No. I live here." He gestured around us. "In the mud, not in the sky where your kind spend their time. The mud is full of murderers and thieves and rapists. That's real. People don't change."

"I've changed. I'm not the man I was."

"No, you're not. But you probably will be again. It's all still there; it's just waiting for the right time. It might never come, but that man will always be there, waiting. Maybe you won't let your guard down far enough again. If you're lucky, maybe you'll never get yourself in a fix where you need to compromise your current lofty principles—but I'm betting, I'm sorry to inform you, your lordship, that it'll happen again. The son of a bitch will be back. And it will kill Elizabeth."

I felt my fists clench. "You think I'd kill Elizabeth?"

"No. I said 'it' would kill her. If you become that man again, she'll die—either trying to save you or because of something you do."

"You don't know what the hell you're talking about."

"I worry about that girl. I've been thinking about this for a while, so I might as well put my cards on the table. She's why I help you, because she believes you've changed and that you'd never hurt her again. Just so you know"—he took the two steps to where I stood—"if you do, I'll kill you myself."

I held my ground. "If you're so sure, why don't you go ahead and try."

We held one another's eyes for perhaps ten seconds, but it seemed an eternity. Then Riordan smiled his lopsided grin. "As much as I'd like to sometimes, I don't come after anyone before they commit a crime." He turned and walked away, through the entrance to the kitchen, heading for the door. "Who knows? Maybe you'll be the exception. Maybe I haven't seen everything."

Ten inches of salty detritus—food, old newspapers, and other assorted garbage—covered the floor of the back bedroom of Flikklund's hideout. As the rest of the house was largely empty, I thought I'd start searching here. We'd shut all the windows and doors, but the house was frigid. I could barely feel my feet. Riordan was back in the cellar looking for evidence of tampering with the gas lines. I was glad to be rid of him, even if it was only for the moment. He was just looking out for Elizabeth, I knew that, but I'd thought I had earned his respect and trust.

The conveyor was louder here than in the cellar. *Boom! Boom! Boom!* It was enough to drive a man crazy without the gas.

I kicked the crusted pile in front of me, and it barely budged. The room had been recently disturbed; that was obvious from the uneven white film atop the garbage. Papers had slipped and slid, unearthing yellowed pages, a blue spherical object that might have once been an orange, and an open sack of what I was certain to be dog shit, though thankfully it was old enough that it no longer stank. Even with my gloves, I was less than enthusiastic about touching anything, so I started near the door, using my shoes to push the pile around.

After a couple of uniformed policemen—including one in a clean uniform, which I assumed meant he was an officer—had nosed around a bit, a pair of young men directed by the coroner carried Flikklund's blanket-covered body out of the cellar and deposited it in the back of a truck. The other cops rode off with them, more than happy to leave Detective Riordan to investigate.

As much of a jackass as he was, Riordan was the only policeman I'd ever dealt with who, once he'd discovered there was no money to be made, wasn't frantic to lay off the responsibility for the case on someone else. The concept of solving crimes or, God forbid, helping to dole out justice, seemed to be a foreign idea to the rest of the force. I suppose to most policemen the job becomes exactly that—a job. They wake up, punch the clock, find a body and drop it in someone else's jurisdiction, punch the clock again, and go to sleep. The next day is more of the same.

I wondered if I could become so inured to the blood, the violence, the death, and I supposed I would. Cultures throughout history have proven it—people will adapt to their circumstances, almost without regard to how horrendous they find those circumstances. With precious few exceptions, men living in a violent, unjust society looked the other way and quietly breathed sighs of relief that it wasn't them under the sword or the gun.

Boots clomped up the stairs. "Found it," Riordan called.

I stepped just out of the bedroom, not trusting myself to speak to him yet. I heard him top the stairs, turn the corner, and walk down the hall toward me.

"There was a crease in the pipe," he said, "like someone had hit it with a heavy object." He was speaking normally, as if he hadn't threatened my life only an hour before. "The hole is a vertical line at the crease, right where it ought to be if the pipe had a weak spot. I can't tell if it was done on purpose or if maybe Flikklund just hit it when he was moving something around."

I didn't look at him. "Hmm" was all I said.

"By the way, the lieutenant said they haven't found Sanford's body yet. I don't hold out much hope for it. The river's running high. Assuming you saw what you say you saw, he's probably halfway to Lake Erie by now." He paused and looked at me. When I didn't respond, he continued. "I've got a friend at the gas company. I'm going to pick him up, have him take a look at this. You want to ride along?"

"No." I returned to the bedroom and busied myself with a pile of trash. "I'll keep looking around."

"Suit yourself."

A few seconds later, the front door opened and closed, and the house was still again. Outside, the conveyor belt creaked and clanked, and the salt chunks pounded into the rail car.

Glancing around the room, I noticed something I hadn't before. Near the middle of the room, a pencil was buried into the side of an old canvas bag that was white with salt. The pencil itself was just as white as its surroundings, so I didn't believe it had been recently placed here, but if I were trying to hide something in this god-awful mess, I'd have marked its spot somehow.

I put a foot atop the garbage and shifted my weight forward, working to keep my balance. Two more steps, and I squatted near the pencil and lifted the bag from the pile. Though the area around it didn't look to have been recently disturbed, the bag wasn't stuck to the rest of the garbage. It was stiff and, when I pried it open, empty. I tossed it aside and dug deeper, disturbing the contents and raising a rotten-egg stink that had been lying dormant under the pile. Garbage, garbage, and more garbage.

I sat back on my haunches and looked around the room again. Across from me, near the wall, lay the only spot that looked truly undisturbed. The white coating atop the pile was flawless and even, while the remainder of the room looked to have been recently trampled. I stood and slipped and slid across the pile, losing my balance and only just keeping my feet. Squatting again, I pulled a newspaper off the top and, voilà, saw a relatively clean white envelope underneath.

The front door opened. *Wow,* I thought, *that was fast.*

I was going to call out when I heard two men speaking. Neither of them was Detective Riordan.

"It's here somewhere," one of the men said.

"So let's find it and get the hell out of here before the cops come back," the other replied.

I picked up the envelope and slipped it into my inside coat pocket, then stood and began retracing my steps across the room, moving as quietly as possible. I slipped my hand up to my shoulder holster and froze—the police still had my gun and knife.

"Look around up here," the first man said. "I'll check the cellar." That voice. It was familiar, but the salt blocks were booming so loudly, it was all I could do to make out the words.

The second man grunted in acknowledgment.

My heart was pounding. For whatever reason, these men were looking for the same thing I was, and they wouldn't have come unarmed.

A pair of boots thumped down the steps. I started for the window, straining to listen for the other man over the sound of the conveyor creaking and the salt blocks booming.

When he stuck his head in the room, I was nearly as surprised to see him as he was me. I'd heard nothing. First impression—a good-sized fellow, dark hair, long nose, blue eyes, tan overcoat, black derby. He cleared his coat with one quick hand and reached for a revolver stuck into his belt. I was too far away to reach him before he shot, so I tossed a handful of garbage at him and ran toward the window.

He fired the gun, the boom deafening. The window shattered half a second before I dove through it. I landed on the crusty salt of the yard and the broken glass of the window. Jumping up, I darted for the back-yard, away from his view. I heard a thump from the bedroom, and he shouted out. He'd slipped on the garbage.

I kept sprinting. I glanced back to see him dive out the window, somersault, and come up running. Fast. I had put at least fifty yards between us. If I could maintain that lead, the odds of him being able to hit me with a pistol shot were astronomical. *If* I could maintain that lead. With his speed, it didn't look likely. I veered left, heading toward the salt mine. If I could beat him to the buildings, I'd have plenty of witnesses. Surely he wouldn't follow me there.

I slowed and jumped high enough to grab the fence's top bar with both hands. Hot pain arced through my burned right hand as I pulled myself up. A bullet whizzed by, cutting through one of the squares six inches from my head. The crack of the report reached my ears a split second later, surprisingly loud over the booming of the salt blocks. I flipped over the side and landed in a heap after the eight-foot drop. As I scrambled to my feet, I glanced back. The man was sprinting like an Olympian, his long strides quickly making up the distance between us. I doubted the fence would prove a serious obstacle to him.

I ran for my life. Even though there had to be people about, not a single worker was in view. The main building of the mining company, an ugly four-story redbrick a hundred yards ahead, was bound to be occupied. I sprinted toward it, crunching through the salty yard, my shoulders involuntarily tensing in expectation of a bullet's impact. The gun fired twice more, the bullets kicking up little explosions of white dust in the ground in front of me, but I made it to the front door of the building without being hit. When I jerked the door open, I glanced back at him. He was perhaps twenty-five yards away, running hard, the gun in his hand. I ran into the spartan lobby. A young man sat at a desk just inside.

Standing over him, I held out my hand. "Give me the door key. Now!" If I could lock the gunman out, it would at least slow him down.

"Sir?" the young man said.

"The key, boy, now!"

"But I don't . . ."

"Then get under your desk. Quick!" I vaulted the half-door that led to the back and bolted down the hallway. A quick exit might give me the distance I needed to escape.

"Now see here," the young man called after me. "You can't—"

I ran through the narrow hallway past half a dozen doors on each side, most of them closed. I was twenty feet from the end of the hall when the front door banged open behind me and a gun fired. The bullet whizzed past, stinging my right ear, and thudded into the wooden door in front of me. I threw it open, ran into a small vestibule, and slammed the door behind me. The back door, and my escape, were only five feet away. I ran to it, turned the knob, and pushed.

Locked.

I glanced back and saw a stairway to my left, leading up. It was the only other way out of the vestibule. I bolted up the stairs two at a time, turned the corner at the first landing and, halfway up the next flight, heard the bang of the hallway door slamming into the wall. A couple of seconds later, shoes pounded up the stairway behind me. At the second floor, I pulled open the door, ran through it, and slammed it shut. This hall was identical to the one below. I darted into the first office on the right, closed the door, and ran to the window.

The hallway door banged open, and his footsteps pounded past me. I shoved the window open and glanced below before climbing through, hanging from the sill, and letting go. When I hit the hard, salty ground, I fell backward, away from the building. I scrambled to my feet and ran for the front gate, at least two hundred yards away. A Model T roadster stood parked diagonally in front of it, a man behind the wheel. He opened the door and began to climb out.

I darted right, ducking into the conveyor building. Three other men stood inside, all working at benches around the room. All three looked at me, startled. The creaking of the conveyor and the booming of the salt blocks into the train car outside were deafening.

The huge conveyor rose from the center of the room, carrying blocks of salt up from the depths and passing through the ceiling. Inside the same shaft, a tall cage stood in front of the conveyor, with steel bars rising fifteen feet on the sides and over the top, and a pair of metal doors, one in front of me, another directly over it. Metal stairs led up to the second level.

The elevator.

I ran to the cage and threw open the metal door. The control panel was affixed to the metal frame just inside the lower entrance. I searched the panel for the right switch, my hands hovering over the surface.

There. I flipped the DOWN switch on the panel, and the elevator jerked to a start. I grabbed a hard hat from a large pegged board on the wall as I did. I watched the doorway, expecting to be shot, but neither of the men made it in time. The cage was small, large enough for perhaps three men. I looked up through the bars, expecting to see a face and then a gun loom over the edge, but the metal floor of the level above me blocked my view and would protect me from bullets. In the midst of the adrenaline coursing through me, I felt a momentary bit of calm.

I'd never met this man, but the way he moved was familiar. Could he have been David's killer? The movements were right, I thought. The killer had been a big man—like Warren Brennan—but seemed lithe and athletic, unlike Brennan. Still, I'd seen him for only a few seconds, and it was dark. I couldn't be certain.

A gun fired, the report echoing loudly in the shaft. The elevator shuddered. The gun fired again. Again, the elevator shuddered.

A cold tremor rose from my gut. He was shooting the elevator cables. I hadn't seen how thick they were or what they were made of. I was more than a thousand feet above the floor of the mine.

The gun fired a third time. This time, the echo of the shot was much quieter, and the elevator barely vibrated beneath me. Now I heard nothing over the creaks and groans of the conveyor, separated by a metal wall from the elevator. I couldn't see below me, but the mineshaft here was rock.

Everything I'd done to escape had been completely instinctual, but now I was jolted into reality—I was under the earth in an incredibly deep hole. The elevator hummed along. The shaft began to tighten around me. I needed out. I couldn't get a breath. I fell to the metal floor of the car and curled up into a ball, squeezing my eyes shut.

Still the elevator dropped. Endlessly, it seemed. Hundreds, thousands of feet, millions of tons of rock above me, the shaft only wide enough for the elevator and the conveyor. My chest constricted. My mind shuttered through horrifying images—being trapped in the black and airless interior of the steamer trunk when I'd been kidnapped, trying to squeeze through the narrow corridor to the secret room at Elizabeth's house, walking through Eloise Hospital's tunnels and crawling through its two-foot-wide water pipes. I couldn't think straight. The weight on my chest was crushing. I couldn't draw even a shallow breath. I was going down. Down into the depths of the mine. Down to my death, my body crushed to nothingness.

The trunk closed in on me. White lights burst in my eyes. Then nothing.

CHAPTER NINE

Hey," a man said. "Wake up."

I opened my eyes to see a man in a hard hat squatting in front of me. He was small, birdlike. A cigarette dangled from his lower lip. He wore a dark suit that, while a bit threadbare, was clean. I was tucked into the corner of a room filled with huge machines. Men moved through the room in all directions. The ceiling soared twenty feet above me. A single bulb lit the room to a dusky ivory. Around me, machinery creaked and moaned and hummed and slammed. My back was propped against a wall.

"Where . . . where am I?" Then it all flooded back. The mine. Twelve hundred feet below the surface. I tried to breathe but instead began to choke.

The man laughed. "Must be your first day. You're lucky it was me found you, not one of the foremen. That'd be your ticket back to the top—permanentlike." From his coat pocket, he removed a little box and, from it, pulled out a cigarette. "Here." He stuck it in my mouth and lit it.

I inhaled the smoke, and it cut a little piece from my panic.

"You got a handkerchief?" he asked.

I nodded.

He pointed at the side of my head. "You must'a hit your head when you fell. Your ear's bleedin'."

I pulled out my handkerchief, held it to my ear for a second, and looked at it. Blood—quite a lot of it—was smeared across the white cloth. *Right,* I thought. *He shot me.* I pressed the handkerchief against the wound and looked around. A train track ran through the center of the room, which was easily fifty feet wide and seemed to stretch on forever in both directions. Huge pillars of stone separated this room from the others around me. The air was clear, clean. I'd expected five-foot ceilings, tight spaces, foul air. I took a deep drag on the cigarette. My chest loosened a bit more. "How long have I been down here?"

"Ten minutes, maybe," he said.

"How did I get here? Away from the elevator?"

"I dragged you. The proletariat has to stick together. Now you better get movin', bub. What sector?"

"What?"

He cocked his head and gave me a puzzled look. "What sector you workin'?"

"I . . . don't remember."

"Well, ain't no way for me to find that out for you. Anyways, I gotta get back to work. I'd suggest you find a foreman and tell him you forgot your assignment." Grinning, he added, "Maybe you'll get lucky and he'll remember what it's like to work for a livin'." He jumped to his feet and started to stride away.

"Thanks," I said.

He grinned at me over his shoulder. "No problem. You pay back another worker, rook."

It occurred to me that I didn't smoke anymore, but I wasn't giving up this cigarette. Taking a deep drag, I worked my way to my feet, crouching even though the ceiling was distant. I took a shaky step in the direction the miner had gone. And another.

He said I'd been here ten minutes. I had no idea how long it took the elevator to ascend and descend again. At the end of the pillar, I peered around the corner. The elevator platform was built as the one above had been, with two levels and a metal stairway for the upper section. It sat—empty—about thirty feet away. Half a dozen men tossed chunks of rock salt from a huge pile onto the conveyor. Four train cars brimming with salt blocks waited, lined up in front of them. The tracks converged here from all directions. The mine itself was monochromatic—white, white, and more white. The train track continued down the tunnel, past dozens, perhaps hundreds more salt pillars all a uniform size, at least twenty feet square. I knew this mine had multiple levels. I was standing below 1,200 feet of rock inside a salty Swiss cheese. My head swam, and I dropped to the floor again.

No! I can't panic. If those men came down here while I was sitting this close to the elevator, I was dead.

I thought about what I would do if I were them. They could follow me down, but the mine was huge, and the odds of locating me in its tunnels were slim. However, I didn't know if they knew that. On the other hand, all they had to do was wait for me to come up. But—no. Someone must have called the police. Riordan would probably be on his way back to Flikklund's hideout by now. He'd hear about the chase and gunfire. Once he discovered I wasn't at the house anymore, he'd know I was involved. He would look for me, out of a sense of duty or—more likely—his desire to protect Elizabeth. He'd probably assume I was the one shooting.

My best chance: disappear down a tunnel, find a safe spot a long way from the elevator, and hide out for an hour. My knees shook at the thought of going still deeper into the mine. It was all I could do now to focus my mind enough to think. No, I would stay here for ten minutes or so and keep an eye on who came down on the elevator. If they hadn't arrived by then, I was getting the hell out of here.

Five minutes hadn't passed before the elevator slid down to the platform, silent in the roar of the conveyor. Six men were packed face-to-face on each level.

"Hey, you!"

I turned around to see a man standing near the other end of the pillar, in a dark suit and hard hat, a notebook in one hand, the other pointing at me. "Where are you supposed to be?" His head was cocked to the side, and I could see him thinking, *Lazy bastard.*

"Sector two." I was hoping they used numbers and not letters or some other designation. I glanced back at the elevator and saw two men in dark suits, nicely tailored, hurrying down the stairway, their faces grim. One was a big man—about the size of my attacker—with dark hair. I spun back, away from them, and took a step to the right to put the pillar between us. *Is it them?* They wore hard hats, but then again, so did I.

The man with the notebook put his hands on his hips. "Then go, for Christ's sake."

Tensing to run, I glanced back to see if the men were coming. No one else down here dressed that well. Was it them?

"Are you deaf?" the man with the notebook asked.

"No."

"Then go." He hooked a thumb over his shoulder.

"Yes . . . sir." I walked past him and hurried away, not looking back until I reached the next pillar. The man with the notebook was no longer in view, but the men in nice suits strode toward me, down the center of the tunnel, just to the side of the train track. The smaller man saw me, nudged the other man, and pointed my way.

Damn it! I cut behind the pillar and ran farther into the mine, trying not to think about where I was going.

The tunnel ended past the next pillar, but it branched off left and right. I stopped in the middle. Right led to a dead end only fifty feet away, everything stark white salt. On my left, a longer tunnel, unlit, a three-foot-high makeshift wooden fence blocking the entrance. The light behind me carried perhaps a hundred feet into that tunnel; after that, nothing but blackness—a place to hide.

I glanced behind me and, seeing no one, bolted to the other tunnel, hopped the fence, and sprinted toward the dark through another of the nearly identical huge white rooms. It was quieter now, the clanks and bangs fading to a low moan.

Lose the men, I thought, *wait an hour, and then get back to the elevator.*

As I entered the darkness, I could make out the shapes of huge boulders before me. Now, at the end of the tunnel, far ahead, I saw a tiny light glowing, like a star in the night sky. A second later, the light began bouncing up and down, growing in size, and it was joined by another. Over the sound of the machinery, shoes scuffled, running through the darkness toward me.

I ducked behind a boulder the size of an automobile and felt around on the tunnel floor for a weapon. My hand touched a baseball-sized rock, and I scooped it up. The footsteps got louder. I peered around the back of the rock. Two men.

How could they have gotten ahead of me? I held the rock near my left shoulder, ready to throw it or strike with it. The men were close now. I tensed, ready for action.

They sprinted past me and ran pell-mell down the tunnel, each holding a flashlight. They wore gray jumpsuits and hard hats—mine employees. Now I saw the big red signs on the tunnel walls.

BLAST ZONE.

Oh, shi—

The earth exploded, throwing me to the ground. Thunder clapped, the sound deafening. Rocks, large and small, shot out of the darkness and crashed into the walls and boulders around me. A dense cloud of dust blew out behind them.

For a minute or two I lay coughing and hacking, staring at the dust settling around me, before I came to my senses enough to take stock of my physical condition. Unbelievably, I was in one piece. My eyes burned, my ears rang, my head throbbed, and my side hurt, but I didn't think any of these were serious injuries. Not knowing if a second concussion would follow, I jumped to my feet and scrambled through the rocks on shaky legs, still coughing out the dust. I rubbed my eyes, only to have them burn more.

When I reached the light, one of the miners saw me and shouted, "What the hell?" His voice was flat and dull, barely audible over the high-pitched tone in my ears.

"You dumb son of a bitch!" the second miner yelled. "Get the hell out of here! You could cost us our jobs." The second man shoved me toward the fence at the tunnel's entrance. "Get moving."

I did as he said, hurrying out and around the next corner. Up the tunnel, only fifty feet away, stood the men in suits, consulting with the man carrying the notebook. All three looked up. The men in suits marched toward me with narrowed eyes and grim expressions. I couldn't run. They'd shoot me down. But would they shoot me here, in front of witnesses?

The men stalked toward me, and the older of them, the big man, said, "Anderson?"

"Why?" I couldn't imagine how they knew my name.

"A cop name of Riordan said you'd have come down here."

"Oh." My mind was still trying to catch up.

"I'm Ryan, the plant manager."

A man ran up behind me. I whirled around to see one of the men from the explosives team. "Wasn't our fault, boss. He musta been hidin'."

"What are you talking about?" Ryan asked him.

"This guy"—he pointed at me—"he musta been hidin' when we blasted."

I looked down at my clothing. It was covered in white dust.

"It's all right," Ryan said. "It's not your fault."

The miner apologized one more time before retreating into the tunnel. Ryan watched him go, then turned to the younger man and made a short slash across his throat. "Both of them," he said.

The younger man wrote something down.

"It wasn't their fault," I said. "They never had a chance to see me."

He took hold of my arm and began walking me back toward the elevator. "It's their job to see people. And I'd better not see you here again."

"Believe me, I had no intention of coming here in the first place, but it was that or get shot. Did the man chasing me get away?"

"Yes, but he didn't shoot anyone. We got the detective a good description of him."

"Good. I'm glad no one was hurt."

He and the younger man marched me back to the elevator. The three of us rode on the lower level, with three miners facing us. My man was exactly my height, and his nose ended no more than six inches from mine. It was an uncomfortable ten-minute ride to the top. Once there, Ryan allowed me to use a bandage from their first-aid cabinet on my ear and then had the younger man escort me to the gate. On the way, I again donned the tinted glasses, glad they had made the journey intact. I walked up to Dumfries and turned left to Flikklund's hideout. No cars stood at the curb.

I thought for a moment. Riordan must have left. If any cops were here, there'd be a transport of some sort. No, anyone who might be there now would be someone I didn't want to meet up with—particularly unarmed. I hoofed it back to Sanders, then up Fort Street to the corner of Oakwood, where I caught a streetcar to take me back to civilization, to a place where people said "please" and "thank you," a place where I could pull out my wallet without getting it lifted, a place where people didn't shoot at me.

Usually.

I fell asleep standing up on the streetcar and was wakened by a hard jolt that threw me against the man in front of me. The edges of my vision were black, everything fuzzy. I was looking at the world through a tunnel. My head pounded. It seemed I hadn't had a good night's sleep in weeks. Even so, I had things to do, particularly finding out from Riordan whether they'd caught the men who were chasing me.

Thinking of Riordan reminded me of the envelope I'd found at Flikklund's. I braced myself against the side wall of the streetcar and snatched the envelope from my coat pocket. I examined it—a white letter-sized envelope, relatively new and clean compared to everything else in that room. I held it up to the light. Papers, perhaps six inches wide, rested inside. I ripped open the envelope, pulled out the papers, and unfolded them.

A set of ballots—from Ingham County, home of the city of Lansing, Michigan's state capital. I looked them over, front and back, searching for some sort of clue to their import, but they were simply ballots for the upcoming election. The first sheet was filled with the standard nonsense, dozens of candidates no one had ever heard of for jobs no one cared about, such as county road commissioner, whatever that was. Of course, mayor and governor and so on were there as well. The choices for president were most prominent, listing Taft—Republican, Wilson—Democratic, Roosevelt—Progressive, Debs—Socialist, and Chafin—Prohibition.

The other two forms were the constitutional amendments. One was some mumbo-jumbo about limited self-government for certain localities; the other, of course, was the equal suffrage amendment, which was tucked into a single tidy paragraph. I didn't know enough about ballots to examine them properly, so I placed them back into the envelope and returned it to my pocket. I would see if Riordan could make heads or tails of them. First, a bath.

When I stumbled off the streetcar at the corner of Peterboro and Woodward, I planned to get myself cleaned up and go talk to him, but I was too damned tired. I needed a nap. I sat at my desk, where I stashed the ballots and envelope in the pencil drawer, and phoned the Bethune Street station. After asking for Detective Riordan, I nearly fell asleep waiting for him to come to the telephone.

Finally another man picked up. "Riordan ain't here."

My vision swam with dark-edged blotches. "Tell him . . . tell him I found what we were looking for."

"Who is this?" the man asked, irritated.

"Tell him Will called and that I found some ballots. I need him to look at them."

"Yeah, I'll tell him." It sounded like he was dismissing me.

"Look, this is important. Tell him. He'll want to know as soon as possible."

"I said I'd tell him." The receiver clicked, and the line went dead. I tapped the hanger a couple of times and waited for the operator to come back on. When she did, I asked for Elizabeth's home number. I had to tell her about Brennan.

Alberts answered and said she was out. Elizabeth hadn't informed him of her plans, nor, he said, sounding quite exasperated, did he have any idea when she would return.

"Please, Alberts," I said, "tell her I need to speak with her as soon as possible."

He agreed to, and, after wishing me a good day, he hung up.

My eyes drifted to the wall opposite the desk, at the picture of Elizabeth and me outside the casino on Belle Isle. The wind had come up, tousling our hair, and Elizabeth was trying to hold hers back from her face. I was reaching around her back to help her, and my hand may have strayed just a bit, perhaps a little lower than her hair. In the photograph, her mouth was opened wide in surprise, but it was framed in a smile. Even from this side of the desk, eight feet from the picture, I could see the spark in her eyes as she was reaching to push me away. Her hand and arm were a blur, which gave the picture a feeling of motion, of being alive. I liked that. It let me pretend it was now, and that she still looked at me that way—with love, rather than pity.

"Sir?" A woman's voice came on the line. "Did you want to make another call?"

"Sorry. No." I slapped the receiver onto the hook and slid the candlestick back on top of the desk.

I walked to my bedroom to remove my clothing. I'd take a bath, change, and go see Elizabeth. I sat on the bed to unlace my shoes but instead fell onto my back. In seconds, I was asleep.

I opened my eyes to the dim gloom of evening. My face felt tight and itchy. I glanced over at my alarm clock. Nearly six. I'd slept through the afternoon, but my head was just as logy and dull as it had been before. I started a bath and, when I turned, glanced at myself in the mirror and burst out laughing. I had gotten some strange looks on the street, but I attributed that to my clothing, which was covered in salt. No. It was my face that attracted the attention.

I looked like a photographic negative of a blackface minstrel. The salt dust covered me completely. I smiled a toothy grin, and the image was complete. Maybe a new vaudeville act for me—I could put on white makeup, dress like a swell, and sing my college alma mater while eating cucumber sandwiches. I supposed, given my work performance and Mr. Hanley's attitude toward me, it might be my best chance at earning a living.

Which reminded me that I hadn't called the factory to let them know I'd be gone today. Well, they had worked it out long before now. Riordan, I remembered, hadn't come by or phoned. Or maybe he had. I'd been sleeping like the dead and might not have heard him. I'd try him again tomorrow.

I was readying myself to step into the tub when the doorbell chimed. I walked to the door and glanced through the peephole. Sapphira stood in the hallway watching the door expectantly through wire-rimmed spectacles, holding a cream-colored floral handbag with both hands. She wore a modest navy blue skirt and a white shirtwaist under a short burgundy overcoat. Her hair, under a small burgundy hat, had been dyed with henna. I hadn't noticed that before. She looked like a telephone operator.

Wondering how she'd gotten past the doorman, I pulled open the door.

She gawked at me, her mouth open, her eyes big and round. My first thought was my salt-white face, but then my eyes followed hers, which were not focused anywhere near the region that included my face.

I was completely naked.

I slammed the door shut and ran to my bedroom. Once I had donned my bathrobe, I had a brief mental struggle regarding whether or not to ignore her and any other callers for the remainder of the night. Deciding to take my medicine, I returned to the door, where she still waited.

I summoned all my remaining dignity and opened the door again. "Hello, Sapphira. What can I do for you?"

"Roger is dead?" Her voice shook.

I glanced to her left and right. The hallway was otherwise unoccupied. I stood aside. "Come in."

She stopped in the foyer, fidgeting with her bag.

"He is, but it looked like an accident. I'm afraid David Sanford was less fortunate."

"David?"

"He was shot to death last night."

"Are you sure?" Behind her glasses, her eyes were wide again, now in fear.

"I saw it myself. I was going to meet him for drinks. He was shot and fell into the river."

"Oh, my God!" She buried her face in her hands. After a moment, she looked up abruptly, her lower lip trembling. "Mr. Murphy is killing witnesses. I . . . I am the only other one."

I assessed her reaction. It seemed genuine. "Come in and sit." I stretched out my arm toward the parlor and followed her in. She walked like an automaton and perched on the edge of the sofa. "Sapphira, why did you come here?"

"I can wait while you dress." She gestured toward my face. "And you have . . ."

"Yes. Thank you. I'll only be a few minutes." I hurried to the bathroom and washed my face before heading back to the bedroom, where I shut the door and threw on a suit of clothes.

When I returned to the parlor, Sapphira stood next to the big oak board on the wall, in which were buried my four throwing knives. She was running her fingertips back and forth along the blade of one of the daggers. When she heard me, she turned and sat on the edge of the sofa.

I would not be offering her a drink. The sooner she was gone the better. I stood across the coffee table from her.

"I came to tell you I am leaving. I cannot stay with that man." Her words were hard, angry.

I sat in the chair so as to be able to meet her eyes. "Why?"

Her gaze dropped to the table in front of her. "He is cruel. He hits me and . . . has his way with me, anytime he wants. I cannot stop him."

"What the hell do you expect? You're a prostitute. Why would he treat you like a lady?"

She winced as if slapped.

I wasn't apologizing. "Before you go, why don't you tell me what you know about David Sanford."

"He started working in the office three or four weeks ago. He shared an office with Mr. Flikklund but spent much of his time in Mr. Murphy's office. He was . . . very friendly."

I heard a "however." "He was very friendly, but . . . what?"

"I think he was trying to . . . seduce me, even after he knew I was Mr. Murphy's. He was friendly, but there was something underneath. I do not know what it was."

"Was he involved in the conspiracy or helping Flikklund?"

She shrugged. "I have not heard anything about either one. Do you know who shot him?"

"No." *Warren Brennan? The big man from Flikklund's house? Someone different altogether?*

She spoke again, her voice tiny, as if she were trying to strangle the words before they left her mouth. "Do you need me to help?"

"I don't need your help for anything, Sapphira. If you want to leave, then leave."

"You cannot do it by yourself. Mr. Murphy is too powerful. He will have you killed."

I shrugged. I wasn't asking her to help.

She was quiet for a moment. "I should stay," she finally said, "with Mr. Murphy . . . Yes?"

"If you can leave, then do it."

"I have almost no money, I have—"

So this was a shakedown? "How much money do you want?"

"No!" she shouted. "I do not want your money. This is not why I came." Shaking her head, she said, "No, I will not leave. I will see Mr. Murphy pay for what he has done. I can do what he wants. For now."

"It's not wise, Sapphira. You see that, don't you?"

"Wise?" She gave me a pained smile. "I am not wise. You know that. I will help you stop him."

"I don't want your help. Get on a train heading west. They still need women out there. I'm sure you'd be very popular."

Silently, she looked up at me with those big eyes, so dark as to be almost black, against a brilliant white background. She had the eyes of a child, a child who could not understand why the world was such a terrible place.

I was hurting her. I just wasn't sure if I cared. Only two years ago, she had led me by the ego nearly to my death, and in the process contributed to the deaths of two other men. I couldn't trust her, but she was cracking my resolve. She repelled me, yet I found myself wanting to protect her. Was she sincere, or was I just easy to manipulate?

"Is there anything else?" I asked.

Sapphira shook her head.

I made a you-first gesture toward the front door. She took the hint and headed for the foyer. I followed and let her out with a polite "Good night," before locking the door and walking back to my den to telephone Elizabeth again. Alberts answered and told me she was out with Miss Pankhurst, who he said was leaving the next evening to return to England. He did not expect them back until late.

"Did you give her my message?" I asked.

"Of course, sir."

"Please tell her again, Alberts. It's imperative that I talk with her."

I hung up and returned to the parlor, where I pried my knives out of the board. Stepping back behind the sofa, I flung the first dagger. The tip of the blade struck the board and buried itself half an inch deep, making a solid and most satisfying thud. I turned and took three steps left, pivoted, and fired the next dagger. It, too, stuck in the board. I kept it up for an hour, running around the parlor like a maniac, spinning and firing knives. Fewer stuck than didn't, and I managed to put a few holes in the plaster, but my muscles thrummed with the activity. I dropped and did one hundred push-ups, barely feeling any pain in my hand, and one hundred sit-ups. Finally, dripping with sweat, I warmed the water in the tub and lay back to relax.

In the morning, I would tell my father I needed another couple of weeks off from work, consequences be damned. Then I would chase down Elizabeth, tell her about Brennan, and bring her, rather than that son of a bitch Riordan, the ballots, so she could have an expert examine them. Next I would compare notes with the aforementioned son of a bitch and find out if he had discovered anything about David or the men who had chased me, or if any clues had been uncovered regarding the conspiracy.

I lay in the tub for more than an hour. Whenever the water began to cool, I let some of it out and replaced it with hot water. I thought— about Elizabeth and Riordan, about the big man who had chased me, about David Sanford and Roger Flikklund, Warren Brennan and Andrew Murphy.

When I finished, I put a new dressing on my ear, which had stopped bleeding completely. Putting on my pajamas, I had a satisfying thought. Throughout my hour-long rumination in the tub, not once did I think about Sapphira.

CHAPTER TEN

Thursday, October 17, 1912

I woke the next morning to the light of a gray day, rather than the sound of my alarm clock, which not only had I forgotten to set, but now showed I was already half an hour late for work. I threw on a suit of clothes, ran to the door, and tried to unlock it, but the key wouldn't budge; it was already unlocked. I threw the door open and ran out, stopping only long enough to be sure I locked it securely before bolting down the stairs and out the front into the cold gray morning.

After pushing onto the first streetcar that came by, I ran into the factory, through the cacophony and seeming chaos of the manufacturing facility, and up to the Engineering Department. An hour late today—the day we were presenting our breakthrough for the 1914 line to George Bacon, Detroit Electric's chief engineer, Mr. McFarlane, the automobile factory manager, and my father. While I had nothing to do with the design, Mr. Hanley wanted to include me in the presentation.

Unfortunately for us all, Mr. Bacon was an electrical engineer and spent his time with the EE's. He was tough, but he was a good man. I'd gotten to know him well on the Detroit to New York tour we'd made in a DE Victoria a few years back. I had chosen to get a degree in mechanical engineering rather than electrical, which left me with Hanley.

My eyes had still been closed when I'd thrown on my suit, a black pin-striped two-piece with a black and gray striped tie and a pair of oxfords, which, as I walked through the door, I noticed were brown. Black suit, black belt—brown shoes. Shit. It would bother me all day.

Again, other than Hanley, who grimaced with disgust, no one even looked at me when I squeezed past them to my desk. I missed Joe Curtiss, Detroit Electric's head mechanic. He'd been murdered, and I had avenged him, but I couldn't escape the guilt, nor could I escape the longing I had for his friendship. Joe always had a smile for me and was always ready to lend a hand. Our friend Elwood Crane, the Detroit Electric battery manager, with whom Joe and I used to frequent saloons, had gotten married and had a little boy. I hadn't spoken with him in months. That left me with no friends at work. Realistically it had left me with no friends at all. I'd botched my relationship with Edsel Ford by trying to keep him out of a mess I'd gotten in with the Gianolla gang, the very mess that resulted in Joe's death. I didn't regret doing that. Edsel might have ended up a casualty otherwise.

I was trying to focus my eyes on the design drawings when Hanley sauntered up to me five minutes before the presentation was to begin. Folding his arms across his chest, he gave me a smug smile and said, "You'll be presenting the new feature to the brass."

"Detroit Duplex Drive," I said. "We've applied for a patent and a trademark, of course."

Outside the room, a press slammed, and the floor shook under my feet. "By offering a dual drive system, we may be able to decrease our range of models. If successful, we won't have to duplicate styles with both front and rear drive."

A number of cities had outlawed the driving of cars from the rear seat, as a result of traffic accidents caused by the driver's view being blocked by someone in front. In my opinion, rear drive was ridiculous for motorcars, and was still around only because traditionalists thought that the interior of a car must be the same as the interior of their old coach—with seats that allowed the passengers to face one another. However, with the coach, a driver sat outside, giving him a perfect line of sight. We had already introduced our 1913 line, which had front-drive models that were selling well. Why wouldn't someone who wanted to drive from the front seat just buy a front-drive car? Apparently, that line of thinking was too simple.

The bosses were peering inside the cabin of the prototype car, looking at the mechanism of the duplex drive system. Both the steering and control levers were duplicated, one in front of the rear seat, as had been the custom in our coupes, broughams, and limousines, with an identical set of controls for a front-seat driver. My father, a stocky man, balding, but with an air of energy and confidence, turned back to me. With no expression whatever, he asked, "How does it work?"

"It's simple, really," I replied. "When one mechanism is in use, the other is nonfunctional. You can see the pedals in front are locked to the floor while the rear pedals are deployed."

"How do you change to the other?" he asked.

I glanced at Mr. Hanley, but he looked away. I was going to have to do this. "Well, that's a bit more complicated," I said.

Mr. Bacon, a small, neat man with dark hair, jumped up into the front seat. "Tell me."

"You have to start in back," I said.

He switched seats.

I looked at my notes. "Fully depress the brake pedals and then lock the control lever in neutral."

He did.

"Let up on the brakes, and pull upward and inward on the knob of the brake-shifting lever to release it, then move the shifting lever back as far as it will go. Now fully depress the brakes to the toe board."

He did all of that as well.

"Before letting up on the pedals, bring the shifting lever forward again to its original position. That will lock the rear pedals and release the front brakes."

He did that, glancing around the seat at the front pedals. I held my breath, hoping the mechanism worked as advertised. It did.

"Is that all?" Bacon asked, as if the process were kindergarten-simple. I didn't think anyone would remember how to change the driving seat, and that all the system would do was create frustration.

"Other than turning the front seat around and the normal start-up procedures," I said.

My father cupped his chin in his hand, glanced at McFarlane, an old

Scot with a long gray beard, and then squared himself on Hanley. "Which of our resident geniuses thought this up?"

"It was Will," Hanley said.

"W-what?" I sputtered. I'd had nothing to do with it.

"Oh, yes," Hanley continued. "He worked late into the night to come up with the mechanism. We'd never have even thought of the idea if it wasn't for him."

My father turned to me and gave me a measured stare. "Who do you know at Ohio?"

"Ohio . . . ?"

"Ohio Electric Cars. I know you read *The Horseless Age*, but it wasn't mentioned until yesterday's edition. Who told you about this?"

"I don't . . . I don't know anyone there."

Disgusted, he shook his head, turned, and walked away, calling out over his shoulder, "Read the *Electric Industry Notes*, gentlemen. Ohio calls it 'double drive.' The feature will be on their 1913 models." He stopped and turned back to Hanley. "Any chance we can retrofit the feature into our 1913s?"

Not able to meet my father's eyes, Hanley looked down at the floor and shook his head. "It's a complete retooling. It'll take us a year."

"Damn it!" my father shouted. "Will?"

"Yes?" I said, inwardly cringing.

"I want to see you in my office. Ten minutes." He and MacFarlane strode away, talking in low but ominous-sounding voices.

I spun toward Hanley. "What was that—"

"Let's go, gentlemen," Hanley said, cutting me off. "We've got a lot of work to do." He turned and started for the office. One of the other engineers, a young Yalie who was Hanley's boy Friday, ran his shoulder into me as he passed, no doubt on purpose. I watched the engineers walk off in a line, all following on Hanley's heels like a gaggle of baby geese.

Mr. Bacon jumped down from the car and clapped me on the shoulder—the shoulder in which I'd been shot a few months before. I tried to keep the wince internal. "Nice work there, Anderson," he said.

"I had nothing to—"

"I meant with the presentation. I know you didn't design that mess."

"Oh. Thanks."

"Hanley's a bastard," he said. "He's probably the one who stole the idea. He had to pass it off when Ohio's announcement became official."

I'd stay neutral. Mr. Bacon was a good fellow, but he was management too. "I don't know who came up with it."

"Keep it up." He smiled. "Unless you want to go back to school. We could use a good EE."

"Thanks, but I think I'm done with school."

We shook hands and parted.

I walked over to the administration building as if on my final march to the guillotine. My father's secretary, Mr. Wilkinson, looked up when I walked in and simply pointed to my father's door before busying himself with the work on his desk. Not a good sign.

Taking a deep breath, I strode to the door, knocked twice, and threw it open. My father glared at me from behind his desk. "Close the door behind you."

I did and walked over to him.

"Sit."

I sat in one of the uncomfortable chairs on the other side of his desk.

"Damn it, Will, do you know how much you just embarrassed me? And Hanley hasn't let up on me since you started in engineering. He was in my office twice yesterday, telling me that you didn't come in again without so much as a by-your-leave. What in the hell is wrong with you?"

I waited for him to blow out his steam. My father normally swore as much as Detective Riordan, so I knew this was serious. "First of all, I had nothing to—"

"I don't want to hear your excuses," he shot back. "I have a business to run, and I can't afford to spend all my time playing nursemaid to you, a man who is clearly incapable of acting like a man."

"What?" I was stunned.

"This is it, Will. I've warned you, and not just once. You're fired."

I stared at him, unable to think of anything to say, any argument that would win him over. He was right. I had to be the worst employee in the history of the company.

"It's for your own good, boy. You've got to learn responsibility."

He was quiet, waiting for me to respond. Finally, I said, "I understand," stood, and left his office.

I took a streetcar home, feeling like a spendthrift for parting with the nickel. I had $2 in my wallet, $54.87 left in my checking account, and $100 in twenties in an envelope in the pencil drawer (one never knows when one might need bail money), plus another $85 coming next week Friday for the last two weeks at work, assuming they didn't dock me for the time I was gone. My $241.87 would last . . . how long?

Trying to work out the math, I watched the buildings go by. Woodward had filled in completely with businesses everywhere there weren't homes. Lots of people with money.

Rent was steep at my address—$60—due the first of the month, gas and electricity another $10 or so. My landlord had the police evict deadbeats, even long-term tenants, after a week of unpaid rent. If I got my full check from the company and spent virtually nothing, I would be able to pay rent in November, December, and January. By February 8, I would be out on the street.

I wasn't going home to live with my parents. I wasn't taking charity from them, or from Elizabeth. I would have to get a job. *Shit.*

Well, that would wait. I didn't need a paycheck yet. In this town, a job couldn't be too hard to find. There were more every day, particularly in the automobile industry. Hell, it would be a cinch to find a job with Phipps-Grinnell, Columbia, Hupps-Yeats, or Century. The pretenders in the world of electrics would be happy to hire an engineer from the most successful electric car manufacturer in the country, not to mention add the Anderson name to their roster. That's not even thinking of the dozens of gasoline motorcar companies in Detroit. I could probably get an auction going for my services.

Unfortunately, the thought of every one of those possibilities turned my stomach. I hated engineering. Regardless, I wasn't going to worry about money. 1913 would take care of itself.

After walking the last block to my apartment, I headed to the den to phone Elizabeth. When I sat at my desk, I noticed the telephone stood in the back center of the blotter rather than the left corner, where I normally put it, but I gave it no thought.

I spoke with Alberts. Elizabeth and Sylvia had taken the train to Lansing to meet with Mrs. Arthur and the other board members of the Michigan Equal Suffrage Association. The ladies were to return for a 5:00 P.M. meeting with their local associates at the campaign headquarters. He added that she specifically said she had the evening cleared to spend with me, and she wanted me to pick her up at headquarters at six o'clock. This was the best news—the only good news—I'd had in a while.

After I changed my shoes, I walked back to the den to get the ballots to bring to Elizabeth. I opened the pencil drawer and, for a long moment, could do nothing more than stare. Then I scattered the contents, scooping out pencils and compasses and rulers and notepads and flinging them away. When the drawer was empty, I fell heavily into my chair, leaning back as far as it would go, failure crashing down on me.

The envelope with the ballots was gone, as was the other envelope with my hundred dollars.

CHAPTER ELEVEN

Sapphira! It could be no one else. I cursed myself. But . . . how could she have known I had the ballots? Of course—the men who tried to kill me. She was working with them. She had to be. They were all working for Murphy.

How could I have let her into my home, into my confidence? I was a goddamned imbecile. *The woman who had helped Cooper!* She must be laughing now at my idiocy.

I shot to my feet, snatched up the telephone, and hurled it at the wall. The cord stopped it in midflight, and the candlestick and receiver clattered to the floor. I swept the blotter, along with my pen and ink-well, from the desk. The blotter sailed across the room, hit the wall, and fell to the floor. The inkwell landed on its side and tumbled across the wood planks, leaking black ink, like a trail of blood.

I paced back and forth. I would kill her. I would get the ballots back, and my money, and I would kill her. One more step toward avenging Wesley McRae's death. A step I should have taken the minute I first saw her. I wasn't going to wait. Flikklund said she lived on Dalzelle Street. I'd find her, and I'd kill her.

How to do it? Gun or knife? Either. Both.

I still had one of my Colts. I ran to my bedroom, fit the shoulder holster over my head, and strapped it on. I retrieved the .32 and checked the load—a full magazine. Riordan had my pocketknife, and I had no holster for the daggers, but I ran to the parlor, jerked two of them from the board, and stuck them in my coat pocket.

I ran to the streetcar stop and shoved onto the first Woodward Line car heading downtown. At the Detroit Electric garage, I ran in, grabbed my key from the board, and drove out squealing the tires. The Torpedo jolted when it bounced down from the garage's concrete for a hard right onto the cobbles.

Ten feet ahead—a hearse. I slammed on the brakes and rocked to a stop, no more than a few inches behind the jet black carriage. Through the large windows I could see a walnut casket seated in a plush white interior. I glanced behind me. A black laquered opera coach, no doubt carrying the family of the deceased, sat just behind. The driver stared daggers at me but said nothing.

I told myself to slow down, that I would get to Sapphira's eventually. If she were there now, she'd be there in half an hour. It didn't take. My mind burned. She had played me like a virtuoso.

After another look at the traffic in front of me, I nudged the car onto the sidewalk and edged forward, scattering the pedestrians, until I reached the first alley on the right. I spun the wheel, tore down the narrow mud track, and slammed on the brakes at the end, watching an endless stream of cars, trucks, and wagons sail past.

Goddamn this traffic! It was impossible to get around in this town anymore. Finally, I jerked down on the throttle and cut in front of a spiffy new Hudson coupé, figuring the owner would brake rather than dent up his new automobile. I was right, though my maneuver set off a cacophony of honks all around. A quick left on Fort and I jumped on the gas again, speeding toward Dalzelle Street.

How am I going to do this? She would almost certainly be living with someone. If I was going to kill her, I couldn't very well just run inside and stab her. There would be witnesses. Even if I took her and did the deed elsewhere, other people would see me.

I sped past other cars and wagons until I hit the Fort Street Union Depot, the downtown freight station. Lines of wagons sat double-parked on both sides, forcing traffic to a single narrow lane in the middle of the road. I threaded the Torpedo around and through the other vehicles, bringing traffic to a standstill. On the throttle again, working my way to Sapphira's street. My tires squealed as I shot left in front of a coal wagon and again when I turned the corner onto Dalzelle.

The street was only four blocks, but I didn't expect cooperation from the Irish, who would close ranks against a "native." It would be worse if I came in with my blood up. I had to get control. I took slow, deep breaths as I drove down Dalzelle toward the site of the new train station. Workers swarmed the building like bees in a hive.

Where would she live? Most of the structures were single-family houses, though, of course, that didn't mean that only one family lived in them. It was likely that many, if not most, had boarders to help pay the mortgage. She could be in any of them. More likely, though, were the two apartment buildings. Both were two-story. One was a Spartan structure with a flat roof, the other next door a little nicer, with a wide porch and gabled roof. I'd start with that one. If Murphy was paying the bills, he probably wouldn't dump her in the cheapest place he could find.

I backed up to the intersection with Twelfth and parked at the curb. I climbed out and started across the cobbles, watching for any sign of Sapphira.

"What'cha doin', swell?" a voice piped from behind me.

I stopped and turned to see a youngster of perhaps seven years, standing with his foot hoisted up onto my rear tire. His trousers had holes in both knees, and he wore a jacket that was at least three sizes too large.

Maybe he could help. "I'm looking for someone," I said.

"Who?" the pipsqueak asked.

"A pretty lady named Helen."

"What'cha payin'?"

"Two bits for good information," I said.

"I'll take two bits." I hadn't seen her before, but behind him stood a skinny little girl a couple of years younger, her dress like a flour sack.

"Get lost, sis." The boy shoved the little girl onto the pavement. She promptly began to wail.

Stalking toward them, I shouted, "Hey, you little scalawag! Let her alone!"

"Aw, what's it to ya, buster?" the kid said, backing away, staying out of reach.

I helped the girl to her feet. She wiped her eyes and looked up at me. "Do you know that lady? She has black hair, and her name is Helen." She nodded. "She's nice."

"Where does she live?"

"Don't tell him, sis," the boy called. "He's a copper."

I looked over my shoulder at him. "I'm not a cop. Cops don't pay for information, do they? They beat it out of you."

"Well . . ." The boy kicked at a loose cobblestone. "I guess."

I dug into my pocket and pulled out a pair of quarters. "I'll give you both two bits if you tell me where she lives."

The girl didn't hesitate. She pointed at the flat-roofed building. "All the pretty ladies live there." Holding her other hand out to me, palm up, she said, "Pay up."

Pasting a smile on my face, I gave them both a quarter. "Now, listen," I said, bending down with my hands on my knees. "When I come back in a few minutes, if my car is in the same shape it is now, I'll give you both another two bits. Deal?"

"Deal," they chimed.

I hurried up to the apartment building, dirty white clapboard, a board in place of the first window to the left of the front door, other windows cracked, one on the second floor with the curtain blowing back from a foot-tall gap in the glass. The building looked the right size to hold six or eight apartments, which I thought would be easy enough to check. I climbed the steps, setting off a tremendous howling of dogs somewhere inside. Claws scrabbled against wood with an insane intensity. I pulled open the exterior door and walked into a dingy lobby.

A slovenly man in a white undershirt sat in an upholstered chair next to the fireplace. Two tired-looking women wearing low-cut dresses sipped coffee on the sofa. The room smelled of mold and damp and heavy perfume. I thought I understood when the little girl said all the pretty ladies lived here, but now I was certain.

"We ain't open till noon," the man said in a voice ruined by whiskey and cigarettes.

"Where does Helen live?"

"She's not doin' business. If ya like her type, Flossy would be perfect for you." He gestured to the larger of the women on the sofa. "Got them great big tits and the tightest—"

"Where?" I pulled back my coat and took hold of my pistol's grip.

The women scurried off down the hall, heads ducked.

"Listen," the man said, "you can't just come in here like this."

I drew the pistol and pointed it at his face. "Do you want to live?"

His eyes went wide as manhole covers. "No—I mean, yes, yes. I wanna live."

"Then tell me where she is."

"S-second floor—third door on the left."

"Now get back in your hole."

"Yes, sir."

I started up the stairs while his footsteps pounded across the floor. A door opened and slammed shut.

I climbed the stairs, heading for the third door on the left. I'd try the nice way first. I knocked.

A few seconds later, the door opened. "No, Harold, I have to—" Sapphira saw me and froze, her hands behind her neck, clasping a silver chain necklace. "Will, what are you doing here?" she whispered. "No one can know about . . ." She trailed off, seeing the gun in my hand.

"Give me the ballots," I said.

"Ballots? What?"

"Don't try to buffalo me, Sapphira. Where are they?"

"Where are what? I do not know what you—"

Enraged, I backhanded her across the face with my bad right hand, knuckles connecting with her cheekbone. Her head snapped to the side, and she fell against the doorjamb and then to the floor, half in and half out of her apartment. She looked up at me, eyes beseeching.

I stared at my gloved hand, arcing with pain, and I crashed back to earth. I'd just hit a woman. But . . . I couldn't stop. Steeling myself, I repeated, "Where are they?"

With a hand held to her cheek, she gasped, "Will, I do not know what you are talking about."

"The ballots you stole from my den last night. Where are they?"

"I did not steal anything." Tears streamed down her cheeks.

"God damn it, Sapphira!" I extended my arm until the barrel of the gun touched her forehead. "I want the ballots. Now."

"I am telling the truth," she said, staring fiercely up at me. "I did not steal anything."

"Where did you put my money?" I figured the ballots would be in the same place.

"What is wrong? I have done nothing."

"Show me your handbag."

She climbed to her feet and staggered inside with me on her heels, the Colt pointed at the back of her head. To say the room was mean would be a gross understatement. It was the size of a ship berth, no windows, no furniture other than an unadorned single bed with a lumpy mattress that looked older than she was. Her clothing hung from nails pounded into the walls around the room.

Her bag hung from one of the nails. I shoved her aside and dumped the contents onto the floor. "Against the wall," I said, gesturing with the gun. She did as I said. I searched her things. Her pocketbook held no banknotes, her change purse nothing more than a smattering of copper. No ballots. No twenty-dollar bills.

I rifled through her clothing and examined the bed. I found nothing. She'd already disposed of it. *To Murphy?*

I stood in front of Sapphira, pistol extended. She seemed to have shrunk into herself. Her face carried the resigned mien of a condemned woman waiting for the gallows.

"Where are they?" I demanded.

"Where are what?" she asked. "I do not know what you are talking about."

I thumbed back the hammer on the pistol and held it against her forehead again.

"Kill me." Her voice was small but certain. "You will do me a favor."

"Who were those men? The ones who tried to kill *me*."

"Will, I have been helping you!" Tears streamed down her face. "I do not know what you are talking about."

Rage filled me. I shoved the barrel of the gun harder against her head and shouted, "Who were they?"

"Hey, asshole," a gravelly voice said.

I turned my head to see the slovenly man in the doorway, not six feet away, aiming a double-barreled shotgun at me.

"Get out of here," he said. "Now."

I kill Sapphira. He kills me. I'd heard of worse trades . . . but I wasn't convinced Elizabeth would be safe without me. I held the gun up, barrel pointed at the low ceiling.

He stepped back, out of the doorway, and gestured with the shotgun. I walked out into the hall but turned back to Sapphira. "I will get them back."

She slammed the door shut.

"Gimme the peashooter," the man said.

"I've got no issue with you. I'm not going to shoot you."

"Yeah, well, I *am* gonna shoot you unless you hand me that gun. That'll get me a pretty penny. Anyways, it's the least you could do after wakin' up all my whores."

I held the gun over my shoulder, and he took it, then jabbed me in the back with the shotgun, pushing me toward the stairs. Seething, I descended the steps and left the building.

He stopped in the doorway. "Next time you show your face, I'm shootin'. Don't forget that."

I stopped at the bank and cashed a ten-dollar check. Even though that dropped my balance under forty-five dollars, I needed walking-around money. I considered returning the Torpedo to the garage and taking a streetcar, but I didn't want to spare the time.

I drove to the Bethune Street police station. I would have to curtail my driving as much as possible until I had a source of income. Gasoline continued to increase in price and was now upwards of thirty cents a gallon, even in the single-purpose "gasoline stations" that were sprouting up on every other corner, and the Torpedo used more of it than any motorcar I'd ever seen. A DUR trolley, while overpriced compared to most big cities, still cost a nickel to travel anywhere in Detroit, and even the interurban trains were a bargain by comparison. Of course, they had no style or speed, both of which the Torpedo had in abundance.

I was lucky enough to find Riordan at the station. He brought me back to his tiny office, choked with cigar smoke, and I sat with my knees squeezed up against his desk. It rankled me that he never so much as checked after the mine incident to see if I still had a pulse. "Did you get my message yesterday?"

"Message?" He sucked on the butt end of a cigar.

As I thought. "It turns out I survived the man shooting at me. See this bandage?" I turned my head toward him. "Bullet wound. He almost killed me."

He only nodded.

"You didn't think it was important enough to find out what happened to me?"

He puffed on his cigar and looked at me with those wolf eyes. "The men chasing you were my concern. I spent the rest of the day trying to run them down."

"It didn't occur to you that I might be able to describe them?"

"Is this why you came here? To critique my detective work?" He blew a cloud of smoke over my head. "I got descriptions from a dozen men."

"I was shot at numerous times and nearly blown up in the mine. You left me there."

Stubbing out the cigar, he said, "The manager sent a boy to tell me you'd come up and were fine. I had asked him to let me know. I'm busy. I hadn't meant to hurt your feelings."

He said it deadpan, but it felt like sarcasm to me. I took a deep breath and let it go. I needed him. "I need to move forward, and to do that I could use some answers."

"Before you do that, I have something you'd be interested in. Hold on." He began rummaging through the papers on his desk until he found the one he wanted. "Here it is. David Sanford floated down to the docks at General Ice Delivery. They're right there at the bend, so they get their share. He had his wallet and identification."

"Shot in the face?"

"Shot in the face."

I wasn't sure if I should be happy I hadn't hallucinated David's murder or if I should be sad that he actually had been killed.

"Can I assume you believe I saw him murdered, or do you think it's a strange coincidence that his body happened to turn up after another of my fits?"

He pulled another cigar from his coat, bit off the end and spat it into the trash basket, and flipped his lighter open. "Let's say I believe you." He lit the lighter and began sucking on the cigar, chuffing away like a locomotive, until the end glowed orange and the office was hazy with smoke that smelled like burning feces.

"Can you take a leap of faith that I also disarmed a man at the suffrage rally who was trying to kill one of the ladies onstage—probably Jane Addams?"

He ignored the question. "Did you know Sanford was a gambler?"

"No."

"Story I heard is he owed over a thousand dollars from some big game, and he couldn't cover the debt."

"Really."

Puff. "The game was sanctioned by the Gianolla brothers."

"That would be one explanation."

"Try this one on—did you know that he just got out of a five-year stint in Joliet?"

"What? David?"

"He was bilking Chicago investors on Montana real estate." Puff.

"Really? He seemed like such a nice fellow."

"Those are the ones to watch out for, Anderson."

"Then I guess I don't need to watch out for you."

Puff. "I wouldn't go that far."

"Okay. You know he was a criminal and he went to work for Murphy, who is plotting to beat Elizabeth. Can you see any possible connection there?"

"Right," Riordan said, fixing his wolf eyes on me. "'The conspiracy.' David Sanford worked for the Michigan Liquor Association for three weeks. He did nothing other than write a few press releases. I'd say he was trying to drum up some money before Sam Gianolla gave him a shotgun enema." He sat back again, pulled the cigar from his mouth, and rolled it in his fingers, gazing at the orange embers. "Now." Puff. "As to your mystery shooter at the rally—no, I don't believe in him. I was there. Don't get me wrong. I don't think you're lying. I think you believe you saw him."

I closed my eyes, counted to five, and opened them again. I would not punch him in the face. "Then tell me this—did you catch the fellows who were chasing me, and have you uncovered anything regarding the danger Elizabeth is in? Not necessarily in that order, if you have another preference."

Riordan just stared at me for a while, not moving. Smoke curled up from the end of his cigar. "I'm not sure I like your attitude."

"I don't give half a shit for what you think about my attitude. Do you want to help Elizabeth, or was your speech yesterday morning just a pile of horse manure?"

His eyes narrowed. "You know what I think of her."

"Then you want me to help you, don't you?"

He was quiet.

"I know as well as you that you can't get this police force to back you in anything. If you don't have me, you don't have anyone."

"Don't pretend you know anything about my life, Anderson," he snapped, mashing out his cigar in the ashtray. "Now, listen."

"Wait. You've talked about it before—the alienation you've had here since my trial. Why is it off-limits all of a sudden?"

"It's nothing . . . it's nothing to do with you. So drop it."

He looked bewildered and sounded sad, two descriptions I'd never associated with Detective Riordan. "Fine," I said. It had been a fleeting thought before, but now I wondered—*Is he in love with Elizabeth?* Was it more than a father-daughter love? He was perhaps fifteen years older, certainly not outside the normal range of lovers or spouses. Yet surely he knew that she was outside his reach in every way. Though it had diminished since her father's dishonesty became known, she had social status, and she had money, neither of which would ever be possessed by this man. He had to know that.

He straightened, and his voice again took on its normal command. "So long as you don't endanger Elizabeth, I'll include you—and I'll try to help you, but you'd better show me some respect."

I looked back at him. "I have no problem showing respect for those who do the same for me. It's a two-way street, Detective."

"Fine," he muttered. "The men from the salt mine got away, and we don't have any solid leads. Elizabeth confirmed that she sent Brennan to Wayne Pavilion to protect you. By the way, nothing has turned up that would make me lean toward believing there's a conspiracy—including the accidental death of a man from the MLA office, and the murder of another who was in hock to the Sicilians." He picked up the crooked cigar he'd mashed out, lit it, and sat back, puffing up a gray cloud that fogged the room.

"Since when do you wear blinders?" I asked. "Oh—and you didn't get my message, so you don't know I discovered what Flikklund had been hiding."

"What was it?" he asked around the cigar.

"Ballots for the upcoming election. From Ingham County."

"Why would he have had them?"

"I don't know," I said.

"Was there something on them that looked suspicious?"

"Nothing that jumped out at me, but I don't know a damned thing about ballots. I was going to show them to Elizabeth, but they were stolen from me."

"Stolen? By who?"

I wasn't one hundred percent certain, but I couldn't imagine it had happened any other way. I sighed. "Sapphira Xanakis."

He sat back, a little smile playing on his mouth. "Have you had enough? Are you ready to turn her in?"

I thought about it. I felt like a heel and a bully for striking her. I couldn't do it. Yet. "I don't know where she is."

"When did she steal the ballots?"

"Last night. She came to my apartment saying she wanted to help me. I left her by herself for a few minutes while I dressed, and she must have—"

"While you dressed?" His eyes bored into mine.

"That's not what—yes, I dressed. I had been getting ready for a bath when she rang my doorbell. So, as I was saying, she snuck into my den while I was dressing and found the ballots. For good measure, she also stole a hundred bucks from me."

His eyes widened. "You let her into your apartment? Lord, boy, are you using that noggin for anything besides a hat rack?"

"I know. I just . . . I thought she was telling me the truth. She's a very good liar."

"Ladies of the evening tend to throw out the occasional falsehood. Most are pretty good at it."

I stood. "Yes, I'm an idiot. Now, can we move on? Elizabeth needs us."

He nodded, pushed back from his desk, and, with a wince, got to his feet. "I'll let you know what I find out."

"Thank you. Now, may I have my gun and knife back? I think I'll have need of them."

"We can check on the way out. They might have made it in."

"That's good to know," I said.

He shrugged. "It's the Detroit police."

I could do nothing about it. I held my left hand out to him. "Thank you, Detective, for agreeing to work with me. You won't regret it."

He looked at my hand for a moment before taking it in his left and shaking with me. "That remains to be seen. I'll work with you until you give me another reason not to. See if you can make it through the day without doing that."

CHAPTER TWELVE

After experiencing the miracle of having my gun and knife re-turned to me by the DPD, I drove back to my building to touch up my shave and change clothes before meeting Elizabeth. Everything needed to be perfect, which meant I would not be telling her about my father firing me. That could wait for another day.

I greeted William the doorman, then took the stairs two at a time and hurried down the hall to my apartment. When I unlocked the door, I remembered that it had been unlocked this morning when I left.

I locked it last night. Didn't I? I stepped through the doorway and stood there, trying to remember.

Yes. I would swear I had. Yet the door was unlocked this morning. Could . . . could someone have broken in last night while I was asleep? Sapphira getting in the building without challenge made it clear it was possible. Perhaps she had told the truth.

I removed the bandage on my ear. The damage was less than I had thought, given the amount of blood I'd lost—just a little nick near the bottom of the lobe. After cleaning it up a bit, I left it unbandaged.

Around half past four it started to rain, soft and quiet at first and increasingly hard over the next hour, the drops smacking against my windows like little fists. I grabbed an umbrella and walked downstairs to drive to campaign headquarters. On the way out, I saw Frank was on now, so I stopped and buttonholed him. "Listen, Frank. A woman came up to my apartment last night without me being notified. You're supposed to phone me, and I let you know whether someone can come up."

"Oh," he said, abashed. "I didn't think you'd mind your sister coming to see you." He worried at the inside of his cheek with his teeth.

"My sister? She wasn't my sister. Did you notice the Greek accent?"

"Yes, sir," he said. "Very becoming." His round face was rapidly turning a bright pink.

He wasn't getting it. "Did you let anyone else up last night?"

"Not for you, sir."

"Just let me know who wants to see me before you let them in."

"Everyone?" he asked.

"Yes. If Jesus Christ walks in that door and asks to see Will Anderson, you are still to phone me for my permission. Have you got that?"

"Of course, sir." Now he was hurt.

"Thank you, Frank." I hoped he understood. With my recent past, I couldn't have just anyone admitted to see me if I wanted to live out the year.

I hurried outside into a cold, driving rain, donned my driving goggles, and drove back to campaign headquarters at a crawl, flipping the knob for the windscreen wipers every few seconds. Unfortunately my goggles had none, and I could barely see. When I arrived, I parked on the street outside the building.

Warren Brennan stood at his post in front of the door. He sneered at me, making no attempt to appear neutral or even professional; he'd clearly had enough of me and didn't care who knew it. The wind and rain likely didn't help his demeanor. He wore the same black duster, but it did not give him enough protection from the elements. His derby was soaked through, as was what I could see of his shirt. The temperature was hovering near fifty, but the wind howling in from the northwest shot him with a stinging rain. He was cold, soaked to the skin, and very unhappy to see me.

All of which, of course, made me pleased as punch, particularly as my umbrella blocked most of the rain that would have been soaking me. I couldn't prove Brennan had anything to do with David's death, and maybe he actually had been there to protect me, but the man had been a thorn in my side from the moment I first laid eyes on him. I had to force Elizabeth to get rid of him.

I gave him an ear-to-ear grin. "Enjoying the weather, Brennan? Eh?"

"What do you want?"

"I'm here for Elizabeth. That's Miss Hume to you."

Without a word, he spun, threw open the door, and disappeared inside. The door lock clicked loudly.

I waited . . . and waited. I wrapped my duster around me more tightly and faced the building to block the wind and rain. After five minutes had passed, I knocked on the door. No one answered. It was the Burnsies' job to admit guests, a task Warren Brennan obviously wanted to stretch out as long as possible.

I had to get him out of the picture. That he was a pain in my backside was my problem, but as long as he was around I feared for Elizabeth. If Brennan was involved in the conspiracy, he would be the conduit of confidential information to the conspirators. And that might only be the tip of the iceberg. He had to go. But how?

Finally he returned, unlocked the door, and slipped out, locking it behind him. "She'll be out in a moment."

"She wanted me to wait outside?"

"I don't have specific instructions." He looked straight ahead like one of the King's Guard at Buckingham Palace. "'Never assume, unless it leads to safer circumstances for your client,' Mr. Burns says."

"You're a real pip, you know that, Brennan? Being a doorman has to be a big step up from slopping shit or whatever you're actually qualified to do." If he hit me now, while he was working, perhaps she'd cut him loose.

Now he turned for me, hate burning in his eyes, rain drubbing his face.

I just smiled from under my umbrella. "Go play with your friends, Nancy. You don't have the balls to have a go at me. Don't make me thump you again."

"I . . ." His face contorted with rage. "You name the time and place." His voice was strangled, barely squeezing from his throat. "Any kind of weapon . . . or bare-fisted. You choose."

I laughed in his face. "You've had your chance, Nancy. If you recall, you knocked yourself out hitting me with a garbage can. Face it, Brennan. You're not man enough."

For half a second, I thought he was going to do it. His eyes flashed, and his right shoulder dipped, but he caught himself. After a deep breath, he stepped back, just to the side of the door, and faced the street. Back to his King's Guard routine. "I know about you," he said. "Playing the gentleman while you drag everyone down. You take drugs, commit crimes, and murder people."

"Go suck an egg, Brennan."

He didn't reply, just looked at me with what I'm sure he thought was a steely gaze. I shook my head and leaned against the wall to wait. A few minutes later, Elizabeth knocked on the door from the inside, and Brennan turned and unlocked it.

Unfurling her umbrella, she squeezed through the door. "I didn't mean for him to wait out here, Mr. Brennan. Goodness gracious. Show some manners."

"Sorry, miss," he replied in a neutral voice. "You didn't say specific where he should be."

"Specifically, you mean," I said.

He shot me a hostile glance.

Sylvia walked out, also opening her umbrella. Elizabeth glanced at her and looked back at me. "Before we go to the flickers, I thought we could take Sylvia out to dinner."

"Wonderful," I said. "Where would you ladies like to dine?"

"I have to be at the station in two hours," Sylvia said. "If you don't mind, I'd like to eat Chinese." She glanced at the King Ying Lo sign across the street. "I've developed a bit of a taste for their dumplings."

"King Ying Lo it is." Perhaps half a dozen Chinese restaurants dotted the downtown area. We'd tried Pekin and Chinese National, but we thought King's to be the best. Bowing deeply with a sweep of my hat, I said, "Your wish is my command."

Sylvia glanced at Elizabeth. "Such a gentleman."

Elizabeth put on a smile but said nothing. It was unlike her. I wondered if something was wrong.

When we crossed the street, I glanced back to see Brennan running to catch up with us, his eyes cutting back and forth, as he assessed threats.

In a short pause in the ladies' conversation, I ducked my head between them. "Can we leave Brennan behind this evening? He gives me a pain."

Once on the sidewalk, Elizabeth turned to face me and said stiffly, "Mr. Brennan is here for Sylvia's protection. I'm much more concerned with her safety than your discomfort."

"Fine." I didn't want to push it. I couldn't afford another barrier between us. I held the door for Sylvia and Elizabeth before cutting in front of Brennan.

Though too ornate for my taste, the restaurant was impressively decorated. The dark walnut tables, chairs, and cabinets were carved with intricate patterns of dragons and curved-tile-roof buildings set in jungles. Silk scrolls hung from the ceiling with painted Chinese characters surrounded by borders of Oriental scenes. The electric light fixtures were intricately molded brass, each with three glowing orbs nearly the size of medicine balls. Ginger and other Oriental spices flavored the air.

We were led to a table by a smiling man, who bowed several times with his palms together in a praying position. Brennan sat at the table with us, watching the people in the restaurant. Thankfully, while the three of us ate he kept his mouth shut, even forgoing the opportunity to comment when, in frustration, I began impaling my chicken on a chopstick, rather than continuing the struggle to pick it up in a civilized manner. I didn't bother with the rice, as my only option was to scoop it up with my fingers. I try to respect the choices of foreign cultures, but I simply don't understand how a people who consume this much rice could come to a consensus on eating it with sticks.

The conversation was light through dinner, other than our discussion of TR's condition. His doctors believed the extent of his injury was a broken rib, although they were unable to remove the bullet and were still concerned about the possibility of blood poisoning or other complications. The Colonel was said to be energetic and in good spirits, and expected to hit the stump again soon. Wilson had offered to stop campaigning while he was recovering, but the Colonel said he expected no quarter, nor would he give any. Vintage Roosevelt.

John Schrank, TR's would-be assassin, had been carrying a grip, in which a manuscript was found that denounced the former president, including statements like, "Down with Roosevelt. We want no king." He'd hang for sure.

As the meal was winding down, Sylvia said, "I'm so sorry I have to leave, Elizabeth, but I simply must return." She turned to me. "My mother and sister managed to get themselves arrested again."

"Arrested?" I echoed. "For what?"

She gave me a wry smile. "Smashing windows."

"Why would they smash windows?"

"They don't feel we're getting enough attention."

I glanced at Elizabeth, but she was leaving it to Sylvia and me. "Seems like a strange way to forward the suffrage cause, doesn't it?" I asked.

Sylvia gave us a naughty smile. "When the prime minister and Parliament are getting their windows broken, it does draw attention."

"Ah."

"I was leaving in two days anyway. We're opening a Votes for Women shop on Bow Street on behalf of the Women's Social and Political Union. The East End hasn't a—I'm sorry, you probably don't know the East End of London—it's a great abyss of poverty, and the women there have no political voice whatever."

"Good for you," I said. "It sounds like a wonderful idea."

She pursed her lips. "I wish my mother and Christabel agreed with that."

"What could they have against it?" I asked.

Sylvia glanced at Elizabeth. In the look that passed between them, I could see they'd already had this conversation. "Their stance is that working women have no time for politics, and uneducated women have little use for it."

I was no student of politics, but I could understand the sentiment.

"If I don't go," she continued, "I'm afraid that Zelie—Zelie Emerson, my partner in crime," she added with a smile, "will have to set up the shop singlehandedly. I can't have her doing all the work."

Smiling, Elizabeth reached across the table and gripped her hand. "We completely understand, Sylvia. I know your fight is far from won, but I believe you've helped us win here."

"Oh, posh," she replied. "I wasn't even able to speak in the city."

Elizabeth held a fist near her heart, which reminded me of Sapphira and our conversation at the Cadillac. "You've helped us all in here, Sylvia. The courage that you and your family have shown has inspired us all, and your encouragement has helped me immensely. We shall win, and you will be a part of that victory."

Sylvia laughed. "I love your enthusiasm, Elizabeth. If only all women shared your perspective, this battle would have been won long ago."

"Get them to stop—" Brennan began, but halted midsentence and looked down, turning red.

"Stop what, Mr. Brennan?" Sylvia asked.

"Stop, er . . . well, stop having . . . pleasing their husbands."

Both women guffawed, having caught his meaning. "The *Lysistrata* approach," Sylvia said with a smile. "Yes, it worked for Aristophanes. Perhaps it would work for us as well, eh, Mr. Brennan?"

"Yes, er, well, that's what I was thinking." Brennan now smiled, assuaged by their reaction.

I wanted to call him on it. He didn't know who Aristophanes was. He probably thought *Lysistrata* was a venereal disease. Not only that, it chapped me that his lack of manners was so well received. Of course, to say so would prove me even more poorly mannered, so I smiled and went along.

"That would win the war," Sylvia said. "Think of it—every woman in the Western world withholding favors from her husband. It would be a week to suffrage!"

When we finished our meal, I took the check and paid, trying not to think of the impact $2.87 would have on my cash reserves. Elizabeth had her Baker Electric, and she insisted on driving us back to the Hotel Cadillac for Sylvia's luggage and then to the Michigan Central Station on Jefferson. While my wallet appreciated the break, my ego was less forgiving of being driven by a woman in an automobile made by our top competitor—or rather the top competitor of my father's company, I reminded myself, as I no longer worked there.

The rain had stopped, and the air was heavy with rotting leaves and a wet chill. The cobblestones glistened with little diamonds, kicked up by the headlights. I pulled my derby down over my forehead and slumped on the box seat in the front left corner, hoping no one recognized me. Brennan squeezed his bulk onto the little jump seat in the right front. Sylvia sat on the bench seat in back, next to Elizabeth, who manned the steering tiller and shift lever. I could see why cities were outlawing backseat driving. How Elizabeth could see over the pair of us—particularly the hulking Brennan—was a bit bewildering to me.

It was a tearful good-bye for the ladies. I was pleased to see Brennan board with Sylvia and even more pleased to see the train leave the station. I enjoyed Sylvia, but the loss of Brennan and the prospect of an evening alone with Elizabeth more than made up for that.

CHAPTER THIRTEEN

Finally, we were alone, back in the car. "Brennan isn't coming back, is he?" I asked.

Elizabeth glanced at the watch above the toilet case in the door, put the car into reverse, and pulled out onto the street. "Yes, he is. As soon as he sees Sylvia off in New York, he'll be taking a train back."

"I don't think that's a good—"

"Will, we can talk about this later. We've only got twenty minutes before the program begins." She pushed the shift lever forward through first to second and then third. The Baker whizzed down the wet road at a sprightly fourteen miles per hour.

She glanced over at me. "What happened to your ear?"

"Oh, just a little nick." I didn't need her thinking I'd hallucinated another gunman.

We were coming up to our turn onto Washington Boulevard, and Elizabeth didn't even downshift. With barely a glance in either direction, she shot around the corner in front of a streetcar, which came much too close for my liking.

I didn't want to wait to discuss my concerns.

"The next rally is only a week away, Elizabeth, and no one has a clue who tried to shoot one of you at the last one. Unless the gunman is discovered, you have to cancel."

"Will, I don't—"

"You need to be more careful. Someone could be trying to kill *you*."

She stared straight ahead and bit her lip. Taking a deep breath, she said, "Listen, Will. We have no one else to take center stage at the rally." Then she added brightly, "Perhaps you could get me Colonel Roosevelt. How about that?"

"Don't be ridiculous," I said.

"Ridiculous?" She laughed. "Give me an alternative, Will. Otherwise . . ." She trailed off.

Otherwise shut your mouth, she was thinking.

I didn't think she had been the target, nor did I seriously believe she would be endangered by speaking at the rally next Thursday. Still, she needed to pay more attention to her safety. We'd discuss it later. For now I'd return to my previous subject. "I think Brennan may be involved in the conspiracy."

"We'll talk about it after the flickers."

"There's more I have to tell you."

She turned right on Fort and began maneuvering around Campus Martius Park. "Can it wait two hours so I can enjoy my evening?"

Chastened, I nodded. Turning onto Monroe, she continued past the Bijou Theater and swung down the alley into a parking yard in the back. Automobiles already filled most of the fifty or so spaces, but she found a spot that would allow her to pull straight through to leave. Children were being killed by a new hazard—parents driving cars in reverse, generally to leave a parking space. Elizabeth always looked for a "pull through." I needed to get into the habit myself, though in my case for a quick getaway, as it seemed everyone wanted to take a shot at me these days.

The Bijou was large as nickelodeons go, with seats for about three hundred people. The chairs, walls, and curtains were all red with gold scrolling. I bought the tickets, and we filed in. Nearly all the chairs were already occupied, though we managed to find seats together near the front.

The piano player banged away to open the show, which started with a "scenic" of the French countryside and was followed by an "actuality" of the Italians and Ottomans signing the treaty that ended their war. After a sing-along led by a pretty young lady with a big, though slightly flat, voice, we watched a comedy about a married couple who went from unhappy to happy in the course of eight ridiculous minutes. Next was an illustrated sing-along of Irving Berlin's new smashes "Alexander's Ragtime Band" and "The Elevator Man Going Up! Going Up!! Going Up!!!" The piano player followed that with an extended Berlin rag interval, and the young lady came back out for another sing-along.

Elizabeth did not warm to me as the evening wore on. She seemed preoccupied. She had a lot on her mind, I knew, with the election only three weeks hence, but I wondered what else drove her mood. I did not want to make it worse by discussing the ballots—or worse, Sapphira being in my apartment—but with as little chance as I had to speak with her, I saw no alternative.

I'd been hoping to get Elizabeth back to my place while it was still mine, but I could imagine the fireworks if she agreed to that and afterward I said, "Oh, by the way, Sapphira stopped by last night while I was getting ready for a bath, so I answered the door naked and asked her in." No, that was the cad's way out. I would tell her after the show and take my medicine.

When the lights went down again for the finale, I reached over and took Elizabeth's hand. (I always sat to her right.) She didn't rebuff me, but she didn't return my squeezes either. I spent the twelve minutes of the new Mary episode, "The Affair at Raynor's," breathing in her scent—vanilla with flowery undertones—and hoping against hope I could somehow salvage the evening.

At the end of the program, she took my arm, and, with the rest of the crowd, we filed outside into the cold wet night and the bright lights of the city. I tried to judge her mood as we walked through the alley to the car, but she was quiet and her face was shadowed under the brim of her hat, her breath steaming out from underneath it in bursts of white cloud. We followed the rest of the crowd through the alley and out into the harsh white light of the parking yard. Floodlights beamed down from buildings on three sides. Three long shadows mimicked every move of the fifty people who walked in front of us, even the clouds of steam, like wispy black smoke on the cobbles.

"So, uh," I mumbled, "we need to talk."

"Yes, we do," she said, still not looking at me.

Automobile doors opened and closed, men cranked starters, and engines turned over. We climbed into Elizabeth's car, and she pulled out into the alley, driving north toward Grand Boulevard.

"Why don't we start with Brennan?" I asked. She made no protest, so I said, "I really believe he's dangerous, Elizabeth. You need to fire him."

"Based on what evidence?" At the end of the alley, she turned left and then right up Woodward.

While she did, I told her about chasing Brennan from David Sanford's murder.

"I sent him to protect you," she replied. "Mr. Brennan explained the situation to my satisfaction. Thomas—Detective Riordan, that is—agrees with me. Mr. Brennan is a solid man."

"*Thomas?*"

She tossed her hair, but it was still too short to have much effect. "That's his name."

"So you've been talking with Riordan?"

"Yes." The air between us had turned decidedly frosty.

It was quiet in the automobile for a few moments, the only sounds coming from outside—the hum of the motor, the little jolts and squeaks of the frame and chassis, and the whir of the tires skimming over the rain-slickened concrete. She slowed and stopped for a trolley at Montcalm Street, yet still stared resolutely out the windscreen, saying nothing. I remembered I'd left the Torpedo on the street by suffrage headquarters, but I decided to keep that to myself.

Finally I asked, "Did he tell you about the ballots being stolen?"

Her eyes narrowed, and her cheeks reddened. "Why don't you tell me about it?"

The street cleared, and she pushed the shift lever forward, moving us through the intersection. Through clenched teeth, I told her about finding the ballots at Flikklund's hideout, being chased through the mine yard, and finding the envelope with the ballots missing the next morning.

By the time I finished, she had stopped at Peterboro, waiting to turn left. "Who stole it?" she asked, her voice a study in neutrality.

She already knew. *Riordan, that son of a bitch.*

"I don't *know* who took it. I have an idea."

"And?" She jammed the shifter up to third speed, and the tires spun as she whipped the car around the corner, bouncing me off the side interior wall. The car rattled down the cobbles toward my building.

Ah, shit. I didn't want to do this. "It was Sapphira, and before you jump—"

"Sapphira." Her voice was steady. "So just how did she steal it?"

I was determined to meet this query with pride. I had done nothing wrong. "She came to my apartment last night. She seemed distraught. I left her alone for a few minutes, and she must have sneaked into my den and stolen it."

Elizabeth jammed on the brake, and we rocked to a stop at the curb, still a block away from my building. "You let her in your apartment," she said.

Even though her voice was quiet and her tone even, I heard these words like the bang of a judge's gavel. Still, I had done nothing wrong. "Had you seen her, you would have done the same."

"Will," she said, "I'm sorry. It's just . . . I know you were attracted to her before. She is a beautiful woman . . . but she and I couldn't be more different."

"I have no interest in her that way. I thought she wanted to help us."

Elizabeth did not switch off the motor.

After a moment, I asked, "Are you coming in?"

She was quiet. Her eyes filled. She bit her lip, trying not to cry. If I hadn't known better, I would have thought her face said that we were finished. Even knowing her, I wasn't sure. Exhaling, she finally said, "All right. I'll hear you out." She pushed the steering tiller up against the side and switched off the ignition and the lights.

I climbed out of the car, walked around the back, and opened the door for her. We walked side by side across the street. She didn't take my arm. Her hands were jammed in her pockets, and she hunched down into her coat, hiding in its dark folds.

From the corner of my eye, I caught a movement to our right. I turned and looked across the street. A figure moved toward us, walking across the lawn in the shadow of the tall trees. Now he was silhouetted against the light from the parlor of the home behind him. He looked to be a large man, and his path would intersect with ours. In the dark, I couldn't discern whether he was watching us.

Now another man moved out from the darkness on our left, between my building and the house we were passing, also moving our way. My senses went on high alert. I looked back again at the first man. He was still on the lawn, perhaps fifty feet away, but continued moving toward us. He seemed to start, noticing us, and his head tilted back in what looked like surprise. His face came into view for a fraction of a second.

It was the man from Flikklund's—the one who had shot at me.

Time slowed.

I cleared my coat, drew the pistol from my shoulder holster, and spun toward him. "Elizabeth!" I barked, now pushing her back, toward her car. "Run!"

She stumbled and fell. I leveled the gun at the man across the street, risking a glance at the second man, who had frozen in place. Elizabeth scrambled to her feet and ran. By the time I looked back to the first man, he had disappeared into the shadows of the trees. "You!" I shouted. "Stop!" Footsteps thudded against the turf, quickly blending into the traffic noise.

I spun and aimed the gun at the second man, who stood frozen in place, staring at me, arms raised, mouth hanging open. Little white bursts of steam shot from his mouth.

"Come out and let me see you!" I shouted.

"M-Mr. Anderson? You're not gonna shoot me, are you?"

His voice was oddly high-pitched. I held the gun on him while scanning the area across the street for any sign of the other man. "Get over here," I said. "Keep your hands where I can see them. Elizabeth!" I called. "We need to get inside—now."

"Will!" Elizabeth exclaimed. I glanced her way. She marched toward me, eyes narrowed. "Put that away. Now!"

I kept the gun on the man and looked across the street again. "Elizabeth, that man"—I gestured across the street—"tried to kill me. This is obviously his partner."

"Who? This boy? He can't be more than fifteen years old."

Now I took a good look at the second man—no, a boy—the boy who lived next door. "I'm sorry," I said. "I didn't know it was you."

"Let him go!" Elizabeth reached up and batted my gun down. "Put that thing away! Now!"

"Yes, by all means." I glanced his way. "Please go."

The boy hurried back the way he had come.

I opened my coat and holstered the pistol. "I was just making sure—"

"There's nothing to make sure." Elizabeth stood close to me, hands on hips. "You know you made that boy urinate in his pants?" she hissed.

I moved around so that I would be between her and the man across the street, should he decide to try a shot. "I recognized the first man. He's trying to kill me. I thought the boy was with him."

"Now someone is trying to kill you? Will, my God." Her voice was filled with anguish, her eyes pleading. "See Dr. Miller," she said. "You need help."

"It looked like they were boxing us in." I shook my head. "Listen, do you trust me or not?"

"I . . . yes, I trust you, Will, the real you, but you haven't been yourself lately."

I looked behind me, feeling like I had a target on my back. "Could we go inside?"

Again, she looked like she would start crying.

"Elizabeth, I'm not crazy."

"I don't think you're crazy, Will, but you're confused. It's the radium, I know it." She reached out and grabbed hold of my arm. "You've got to promise me. You'll see Dr. Miller. As soon as possible."

"Sure. Fine. Now, please could we get out of the street?"

"I . . . should go," she said.

"I've had a few fits, but other than that my brain is working fine. This was not a hallucination. Okay, I was wrong about the boy, but I am one hundred percent positive the man is the same one who shot at me at the salt mine."

"Honey." She hugged me and then stood back. "I love you, Will. I want to help. It's just the radium, I know it."

"So you think I'm crazy for trying to try to protect you?"

"No. Will, listen." Her eyes wide, she shook my arm and enunciated as if talking to a three-year-old. "I don't think you're crazy. I think you're just a little mixed up right now."

"My mind is working normally."

"Please. For me. See Dr. Miller."

"Fine. I will as soon as I get a chance."

"We'll talk tomorrow," she said and backed toward her car. I mirrored her movements to stay between her and the other side of the street. At her car, she unlocked and opened the door and climbed in.

I stepped in close. "I still need to explain to you what's been happening."

"I'll phone you tomorrow, Will. Get some sleep." She closed the door, switched on the car, and pulled down the steering tiller. With a glance behind her, she pulled out onto the street.

I watched her drive away. A heavy raindrop splattered onto the brim of my derby, followed by another, and another. The Baker turned left onto Second Street and disappeared behind the houses on the next block.

CHAPTER FOURTEEN

Why couldn't she see? I turned and headed up the sidewalk, sloshing through the rain on the way to Woodward Avenue. I turned right and marched past the streetcar stop, my hands jammed into the pockets of my duster. If I left the Torpedo in the street downtown all night, I'd likely be short one car by morning. Any sane person would have taken a trolley rather than hoofing the two miles in the rain, but then I wasn't sane, was I? I had been driven mad by radioactivity.

What the hell was wrong with her? Miss High and Mighty, leader of the suffrage movement. *Bullshit.*

In forty-five minutes, I'd reached my car, which was still in one piece, and drove it back to the Detroit Electric garage. I dropped it and left before anyone could accost me. I'd been parking there free as a job benefit, but I didn't think the space would be available to me any longer. I'd have to find a new place to store the Torpedo. Or I could sell it—which, as much as I loved the car, I would do before I sold Elizabeth's diamond.

I walked back up Woodward in a steady rain, my duster soaked through, derby a sodden lump of cold felt, stockings sloshing in my shoes. I was nearly home, passing the Addison Hotel on Woodward and Charlotte, when I heard the strains of wild jazz coming from inside. Odd. The Addison was a very posh establishment, and I'd only heard waltzes and the like when I frequented the place in the past.

I glanced at my watch. 1:15 A.M. Earlier this year, the city made it illegal for a saloon to be open between the hours of midnight and six in the morning, though it was a law followed less stringently than the jaywalking ordinances. Serious drinkers could find an open saloon at all hours without a great deal of effort. As was the rule in Detroit, so long as the right palm was greased, any law would be ignored.

I stopped and listened. A trumpet blared, screeched. A saxophone jumped in, running up and down the register. A trombone howled and then a banjo twanged. The doorman watched me stand out on the sidewalk in the rain while he faced me under the canopy in his dry green uniform with gold piping.

I didn't think about it for very long. My alternative was returning to my empty apartment. I passed the doorman in a daze and walked across the marble lobby to the ballroom at the far end. The music swelled, crazy, out of control.

I entered the dimly lit ballroom, and a Negro man took my dripping hat and duster. In front of the band, dozens of couples whirled across the dazzling Florentine glass floor. Most of the men wore tie and tails, but I wasn't entirely out of place, as some also wore suits, though all were much dryer than mine. The women dappled in layered dresses in eye-popping turquoise, emerald, and orange.

High society had fallen for jazz. Unlike all of my previous experiences with jazz music, the band was white, as was everyone else not in a hotel uniform. The long maple bar sat against the side wall. A few stools were open, and I took the one nearest the band, swiveling in my seat to watch them.

"You look like you could use a warm-up, Mr. Anderson," a man said, nearly shouting to be heard over the music.

I turned to see Henry, an older man in a red vest, leaning over the bar toward me.

"Old Tub neat?" he asked, brandishing the bottle. "Double?"

I nodded without thinking, and he poured me at least four fingers of bourbon, nearly filling the glass. "On the house," he said. "Haven't seen you for a while."

I picked up the glass and stared at the beautiful amber liquid inside. "Two years," I muttered.

"Pardon?" he shouted.

"I said it's been two years since I've been in."

"Do you still live around the corner?" he asked.

I nodded and held the crystal glass under my nose, breathing in the sweet scent.

"Why haven't you been around?"

I looked up at him. "I've been staying away from liquor."

"What changed your mind?"

I gazed again at the bourbon and just shook my head.

"What do you think of this racket?" He gestured toward the band.

"I like it."

He raised his eyebrows, indicating his lack of agreement, but smiled and said, "It's good to see you again, Mr. Anderson."

"You, too, Henry." I picked up the bourbon and held it up to look at it against the light, and then, once more, I breathed in the aroma. My mouth watered. I took a sip, let the sweet whiskey linger on my tongue, then trickle down my throat. I closed my eyes and took another.

A rush of pleasure was counterbalanced by one of shame. I pushed that aside. Elizabeth had no right. I'd done nothing wrong. She was the problem, not me. And damn it, if I wanted to get drunk one time in two goddamn years, then that was my business.

Henry had moved down the bar. I got his attention, and he hurried back over. "Say, Henry, what brand of cigarettes would you recommend these days?"

"If I was you, I'd ask the young lady there." He pointed behind me.

I turned my head. A lovely young blonde stood three feet away, carrying a tray filled with cigarettes, cigars, and chewing gum. Her hair was piled in a tight chignon, but it was easy to see it was long and lustrous. She stood at least six feet in her heels and had the kind of form a man would kill for.

Turning all the way around, I leaned in to speak to her. She had to bend down to put her ear near my mouth. A waft of her scent— Oriental and exotic—moved in with her. "I haven't smoked cigarettes in a while," I said, "but I'm planning to start up again. What would you recommend?"

"I like Murads, myself," she said, holding up a pack. Her voice was high and pouty, babylike.

Aggh. The voice that would sink a thousand ships. Now I knew why she was selling cigarettes for a living. "I'll try them," I said. I'd always thought Murad made a mediocre cigarette, but what the hell.

"Certainly, sir." She opened the pack and shook one out for me. Once I had fumbled it up to my mouth, she lit it, and I inhaled the smoke and held it in my lungs, luxuriating, then blew it out toward the high ceiling. I dug a dollar from my trouser pocket and laid it in her palm.

She tucked it into a little jeweled purse on her tray and, without the offer of change, gave me a knowing smile. "Is there anything else I could get for you?"

The way I was feeling, had it not been for her voice, I might have been tempted to explore her meaning. Instead, I thanked her politely and turned back to the bar. The band finished the song and announced they were taking a break, which was all right with me. I'd heard a lot of jazz bands since the night I first heard jazz at the Bucket, but I had never heard a more talented band than that one. It was sad, really. When one's first experience with something is the best one will ever get, every other is a disappointment. Which put me in mind again of my problems with Elizabeth.

Henry excused himself and moved down the bar to serve someone else. The bourbon didn't last five minutes, even though I was trying to pace myself. Henry asked if I'd like another, and I told him I would. He poured me another stiff one, and I drank that with purpose, keeping my face pointed toward the bar, in case anyone who knew me was here. I was not in a talking mood.

The band came back after I ordered my third drink. I was on my fourth cigarette when, behind me, a woman said meekly, "Will, please talk to me."

I turned to see Sapphira standing behind my stool. Makeup was caked around her left eye, which still looked darker than the rest of her face. "I need you to understand," she said.

I spun around and hunched down, elbows on the bar, burning with anger. The stool next to me scraped on the floor. I felt the weight of the gun in my shoulder holster, hidden under my coat. In my peripheral vision, I saw her slide onto the stool and beckon Henry.

He leaned over the bar. "Yes, miss?"

"Whiskey, neat," she said.

"Yes, miss." He didn't show a visible reaction to a woman ordering a drink at the bar, but it couldn't have been a normal experience. It wasn't that women didn't drink; they just didn't drink in public. He poured the whiskey and slid it across the bar to her.

I slugged down the rest of my drink and took an angry pull on the cigarette. "Are you here to gloat?"

She didn't answer.

"Well? What do you want?"

Still nothing. I turned to her. She stared at the whiskey glass but didn't drink. Her long black hair, swirled atop her head, was dry, but the collar of her lavender dress was soaked and clung to her cleavage and the tops of her breasts.

"Sapphira." I didn't want to give her the satisfaction, but I couldn't hide my exasperation. "What do you want with me?"

Turning to me, she said, "I want to help you."

I searched her face for some sign of truth, but she had lied to me so well I didn't know how I could possibly recognize it. "What happened to the ballots?" I asked.

"I do not know what I can say to convince you. I know nothing of ballots."

I'd heard that enough. "How did you happen to turn up here tonight?"

"The doorman said you were out. I waited outside your building for an hour before I finally gave up. I was waiting for the trolley when I saw you standing out front." She nodded toward the hotel's entrance. "I have been trying to work up the courage to speak with you."

"How do you propose you help me?"

"I can get you information on Murphy."

Henry appeared with the bottle of Old Tub, his eyebrows arched. I nodded, and he refilled my glass. "Why don't you do that, then, Sapphira? Let me know when you have something useful for me."

She grabbed my arm and jerked me closer to her. "Listen to me." She had taken as much offense from my tone as I had intended.

I met her eyes, wondering if I could hit her again. When I looked at her, I saw Wesley McRae. I was responsible for his death, and every time I saw her I was reminded of that fact.

She let loose of my arm. "Mr. Murphy will kill me for talking to you, but he must be stopped. I can spy for you. If you would stop being such a pig."

It wouldn't cost me anything to listen. Still, I didn't answer. Instead, I made a gesture that said I didn't much care one way or the other.

Sapphira appraised me for a second before continuing. "First I need to tell you something. I want you to understand. I was not always a . . ." She lowered her voice. "A fancy lady." She took a sip of the whiskey and shuddered. When she spoke again, she continued so quietly I could barely hear her. "When I was thirteen, a man came to my father and told him he could get me a stenography job in New York. He—my father—was a fisherman and did not make enough money to support us. He chose to believe the man. I was excited. There was nothing for me in Chilistra. What did I know?"

I glanced at her.

Her eyes were cast down at the bar again. "They brought us across the Atlantic Ocean in the hold of a ship—thirty-seven girls, all between twelve and fifteen years old. Every day for three weeks they injected us with morphine and raped us. I don't know where the boat landed, but they brought us to Detroit in a freight car and then split us up." She looked at me and smiled weakly. "I was lucky. I got to work a house, not on the street."

I was determined not to react to her, but my resolve was weakening. "White slavers."

"So they call them," she said.

I sipped at my bourbon but said nothing.

"*Will*," she said, then waited until I turned back to her. "I know you can never forgive me for helping John Cooper. I do not expect forgiveness for anything I have done, not from you, not from God. But you, tell me this. Do you forgive yourself for what you have done?"

I grunted out a laugh. Forgiving myself was not on the agenda.

"Do you forgive people who wrong you? Beside me, I mean?"

I took a stiff drink and thought about the question. "I . . . I guess I don't think about it much. When things go wrong, they're usually my fault anyway." I picked up the pack of cigarettes from the bar, shook one out, and offered it to her. When she took it, I lit it and another for me.

The band started up with another New Orleans tune. Sapphira blew the smoke out the corner of her mouth and leaned closer so I could hear. "You sound like a poor man."

"What do you mean?" I finished off my drink.

"When you are poor, you are raised to believe that God is punishing you because you are a sinner. Everything is your fault. The rich are different. My . . . clients . . . they always believed God wronged them. They had everything, always had everything, yet they were sure they were being cheated."

I held the cut crystal glass in both hands, tilting it back and forth on the bar. "So how did you get out of . . . you know, that life?"

"You say that like I am out of it."

I shrugged. "You're working in an office."

"You do not know what my life is."

"Had you been working for Murphy before? Was he involved in the"—I lowered my voice—"prostitution?"

"He *saved* me." Sarcasm dripped off her words. "He bought my freedom. He was a client. Now he owns me."

"Do you have any evidence that would get Murphy locked up?"

She shook her head. "No, I—"

Someone slapped my back. "Why, it's Will Anderson!" Edsel Ford stood next to a pretty girl about his age, that is, around twenty. I swiveled around on the stool and stood. The room swayed, but I caught my balance and tried to look sober. "Hi, Edsel." I shook his hand and ignored Sapphira. I wondered what Edsel had seen. We had been so close together that our heads had practically been touching.

"This is Eleanor Clay." He turned to the girl. "Eleanor, my friend, Will Anderson."

Now I remembered her. "Yes, Eleanor," I slurred. *Yeshh*. I started articulating carefully. "We met a few years ago, at the car show, if I remember correctly. You're J. L. Hudson's niece, right?"

"That's right," she said. "Oh, of course, yes, that's where we met." She was being polite. It was clear she didn't know me from Adam. I remembered her because she was attractive.

"Is Elizabeth here?" Edsel's eyes landed on Sapphira, who hadn't—and didn't—turn around.

"No, I just stopped in for a minute. I was passing and heard the music."

"Would you like to sit with us?" he asked. "We're here with some friends, but we've got room at the table."

"Thanks, Edsel, but no. I've got to be going."

"Oh, yes, work in the morning. Good for you."

Something like that, I thought. "It was really nice to see you, Edsel. It's been too long."

"Eleanor and I would love to get together with you and Elizabeth," he said, smiling. "I'd like to catch up on your more recent adventures. I doubt you've been sitting home with your knitting."

I laughed in spite of my mood. "No, no misshapen sweaters on my sofa."

He clapped my shoulder, leaned in closer, and spoke into my ear. "We need to get together, Will. Don't be a stranger."

"Thanks, Edsel. Enjoy your night." I turned to Eleanor. "It was nice to see you again."

"You as well," she replied, and they walked away, arm in arm, heading for the other side of the room.

I sat again. Sapphira stared straight ahead.

"Thanks," I said, now maintaining my distance. "It would have been awkward . . ."

"I am always awkward," she replied.

"Listen, Sapphira—"

"Please do not call me that name." Her eyes burned into mine. "That is a whore name. My given name is Helen. *Please* call me Helen."

I took in her face, now sharp angles but still beautiful, her dark, mysterious eyes, enticing lips. I saw a schemer, a survivor, but God help me, I thought I also saw a real person. "I'll do that. I'm sorry for what you've been through, Helen."

Tears shone in her eyes.

"I can't imagine how lonely a life like yours must be."

She nodded. A tear dripped onto her lap.

"Do you still . . . have any hope?"

"I hope the bastards will pay for what they have done."

"For yourself, I mean. Do you think you have a chance for a better life?"

She laughed, but it was more a sob. "Revenge would be better."

I leaned in closer to her and spoke quietly. "No. Do you think you can ever be happy?"

She smiled. "Happy? Rich people think about being happy. People like me think about surviving. I have survived. And I will see Mr. Murphy dead or in jail."

I took a drag on my cigarette and got Henry's attention to order another drink for each of us. "Have you remembered anything about David Sanford that might help me?"

"No. I did not know him."

"How did he get the job? Did he know Murphy?"

"No, but his brother did. He talked to Mr. Murphy."

"Wait. His brother?"

She nodded. "Eli."

I turned in my chair so I could study her closely. "How do you know him?"

"He was a client. He got me to Chicago on a freight train after you . . . killed John."

Henry slid the glasses in front of us and removed the empty ones.

I waited until he moved away again to ask, "When did he talk to Murphy?"

"A month ago. Mr. Murphy hired David right away."

"And you haven't seen Eli since?"

She shook her head.

Thinking out loud, I said, "So . . . he could have moved to New Mexico after he talked to you." I looked at her again. "Did he say anything about moving? Or gold mining?"

An inward-looking smile crept onto her face. "Gold mining? No, but he might try that. He always had a crazy plan to make a lot of money and come and take me away."

"Huh. So Eli talked Murphy into hiring David."

"I think. Mr. Murphy said no press man ever came so cheap."

"Interesting. He really wanted to work for the MLA. Do you know why?"

She shook her head.

I took a sip of bourbon. *Goddamn, that's good.* "Maybe he thought it would be good exposure, help him find a long-term job."

"Maybe."

David, I thought, *what was going on in that head of yours? Why the MLA?* Two people might be able to answer that. One was dead, the other in New Mexico.

"Now I must go," she said. "I have work in the morning."

I turned on my chair and regarded her. "I'll be able to find you at the MLA office?"

"If you need to speak with me, write or telephone the office. Mr. Murphy must not find out I am helping you."

"When are you there?"

"From 8:00 A.M. to 5:00 P.M., except for lunch."

I nodded. "Good. Is there anything else you ought to tell me?"

She pushed back her chair and stood. "That is what I know."

"All right. I'll be seeing you."

She walked toward the door. Once she was gone, I gulped my drink, dropped a five-dollar bill onto the bar, and shouted my thanks to Henry. I retrieved my wet coat and hat and walked out into the cold night, fortified against the weather. Down a block, turn left, and follow the sidewalk to my building, which, other than a soft glow from a few windows and the lights of the lobby, was dark. Trying to be quiet, I opened the door and walked in. The walnut desk was unmanned. Frank was nowhere to be seen.

"What the . . . ?" I stumbled up the stairs and crept down the hall to my apartment. The door was cracked open, just far enough to see a black line along the edge of the white door. I stopped and stared while my brain caught up. I hadn't left my door open.

Even drunk, I remembered for certain. I had locked it on the way out.

CHAPTER FIFTEEN

Friday, October 18, 1912

Jerking my gun from the shoulder holster, I pushed the door open, crept into the foyer, and listened. A motorcar puttered by on Second Street. My apartment hummed, low and quiet—electricity. No other sound. I switched on the light.

A semicircle of white powder stretched out on the walnut floor from the entrance to the kitchen. A wooden spoon lay on the floor against the opposite wall. A copper pot sat upside down between them. I walked heel to toe out of the foyer to the kitchen entry and peeked in. The icebox and all of the cabinets were open. The linoleum floor was nearly covered by the white powder, explained by the flour bag tossed on top of it. Shards of a milk bottle shone on the floor, the milk bubbled up in the flour. Pots, pans, silverware, food—everything—strewn across the counters, sink, and floor.

Next, the dining room. The table lay on its side, two legs snapped off, the chairs around it on their backs or sides, also lying on the floor.

I headed down the hall to the parlor and flipped on the light. Brown horsehair blanketed the room. Cushions were torn and thrown everywhere. Long slashes ran across the backs and seats of the sofa and chairs. Worst of all, Wesley McRae's Victrola lay smashed on the floor, the records in pieces all around.

In a rage, I ran from room to room, searching the closets, the bathroom, everywhere someone might be hiding. No one. Whoever had broken in was gone.

My bedroom and den were in similar condition—everything smashed, torn, broken, ripped to shreds. Nothing appeared to have been taken. I had little of value, but what I did have was still here. Elizabeth's ring lay in its box on the floor, and my gold watch, chain, and cufflinks were strewn around my broken jewelry box.

The ballots.

It was the only explanation. Whoever had broken in hadn't known the ballots had already been stolen.

I stood still and listened, breathed. The building hummed, then creaked as it settled. Downstairs, footsteps pattered across the floor. I inhaled deeply. There, in the background . . .

I waved air toward my nose, moving around the apartment. Smoke . . . what kind? In my den the smell was more distinct, though still so minimal as to make me think it might be my imagination. Sweet, not cigar, not cigarette. Sweet pipe tobacco. Old English? I inhaled deeply, thinking of the smoke around Andrew Murphy at the suffrage party, around David in the saloon afterward. Yes. Yes! This was Old English.

Murphy himself had come to steal the ballots? Or was the man from the salt mine also an Old English smoker? Either way, they had determined I was not in my apartment, perhaps from sources within the suffragists—like Warren Brennan. It seemed we had interrupted them, so they simply waited until I left again. Or, I supposed, they could have already searched my apartment, and the man from the salt mine was returning for something. It didn't really matter. They'd gotten nothing, because there was nothing to be had.

I wandered back to the door and closed it before heading to the parlor and throwing my hat and coat on the remains of my sofa. I lit a cigarette and sat on the window ledge, looking out at the city lights. The rain clanged off the fire escape and thrummed on my windows, leaving long punctuated streaks. I was drunk, bone-tired, and confused beyond my abilities.

When I finished the cigarette, I flicked the butt out the window and sat on the floor next to the Victrola. One side had been pried off it, and the arm hung off the top by a wire. I picked up the case and hugged it to me.

Wesley McRae. The best man I would likely ever meet; a man whose life defined courage. My last link to him lay broken on my lap. I hoped he was in heaven, but I hoped more that he hadn't been able to watch the mess I'd made out of my life.

Shit. Shit, shit, shit.

I wondered about Helen. Could she have been involved in this? But then, she knew I didn't have the ballots. I couldn't imagine any other reason someone would destroy my apartment. It made no sense. Could she . . . really be on my side?

I stood up, threw on my coat and hat, and headed outside again.

The ballroom at the Addison would still be open. Henry would be happy to sell me a bottle.

When I woke the next morning, tangled in the blankets on my ripped-up bed, my head pounded with twice the usual intensity. I sat on the edge of the bed, head in hands, feeling the hard patches of scar tissue against my face, and the corresponding ache in those fingers from the pressure.

Elizabeth.

I rubbed my eyes and thought. Was I doing this simply to prove to her—to everyone—that I was right, or were my motives pure, my desire only to protect the one I loved? Then again, whose motives *are* pure? Isn't every act motivated by the self, by the feeling of satisfaction, joy, or pain that act might bring?

I sat up. I knew one thing for certain: Both Elizabeth and the cause for which she fought were in danger. I would try to protect both. I wouldn't think any farther than that. What happened next would happen.

Now . . . who had ransacked my apartment? They had to have been looking for the ballots.

Someone else had already stolen them.

That meant two different groups wanted them, and they weren't communicating. Yet both knew I had taken the ballots from Flik-klund's hideout, which left . . . who?

Sapphira knew I didn't have them. So did Riordan and Elizabeth. Who might think I did? The man from the salt mine, obviously, who my gut said worked for Andrew Murphy, and . . . Riordan might have talked to someone about my fears, but I doubted it. I was crazy, after all. After that, I drew a blank. The man from the salt mine tried to steal them last night; that seemed a safe bet. Unfortunately, I had no idea who he was or whether he really worked for Murphy. I had even less of a clue who his competition might be.

I got out of bed. I would start by searching for fingerprints. Given that a suspect had to be in custody in order to make a comparison, the odds were long against it being any help, but I had to start somewhere. My magnifying glass lay on the floor of my den but had made it unscathed from its trip across the room. I started in the most promising location—the kitchen. A few lines that might have been made by fingers smeared the flour on the kitchen counter, but I saw no evidence of prints. The flour on the linoleum had been shifted by feet, but nothing like a footprint was apparent.

I could call Detective Riordan or phone in the attempted burglary to the Detroit police. However, with my history, the odds against the Detroit cops making a serious investigation were astronomical. They wouldn't catch the intruders anyway.

This was my problem.

I set a pot of coffee to boil and walked back to the parlor to start cleaning. I threw out the cushions and as much of the horsehair as I could scrape up, then started organizing my books and magazines that were scattered across the floor. This was good mindless work for me, giving me something on which to concentrate other than Elizabeth, my job, or the seemingly endless parade of idiots who had been inserted into my life in the past few weeks.

I spread sheets over my sofa and chairs, giving my parlor the aura of an abandoned house, but at least it brought a little order to the place. While I worked, I thought. It made sense that Andrew Murphy was pulling the strings, and all roads led back to the MLA office. Two of his employees had been killed. I needed to get to Murphy, find him out, and end the conspiracy. He'd never talk to me, though, and David was the only person in that office I had known.

A cover of a *Popular Electricity* magazine jolted my memory. A few months back—right about the time the Burns investigation came to light with the arrests of the aldermen—they'd run an article about Detective Dictographs. I dug through the stack until I found the June issue.

There. The article was entitled "Eavesdropping by Science." I dropped to the floor and reread the article. William Burns had become a household name through the use of this device. The Dictograph used a small sound collector, which could be hidden any variety of places, to convey voices and other sounds to a second location by way of a pair of wires. There, a detective would listen with a telephone receiver and take down everything being said. I remembered, though, that the Burns men had actually recorded voices in the alderman case and used those recordings in the preliminary hearing. This article said nothing of that.

I needed evidence of the conspiracy. Were I able to get hold of a Dictograph, plant it, and write down the conversations, I'd get laughed out of court. I would have to enlist someone whose testimony would be considered credible, which meant I'd have to hire a notary or recruit one of the Burnsies to assist me, neither of which was feasible. I needed to get my hands on a Dictograph as well as the recording device. I couldn't ask Brennan to get me one. I couldn't ask Elizabeth to ask them for me. I certainly couldn't afford to buy one, nor, even if I came up with the money, did I want to wait for one to be shipped.

I was getting ahead of myself. I didn't even know if there was a spot near Murphy's office to install the recorder. For that matter, even though I knew the Dictograph was small, I had no idea of the size of the recording device. I would need a closet or the like to place the equipment, and it would have to be near enough to Murphy's office that I could run wires between them. If that wasn't enough, the location had to be a place that would be ignored by the staff. In a closet, a janitor could discover it.

It looked to be a long shot at best, but it was worth making a trip to the MLA office to find out for sure. Perhaps Sapphira—Helen—*could* be of help after all.

After phoning the landlord to complain of the abominable service provided by our alleged night doorman, I threw on my coat and tinted glasses and walked down to the streetcar stop, pushing onto the first trolley heading downtown. The sun shone in a brilliant sky, and today the wind was dry and brisk. I breathed deeply of the autumn air, fresh-smelling after the rain. By the end of the day, coal smoke and horseshit would overpower the fresh air, so I tried to enjoy it while it was here.

Ten minutes after I stepped on the streetcar, we reached Michigan Avenue, across from city hall. I climbed off and crossed the street, nearly getting run over by a matronly woman in a brand-new hunter green Detroit Electric Model 25 extension brougham. She hurtled in from Monroe, apparently unable to slow as she tore down the circular drive around Campus Martius Park and flew past me, wide-eyed.

Bravo, I thought. *They're still selling—and this woman might need another one soon.*

I walked up to city hall, around the semicircular lawn in front of the grimy sandstone structure. It had been years since I really looked at this building. It was such a fixture in my mind from my childhood that I didn't even see it anymore. I remembered it as cream colored, but coal ash had long ago turned the building gray, particularly in the textured blocks that alternated with the smooth stones on the massive building. A pair of plugged cannons captured from the British in the War of 1812 stood at the sides of the stairs. Five large arches and two small ones, mimicked on the balcony above, covered the entryway. Statues of various figures from Michigan's history pocked the exterior, like a small army of the despairing readying themselves for the jump to oblivion.

When I reached the shadow of the building, the bell tolled its long clamorous gong, and I glanced up at the clock just below it—11:30. Nearly lunchtime. This might be an opportune moment for some investigation. I hurried past to the twenty-three-story Dime Building. Its fascia, smooth and clean, was white brick, and its U-shaped upper levels created a twin-tower effect that, on a sunny day, showered the sun's rays through the skylight onto the third floor's central court.

I opened a windowed brass door and stepped inside, past a pair of bank guards. I kept my glasses on, eyes front. For a bank, it was a noisy place. The tall ceiling and unforgiving stone surfaces amplified the footsteps of the dozens of people clacking across the white marble floor, their voices echoing over and over, as if the throng were quadruple its size. The bank lobby lay in front of me, a cool collection of white marble—the long antiseptic floor, tellers' cages of brass wrapped in white rock, huge pillars towering overhead. On the right, a marble staircase curled up to a second-floor landing. Still right of that was the guard's desk, behind which a grumpy-looking man sat, eyeballing the folks passing him.

I removed the glasses and slipped them into my coat. Leaving my hands in my pockets, I passed the guard and turned left down the hall. I wanted to get a look around, and I needed to find the MLA office. I doubted it would be on the first floor, but I looked just the same, marching down each of the halls as if I had purpose, and slipping past the intersection so the policeman wouldn't notice me.

Nothing but bank offices on the first floor. I found a building directory, which showed the MLA to occupy rooms 218 and 219. On the Michigan Avenue side of the building, I took a smaller marble staircase to the second floor, and voilà, there it was, the last doorway in the hall, on the building's corner. A brass nameplate attesting to that fact was affixed to the closed door. Only one other office adjoined it. I walked twenty feet down the hall and came to another closed door, on which a nameplate read, MICHIGAN LIQUOR ASSOCIATION—ACCOUNTS. Flikklund's old office. I wondered—had they filled the position yet?

I glanced at my watch again—11:50. I'd wait until after noon to try to look around Murphy's office, and I couldn't very well stand here waiting for his employees to file past me. I knocked softly on Flikklund's door, trying to think of a reason to be here if someone answered. No one did. I turned the knob and tried to open it—locked. This could be the perfect setup. If this office were empty, it would be the ideal place from which to do surveillance. I could wire from one to the other—

Murphy's door opened. I turned away and began walking down the hall. A pair of men headed the other direction and were soon pounding down the stairway. The door opened again, and a loud conversation was carried out into the hall. I stopped and glanced back.

Andrew Murphy waddled out berating a pair of young men. The two gargantuans I'd seen with him at the party followed behind, looking relieved that Murphy was taking someone else to the woodshed. Murphy's pipe was clenched in his teeth, obscuring his words. ". . . haf to be compwete idiuss to'f missed it." He started for the stairway, and the men scurried along behind him. He pulled the pipe from his mouth. "You are supposed to be college graduates," Murphy spat. "Of what, the P. T. Barnum school of . . ." His voice blended in with the general hum of conversation as they disappeared down the stairs. Too bad. I was very curious where he was going with that.

I was afraid I had missed my opportunity to actually get inside. If everyone left for lunch at noon, the door would be locked. I turned and walked back down toward the office and tried the door. It was unlocked. I ducked inside.

The pretty girl at the front desk looked up at me behind wire-rimmed spectacles. Her dark hair was tightly fastened atop her head like a helmet—a serious woman's hairdo. She wore a starched white shirtwaist. In every way, she looked like an office girl.

Nonetheless, it was Sapphira.

"Hello, Sapph—Helen."

Her eyes darted around the office. No one else was in sight.

"Are you the only one here now?" I asked.

"I think one of Mr. Murphy's men is still in his office," she whispered.

I nodded. The walls were ivory plaster with oak wainscoting, the floor covered in a new burgundy carpet that smelled of chemicals. A pair of desks sat against the wall between the large windows. A hallway on the right headed toward the corner of the building and what I was sure to be Murphy's office. I ducked my head down the hallway. The office door was closed, and the opaque white window in it was dark.

I leaned over the desk and whispered, "Does anyone work now in Flikklund's old office?"

She shook her head. "No. Why?"

I ignored her question. I didn't trust her nearly enough to share my plan. "How late are people in this building?"

"Most leave at five thirty, but there are always people here later."

"I have to get in here at night. Is that possible?"

"Without a key?"

"Unless you can get me one."

She thought, then shook her head.

"You don't have a key?"

"No." She glanced back, down the hall toward Murphy's office. "Mr. Murphy is the only one."

"Could you steal it?"

Her brow furrowed. "No," she whispered. "Mr. Murphy is afraid everyone will try to steal his things. I cannot get near it."

"This is really important. I need a key to get in the building and to get in these offices."

"I do not know how, Will. He knows better than to trust me."

"Do what you can, Helen. I'm counting on you."

"I will try."

"That's all I can ask. What I'm planning could put these men in jail and free you, but I have to be able to get in here. I'll be in touch tomorrow."

She nodded.

Murphy's office door opened, and I took that opportunity to leave. It wouldn't do for me to be recognized here. I hurried out into the hall and down the stairs. I had to keep moving forward. One way or another, I would get into this building once I had procured the machine. If I was lucky, Helen would get me the key.

I knew I couldn't count on good fortune shining down on me, though. I would have to make my own luck.

On the streetcar I was struck by a thought: People at Detroit Electric would know I had been fired, but it was unlikely that anyone else did. My father wasn't going to publicize the fact that his only son was an ignoramus. If I were to stop by the National Dictograph office, why wouldn't they sell me a machine for my father's company? I had a business card, and I shared the owner's name. If I told them I wanted a Dictograph and a recorder, they would sell it to Detroit Electric on terms, which would allow me the use with no money down. It would take weeks before anyone realized they'd been hoodwinked, and hopefully before then I would have my incriminating recording and have returned the machine for a refund due to poor performance or some such thing.

It was worth a try. Worst case, I'd sell the Torpedo.

For today, however, my car was the perfect accessory for the up-and-coming executive I would try to portray. If all went according to plan, it would also serve to transport the equipment back to the Dime. I picked up the Torpedo from the garage and drove to the National Dictograph office on Lafayette, where I pulled to the curb and breezed into the store pulling off my glasses.

A smell of ozone, machine oil, and furniture polish greeted me along with a compact, clean-shaven man, who stood up from his desk when I entered. He allowed me a brief smile, the kind retail clerks are taught to communicate professionalism with a touch of friendliness. "What might I help you with, sir?" he asked.

I answered in my best Detroit Brahmin voice. "I'm with the Detroit Electric Automobile Company, and we are in the market for a recording Dictograph."

"Yes, sir. Tell me, sir, are you planning on using the sound collector and recording device in the same office, or will the setup be for you in one office and your secretary in another?"

"That one. Separate offices."

"Yes, sir," he said again. "Right this way." He led me to the rear of the store, where a black leather case sat on a mahogany stand. The case was roughly the size of an extra-wide briefcase—easily transportable. He opened the top. A number of devices lay strapped to a green velvet panel: a telephone receiver, a black disk about three inches around, and a black metal box with an electrical cord, along with a little stand and some neatly coiled wires.

"Are you familiar with the operation of a Dictograph, sir?"

"No, not really. I understand the general idea."

"Yes, sir. It's very simple." Picking up the disk, which was only about three-quarters of an inch deep, he said, "This sound collector is placed in a stand on the executive's desk." As an aside, he added, "Stands are available in seven attractive finishes, one sure to match your decor."

While he talked, I pulled a cigarette from the pack of Murads in my coat and tapped it against the side of the pack. "Fine," I said. "What else?"

After he lit my cigarette with his lighter, he produced a sparkling-clean ashtray from a nearby cabinet. "If the Dictograph is being used for normal dictation, that is, to a secretary who will transcribe the information, the executive speaks into the sound collector. The sound is electronically transmitted via these wires to this box, where the heart of the Dictograph lies." He gestured over the box like a magician. "With the receiver connected, the secretary hears everything in breathtaking detail and clarity."

Digesting the information, I took a long drag on the cigarette. Harsh Turkish tobacco smoke scorched my throat and lungs. Now I remembered why I didn't care for Murads. Well, I had paid for them. I blew the smoke out the corner of my mouth, masking my distaste. It wouldn't do for my performance. "This device doesn't actually record the dictation."

"That's correct, sir. For that you need a telegraphone." Turning, he made an expansive gesture to our left, where a wooden console, approximately thirty inches in all directions, sat on a table against the wall. "This amazing machine is the telegraphone."

He opened the top of the one nearest us, a handsome mahogany model. A large reel of wire, about six inches around, lay on the left side, and the wire wound into a raised section through a channel and then to a take-up reel on the other side. Four switches—on/off, record/play/stop, fast forward/fast rewind, and speed—and a large National Dictograph plaque were the only other features.

He talked about recording time, which could be as long as an hour, and spent fifteen minutes trying to impress me with his product knowledge. I heard only a fraction of it. I wanted to get the machines and get the hell out of here.

When the clerk came up for breath, I fit in, "How much do telegraphones weigh?"

He seemed a bit nonplussed by my question but had a ready answer. "Approximately sixty pounds, sir. It depends on the type of wood. They vary by a pound or two."

I smoked and thought. Sixty pounds. I would be able to carry it by myself. "And what do these devices cost?"

He worried the edge of the console, trying to rub off some invisible smudge. "The Dictograph is twenty-five dollars a month with a one-year contract. We require a one-hundred-fifty-dollar security deposit. Telegraphones are sixty dollars a month with a one-year contract. For that, a deposit of three hundred dollars is required."

"Oh. You rent them?" *Better yet.*

"Yes, sir. Rental only. That way we're able to upgrade our customers as soon as new models are available. You will never have anything but the latest technology."

I ground out the cigarette in the ashtray. "All right, that sounds acceptable. I'd like to put this on account."

"I'm sure we can make those arrangements, sir. I'll get a credit application for you." He scurried off, no doubt counting his commission.

I marveled at the machines. The twentieth century's incredible explosion of technology was changing life by the day. Just when it seemed that everything had been invented, here came another mind-boggling invention. Who'd have thought it possible?

The clerk returned half a minute later with a legal sized document. "If you would please complete this form and return it to us along with a corporate resolution, a purchase order, and four hundred fifty dollars, we can arrange a delivery."

I summoned up a privileged person's indignation. "Surely you know of our company. Why, we're the largest electric car manufacturer in the world. I simply cannot believe that our credit is not good enough for such a small purchase."

"Sir, I apologize, but security deposits are required from all of our clients."

Hands on hips, I said, "So if Mayor Thompson walked in here, you'd make him pay?"

The clerk's face remained impassive. "Yes, sir."

"Hmm." If I sold the car and faked a corporate resolution and purchase order, I might be able to rent these things. I gave him a sidelong glance. "Would it be any less expensive if I picked it up rather than having it delivered?"

"No, I'm sorry, sir, but we deliver and calibrate all the machines. Telegraphones are a bit fussy, I'm afraid, and they must be set up by a professional."

"Are you saying you wouldn't let me take one with me if I brought you the money and all the infernal paperwork?"

"That's correct. I'm sorry, sir, but National Dictograph is committed to quality, and we cannot allow that reputation to be besmirched."

Even if I had $450, I would leave an evidence trail long enough that even my father would press charges against me. It didn't matter anyway, since my liquid assets totaled approximately 10 percent of that. Picking up the credit application, I said, "I'll get our people on this. We'll be in touch."

"You may want to put down a deposit, sir. Dictograph/telegraphone combinations are the rage right now. We're fortunate to have a few available at the moment. All the publicity William Burns has been receiving has been wonderful for our business."

"I'll take my chances." I left the store, his business card and credit application in hand. At the first alley, I wadded them up and threw them in the general direction of a garbage can. The paper landed atop a pile of garbage and the contents of someone's chamber pot, the odor of which assaulted my nose. *Shit*. Which was exactly what my chances were of landing a Dictograph and telegraphone.

Total shit.

CHAPTER SIXTEEN

I spun and hurled a dagger at the wall. The point buried in the wooden target. The knife quivered and then was still.

What about Riordan? The Detroit Police probably had at least one Dictograph. If he couldn't get that, he could ask the Burns Agency to use one of theirs. I just had one problem with that—I couldn't convince myself he was on my side. No. I had to figure out another way to get the equipment.

Anyway, that wasn't my only problem. Warren Brennan still worked in close contact with Elizabeth. I couldn't have been more positive that he was scheming against her and her cause, but she just wouldn't see it. I couldn't trust Riordan with my scheme, but maybe he could change Elizabeth's opinion of the man.

I phoned the Bethune Street station. Fortunately, or perhaps not so fortunately, Riordan was in. When he answered, I identified myself and said, "I need a favor. No matter how you answer, I need to know you'll keep this between us. I don't want Elizabeth to know. Will you agree to that?"

He sighed. "Are you going to confess to a past or future crime?"

"No." I didn't trust him nearly that much.

"Why not." He puffed on his cigar. "It's been a slow day."

"Could you try to talk Elizabeth into firing Brennan?"

"You should forget about him," Riordan said. "I checked him out, and he's clean."

"What you mean is he hasn't been caught yet."

"Paranoia scares people, Anderson. Especially women. Do us all a favor and move on. Don't you have work to do or something?"

"No . . . I got fired."

"You got fired? From your old man's company?" He sounded just as incredulous as he should have.

"I don't want to talk about it."

I could just see him smiling. "Only you." Tobacco crackled as he took another puff on his cigar. "Is that all?"

"I can't imagine why you won't protect Elizabeth. She could replace Brennan easily enough. Where's the harm in recommending she put someone else in his place?"

"You're barking up the wrong tree, Anderson. Just leave it."

My face was hot. "So that's it? You're just going to let this go?"

"Yep."

I closed my eyes and took a deep breath. "Did you know that David Sanford had a brother named Eli who lived in town until recently?"

"As a matter of fact, I did. Hold on a minute."

The receiver clunked down onto his desk. I waited, listening to the muted sound of a police station—men laughing and cursing, footsteps tromping up and down the hall, a jingle of keys. On the other end of the line, a lighter snapped open with a metallic click, followed by the scrape of the wheel against the flint. Now Riordan sucked and sucked, and I pictured the cloud of smoke billowing around his head.

"Eli Sanford, date of birth 7/16/1891. No criminal record. Why? Do you think he's involved in your little conspiracy?"

"My 'little conspiracy'?"

"Look, Anderson. You've got to understand that your head's not working right. You seem to be the only person who thinks there *is* a conspiracy."

"You should see my apartment. Someone completely destroyed it trying to find the ballots."

"You're not drinking again, are you?"

I wanted to reach through the telephone and pull out his liver. "Let me ask you straight out, Detective, because I know that's how you like it. Are you obstructing me? Are you trying to keep me from figuring out what's going on here?"

"That's insane. Maybe you ought to go on back to Eloise for a long rest."

"Really? You won't help me figure out who's involved in the conspiracy. You won't even help me get rid of a man who I am certain means harm—at least to Elizabeth's dream, if not to her."

"Listen, you," he said. "Stop bothering me." He slammed the receiver onto the hook.

I hung up and sat back in my chair. This was so unlike the Detective Riordan I knew. Yes, he was a jackass, but he was dogged to a fault and always on the side of the just.

Was I crazy?

I had suffered prolonged radium bombardment to my brain. Had it caused hallucinations, paranoia, insanity? Did I feel different? My head hurt, yes; my eyes were sensitive. Swaths of time randomly disappeared from my memory. My thoughts, though . . . shit.

Was I crazy?

How in hell was I supposed to know that? I thought I was thinking normally, but in my experience crazy people think the same thing.

I wandered into the kitchen and went back to cleaning. Both Elizabeth and Detective Riordan thought I was paranoid. They wouldn't help me. I had to think, create a plan, foil the conspiracy, and win Elizabeth back. How would I do that?

David was dead, and his brother might have the information I needed.

Warren Brennan was poison. For some reason, I was the only one who saw it.

Thomas Riordan—something was not as it seemed. He loved Elizabeth. Like a father, he'd said. I wondered, did he love her in another way? Was he simply trying to get rid of me so he could make a play for her? No, that was ridiculous. He was married. He was much older. More importantly, he was a cop, and she an heiress. Then again, love makes a person do strange things.

I laughed. I needn't look any farther than myself for examples of love leading to insane behavior. I loved Elizabeth as I could never love again. Hopefully when the election was over and suffrage prevailed, she'd come to her senses.

Or, I imagined, since it meant returning to me, I would need her, once again, to lose her sense completely.

I mopped the kitchen floor, thinking about Riordan suggesting I was crazy enough to need Eloise Hospital. *Jackass.* I never wanted to see that place again. Dr. Beckwith had nearly killed me with his goddamn "therapy." I was happy to think that, assuming he didn't have friends in high places, he would get what he deserved.

Courtesy of a telegraphone.

Of course. He'd recorded the evidence against him. In his office.

At Eloise.

The device would almost certainly still be at Eloise Hospital. Beckwith's son, Francis, had had complete run of the place, prowling the tunnels and back alleys of Eloise at all hours. He could get me in.

I slapped the mop back into the dirty water. No. It was unthinkable, irresponsible, immoral. Still . . . Francis and I had made it together through an incredibly dangerous obstacle course, trying to escape from Eloise Hospital. He was strong. He would—probably—work with me. He was certainly intelligent enough to make his own decisions, though I'm sure an alienist or psychiatrist would say that other reasons prevented him from making sound judgments.

I wrung out the mop, flopped it back onto the floor, and scrubbed at the amalgamation of liquids and powders on the linoleum. *Ultimately, it doesn't matter,* I thought. Without Francis, I couldn't pull this off. If I were unable to discover evidence of the conspiracy, Elizabeth's dream could go up in smoke, and if what I feared was true, the results could be even more devastating.

If we could break into Eloise—which had to be less complicated than breaking out—and "borrow" the machine, perhaps I could get it into the Dime Building and record Andrew Murphy. He was at the heart of the conspiracy. He had to be.

Heading into my bedroom to dress, I thought about strategy. I would tell Alberts or Mrs. Hume—hopefully, not Elizabeth—that I would take Francis out tonight for dinner and a walk along the river. He needed company, as he was used to interacting with hundreds of patients every day. They wouldn't want him to become morose and withdrawn, would they?

I convinced myself. We'd see if my patter would convince the Humes.

This was my best chance of bringing down Murphy, ending the conspiracy, and helping Elizabeth win suffrage. When I did that, she would see, see that I'd been right all along. Everything would change. If not . . . there was the bottle, and after a single night it already felt comfortable. I knew it would lead nowhere good, and I would be throwing away my life yet again.

Frankly, I didn't care. Without Elizabeth, oblivion was the best answer.

I sat at my desk in the den, thinking. I had to be certain the Dictograph and telegraphone hadn't been removed from Eloise. It seemed possible that the police would have confiscated it as evidence, since it was highly unlikely the authorities out there in the hinterlands had a device that would play back the recordings.

I picked up the telephone and asked the operator for the main switchboard at Eloise Hospital. She sounded older, unsure of herself. She asked me to wait and then cut me off. I hung the receiver on the hook and pulled it off again, waiting for another operator. This time, I got a young sprightly-sounding girl, which was much more the norm. I sat back, waiting for the long connection to be made. Older folks didn't have much of a chance with today's technology. I was glad I was young enough to adapt, as many older people were having a terrifically difficult time with telephones. When a woman at the Eloise switchboard answered, I asked for the administrator's office, and again waited, though this time for only a few seconds.

"Eloise Hospital administrator's office," a woman said.

In a lower-class Irish accent, I rasped, "Yeah, this is Detective O'Rourke, Detroit police. Do you still have that dictation recordin' thing?"

"A recording thing?" She let the words hang in the air.

"Yeah, the telegra-thing Beckwith made the recordin's on. You know, the ones what got him locked up."

"Oh, I see," she said in a small voice.

"Well? Do ya or don't ya? I ain't got all day."

"Have the telegraphone?"

"Yeah, and the Dictograph. Jaysus, lady, am I speakin' Chinee or somethin'?"

"It's still here."

"That's all I was askin'." I hung up the phone. I don't like treating people rudely, but had I been polite she'd have known I wasn't a cop.

So they still had the equipment. Now I just needed to steal it.

I caught a streetcar to Jefferson and then east to the stop nearest the Humes' house.

Elizabeth would almost certainly be working. For the first time ever, I was going to her house hoping she *wasn't* there.

Alberts led me to the living room, where Mrs. Hume sat on the straight-backed white sofa. He joined her, and I sat on an upholstered chair on the other side of the coffee table. Elizabeth, fortunately, was working. Bridie Kelly had taken Francis and Robert for a walk, which was fine with me, as I wouldn't risk asking Francis to help me while we were here. He was volatile, and the request could send him into a fit, which I would then have to explain. I'd rather do it elsewhere, where I had better control of the circumstances. Tonight would be perfect.

I glanced at Mrs. Hume and almost didn't recognize her. She had been beautiful, but whatever caused her dementia had also taken an incredible physical toll. She looked tiny, vulnerable. Her face had been stretched and pulled into a papery roadmap of bruised-looking skin punctuated with multicolored blotches and moles. Alberts had fared better. His skin was still stretched tight, though it had assumed the same papery aspect. As usual, he wore his butler's black tuxedo, which belied the paternal role he'd taken in the family since Judge Hume's death.

I laid out my story, peppering it with phrases like "It will be good for him," and "Francis and I became friends in there; we really did," and "Oh, it's nothing, really. Just trying to do my part."

In order to secure their approval, I probably would have said I was prepared to adopt Francis, but fortunately, it didn't come to that. They agreed that the experience might be good for him, though Alberts added gravely, "Just so long as *you* know what you are getting into."

"I spent quite a lot of time with him at Eloise. I think I know him pretty well."

Alberts raised his eyebrows a fraction of an inch, which for him was the equivalent of a look of astonishment. "I will frisk the young man before he leaves. Just when I think all the weapons are hidden, he digs up a dirk or a cutlass. I hadn't even known the judge had them."

"I'd appreciate that." Before I left, I asked when they expected Elizabeth home. I would need to pick up Francis prior to that time. She wasn't expected until well into the night, so I felt safe in saying I would come for him around seven.

When I returned to the Humes' home, Bridie was sitting on the porch swing with Francis, or should I say Blackbeard, illuminated by the electric lights. He wore the black tricorner hat with white piping and a long scarlet coat with gold buttons. His "beard" had sprouted into a mess of scraggly and nearly transparent hairs.

We would not be inconspicuous. Still, I was pleased to see no evidence of a sword or pistol.

They stood as I approached up the walk, hunching into my coat to stave off the cold. Bridie was a solid, fresh-faced Irishwoman of about thirty with a faint splash of freckles across her nose and cheeks. She wore a nondescript blue overcoat and black buttontop boots. Francis held a black briefcase. Their breath, Bridie's slow and steady, Francis's shooting from his mouth like he was angry with it, made clouds around their faces.

"Good evening, Bridie." I had called Bridie Mrs. Kelly when we first met. She asked that I not do it again as it reminded her of her dead husband. I had assumed she associated the name with her loss, but Elizabeth said she was so pleased to be rid of him that even the mention of his last name filled her with revulsion. I supposed she was not the first to suffer that malady.

I grinned at Francis. "Are you ready to go?"

"I am ready to go, John Doe," he said in that strange monotone of his, his face betraying no expression whatever. I'd never heard another person talk like a terrible actor reading someone else's lines, but, other than when he was angry, Francis's words seemed to come from some-place else. He turned to Bridie. "Good-bye, Bridie Kelly."

"Now Francis, you listen to Mr. John"—she winked at me—"and do as he says, you hear me?"

"Edward. Teach."

"Right," she agreed. "Edward."

"I am not a child, Bridie Kelly," Francis said in his odd quack.

"You know you act like one sometimes, don't you?"

Squaring off on her, he put his hands on his hips. "You are an ignoramous." He spun and marched across the porch to the steps.

Bridie smiled at me. "He's in good form today, should be no trouble at all."

"I can handle him, I think. I just need to keep track of who he is."

"John Doe, I am hungry!" Francis called from the bottom of the steps.

I winked back at Bridie. "Can't keep the Pirate King waiting, now, can I?"

"I'll be here tonight with nothing to do," she said. "Robert went to bed early, so I'll just be reading. Bring Francis back whenever you get tired of him."

"We might be late."

"That I doubt," she said.

"John Doe!" Francis barked.

"On my way." I turned back to Bridie. "Have a nice evening."

"I think you'll need more luck than I on that account," she replied with a smile.

I headed down the steps and front walk and met Francis at the little white wooden gate. "Are you ready for a night of adventure?"

"We need to leave," he said in a low voice.

"All right." I studied his face. Something was troubling him. I opened the gate, and we walked to the car.

Francis remained quiet as I started the car, but as soon as we were in the Torpedo, he said, "Drive one hundred yards and stop at the curb."

Fingering the handle of the case on his lap, he glanced back at the Humes' house.

"Why?"

"Just do it!"

"All right." I pulled out and stopped a couple of houses down.

Francis's eyes remained fixed on the Humes' home. I craned my neck and looked around him to be treated to a most unusual sight. A hat sailed out to the ground. A knotted line of sheets flew out a lit second-story window, making an escape rope to the ground like something out of the flickers. A man—Robert Hume—leaned over the ledge, worked his way out the window, and, clinging to the sheets, inched toward the ground. I wanted to yell at him to stop, but he was already hanging outside. I was worried for him, but I also worried for Elizabeth . . . and myself. What would she think if Robert sustained serious injuries with me sitting here watching?

Yet I could do nothing to stop him. His gangly form reminded me of a praying mantis as he descended, hand under hand, legs clenched around the sheets. In the dim light, I watched the whole procedure open-mouthed. He hugged the sheet until he was on the ground and had his balance. Once he'd gotten his bearings, he found his hat, a fedora. With a hand over the top of it, he ran toward us with a fervor only approached by those with hell-hounds nipping at their heels.

He and Francis had obviously worked up this escape plan, and I was simply the necessary transportation. Could I bring both of them? Adding Robert to the mix exponentially increased our chances of being caught. I supposed Elizabeth would be able to get either out of jail with little difficulty, but it would surely add a few years to my sentence.

Well, in for a penny . . . I looked at Francis, who was still watching Robert running toward us. "You two are planning on going back tonight, right?"

He didn't answer. Robert slammed into the side of my car and scrambled to get inside.

"Hey, watch the paint," I protested as he squeezed in next to Francis, panting and wheezing. I was pleased to see he wore an ordinary pair of brown trousers, a white shirt and collar, and a navy blue overcoat, rather than an outfit matching Francis's.

"Go! Go! Go!" they shouted, staring back at the Humes'.

I pulled away from the curb, thinking I'd phone Bridie as soon as I had the chance. I hadn't really thought we'd be ready to take on Eloise tonight anyway. Tonight we'd plan.

"Huzzah!" Robert shouted.

I leaned forward so I could see him. "Nicely done, Robert."

He looked down at his lap with a tight inward smile.

"Arrr," Francis growled. "Escaped you from the brig, I did." Again, the words were said without affect.

"You two are planning on going back tonight, right?" I asked again.

"We will return when we have our plunder," Francis replied. Robert watched him and nodded at me when Francis finished.

"And your plunder is?"

Francis's mouth puckered as he looked at me with disdain. "Treasure, of course. We must plunder for treasure."

"Hmm." I had an idea of what could become a treasure for me. Now I just had to get them on board, so to speak. I have to admit I was impressed with them. These were two solitary men who had difficulty communicating with others, and Robert was as timid as anyone I had ever met, yet somehow they had formed a bond and were working together.

"Supper, gentlemen?" I asked.

"Yes," Francis said. "All of this pirating has left me starving."

"What sort of food would you care for?"

"Is it true," Francis asked, "that a servself has all the food out, and you can take everything you want?"

"It is," I started, "but—"

"A servself!" Robert chimed in.

"Aye, matey," Francis agreed. "A pirate wants his plunder."

I could see this was an argument I would lose, so I headed downtown. I parked at the curb and we hoofed it to the Avenue Servself on the corner of Jefferson and Woodward. The food was better, if only marginally, than the standard cafeteria, and they had a pay telephone near the restroom.

The restaurant was the first floor of a two-story redbrick, with apartments above. The interior was overwhelmingly pink, with patterned wallpaper and plaster ceiling both in that soothing color, which I thought might calm the boys, who practically vibrated with energy. The restaurant smelled of beef gravy. We walked up to the counter, above which hung a large white sign with SERVSELF emblazoned in flowery yellow script, and food prices in no-nonsense black print on either side. Of course, everyone's eyes tracked us to the counter, and a low buzz of conversation started up. A pair of young men snickered. I tried to ignore them. The boys didn't seem to notice anyone at all.

I hung my hat on one of the wall-mounted racks and asked Francis and Robert to do the same. Robert complied, not able to take his eyes off the plates of food in front of them. Francis marched imperiously along the counter, eyeing the booty. Rather than invite Armageddon, I let it go.

I took three trays, handed one to each, and gestured for them to begin. Both piled their trays high. Each took one entree and a bowl of soup and then loaded his tray with desserts. When they could fit no more, a woman behind the counter totaled them up, and they headed for one of the small round wooden tables, Francis with his briefcase tucked under an arm. I took a hamburger sandwich with a baked potato and corn and filled up three coffee mugs before bringing out my wallet and paying for the feast. Our meals came to just under two dollars, which left me with nothing but a smattering of coins. I told myself it was an investment. Crack the conspiracy and my life would pull back together.

I set my tray on another table and squeezed my plate onto the one the boys had chosen, crowding their plates, all of which they carefully guarded with one hand while inhaling the nearest dessert. Excusing myself to use the telephone, I left them to their glorious gluttony. The pay telephone was a box screwed to the wall, so I was able to keep an eye on the boys while making the call. Alberts answered. I told him what Robert had done and recommended that Alberts pull up the sheets from the bedroom window to keep the boys from reentering the house that way. He said he'd take care of it.

When I wished him a good night, he asked, "Would you like to bring them back now?"

Sticking with Francis's nautical theme, I declared, "I have not yet begun to fight."

He chuckled and wished me luck.

I ate most of my supper before bringing up the topic of adventure.

Robert and Francis were tucking into their third piece of pie and fourth bowl of pudding, respectively. Francis already had a gooey brown smudge on the lapel of his scarlet coat.

"I have to work out some details," I said, "but . . . are you boys interested in having an adventure?"

They both gave me stony stares, mouths glistening with food. I didn't take it as a no, since neither of them made a habit of giving away his thoughts with a facial expression.

"This is a secret mission, and if you are going to help, I must swear you to secrecy."

"I do not like secrets," Francis said.

My plate was teetering, on the brink of falling into my lap. I set it on the table behind me and leaned in toward the boys. "I know that, but you and Robert shared a secret tonight with him leaving the house to come with us. That wasn't bad, was it?"

"It was bad," Francis said. A half second later, his eyes lit up. "Pirates like to be bad."

"Wouldn't you like to have a secret adventure with just Robert and me? No one else would know."

He looked at Robert before saying, "Yes. I would like a secret adventure."

"Robert?" I asked. "What about you?"

He nodded and, looking down at the table, smiled. "I like secrets."

"All right," I whispered. "I just have to get my hands on a key, and we'll start it. Maybe later this week."

"A key?" Robert asked. "To what?"

"Robert can pick locks," Francis said in a normal tone. "He could get out of the buildings at Eloise and break into any room in the hospital."

Several people again turned toward us. I smiled at them and waved them back to their suppers, trying to convey a sense that I was humoring these lunatics. However, my smile was real. This could be perfect. Sapphira—Helen—said she couldn't get a key to the Dime Building. Robert could potentially get us in both places.

"Maybe . . ." I started. "Maybe we could do this tonight."

"Ah, an owl job," Francis said.

I gave him a sidelong glance. Well, he *was* a reader. "Uh, yes. We'll have to do this at night."

Francis's mouth tugged to the side in annoyance. "We have to do what?"

I leaned in close to them. "Steal some surveillance equipment and install it at the Dime Building." Glancing at Robert, I asked, "Do you think you can pick the door locks at the Dime Building?"

He pursed his lips and nodded with a casual confidence, then leaned down low over the table. His shirt pressed into the remains of his pie. "Are we spying on somebody?" he asked in a hoarse whisper.

"Yes," I whispered back. "The director of the Michigan Liquor Association."

"That sounds boring," he whispered.

I cut my eyes from him to Francis. "It won't be. He's a criminal."

They both nodded.

"This will be dangerous," I whispered, "because there will be guards in the buildings, and they will have guns."

"I don't like guards," Robert said. "Or guns."

"I am not afraid." Francis's right cheek contorted with a tic.

"It will mean going back to Eloise Hospital," I whispered. "Sneaking in."

Robert's eyes widened and began to fill with tears. "Nooooo!"

People spun in their seats, staring at us.

"I'm not going back to the Hole! I'm not going "

"Shh, Robert. Shh." I put my hand on his shoulder. "It's all right. I won't force you to do anything. I'll get a key to Eloise . . . somewhere."

Robert quieted to a sad little whimper. The other customers turned back to their slop.

"Why do we need to go back to Eloise Hospital?" Francis asked.

"For the equipment. Your father had dictation recording equipment that—"

"The Dictograph and telegraphone," Francis said.

"Well . . . yes." I was surprised he knew.

Francis thought for a moment. "Shiver me timbers," he said, with absolutely no inflection. I decided pirate lingo needed some enthusiasm behind it to be effective. "Is that all we need to do at Eloise Hospital?"

I nodded.

"You must go, Robert Hume," Francis said. "We must help John Doe. It is the pirate code."

"The pirate code?" Robert sounded unsure.

"We are a crew. We do or die."

"I don't want to die," Robert said in a tiny voice.

"Then you just have to do," Francis replied.

"Oh," Robert said. "Okay."

CHAPTER SEVENTEEN

Francis shoveled another spoonful of chocolate pudding into his mouth. "Have you ever used a telegraphone?"

"No," I answered. "I've seen one but never had the chance . . ."

He looked at Robert and spun a finger in the air near his temple. Robert ducked his head and had a private smile.

"A telegraphone," Francis said, "is the dictation recorder, you dunce."

"Yes, I know that, but—"

"Do you use bean cans and strings at your fancy office?"

"There's no reason to be nasty about it. We have speaking tubes at the office. Just like everyone else does—or nearly everyone," I added before Francis could correct me.

He stared at me, cheek muscles rippling with little twitches, his face expressionless. "The operation is very simple. You thread a wire through the center onto a take-up reel, turn on the machines, and flip the recording switch."

"From a sound collector," I said.

Francis again looked at Robert and made the same gesture. This time I ignored him, but Robert pushed aside his current pie plate and buried his face in his arms atop the table. I waited him out.

Robert peeked up from the nest he'd made with his arms and

whispered, "You hook the telegraphone to the Dictograph. The sound collector connects to the Dictograph."

"How do you two know so much about these things?" I asked.

"I fixed all the equipment at the hospital," Robert said. "Telegraphones mess up all the time."

Francis scowled at him. "I fixed some things!"

"I was the fix-it man. That's what your father said."

"My father is an imbecile!" Francis shouted. "And so are you!" He stood up, trembling, and his hat slipped to the side.

"Francis," I said, "it's all right. I'm sure you are also a good repairman."

"I should smash you to smithereens," Francis growled at Robert, holding his briefcase out to the side, as if he were going to bash Robert over the head with it.

Robert ducked his head, put both hands over the back of his neck, and began rocking back and forth, chanting in a low, plaintive voice, "I'm the fix-it man, I'm the fix-it man, I'm the fix-it man."

I stood and placed myself between the two of them. "Francis, calm down. Robert didn't mean anything by it."

Pointing at me, Francis shouted, "You are also an imbecile! You are both complete . . ." His face turned bright pink as he searched for the word, finally settling on, "imbeciles!" He spun and marched to the door, threw it open, and hurried out into the night, briefcase tucked under his arm like a football.

"Robert, come on, we can't lose him."

Rock. "I'm the fix-it man." Rock. "I'm the fix-it man." Rock. "I'm the fix-it man . . ."

I tugged at him, but he wouldn't stand, just rocked and chanted.

"God damn it, then, you stay here." I ran out the door and swiveled my head, looking at everyone on the street and sidewalk. *There!* Scarlet coat, black hat, crossing Woodward, heading west. He looked like he was trying to skim over the ground while bracing for an impact. I ran after him. When I caught up, he was hurrying along Jefferson, going who knows where, staring straight ahead, jockeying through the crowd so that no one would touch him.

"Francis, come on. He didn't mean anything by it. Robert is your friend. Listen, we'll forget this whole stupid idea. We won't go to Eloise."

Sneaking peeks at me, he began to slow. "My name is Blackbeard."

"Yes, I'm sorry. Blackbeard. I don't know what I was thinking anyway. Bringing the two of you into something like this."

He stopped and looked me in the eye. "I am having an adventure."

I tried to discern his meaning. "You want to help me?"

"I want to do something fun."

"You think breaking into Eloise and the Dime Building will be fun?"

There was a gleam in his eye that I thought was real, not his regular put-on look. "It will be a riot."

On the way back to the restaurant, walking side by side with Francis, I seriously questioned my sanity. Who in his right mind would bring a pair of schizophrenics to a burglary? I had to be nuts. Particularly because I wasn't planning to put the kibosh on the plan, though I thought hard about it. I thought—I hoped—that Francis meant the word "riot" as slang, rather than its traditional definition. The thought of the other meaning set my head to pounding again.

Thank God, Robert was still at the restaurant when we returned, sitting at our table, picking up crumbs and stuffing them into his mouth. When we sat, he looked up at Francis shyly, seeming to try to judge his mood.

"All right, back to the plan." I turned to Francis. "The telegraphone's in your father's old office?"

"You should ask questions in the form of questions."

I sighed. "*Is* the telegraphone in your father's old office?"

"Yes."

"Can you and I get inside the hospital and get the telegraphone and Dictograph out?"

He thought for a moment, glancing at Robert and away again. Robert scratched his cheek and said, "The Dictograph is easy. The telegraphone is heavy."

"Right," I said. "I've seen one. The man said they weigh sixty pounds."

"No," Robert said. "This one is built into a table with a shelf in the bottom. It's heavier than that."

"How heavy do you think it is?"

"One hundred pounds?" He arched his eyebrows at Francis.

Straightening his long coat, Francis said, "I would estimate it at one hundred twenty pounds."

Still achievable, I thought. "Francis, would you be able to carry it with me?"

They both looked at me doubtfully.

"Hey, I'm pretty strong," I said.

"Francis and me carried it." Robert looked me up and down. "Maybe you could hold up half. Maybe."

"Okay, so assuming we can carry it, we'll have to get it out of the hospital and into the . . ." It would never fit in the car with the three of us. I wasn't sure the behemoth would fit with just two of us. Could I go to the Detroit Electric well one more time? I looked at Francis. "Assuming I can get my hands on a large enough vehicle, how would we get the equipment out of Eloise?"

"That will be simple." Francis set his briefcase on the table, opened it, and began sorting through papers. He pulled out a hand-drawn map of the Eloise Hospital grounds, pushing plates to the sides to set it on a clean section of table between us. "We can drive in the back gate by the freight station—here." He pointed to the spot, and then his finger trailed down the page. "We will have to walk in past the river because the policemen will see the car if you drive to Building A. If we go in one to two hours before the policemen change shifts, no one will notice."

"There are no guards at that gate?"

"No. Never."

"Okay," I said. "What time do the policemen change shifts?"

"Midnight and every six hours."

"That sounds like it'll work. What tools do we need?"

"A screwdriver," Robert said.

"We will need a flashlight," Francis added. "Depending on the installation, we may need additional supplies."

"We might as well get it all now," I said.

Francis's cheek twitched. "Are you planning to install the sound collector in one room and the Dictograph and telegraphone in another?"

"Yes."

He used a forefinger to push his eyeglasses up farther onto his nose. "You will need a drill."

"Anything else?" I asked.

After musing on it for a second, Francis said, "We will need a spool of wire—and glue if you have to attach the wires to walls."

"I have all of that at home." Time was of the essence. If Robert could pick the locks at Eloise and the Dime Building, we didn't have any preparation left to accomplish. I looked from Francis to Robert. "Are you willing to try this tonight?"

Robert didn't look up from the table, but he smiled his private smile and nodded.

"I am ready," Francis said.

"All right. Let me see if Mrs. Hume will let you spend the night with me." I walked back to the telephone, hoping Elizabeth hadn't shared her current feelings about me with her mother.

My fears were quickly allayed when Mrs. Hume came to the telephone. She thought it a splendid idea for the boys to spend the night, so long as I was certain I could handle them. She sounded fine—lucid and pleasant, which made me hope Elizabeth had a chance to spend some time with her tonight. These moments were fleeting. Elizabeth needed to speak with her mother, not the lost soul she so often became.

I returned to the table and laid out the plan to Francis and Robert in simple terms. When I finished, I added, "Now, again, the most important thing to remember is, be . . . very . . . quiet."

I had to keep reminding myself I was doing this for Elizabeth. Otherwise I would again get caught up in the notion that the plan was completely insane. I was going to break into an asylum with a pair of lunatics, steal a Dictograph and telegraphone, spirit them into the Dime Building while carrying heavy and delicate machinery, install a sound collector in a criminal's office, wire it back to the telegraphone in the room behind, and get out without being noticed.

Well, what the hell? I thought. *Doing something this crazy won't get me thrown in jail. I'll bet there's still a nice padded cell at Eloise Hospital for me.*

Now for an appropriate vehicle. Not only was the Torpedo too small to fit all three of us and the equipment, it had a louder engine than any other car I'd heard. Normally, I didn't mind announcing my presence, but if I was able to secure an electric, we could make a silent, or nearly silent, approach on Eloise. The old Victoria I used to drive had no more space than the Torpedo. A DE truck would be just the thing.

I left the boys on the sidewalk and drove the Torpedo into the garage, where I pulled it into its normal spot, amid 150 or so Detroit Electrics, lined up along the walls like horses in stables, all facing out so they could be easily connected to the charging stations behind. The odor of ozone hung heavy in the air, like the smell of an approaching thunderstorm. I breathed deeply. This smell of electricity was perhaps my favorite.

Climbing out of the Torpedo, I thought it a good sign that no other car had taken my place thus far. I scanned the garage, looking for a panel truck like the one I'd used for nastier business a few years before.

A rangy young man whom I didn't recognize walked up to me, wiping his hands on a white cloth—not a rag. Detroit Electric employees did not use rags. The name embroidered on the breast of his white one-piece uniform read PETERSON. With a smile, he eyed the car through smudged wire-rimmed eyeglasses. "Is it true? This was Edsel Ford's?"

I nodded.

"How fast does she go?"

"I've had her up over fifty," I said, a little grin sneaking onto my face. I had an idea. "Say, would you like to take her out for a drive?"

His eyes widened. "Gosh, Mr. Anderson, I don't . . . well, I work until six anyway."

"I'll tell you what," I said. "I'll take one of the company trucks—I need to move some furniture for a friend. When you get out tonight, just take the Torpedo. Bring it back in the morning. I'll have the truck back by then, too."

He kept smiling at the car. "That would be nice, but I have a day job. I wouldn't really have time to drive her."

"You work until six, *and* you have a day job? When do you sleep?"

Grinning, he shrugged. "Sundays."

"Well, maybe you could keep it for another day. I wouldn't mind. So long as I could hang on to the truck." *Might take more than a day to get everything done.*

"I could . . . maybe . . ."

"Is there a company truck here? One that we own?"

He glanced around the cavernous room and craned his neck toward the back, where half a dozen men were washing the exteriors of a row of cars. With a look of regret, he shook his head. "No, nothing." Then his eyes lit up. Snapping his fingers, he exclaimed, "The old 601! Elwood—Mr. Crane—keeps that upstairs to tinker on. Want me to check?"

Clearly this lad didn't know I'd been fired. "I'll go up with you."

We walked to the back of the garage and took the stairs to the second floor, where we wended our way through a couple of dozen Detroit Electrics, which sat in various states of repair. Elwood Crane was in charge of battery technology and manufacture. He was responsible for our own lead-acid batteries as well as overseeing the quality, installation, and testing of Mr. Edison's nickel-steel batteries, which had been supposed to revolutionize the electric automobile industry. Turns out men are just not that impressed by a hundred-mile range when, instead, they can rev a motor, spew out a cloud of malodorous fumes, and make a lady swoon. An electric had little swooning potential.

As we walked toward the battery department, I realized I was no different than the rest. Edsel had sold me the Torpedo for only five hundred dollars, whereas purchasing a Detroit Electric would have cost at least four times that much. However, I wouldn't have bought a DE had I had the money. I wanted speed, derring-do, panache. An electric—a "lady's car"—had none of these traits.

Tucked into the corner just outside the battery room was an old panel truck. The 601 was the least stylish vehicle ever produced, essentially a big black box with a piece cut out of the front, into which a bench seat had been installed and, in front of it, a steering wheel. Because the batteries were under the seat and the motor underneath the chassis, a single three-foot-tall wooden panel was all that stood between the driver and any obstacle ahead.

The truck looked no worse for the wear, but when I raised the seat I saw that the batteries had been removed. The young man looked around the room. "I don't know what else there is." He sounded dejected.

"I can grab some batteries," I said. "I've put them in plenty of times."

"Oh. Okay, then."

I pulled out my key ring, slipped off the Torpedo key, and held it out to him. "I'm sure you've got work to do. I'll take care of this."

He took hold of the key, but I didn't let go.

"I love that car," I said. "It's my baby. Don't let anything happen to it."

"No, sir." His eyes shone. "You have my word, Mr. Anderson."

I let go of the key and held the same hand—my left—out to him. "I'm Will."

He reached out with his right and shook my hand clumsily. "Melvin—Mel. Glad to meetcha." Reaching into his breast pocket, he said, "Listen, if you ever have a bug problem, give me a call." He handed me a business card for Peterson Pest Exterminators. "I'll do it at cost. No problem."

"Thanks, Mel. I don't currently have a need, but you never know." I tucked the card into my pocket.

He walked back to the stairway with a spring in his step. Few men had driven an automobile in excess of thirty miles per hour. I had a feeling Mel was going to test the limits of the Torpedo. That was fine with me. That's what Edsel and his crew had built it for.

Inside the battery room, dozens of stacks of batteries perched on shelves that lined the walls, all connected to charging stations. Virtually all were our own batteries, but two of the stacks were Edison's, which is what I wanted for the drive to Eloise.

I disconnected the cables and loaded five of the batteries onto a hand-truck, wheeled it out, and stacked them on the floor. I did the same four more times and then, one by one, loaded the batteries into the compartment under the truck's seat. When I finished connecting them, the meters on the dash showed a full charge, which meant I could expect a minimum of one hundred miles—and likely at least half again that much—before the batteries would need to be recharged. More than enough for the drive to Eloise. I hadn't thought of this before, but I realized I would also save a fortune in gasoline. Driving the Torpedo out there and back would burn through two or three dollars of gas, as opposed to the free electricity—or at least, free to me—that I was stealing from my father's company.

I switched on the truck, wheeled it over to the elevator, and rode down to the main floor. Mel was unhooking the cables from a blue 1910 limousine and waved as I drove past. I pulled out onto Woodward and picked up the boys, then headed uptown toward my apartment.

I'd stolen a truck, which was the one simple part of the plan. Each additional step would be increasingly dangerous. We'd see if Black-beard's crew would *do*.

The alternative was unthinkable.

Francis walked into my apartment ahead of Robert and me. He contin-ued down the hall to my parlor. "Your house looks like a dump for garbage!"

"Yes, I know," I said, opening the door to my front closet. "Someone tore my apartment to shreds last night."

"Your apartment is not torn," Francis said. "However, your couch and chairs are torn, your Victrola is broken, the records are smashed . . ."

I tuned him out. My hand drill stuck up from the mess on the closet floor. I pulled that out and dug for my drill bits. When I found them, I interrupted Francis's continuing inventory of my torn, broken, and oth-erwise destroyed possessions. We discussed the theft and the installa-tion, and, after switching on both of my Eveready to be sure the batteries were strong, I packed two small canvas bags. One held our burglar kit—the Eveready and two screwdrivers. The other was to be our installation kit—the drill and bits, two 100-foot spools of wire, one insulated with black fabric, the other with white fabric, and a quick-drying glue.

Everything set, I turned to Robert. "Are you certain you want to do this?"

His brow furrowed, and he glanced at Francis, who glared at him, daring him to say no.

"It's all right if you don't," I said. "It's up to you."

Robert's face screwed up as if he were going to cry; then slowly his face relaxed, and he shrugged. "I want an adventure."

"All right, then. Don't worry. I'm going to take care of you."

We walked down to the truck and loaded our bags into the back, which contained, I now saw, a stack of perhaps a dozen packing blan-kets. I hadn't considered the possibility of damaging the equipment on the drive, so this was a relief before I even recognized we had a prob-lem. We all climbed in and began the long drive on Michigan Avenue to Eloise Hospital, which was nearly twenty miles west of the city.

The warm, sunny day had turned to a cold, clear night. Even though it wasn't windy, the front of the truck was completely open to the elements, and, at eighteen miles per hour, we were generating plenty of our own wind. I'd forgotten goggles, so our eyes teared, and the cold clung to us like death.

Francis sat next to me huddled in his coat, his tricorner tugged down tight to his brow. On the other side, Robert curled up into himself, occasionally letting out soft moans that I knew had nothing to do with the temperature. I tried to reassure him, but he gave no indication that he'd even heard me. Other than Robert's moaning, they were both silent on the ride, but I could see their apprehension begin to ratchet up as we neared their old home. Away from the city lights, the heavens were filled with stars, virtually forming a soft white blanket in the night sky.

Finally, the hospital loomed before us, floodlights illuminating the grounds and the huge redbrick buildings that housed Wayne County's insane, tubercular, and indigent. Building A, our target for the night, lay before us, one of the redbrick monstrosities, tantalizingly close to the front fence. Unfortunately, our way in was at the opposite end of the hospital, which meant a lengthy journey on foot carrying the equipment.

Pulling off the road with the hospital grounds still a hundred yards distant, I looked over at Robert. "Last chance for us to stop."

He said nothing.

"Robert?"

His voice was barely a squeak. "I want to have an adventure."

"I'll protect you, Robert. You'll be safe."

He looked far from convinced, but he nodded. I thought he was trying to prove something to himself.

I shut off the truck's lights and drove around the grounds on the dirt road that hugged the fence on the side. Turning left, we followed the road around to the back center, where the freight trains were unloaded. A single floodlight shone down on the gate, tight squares of twisted wire topped with four strands of barbed wire. A heavy padlock, red with rust, locked the gate.

I shut off the engine and listened. In the distance, a dog barked. When the sound faded, I heard only my companions breathing and the wind rustling the branches of the nearby trees. "So long as we're quiet, we'll be fine, fellows," I whispered. "If we get caught, just raise your hands and don't try to run. Okay?"

"Okay," Robert said.

Francis was silent. I knew I'd never get him to agree, so I turned back to Robert. "Can you unlock that gate?" I whispered.

"Yes."

"Would you do it? Now?"

"Y-yes."

Robert and I stepped out of the cab. Pulling something from his pocket, he made a halting advance toward the gate. I stayed by his side, murmuring to him that we'd be all right, and that I so appreciated his help. In the light by the gate, I saw now that he had a pair of hairpins. He knelt by the gate, stuck the pins into the lock, and began manipulating them. His face was tight with concentration, but he looked more confident than I'd ever seen him. Francis stood over us, his briefcase clutched to his chest.

That Robert was in his element was proven in about fifteen seconds, when the lock clicked open. He looked up at me, burped, and said, "There you go."

"You are amazing." I helped him to his feet and shook his hand. "That was incredible."

Francis pulled the padlock off the gate and stood with his hands on his hips. "Are you ready to go in?" The tension seemed to be overriding his pirate affectation.

I pulled the gate open, started the truck, and drove in first speed onto the hospital's grounds, stopping where Francis stood just inside. "Could you close the door?" I asked.

"Yes." He turned and began closing the door.

"Don't latch it, though. We may need to get out of here fast."

"I am not a numbskull."

I tried to say the right things, but he clearly was in a mood, which could be real trouble by the time we got to Building A.

Francis climbed onboard, and I started up at a crawl. The truck was silent other than the quiet hum of the motor, the solid rubber tires rolling over the macadam, and the occasional squeak or creak of the suspension. Keeping an eye out for any sign of trouble, I turned right and passed two buildings, both dark and quiet, and turned left to take the street that led down to the river. We passed the tubercular sanatorium, a long, low white building where I'd received my radium treatment. I shuddered and looked away.

It looked like Francis had been right. The police were all back at the station, waiting for the shift change.

Of course, the police station was in Building A, our destination.

CHAPTER EIGHTEEN

I parked the truck by the river in the shadow of the trees, as close as I could get to Building A and still have cover. I suspected they left the trees to hide the consumption patients from the insane and vice versa. In the dark, the river was invisible, but the water burbled and whispered with ghostly voices. *Eloise's dead,* I thought, *crying for rescue.*

Even though my principal tormenters had been arrested or fired, I couldn't escape the strangling constriction of my throat or the lead weight in my gut. I was petrified. For the rest of my life, a shiver would run down my spine every time I thought of this place or, for that matter, heard someone mention the name Eloise.

I turned toward the boys. "The rule here is we whisper, all right?"

"Who has that rule?" Francis asked, of course not lowering his voice.

"We do," I said. "If we are caught we will all be in big trouble. All of us."

Neither of them replied, but I thought Francis took my point since he didn't argue. I coaxed them out of the truck and waited, tool bag in hand. Francis appeared, holding his briefcase to his chest with both arms.

"Francis," I said, "you have to leave your briefcase here. We've got—"

"You are not going to trick me into having my maps stolen," he said. "My briefcase has not left my side since I left Eloise Hospital."

"But we have to carry the telegraphone and Dictograph. You'll need both hands."

"You are not taking away my maps."

I took a deep breath and exhaled. "Fine." We skulked across the wooden bridge and hung near the trees, heading left along the river to stay out of the lights, should anyone be taking a nighttime stroll. We followed the river all the way to the fence before turning for the front of the asylum. I was uneasy for more than the expected reasons. Something about the hospital seemed wrong, but I couldn't place it.

"It's c-cold," Robert whispered. The white clouds of his breath huffed out in rapid bursts, like an overtaxed steam engine.

"Yes, it is," I whispered back.

"I'm afraid."

"It will be okay." I put my arm around him.

"N-no." He ducked out from under my arm. "Don't touch."

I stepped back. "All right. Just know that I'm going to protect you. Nothing bad will happen to you here. Trust me."

"O-okay."

We walked side by side by side as we approached Building A. The closer we got, the more Robert shook. He began to make little whimpering sounds.

"Robert," I said, "do you want me to take you back to the truck—or get you out of here?"

"I d-don't feel so good."

"Are you all right to go on?"

"I-I-I just wanna g-go."

I stopped and began turning him around. "All right. Come on."

"N-n-no. I-I wanna go with you."

"To Dr. Beckwith's office?"

He nodded.

"Okay. But, buddy, you've got to be quiet. We're a trio of buccaneers on a mission."

He stared at me. A pair of floodlights reflected white pinpoints in his eyes. "Okay, Will."

Francis shook his head and groused, "Are you ready to go?"

"I think we are. Robert, what do you say?"

"O-okay, Will."

We hurried the rest of the way along the fence until we reached the thirty yards or so of open lawn that led to the side of Building A. Dr. Beckwith's office was on the opposite end of the building, on the second floor. The police station sat in the middle of the first floor, above the dungeon that the administration called solitary confinement, but everyone else called the Hole.

Assuming nothing had changed in the past month, the buildings were all unlocked from the outside, as no one tried to sneak *in*. They were locked, however, from the inside, preventing patients from absconding in the middle of the night. We'd enter on this side and take the stairway to the second floor, where we would cross to Beckwith's office, the theoretical location of the Dictograph, and his secretary's outer office, the location of the telegraphone. Robert would get us out.

A truck roared past on Michigan Avenue, in front of the building. I realized what had been making me so uneasy. When I'd been here a few months ago, the windows were left open at night, and it was never quiet. The sound of the patients' howls, screams, and even snores filtered from room to room, building to building. Now all I heard was branches rattling with the wind and the rumble of far-off traffic.

"All right," I said. "If we get caught, you say I made you come with me. Have you got that? Both of you?"

They did.

"Let's go. Complete silence now, boys."

Francis led the way across the lawn. The grass was long and slick, matted in wavy indentations. I looked behind us and saw three lines of shadowy tracks in the grass. Hoping no one came by here soon, I walked a little faster, coming abreast with Francis. Robert stayed at my side. We stepped up on the concrete pad at the entrance with barely a sound. Francis leaned in and looked through the little window in the door before twisting the doorknob and pulling. The door didn't open. He turned, eyebrows knit, and exchanged a glance with Robert. An owl hooted in a nearby tree, and I nearly jumped out of my shoes.

They'd begun locking the doors from the outside, too. Robert knelt by the door and manipulated the pins, and within half a minute the lock clicked. Robert stood again, whimpering and holding his stomach.

"Are you all right?" I whispered.

"I don't feel so good," he replied.

Francis opened the door and walked in. I held it for Robert and followed the two of them inside. A blast of heat greeted us. The air was stale, dry, and very hot.

As the door clicked shut behind us, the full import of the moment struck me. Francis, Robert, and I were inside Eloise Hospital, the insane asylum that only a few months ago had nearly claimed all three of our lives.

We stood just inside the entrance for a moment, watching and listening. The long hall was dark until its intersection with the center hallway, which was brightly lit. The brilliance of the lights threw long reflections off the hall's polished marble floor. The police station was just around the corner. Bedsprings creaked; the faint sound of conversation rose and fell, not loud enough to be recognizable as men or women. Of most concern, above us, someone walked along the floor, moving in our direction.

I glanced at the boys, who were both looking at the ceiling, their eyes tracking the sound of footsteps as they got closer. I touched their arms and pointed to the back of the stairway. No hiding place was apparent, but the area was completely dark. So long as they stayed quiet and the person above us didn't switch on the lights, we'd be fine.

They crept with me around the stairway, and we huddled next to the wall, my shoulder touching Robert's, which was shaking badly. The man's slow and heavy gait pounded on the floor over our heads—now he tromped down the stairs. I prayed Robert could stay quiet. A bead of sweat trickled down my face, and I had a nearly uncontrollable urge to remove my overcoat. The man turned at the landing and walked down the stairs next to us. At the bottom, he didn't hesitate; he just started down the hallway. His green uniform flickered into view—a guard on rounds. Hopefully this meant he wouldn't return for a long while. When his footsteps faded, we shrugged out of our coats and crept around the stairway. A flood lamp beamed in a window from above, throwing a wide stripe of yellow onto the first landing.

Robert hiccupped but covered his mouth with his hand, so that the sound was muffled. We began climbing the stairs, the soles of our shoes scuffling softly on the marble. Halfway to the first landing, Robert stopped and grabbed at the banister, as if the stairway were a ship swaying beneath him. "I think I'm going to vomit," he moaned.

"Shh!" He didn't sound good, but we couldn't stop now. "Go," I whispered. "We've got to get up the stairs." I grabbed his arm, trying to hurry him.

"I really think I'm going to—" Robert gagged as his foot hit the landing. He stepped into the beam of light and erupted. Chunks of apple, peach, and blueberry pies mixed with a froth of stomach fluids exploded from his mouth. As vomiting goes, Robert's was of the blue-ribbon variety, with a tight multicolored geyser carrying easily four feet before splashing off the wall. His second spasm sprayed me with foam. My immediate concern, however, was the sound he was making, a god-awful choking moan that echoed through the quiet space like the rising of the dead.

I grabbed him, turned him around, and pushed him up the steps. When I picked up his coat, I missed his third volley, but on the way up, his fourth, fifth, and sixth offerings spattered the stairs. All the while, he kept up the moaning and groaning, now accompanied by a soupy-sounding gurgle in the back of his throat. At the top of the stairs, a little sign for a men's toilet was posted over the first door.

"In here." I pushed him inside the room. God, it was hot. Just enough light crept in through the opaque window in the door that I could see three stalls in the back. By the time we reached the toilet in the first stall, Robert had run out of pie, and so only coughed up the remaining mucusy spittle. When he finished, I sat him on the floor in front of the toilet and squatted down in front of him. "Stay in here," I whispered. "I'll be right back. And remember. You've got to be quiet."

His answer was a moan—a quiet moan, but a moan nonetheless.

I hurried to the door and opened it. "Francis?" I whispered.

"What, John Doe?" he whispered back. He stood just outside the door, staring in at me.

I stepped into the hall but held the door open so Robert wouldn't think I was abandoning him. A light down the hall glared off Francis's glasses, coloring the lenses white. "Have you heard anything?" I whispered.

"I heard Robert vomiting," Francis whispered back. "You smell terrible."

"Yes, I know. Have you heard anything else?"

His mouth flickered his annoyance. "There is always noise inside Building A."

"Right," I whispered. For Francis, every question was a literal one. "Okay, have you heard anything I should be concerned about, such as an alert or a guard coming up?"

"No."

"Good. Let me listen for a second." Amazingly, I heard nothing. Robert's gagging had seemed loud enough to wake everyone, even county employees sleeping on the job. "Will your father's office door be locked?"

A man's voice rang out from the stairwell behind us. "Goddamn! What the hell?"

We froze.

Francis and I stood in the dark hallway, our eyes fixed on the stairs.

"Coleman!" the man shouted. "Shit, it's all over my goddamn shoes! Coleman! Get over here!" The man began stomping up the stairway that stood only a few feet from our position. Francis stared at me. I put a finger to my lips and motioned him inside the bathroom. I followed him, pulled the door shut, and locked it.

The footsteps pounded directly to the door. The knob rattled. "Goddamn it," a man—the same man who had stepped in the vomit—barked. Keys jingled.

I herded Francis and Robert back into the last toilet stall. I'd just latched the door when the man outside swung the door open and flipped on the light. I climbed onto the toilet seat, crouching, and motioned for the boys to do the same. They climbed on and turned so that they were facing away from me, Robert bracing himself on the plaster wall behind the toilet, and Francis with his hands on the wall to the side. Despite my fear, I was impressed with them. Years of sneaking around asylums stood them in good stead for this operation. They were silent.

Fortunately, the guard wasn't. He muttered to himself from the moment he walked in. "Goddamn stink. All over my goddamn shoes. I'm reporting that goddamn Coleman. Son of a bitch can't even clean up some goddamn puke." He turned the water on full-bore in the sink and tried to clean his shoes, all the while cursing Coleman, Coleman's apparently unwed parents, and the day Coleman was born. Next, he slammed open the first stall door. A belt buckle clanked, clothing rustled, and muttered curses accompanied the ensuing grunts and toilet noises.

We crouched, balancing on the seat, dead silent. Finally the man finished, flushed the toilet, and left. On the way out, he flipped off the light.

After waiting another minute, we climbed down and left the crowded stall. I opened the door to the hall, using the tips of a finger and thumb to avoid at least some of the guard's germs, and peeked out. He was gone.

I turned back to Robert and whispered, "Are you ready?"

The boys stood side by side in front of me, silhouettes now in the dim light that leaked in from the hallway. Robert hesitated, finally nodding. His rancid breath crossed the space between us, and I made him get a drink of water from the sink before whispering, "Okay, let's go," for what seemed like the hundredth time.

We started down the hallway, heading for Dr. Beckwith's old office at the other end of the building. Below us, a man howled, a long, low note, rising at the end like the cry of a wolf. The hairs on my arms stood on end. I wondered about the men I'd gotten to know here. I had to visit them. As soon as this was over.

Behind us, downstairs, the guard began shouting again. "How did you miss this, you goddamn idiot?"

The other man, presumably Coleman, said something I couldn't discern, and the guard went back to berating him. It didn't sound like they were coming upstairs.

We turned down the last hallway on the left, and the administrator's office stood before us. The sound of the guard's voice was gone now. Francis tried the knob. It was locked.

I held the beam of the Eveready on the door lock, and Robert made short work of it. We entered the office. Light streamed in the pair of large windows on the side, bathing the room in dull yellow, rendering the furniture and walls gray. The shapes coalesced—a desk and chair, and behind them a credenza, next to which sat the telegraphone, which was much larger than the ones I'd seen at the store. This machine and the table on which it sat created a four-foot-tall contraption, and it was at least six inches wider and deeper than the machine at National Dictograph. I guess not all of their clients always had the newest technology.

Still, the room looked as I remembered it. I hadn't known what a telegraphone was when I'd waited in this office for Elizabeth to speak with Dr. Beckwith.

Elizabeth.

It seemed so long ago, yet it was only last summer. Would I have another summer with her?

Francis set his briefcase on the desk, and he and Robert hurried to the telegraphone. "Give me the screwdriver," Francis said.

"I want to do it," Robert whined.

"That is not accept—"

"Boys," I said sternly then whispered, "You've got to be quieter. Look, how many screws do you need to unscrew?"

"Four," Francis said.

"Why don't you trade off, then? Francis can do the first and third, and Robert can do the second and fourth."

"Fine," Francis muttered. "Robert is the fix-it man, Robert is the fix-it man." Now he was sulking.

"Francis, please," I whispered. "We need to get this done and get out of here."

"You are an imbecile," he said.

Leave it to Francis to state the obvious. I handed him a screwdriver and held the light for them. Fortunately for all of us, once Francis had removed the first screw he handed the screwdriver to Robert, who unscrewed the one next to it. Francis picked up a black box, not much larger than his briefcase, from the top of the credenza, flipped it over, and removed one of four screws from the back of it. Robert got the one next to it, wrapped the pair of thin wires they had freed around his hand, and handed them to me.

"Now we get the sound collector from my father's office," Francis said.

I followed them through the door of the inner office. From the desk, Francis picked up the sound collector. A pair of wires ran from it to the floorboards adjacent to the outer office, where they disappeared. He gave a pull on the wires. They obviously weren't attached to anything now, because he was able to quickly retrieve them from the wall.

"Perfect," I whispered. "I could not have a better team to work with."

"Blackbeard's old crew was far superior," Francis said.

"You've got me there," I whispered back. "Let's go."

We returned to the outer office. Francis began rooting around in the credenza and, seconds later, pulled out a black case, which I recognized as a Dictograph case, and then a cardboard box. "We need the wire reels to record on," he explained as he set the box atop the desk and began packing the pieces of the Dictograph into the case. "You two carry the telegraphone. I will carry the Dictograph and the reels."

"We'd better put on our overcoats, boys," I said. "We might not get another chance."

Once we had donned our coats, Robert and I pulled the telegraphone away from the wall. One of the legs scraped, making a little screech before I could stop. I held up my hands to keep them quiet and listened. Nothing. "Robert," I whispered, "do you want the top or the bottom?"

He elected to take the bottom. We picked up the machine, which weighed at least 120 pounds. Pain shot through my injured hand. This was going to be a very long haul back across the river. I strengthened my grip, and the machine rocked in Robert's hands.

"The telegraphone is very delicate," he scolded. "You have to be careful with it."

"I'll try."

Francis opened the door and peered out. "The coast is clear."

We followed him into the hallway, me walking backward, glancing back to both sides looking for clearance. Francis stopped at the corner and peeked around before waving us forward. The trip down the hall seemed much longer than it had earlier, but we made it to the stairway without incident. Francis crept down the stairs, as silent and stealthy as the pirates of whom he was so fond, returning a few seconds later to wave us ahead again.

When we reached the bottom of the stairs, we set the telegraphone down, and Robert picked the lock again. Francis held the door for us as we carried out the machine. The cold air washed over me, and I sighed with relief. My shoulders and neck ached. Robert was thin and spindly but showed no sign of fatigue. We hurried out into the shadows near the fence.

"Stop, Robert," I said. We set down the machine, and I stretched my sore muscles.

"Come on, mateys," Francis said.

After a deep breath, I said, "Okay, I'm ready." We picked up the telegraphone again and carried it along the fence and the tree line by the river until we reached the bridge.

While Robert and I rested in the shadow of the trees, Francis scurried up onto the wooden bridge and looked around. "There is no one in sight. Come now."

A few hundred feet more, I thought, and then I can set this goddamn thing down for a good while. We started again and were perhaps twenty feet onto the bridge, about a third of the way, when I heard an automobile engine coming toward us. I looked up to see a pair of headlights. The car was still a couple of hundred yards away, but it would be on us before we could cross the bridge.

"Robert," I said, "we've got to go back." I started turning around, coaxing him to move in the right direction. He just stared at me, uncomprehending. "Please, Robert. We've got to hurry!" I kept turning, and I could see he finally understood, but by the time he started to turn around, one of the machine's legs slipped out of his hands, and a corner of the telegraphone dropped a foot, hitting the bridge with a thump and the tinkle of glass.

"Robert, pick it up, please."

The car kept coming. Its headlights were less than a hundred yards away and gaining quickly. Robert lifted the telegraphone, and we waddled back as fast as we could while carrying it between us. My hand felt like it was going to explode.

"Come on, Robert, come on!"

Francis was already on the other side. I hoped he had the sense to stay hidden.

Fifty yards away now. The car passed under a streetlamp. It was a dark—blue or black—Packard.

The Eloise police drove blue Packards.

"Robert, I'm turning to your left as soon as we reach the end of the bridge. We're going to take about five steps down into the depression and fall flat to the ground. Got that?"

"Yes." His eyes were wide with panic. "I'm not going to the Hole," he muttered. We reached the end of the bridge, and I made a 180-degree turn onto the lawn. All the while, he repeated those words, "I'm not going to the Hole," like a Hindu mantra.

A few feet farther, we dropped the machine, fell to the ground, and hugged the earth. I peeked up and saw the Packard moving toward the bridge at a crawl. A cop looked out the driver-side window. We were cloaked in the black of night, but only a few seconds before, we had been visible under the streetlamp.

The Packard slowed still more, and, at the base of the bridge, it stopped.

The driver's door swung open. On the other side, the passenger door opened with a creak.

CHAPTER NINETEEN

I could do nothing other than hope they searched the other side first. The driver sauntered along our side of the bridge, looking for movement in the shadows while he slapped an Eveready against his palm and switched it on and off to no effect. The other cop joined him.

"I told Sarge we needed new Evereadys," the first cop said. He bent down and banged it against the wooden slats. Now below the level of the bridge, what I heard was the echo of a hollow *tap, tap, tap*.

"You sure you saw something?" the second man asked.

"Yeah. Somebody was walkin' on the bridge. Looked like two guys. Carryin' somethin'."

"If you say so. I didn't see anything."

"Maybe if you wore your peepers once in a while."

"I told you," the second cop said with an edge to his voice, "they're broken."

They turned and walked to the other side of the bridge, the first cop saying, "If they're broke, get 'em fixed."

"Hah!" the other man barked. "On what we get paid?"

We had to go. It wouldn't be long before they searched this side. Now the telegraphone was the least of my worries. I had to get Francis and Robert out of here.

The river. It was only perhaps ten feet across. I'd never really looked at it, but I thought it was shallow as well. I nudged Robert, wiggled over close to him, and spoke into his ear. "How deep is the river here?"

"It's cold."

"I know it's cold, but it's not very deep, is it? The car is right on the other side. We could get out of here."

After a few seconds, he whispered back, "The water is dangerous because of the rocks. It's easy to slip and hit your head." He said it like his "fix-it man" phrase, as if he had been forced to memorize it by rote.

"But it's shallow?"

"Yes."

"We have to cross. We can get out of here."

The cops were still chatting on the other side of the bridge. I got up into a crouch and began to scuttle toward the river.

"Psst!" Robert hissed.

I turned back to him.

"I am not leaving the telegraphone here," he whispered. "I must fix it."

"No, your safety is more—"

"Pick it up."

A weak light illuminated the trees on the other side of the river. "Finally," the first cop said. He swept the sickly yellow beam over the lawn and into the trees. The Eveready wasn't much good, but if he shone it on us, they'd have no trouble picking us out.

"Okay, Robert," I whispered. "Let's go—but slowly. Go at my pace." We both lifted from the bottom, and again I walked backward, but this time with a foot probing behind me before I set it down.

I glanced over at the cops, who were still on the other side, wandering up to the end of the bridge, the flashlight beam playing over the limbs, the trunks, the water.

My foot hit a rock, and I adjusted my path to the right. There. The next step, a little splash into a few inches of water. I shifted my weight back, atop a few rocks that seemed stable. "I'm in the water now, Robert," I whispered. Another step, feeling behind. There. Icy water swirled around my ankle, filled my shoes.

The cops kept chattering to each other, not the best idea when one is trying to flush some suspects, but I'd never been impressed with the professionalism of police forces in general. Anyway, it worked to our advantage.

Another step back, feel, shift. My foot slipped. The machine tipped left. I nearly fell but caught myself at the last second. Somehow we both managed to keep hold of the telegraphone. My feet and shins ached from the cold. Another step, and another, up to my knees now, and then the river began to shallow. Step back, feel, shift, back, feel, shift.

The flashlight beam weakened still more, faded. "Piece of crap!" the first cop exclaimed.

We kept moving. Suddenly, the machine became weightless in my hands as it tipped over toward Robert. He fell hard into the river, on the rocks, but somehow the machine was still above the water. Even though he must have been completely submerged, or nearly so, he was holding the telegraphone up, as if he were sacrificing himself for the machine. I bent down, wrapped my arms around it in a bear hug, and lifted it off him. He splashed up out of the water, and we hurried to the other side, me still carrying the telegraphone by myself, strengthened by panic.

On dry ground, I muscled the machine up the short embankment, and there, silhouetted against the lights of the tubercular sanatorium, was the truck. Next to it stood the silhouette of a single man wearing a strangely shaped hat. Francis.

The cops had returned to the other side of the bridge near their car, and had disappeared from the light of the streetlamp. I thought they were now where we had lain on the grass.

Robert shook and shivered, teeth chattering. I shrugged off my duster and wrapped it around him. Francis and I pushed the telegraphone into the back of the truck, and I closed the door and latched it as quietly as possible.

"Let's go," I whispered. "Climb in."

We wouldn't be able to outrun the Packard, so we had to make a silent getaway. I switched on the truck and slipped the shift knob forward one notch. The truck started moving with a little lurch and a creak but was otherwise inaudible over the river's babbling. To stay out of the light of the streetlamps, I drove on the grass for as long as I dared, crawling along in the dark, but I couldn't see the lawn in front of me well enough to keep it up. All we needed was to hit a rock or a large bush to get stuck. When we were about a hundred yards from the bridge, I angled back up onto the pavement, looking ahead and then behind.

The Packard still sat on the bridge.

I heaved a sigh of relief. My feet felt like frozen lumps of rock, and my legs throbbed with pain.

"Hey! Stop!" a man yelled behind us.

I looked back again. The headlights of the Packard flared. I threw the shift lever all the way forward and was thrown back against the seat. We tore down the road. I looked back. The Packard was just getting off the bridge. I thought we had a chance. I slowed just enough to make the corner without tipping, and we hurtled past the sanatorium, then made a sharp left to the gate.

"Hold on, boys!" I didn't slow, and the truck burst through the gate and roared out onto the dirt road.

Francis kept his neck craned to see behind us, one hand over the top of his tricorner hat. "They are getting closer."

I left all the lights off and didn't take the corner that led around the side of the hospital's grounds. We bounced onto a grassy two-track, rattling down the stone-pocked road. Our cargo bounced around as much as we did, and I had little hope for its condition. However, that was not my foremost problem. I glanced back, hoping to see the Packard's lights disappear as it followed the well-traveled road around the hospital, but they only got larger.

The road in front of us was defined in the outlines of trees on each side, a dense forest through which a narrow track had been cut. Branches scraped along the sides of the truck. My eyes flashed from one side to the other, looking for a space to pull in, to hide from the policemen, but we were in a forest of huge trees and dense undergrowth, with no roads or trails cut in, at least that I could see.

"They are getting closer!" Francis shouted.

The trees around us and the road ahead were brightening as we became bathed in the Packard's lights. With no reason now to do otherwise, I switched on the headlights and kept the truck moving as fast as it would go. The Packard was right behind us, but the policemen were stymied by the narrow road, as they had nowhere to pass to try to cut us off.

The road turned hard left. "Hold on, guys!" I shouted and spun the wheel, holding on with all my strength. The tires on my side lifted off the ground—an inch, two inches, six inches. I braced myself for the crash, and as the road straightened out I turned the wheel right, just enough to throw the truck's weight back toward center. We slammed down onto the road, and the back end fishtailed, banging off trees on the right and then the left, but we still moved forward at full speed. I glanced back again. We had gained a good twenty yards on the Packard, but still it came, relentless.

"Why are you chasing us?" I shouted. "You don't even know what we were doing!"

Now the Packard was ten yards back and gaining.

"Get down off the seat!" I shouted to Francis and Robert. "Sit on the floor! Now!"

They both immediately complied.

"Brace yourselves!" I pulled the shift lever all the way back and jammed my feet on the brakes. The truck slipped a bit on the grass and dirt, but the parking brake engaged by the shift lever and the normal front and rear brakes locked down the tires immediately.

The Packard smashed into the back of the truck. The steering wheel slammed into my chest. A split second later, I was flying over the top of it. I gripped the wheel as tightly as I could, wrenching my arms as I flew up over the front panel of the truck. I flipped down onto the road. The truck slid forward another couple of feet, banging into my shoulder, but stopped before it did much damage.

Someone was screaming—Robert. I pulled myself to my feet and jumped back in the truck. He had tucked himself into a ball with his head buried in his hands. He screamed, with fright and shock, I thought. I saw no blood. Francis lay on the floor of the cab, his hand clawing for the seat, and quickly climbed up next to me. Praying that the truck suffered no serious damage, I pushed the shift lever forward. Nothing happened. I pulled it back and tried again. Again, nothing.

Oh, my God. We're going to be caught. We'll have to run.

I tried pushing the lever to second. The truck leapt forward, lurching into motion with a series of creaks and pops. Robert's screaming wound down to a sad little whimper.

I looked behind us. The Packard sat on the trail at an angle, the hood popped open. Steam poured from the radiator, creating a rolling fog that quickly obscured the car from my view. The policemen walked through the fog and moved toward us a bit unsteadily, but they looked all right. More importantly, they were getting smaller by the second.

"Robert? Robert? Are you all right?" I shifted to third successfully and tried to move the lever ahead into fourth. It stuck. I was afraid if I pushed too hard I would disable the vehicle. Twelve miles per hour was the best we were going to do now. If the police were able to fix their car, we'd be caught in no time. I glanced down at Robert, but it was too dark to make out his condition. "Robert? Talk to me!"

His head lifted. In the glow of the amp- and voltmeters, tracks of tears glistened on his cheeks. "I'm f-f-freezing."

"You're not hurt, though?"

He shook his head.

"Okay, we'll get you warmed up in just a minute. You were very brave. You, too, Francis. Are you all right?"

I was glad to see that his hat had stayed on. He would have forced me to go back for it otherwise. He stared straight ahead in a stony silence, then said, "Rammed us amidships, they did."

I breathed a sigh of relief, tempered by the groans and pings and shrieks coming from the underside of the truck. I hoped it held together long enough to get us to Detroit. Francis and Robert both sat on the seat now, silent. I was silent as well.

Half a mile ahead, I turned right at a main road, and right again on another that led us back to Michigan Avenue. I pulled off the road and ran around to the back of the truck. The bumper was gone, the back doors were crumpled, and a long crack ran down the center of the bed. The box had been pushed forward on the chassis, tilting the front end up a few inches. I pushed against the side, checking if it was stable. It felt so, but who knew what might happen? This would cost more than my Torpedo would bring. I'd give the car to my father or sell it and give him the money. Somehow I'd work off the rest.

Fortunately, the blankets hadn't fallen out. Robert stripped to his underwear, and I helped him dry off and then wrapped him in layers of blankets, saving one for Francis and one for my feet. I threw my shoes and stockings and Robert's clothing into the back of the truck, then inspected our haul.

The box containing the wire reels had broken in transit. It looked like we had lost most of them, but six remained, spread over the bed of the truck. I gathered them and popped open the Dictograph's case. When I ran the Eveready over the contents, nothing looked damaged or even disturbed. The telegraphone had not fared as well. The front right corner of the wooden top had broken off, one of the legs had snapped, and we'd already broken some of the internal workings prior to the "accident," which certainly would have done additional damage. My heart sank. All of this might have been for naught. I hoped Robert was the "fix-it man." because this machine would certainly require one.

We started again on our journey back to the city. An all-night Western Union office was open in Dearborn. I stopped there and, under a fake name, wired the Eloise Hospital police force that one of their cars had crashed, giving them the approximate location. I wondered, now that Beckwith, the one who had used the dictation equipment, was gone, if anyone would even notice we'd stolen it. If we were lucky, the cops would assume we were kids breaking in on a dare. It couldn't be unusual. I'd certainly done my share of stupid dares when I was younger.

Didn't seem like I ever stopped, now that I thought about it. Perhaps I would have to look at maturing.

Not quite yet, though. I still had work to do.

As we neared the city, I slipped my watch from my inside coat pocket and glanced at it—2:35. This had gone far enough. I wasn't going to endanger these young men any more than I already had. I'd figure out some other way to get the machine into the Dime Building. "Robert, Fran—sorry, *Edward*, I'm sorry I put you in this situation, but it's not going any further tonight. Would you like to spend the rest of the night with me, or would you prefer that I brought you home?"

Francis sat up straight and looked at me. His thin face began to turn red. "We will go with you—to the Dime Bank Building."

"I appreciate that you want to help, Francis, but—"

"We have not finished the deed yet. We are a crew. We must finish what we started."

"I'm going to think about the best way to get in. Breaking in at three in the morning sounds like a pretty bad idea now. Anyway, Robert's clothes are still wet."

Glaring at me, Francis said, "We . . . will . . . *finish!*" He ended the sentence on a shout.

"Listen," I said in a soothing tone, "I was irresponsible to bring you along with me. I could have gotten you killed. I won't let you risk your lives." I shook my head. "You can't help me anymore."

"No! You listen to me." His hands balled into fists. "My father told me that I cannot do what I want." Francis brought his fists up in front of him and stared at them, seemingly captured by the sight, then dropped his hands and looked at me. Quietly, he added, "You cannot tell me what to do."

"Will?" Robert said in a tiny voice.

"Yes?"

"We need to help you. And Lizzie."

"Do you both realize that you could die? Or go to prison if we got caught?"

Robert looked at me, his face screwed up as he tried not to cry. "You are wrong."

"You will not get in without us," Francis said. "Robert can open the doors. You cannot carry the machines by yourself."

"I'll put my clothes back on," Robert said. "I'm warm now."

He looked like he was still shivering, but I didn't say so. "The telegraphone is broken," I said. "What's the sense of bringing it in now?"

"Once it is in there," Francis said, "we will be able to fix it. People can get into the building during the day."

"Let me think for a minute," I said.

"You need our help," Francis said.

I sighed. "You're right. I can't do it without you." Shrugging, I looked over at the boys. "Shall we?"

We drove down to the Dime and stopped in the shadow of city hall, in front of the bank entrance on Griswold. In the brightly lit interior, a guard with a gun on his hip stared out the door at us. I started the truck moving again and pulled onto Fort Street, only to see another guard at that entrance.

"This is crazy," I whispered. "We can't do this. We're trying to break into a bank. They'll kill us."

"John Doe," Francis said, "if we shoot the guards, we will—"

"We're not shooting anyone. We're leaving. Now." Pulling away from the building, I said, "Don't worry. We'll figure out another way." I tried to sound upbeat, even though I had absolutely no idea what that other way might be.

I drove back to my building and parked across the street. We decided to bring the telegraphone inside to fix it. When Robert and I picked it up, little pieces of glass tinkled against the back, sliding up and down with our motion, as we lugged the machine into the lobby.

A thin young man in the blue and gold doorman uniform stood behind the desk. He walked around it, smiling and pointing his finger at me like a gun. "Mr. Anderson, right?" Acne had swollen and pitted his face, turning his cheeks and forehead crimson.

We set down the machine. "Yes, good guess. And you are?"

"Ralphie," he said. "Frank got fired. And it weren't no guess. I seen you in the papers."

"It's nice to know of my celebrity." Of course, my picture had only been in the papers during my murder trials. "Listen, don't let anyone up to my apartment without clearing them with me first."

"Sure thing." Smiling, he gave me a little salute.

I thanked him, and we hustled the machine up the stairs. Fortunately, none of my neighbors came out to investigate the noise. They tend to be suspicious of me and would probably phone the police if they saw anything out of the ordinary.

We carried the telegraphone inside and set it in the parlor, propping the corner with the broken leg atop a pair of wooden crates. After I got Robert dry clothing to change into, I chipped off some ice and poured ginger ales for both of them. My head throbbed a steady beat, and the boys looked worse than I felt. They sat with their drinks in the used-to-be upholstered chairs across the coffee table from me. Francis, still wearing the Blackbeard garb, stared straight ahead, his body rigid, his hands clasped atop the briefcase on his lap.

"Tickles my nose," Robert muttered.

An uncomfortable silence fell upon us.

I supported my head in my left palm, my elbow on the sofa arm. A dull throb pulsed from the space behind my eyes. We had a working Dictograph—as far as we knew—and a positively broken telegraphone. Now, it was just a matter of fixing the telegraphone and slipping the equipment into the Dime Building—which was guarded day and night and impossible for us to break into, and my only confederates were a pair of young men who were "schizophrenic with autistic tendencies."

Something small moved at the edge of my peripheral vision. A little black spider scuttled toward the far edge of the end table next to me. I slapped my hand down on the table, just missing the spider as it disappeared on the other side.

Francis looked up. "Could we bring the equipment into the building during the day? We could hide and install it at night."

"I don't know," I said. "Hiding in the building would certainly increase the chance that we'd get caught. We've taken too many chances already."

Damn it. We were so close. How could we do this? We had to go in during the day, but we would need anonymity—and someone to unlock Flikklund's office.

The spider broke for the other side of the room, hurrying across the open floor. A crazy thought spun into my head. *Peterson Pest Exterminators. Yes. That could work.*

I looked at the boys. "We might be able to get them all to leave the office during the day. We could wire the equipment without anyone knowing."

Robert glanced up at me. "How?"

I smiled at him. "The MLA office is about to have an insect infestation."

CHAPTER TWENTY

Saturday, October 19, 1912

I set the boys to figuring out what had broken in the telegraphone and headed to my den to make a telephone call. The odds were reasonable that the Detroit Electric folks were on the lookout for me, so when the telephone was answered, I disguised my voice, growling, "Could I talk to Mel Peterson?"

The man on the other end hesitated, then said, "Please wait." DE employees were not supposed to take personal telephone calls.

About a minute later, the sound of the telephone jostling was followed by "Hello? This is Mel."

"Good morning, Mel, this is Will."

"Oh, hello, Mr., uh, Will. Did you—do you need your car back?" I could tell he didn't want to ask.

"No, I just have a strange request for you. Do you have uniforms for your day job?"

"Yes, sir. Modeled 'em after our DE uniforms."

"Could I borrow three of them for a few days? Some friends and I want to do some Halloween guising for a party."

He didn't answer.

"I'll pay you, of course," I said. "How about two bits a day for each?"

"How long would you want them for?" He sounded reluctant.

"Two days—three at the most."

"Well, sir, I, uh, I don't know."

He obviously knew at least a little of my reputation. "Five bucks," I said. "Five bucks, and no more than three days." I couldn't afford it, but I didn't think he could afford not to take it. Five dollars was nearly a week's pay from his DE job.

"Oh. Well, I suppose I could."

"Great. One more request. To pull this off, we also need some bugs. They're harder to find this time of year."

"Well . . . I've got a job this morning. Supposed to be some monster cockroaches. The buggers are hard to catch, though. We usually just gas 'em and clean 'em out the next day."

"Would it be possible to slow them down but not kill them?"

"Well . . . I suppose so. We could use less gas in part of the house."

"Perfect. I'd like to get half a dozen or so that are still alive. That would be ideal."

"You never know what you're gonna find, but it could work out." Mel gave me the address and said he'd be there at eight with the extra uniforms.

I hung the receiver on the hook and set the candlestick on the desk. Was that everything? My head was fuzzy, the area behind my eyes heavy and burning, my vision tinged with black. I couldn't think anymore. Sleep. An hour and a half was better than none.

Robert slipped into the den. "I figured out what was broken."

"Oh. Good." I pushed myself to my feet. "Let's see." I gestured toward the hall.

Francis now lay on the sofa, sleeping, his chest rising and falling, little snoring sounds escaping his lips. The back of the telegraphone stood propped against the side of a chair. On the table next to it sat the jagged remnants of a pair of tubes. Robert picked them up carefully and held them out in his palm so I could inspect them. "Two De Forest audions broke when you dropped the machine," he whispered.

"Wait," I said. "When *I* dropped—"

"They are easy to replace," he continued, "but I don't have any."

I decided that, regardless of who had dropped the machine, I needed to shoulder the blame for *everything* that had gone on tonight. "Okay. How is the rest of it?" I asked.

"I can't tell. Nothing else looks broken, but the machine will need to be tested."

"Can you do that?"

"Once I've replaced the audions."

"Great. I'll pick them up this morning on my way back. Get some sleep now."

"Can I sleep in your bed?" he asked.

"So long as you don't mind if I join you for a little while."

He shook his head. "No touching."

"No touching," I agreed.

I didn't even remember climbing into bed, only the alarm going off what seemed to be a second later. I shut it off, climbed out of bed, and started some coffee, then washed and dressed. These tasks were punctuated with trips to the kitchen for more coffee, which I diluted with cold tap water so as to get it down. Tepid, weak coffee, but coffee nonetheless. Robert and Francis slept like the dead, unmoving while I bustled back and forth.

I looked at my watch, grabbed my checkbook, and headed for the door. It was time to get some bugs.

The house was a white clapboard two-story in Black Bottom, the muddy lowlands near the edge of the city that had become home to Detroit's small Negro community. A well-tended garden rimmed the exterior of the home with evergreen shrubberies. The paint was relatively fresh, making the home stand out from its neighbors, mostly ramshackle frame houses with added-on rooms and lean-tos in crazy configurations.

When I strolled up to the porch, Mel walked out the front door, wearing a white one-piece uniform with PETERSON PEST EXTERMINA-TORS embroidered on the breast. "Hello, Mr. Anderson—Will."

His forehead furrowed, and I realized he was looking at my eyeglasses. I extended my left hand, and he took it. "Good morning, Mel. I appreciate your help." When I released his hand, I reached up and touched the rim of the dark glasses. "Light sensitivity," I explained. "No disease or anything. The doctors expect it to be temporary."

"Oh, yes, that's . . ." He was flustered. I waited him out. "Hey," he said, "did you hear Roosevelt is going home on Monday?"

"No, I hadn't."

"The doctors want him to stay on his back, but it won't be long now. Heck, the election is only a couple weeks away. He can't stay home."

"Are you a Roosevelt fan, Mel?"

"Why?" His tone was suspicious. Talking politics with the boss's son could be hazardous to his continued employment—or so he thought.

"I'm voting for him," I said.

He gave me a relieved smile. "Yeah, me, too. Okay, well, I've already got everything set up. Are you ready?"

"Sure." I followed him onto the porch, where three white coveralls, folded into squares, lay on a wooden chair. He asked me to put one on. We talked about the Torpedo while I pulled it over my suit. Mel was crazy about cars and asked me to let him know if any mechanic jobs opened up in the company. With a pang of guilty conscience, I told him I'd keep my ears open. When I finished buttoning up my uniform, we headed into the house, which was as nicely kept on the inside as out.

"Watch the water," he said, pointing to an earthenware jar, perhaps a foot tall, that sat atop a pile of newspapers in the middle of the hallway. We passed it, and he pushed aside a blanket hanging at the end of the hall and walked into the kitchen, where an identical jar had been placed on more papers in the middle of the floor.

"We're going to start here," he said. "I'm going to use a small dose of gas and then we'll come back in and see what we got." First, he taped the blanket in place around the entryway. From the counter, he took a bottle and a small paper bundle and set them on the floor next to the jar. Looking up at me, he said, "Hydrochloric acid and sodium cyanide. The bugs don't like this stuff, and neither do people, so we need to get out of here fast. Why don't you open up the back door?"

I took the uniforms to the door and held it open. He poured some acid into the jar, tipped in some cyanide, and mixed them with a long-handled wooden spoon from the pocket of his uniform. Gas immediately began to rise from the jar in a white mist. As soon as he finished, he jumped to his feet and we hurried outside. He slammed the door shut behind him.

"We'll give it ten minutes," he said, "and then see if we've got anything. We go much longer, they'll have already given up the ghost."

"Isn't it dangerous to go in that quickly?"

He shrugged, smiling. "I wouldn't normally do it, but how else are you gonna catch a monster cockroach?"

We talked about cars until he was ready to return. He stood at the back door, peering in through the glass. "Yep, see a few crawling. They ain't gonna last long once we get 'em." He glanced back at me. "In and out as fast as possible. You ready?"

I nodded.

He pulled a pair of small burlap bags from his uniform pocket and gave one to me, then threw open the door and ran inside. I took a deep breath and followed right behind. Eight or ten cockroaches in varying sizes stumbled across the floor, trying to escape the gas. He scooped one off the floor and then another. I grabbed three roaches off the blanket separating the rooms, each at least two inches long, stuffed them in the bag, and ran back outside, with Mel right behind me.

"I got four big 'uns," he said, thrusting the bag toward me.

My eyes were starting to hurt, just a small irritation. I smelled bitter almonds—cyanide. I tied off the bags to keep the cockroaches from escaping and thanked Mel for all his help before jumping on the step of a streetcar, carrying with me three uniforms, two bags of cockroaches, and the odor of bitter almonds in my nose.

The audions cost three dollars at National Dictograph, an amount with which I would not have been remotely concerned only a few days before, but this morning trading a three-dollar check for a pair of tubes dropped a lead weight in my gut. Change in my pocket and now less than forty-two dollars in my checking account. I would have to sell the Torpedo one of these days, something I dreaded. I'd sell it when no option existed other than selling Elizabeth's ring, and not a moment sooner.

On the way home, I tried to puzzle out motives and connections.

Motives—Murphy was easy. He wanted to beat the amendment. David Sanford was still murky, Warren Brennan the same. It was easy to fall back on money as their motive, but it was still an admission that I had no idea what it really might be.

Connections—something tied together Andrew Murphy, Warren Brennan, David Sanford, and the man from the salt mine. I'd be damned if I could figure what it was.

A germ of an idea began to niggle at the edges of my mind. Eli Sanford was still a complete mystery to me. He'd been in Detroit while David was in jail. Was it possible that he was the thread that connected these men? Helen told me Eli had gotten her out of town on a freight train. He'd grown up in a well-to-do family, and I doubted many people with privileged backgrounds knew anything about hopping trains. I'd ask her how he did it. If he had anything to do with the Wabash line, I might just have my common thread.

When I walked in the apartment, Francis and Robert were waiting for me, excited to see the "monster cockroaches," so I opened the bags and let them take a look. The bugs were still alive though hardly robust.

The boys had already finished off my box of Toasted Corn Flakes, so I settled for two more cups of coffee while Robert replaced the telegraphone's broken audions, made a number of adjustments, and finished putting it back together. Next, I helped them into their exterminator uniforms, and, after winning—surprisingly—a short altercation with Francis regarding the inappropriateness of wearing his scarlet coat and tricorner hat to exterminate bugs, we tucked the pirate garb and telegraphone into the truck and climbed in. I was just hoping the truck still ran.

It started, a good sign, but when I moved it through first to second speed, the truck was slow to respond, creaking and groaning like mad. The truck continued to slow, but eventually found its equilibrium in third speed at somewhere around five miles per hour. Now that the city speed limit had been raised to fifteen, none of my fellow commuters seemed to be too pleased by that, judging from their honking, curses, and gestures as they passed.

"Can either of you drive?" I asked.

They both raised their hands like eager students at a primary school. "Me, me!" Robert said.

"You cannot drive, you nincompoop," Francis scoffed. "You have never driven an automobile in your life."

"Francis," I said, "be nice, or I won't let you participate. You need to get along with others, and calling them names is not a good way to do that."

"*You* are a nincompoop," he muttered.

I ignored that. "Have you driven a truck?"

"Yes. My father let me."

"Okay. Good."

Even though the truck began to sputter along in a herky-jerky rhythm that threw us forward and back in the seat, it took only a few more minutes to reach Campus Martius, and Robert spotted a place to park a block from the Dime Building. The boys waited in the truck while I walked to the building with my bags. A bright red 1913 Abbott-Detroit limousine sat empty, double-parked by the entrance. I thought it unlikely to be a coincidence. It had to be Murphy's. I passed it, walked inside, and, from one of the pay telephones in the lobby, called the MLA office and asked for Helen.

When she came on, I said, "Helen, It's Will. Don't talk. I need you to come down to the pay telephones in the lobby. Right now." I hung the receiver on the hook and sat in the booth with my cockroaches. I risked opening the bags and shaking them to see if the roaches were still alive, and they moved around in a halting lumber, not their normal skitterish behavior. I actually felt bad for the cockroaches, subjecting them to this torture, though I would never have admitted it publicly. Even though men's and women's roles were changing, a man with those kinds of thoughts would still be branded a Nancy.

Helen turned the corner a few minutes later, wearing a tight yellow skirt and white shirtwaist that really emphasized her curves, particularly as she was not wearing a corset. I tried not to stare as she jiggled toward me on high-heeled button-top boots.

She stopped at the booth and glanced behind her, as if looking to see if she had been followed. "What is it?"

I explained what we were going to do in the most basic terms, going into little detail about the Dictograph and telegraphone. The cockroaches didn't have much time left. "First, I need you to let these bugs loose in your office." I held the bags out to her.

She wrinkled her nose and looked at the bags, in much the same way as, well, as one might expect a woman to stare at bags of insects.

"Let the bugs out secretly and then scream like a maniac. When everyone panics, tell them you saw an exterminator on the main floor. Run down to get us. We'll be waiting at the bottom of the stairs. I'll take care of the rest."

"Us?" She glanced around.

"I have some partners. We'll be ready in ten minutes. And listen. I have questions for you. Could we meet later today or tonight?"

The corners of her mouth tugged downward. "No. Mr. Murphy is taking me dancing tonight."

"Do you want me to get you out of here?"

"No. I am helping you."

"You could escape."

"No."

Stubborn woman. "All right, then. One question—you said Eli Sanford got you out of town on a freight train. How did he manage that?"

"He worked for the railroad."

A tingling started at the base of my skull. "Helen, what railroad did Eli Sanford work for?"

She looked puzzled. "It . . . it was the Wabash, I think."

The revelation hit me like a sledgehammer. I was afraid to ask the next question for fear it would take away what I had just gained. "What did he do for them?"

"Security. That was how he got me on the train."

"Well, I'll be damned."

Brennan and the Sanford brothers and the MLA. Like this: Eli Sanford and Warren Brennan work together on the Wabash/aldermen case, Eli puts in a word to get David the job at the MLA. Maybe Eli has some dirt on Brennan or vice versa. For some reason they decide to all throw in together on beating the amendment any way possible. For what reason? Money? The MLA members stood to lose millions of dollars a year if suffrage passed and prohibition followed. Paying these three fellows—even paying them a lot—would be no more than a drop in the barrel. As soon as I had a spare hour, I was going down to Union Depot and talk to the Wabash people, see what I could dig up about Eli.

"Will?"

I snapped back to Helen.

She looked behind her again. "I have to get back. Now."

"All right, here." Again I thrust the bags at her. "Take these, let them loose in the office."

"What . . . what kind of bugs?"

"You don't want to know."

Lips pursed, she took hold of the bags with a thumb and forefinger and held them away from her.

"You'll have to hide them on the way in," I said.

She looked down her front, then back at me.

"They're already three-quarters dead."

She didn't look any more convinced.

I shrugged. "It's for a great cause."

After a deep breath, she nodded and hurried away, and I ran outside. When I reached the truck, I startled Francis and Robert, who were deep into a discussion. They quieted immediately. I covered the telegraphone with a blanket, and Francis and I picked it up and set it on the sidewalk. He reached back in for the Dictograph and our bag of tools and supplies. The bag rattled as its contents shifted in Francis's hand.

"You carry the telegraphone with John Doe," Francis told Robert. "I need to carry my briefcase."

Robert simply moved around behind the machine and waited for me. Francis balanced the Dictograph, the box of wire reels, and our bagged supplies atop his briefcase, and we lugged the equipment to the door.

"Remember," I said. "Let me do all the talking."

They nodded. Robert and I lifted the machine, Francis held the door, and we waddled to the stairway nearest the MLA office, where we set the telegraphone on the floor, balancing it on the three intact legs, and waited.

We didn't have to wait long for the screams, which sounded like at least three voices. They were followed by shouts from both men and women, and then Helen came running down the stairs. "Ready."

I turned to the boys. "All right, you stay here. Don't talk to anyone. Just wait for me." Helen and I climbed the stairs and turned the corner. Andrew Murphy, looking green around the gills, his pair of thugs, and a severe looking gray-haired woman stood outside the door to the MLA office. Sauntering up to them, I said, "Hear you got cockroaches." Before anyone could respond, I added, "Yeah, downstairs, too. Big ones. Biggest I ever saw, in fact. But it's your lucky day. I can get rid of 'em fast."

"We have to work in that office," Murphy said, pushing toward me. "We can't wait for fumigation."

"Fumigation?" I snorted. "Nobody uses fumigation anymore. Everybody knows electricity is the way to kill 'em."

Murphy chomped on the stem of his unlit pipe. Behind him, the Nordic man lit a hand-rolled cigarette. "Electricity?" Murphy repeated.

"Yeah. We use an *Electro-Insecto-Annihilator.*" I raised my eyebrows, signifying that they should be impressed.

"Oh, one of those," Murphy said. "Right, I read about that. *Popular Electricity,* was it?"

I shrugged. "Dunno. Don't read much." This was getting to be fun. "Anyways, it shoots out electricity that kills 'em quicker'n you can say Jack Robinson." I snapped my fingers. "But"—I arched my eyebrows— "in people it causes sterility and"—I leaned in toward Murphy and lowered my voice—"im*pot*ence, if you know what I mean." I raised my good hand up near his face and demonstrated a wilted carrot with my forefinger. "And that's the lucky ones. It could kill you. The area needs to be clear."

Wide-eyed, Murphy asked, "Won't the electricity start fires?"

"Do you think I'd bring a machine in here that would burn the place down? Of course not. It's a different frequency. I don't understand the science, but the thing works like a son of a—" I looked around and pretended to just notice the women. "Beggin' your pardon, ladies." I tipped my derby and turned back to Murphy. "Let's just say the thing really works."

"Hmm." He rubbed his chin. "How long does it take?"

He was sold—this idea wasn't that far off from other machines scientists had dreamed up using electricity. For most people, electricity equaled magic.

I thought for a second. "Coupla hours. What time is it?"

He reached into his coat, pulled out a gold watch, and flipped open the lid. "Almost eleven."

"All right." I held my chin in my hand, pretending to think. "We're supposed to work on the first floor before we go—"

"No," Murphy said. "They can wait." I could see him imagining one of the monsters jumping out from a desk drawer.

"Well," I said. "I don't know . . ."

Murphy pawed at his coat pocket and pulled out a large billfold, from which he extracted a twenty-dollar bill and thrust it at me. "Now."

"I got some brand-spanking-new fellows here, who ain't never done this before."

"Bill us at full price. Double."

Shrugging, I plucked the banknote from his hand and tucked it into my breast pocket, silently blessing him. "You're the boss. All right. I just gotta get my guys and the machine. You all take a couple extra hours for lunch. We oughta be finished by two."

"It won't damage anything?" the dark-haired thug asked, rolling a cigar in his fingers. I decided he was "Pepper," and the Nordic man was "Salt."

"Nope."

Murphy squinted at me. "There's no residue?"

"Nope."

"And it will be safe to come in by two?"

"Yeah." I shrugged. "But if you're so worried about it, maybe you oughta call one 'a them old-fashioned exterminators to spray cyanide and acid all over the place."

"No, no," he said quickly. "That won't be necessary."

Pepper lit the cigar and blew the smoke my way. I coughed and waved away the cloud. His cigars smelled even ranker than Riordan's, who had held the world's record until now. No chance bugs could survive in that office.

I nodded toward the door. "Unlocked?"

Murphy said it was.

When I pulled the door open a couple of inches, everyone but Helen took a large step backward. Closing the door, I gestured to Flikklund's old office. "How about that one? We need to be thorough."

Murphy looked at Salt. "Unlock it."

After he unlocked Flikklund's door, I shooed them all away. Helen winked at me and followed the rest down the stairs. When they were gone, I ran down to the first floor and told the boys this was it—our chance to continue the adventure.

CHAPTER TWENTY-ONE

F rancis let us in and closed the door behind us. Light streamed through two windows in the back. The office was spacious, with a pair of oak desks. The larger of them near the windows facing forward, likely Flikklund's; the other, which must have been David's, rested against the left hand wall, nearer the door. An old scent of bay rum aftershave and Old English tobacco lingered in the air.

I directed Robert to the back of the office, where we set the telegraphone behind Flikklund's desk, propped between a credenza and the corner that adjoined the MLA office.

I took a deep breath and exhaled through my nose. "Listen, fellows. If we run into any trouble, scatter, take off your uniforms, and get out of the building. Make your way back to Elizabeth's house. All right?"

"We are not babies, John Doe," Francis said, his voice rising. "We know how to be sneaky."

"I know you do, Francis. Thank you—both—for helping me."

"You're welcome," Robert said.

Francis stared into my eyes, judging, I think, whether I was being condescending. I must have passed the test, because he said nothing further.

I opened the Dictograph case and removed the sound collector and wires, and we marched out of Flikklund's office, down the hall to the MLA's. Salt stood by the staircase, watching us. I pulled open the door and waited for a second, expecting a cockroach to jump out at me. Instead, three of them lay upside down, unmoving, on the carpet. "The electricity is working already," I said to myself.

The boys traded a puzzled look but didn't ask me about it. I closed the door behind us and said, "Let's see what we're working with."

We traipsed down the hall toward Murphy's office at the corner of the building, out of sight of the little lobby, on the way passing two more dead roaches. I picked them up (there are advantages to always wearing gloves) and tossed them over by the door, in case anyone wanted to investigate the results of the Electro-Insecto-Annihilator.

I headed back down the hall, where the boys waited quietly. A large brass name badge was screwed onto the door—ANDREW MURPHY, DIRECTOR, MICHIGAN LIQUOR ASSOCIATION. I looked back, trying to establish a path that would stretch across the distance between Murphy's office and Flikklund's wall—about twenty feet of open space. A pair of desks sat along the wall, their backs to the windows. It might be tricky, but I thought we could make it work.

I opened the door to Murphy's office, and we walked inside. The room was huge and cold. One of the three floor-to-ceiling windows was cracked open, I imagined to clear some of the smoke while they were out to lunch. The air was hazy with an amalgam of burnt tobacco—Murphy's pipe tobacco, Salt's cigarettes, and Pepper's nasty cigars over the top, souring it all.

Plush blue carpeting covered the floor, muffling the sound of our footsteps. The front fifteen feet of the office—the area from which the wire would exit—contained a sitting area and built-in walnut bookcases. Six-to-eight-foot-tall potted palms were placed in every corner and between the windows. A gigantic walnut desk sat in the back of the room in front of a long credenza, also walnut. In front of the desk was a pair of burgundy club chairs, and behind it loomed Murphy's matching, but much taller, swivel chair. The desk was topped with a huge black marble ashtray, pipes set into three of the six cutouts around the outside. Four cigars and a dozen cigarettes lay mashed out in the middle of a pile of gray ash. Murphy and his men were smoking with determination.

"You boys know this better than me," I said. "Where should we put the sound collector?"

They wandered around the room, picking up books and peeking behind the palms. Francis picked up a bust of Socrates from the credenza and sniffed it. "The sound collector is sensitive enough to pick up normal conversation within a fifteen-foot radius," he said. "It will need to go in the middle of the room, so that it can collect the sounds from voices at the desk as well as in the sitting area."

I glanced up at the ceiling, at the light fixture in the center.

"No," Robert said. "No access."

I looked over at him and saw he was talking to me.

"It was a good idea, Will," he said, trying to sound encouraging, "but there's no way to run a wire inside the ceiling." He looked over at Francis. "Pot."

"Pot," Francis agreed.

They met at the palm nearest the center of the room, between a pair of windows. Their eyes trailed down the wall to the corner. I peered out Murphy's door, craning my neck around the corner to see where the wire would exit the room. A file cabinet stood there, the perfect cover. I walked over and pulled the cabinet out a couple of feet before returning to Murphy's office, where Francis and Robert were already busy with the installation. Francis had retrieved the glue and was applying it to the back of the sound collector. Robert had rolled the palm away from the front corner and lay on the floor, drilling a hole into the bottom of the wall.

Without looking at me, Robert said, "Will, you run the wire from the pot to this corner. Peel up the carpeting—carefully—and hide the wire underneath."

I got the wire and did as he asked. By the time I finished, Robert had the hole drilled. While Francis held the sound collector in place at the back of the pot, waiting for the glue to dry, Robert fished the wire through to the outer office. He and I pocketed as much of the sawdust as we could and whisked the rest across the carpet before replacing the palm. Francis, finished with the sound collector, walked into the next room and began pulling the wire through. When it was taut, I thought we were finished in Murphy's office, but I examined everything closely before leaving. It looked perfect.

We crossed to the other side of the office and moved the filing cabinet out of the corner adjoining Flikklund's office. This time they let me drill the hole while they tucked the wire under the carpeting.

I was nearly finished when the outer door opened. I turned my head to see Andrew Murphy staring at me with his hands on his hips, pipe clenched in his teeth. Salt and Pepper flanked him, behind on either side.

Murphy jerked the pipe from his mouth. "What are you doing?" he demanded.

A thrill of panic shot through me. Then—*bluff.*

"My God, man!" I shouted. "In or out, but close the door!"

He eyed the pile of roaches on the floor and swayed forward, but didn't step inside. "What? . . . Why?"

"I'm nearly through to the nest! Close the damn door!"

His mouth fell open, and then it closed, and then it opened again, but no words came out other than a meek "Sorry." He slammed the door shut.

Grinning, I looked back at Francis and Robert, expecting to see smiles. They stared back at me with dumbfounded expressions.

"The nest?" Robert ventured.

"Yeah, pretty good, huh?" I laughed. "Scared the bejeepers out of him."

"There's not really a nest?"

"No, I just said that."

"A lie." Robert gave me a disapproving look.

"Yes, it was. Now we'd better get finished. I don't want them coming back."

I got the hole through, and it took the boys only another minute or so to finish tucking in the wire. Francis fed it through into Flikklund's office. I unbuttoned my uniform far enough to reach my watch, and I pulled it out—just after noon. We had plenty of time. We walked back out to the hall, where Murphy stood with his thugs near the staircase. I sent the boys into Flikklund's office and headed over to give Murphy an update.

"Are you done?" he asked, his eyes twitching between me and the office door.

I shook my head. "I told you it would take a couple of hours. The machine is working now in there"—I hooked a thumb over my shoulder at his office—"while we get at the rest of the infestation. Now, while I'm workin' on that, I need you fellows to make sure no one goes into that office. If they do . . ." I slashed my hand across my throat.

Murphy was cocking his head at me, forehead furrowed. "Have you and I met before?"

I thought he hadn't noticed me at the suffrage fund-raiser, but perhaps I was wrong. Of course, he might also be remembering one of my headshots in the newspaper. Formula for the day—bluff and hope for the best. "Nope," I said. "I got no idea who you are." Before he could say anything further, I spun and headed for Flikklund's office. "Remember, keep everyone out of there. Otherwise, you're gonna have a death on your hands."

And for you, Murphy, I thought, *it won't be the first.*

When I opened the door, Robert was placing a reel of wire onto the telegraphone. He stopped and looked at me, then went back to work, feeding the end of the wire through the machine's apparatus and onto the take-up reel. That done, he flipped the switches that powered on the machines. They had apparently connected everything while I chatted with Murphy.

"We're ready to test," Robert said.

"Fantastic. Okay, wait here just a minute."

"One minute?" Francis asked. "Precisely?"

"No. Just wait. I'll come back and tell you when I'm ready for you."

"That is a very different instruction than to wait one minute."

"You're right, Francis. Sorry. I'll try to communicate more clearly."

"Just say the truth," he scolded.

I took a deep breath, walked back to the door, and made a point of hurrying out, slamming it shut behind me, shaking my head.

"What?" Murphy asked. "Is it bad?"

"The first office is bad. This one is worse. A lot worse."

"Do what you have to do. We don't need that office anyway, not for weeks."

"All right," I said. "I'm going to have to use poison. Until today, I'd never seen a bug too big for the Insecto-Electro-Annihilator. I don't know what you're feedin' 'em, but—"

Murphy was drawing on his pipe but stopped abruptly and squinted at me. "I thought it was the *Electro-Insecto*-Annihilator."

"Yeah. That's what I said."

"No, you said Insecto-Elec—"

"Do you want to get rid of the goddamn cockroaches or not?" I demanded, scowling at him.

"Yes. Of course." He seemed to shrink into himself, as he imagined the bugs still crawling around his office.

"So like I was sayin'. I swear I saw one this big." I held my hands in front of me, about six inches apart. "I can keep the fumes out of the other offices, but this one is going to have to be quarantined for three weeks." By then, the election would be over, and I would either have what I needed or not. If not, it would be too late to accomplish anything anyway. "Have somebody make a big sign—keep out, poison—like that."

He nodded.

"Almost time to go back and take the first check of your office," I said. "One of us will be headin' over there in a minute." I knew that, unlike Francis, they wouldn't try to pin me down on the meaning of the phrase. I walked back to Flikklund's office, jerked the door open, and darted inside, slamming the door behind me.

Francis was sitting in David's chair on the side. "Take a look at what I found." He held up his hand. A pair of keys dangled off a little key ring.

"What do they open?" I asked.

"This one"—the smaller of the two—"locks and unlocks the desk drawers, and this one locks and unlocks the office door."

"Really?" I said. *Perfect, perfect, perfect.*

"Do you believe that I am lying to you?" Francis demanded.

"No, not at all. I just can't believe the luck. This is—"

He leapt up from the chair, his face turning red. "It is not luck when I search a drawer and find two keys!"

"No, you're right. Thank—"

"You are an ignoramous! Do you hear me? You are an ignoramous!"

"Francis." I held my hands up in front of me, palms down, gesturing for him to quiet. "I understand. You are the one who—"

He threw the keys at me. They bounced off my chest and fell to the floor. He stomped to the door and reached for the knob.

I took hold of his arm. "Francis, no. You can't—"

He wound up and threw a wild right hook at my head. I ducked under it, spun him around, and held him in a bear hug from behind, gripping my right wrist with my left hand. Screaming, he kicked my shins and reached back, pulling my hair. It hurt, though no more than the pain shooting from my wrist. I held on. He bent over, lifting me off my feet, and ran backward, slamming me into the wall. The air went out of me in a whoosh, but I didn't let go. We crashed to the floor on our sides. Francis thrashed around, clawing at my arms and hands with his nails. Fortunately, my shirt, uniform, and gloves took the brunt. The screams were deafening. As I was buffeted back and forth, as if I were holding onto an enraged tiger, I realized two people were screaming— Francis *and* Robert.

I climbed on top of Francis, pinning him to the floor. He kept thrashing. His eyes were wild, unfocused.

"Francis, look at me."

"Noooo!" he howled.

"Francis! Francis! Look at me."

"Get off! Get off!" He was crying, mucus running into his mouth. "Get . . ." He began sobbing. His muscles went limp. I climbed off, and he curled into the fetal position, crying with heart-wrenching sobs. "Don't . . . don't touch . . ." he kept repeating through the sobs. Robert had quieted.

My eyes were pooling with tears. "I'm sorry, Francis, I'm sorry." I wanted to touch his arm or rub his back but knew it would bring on another fit. I sat up and looked at Robert. He was sitting against the wall in the corner, rocking back and forth as quickly as he could. I got him up into Flikklund's chair but didn't touch Francis, who by now had quieted and simply lay curled up on the floor. I sat in David's chair and waited.

After a few more minutes, Francis climbed to his feet, sniffling and straightening his clothing. I stood and offered him my chair. He sat, but when he did, he looked up at me and muttered, "I still think you are an ignoramous."

"You're right about that," I said. "Okay, I'm going to go out and see what we're dealing with."

Neither of them responded.

"Francis, Robert, listen to me." I waited until they met my eyes.

"You might need to escape. If I yell for you to run, get down the stairs and outside as fast as possible. Get back to the Humes' house." If Murphy was going to have me arrested, I at least wanted the boys to have a chance to get away. "I'll be back in a . . . shortly," I said.

I walked out of the office and shut the door behind me, this time to an audience of a dozen people standing in the hall, their attention glued to me. At the end nearest the stairs stood a pair of uniformed Detroit policemen, their hands resting on the butts of their guns. I readied myself to create a distraction, to give the boys a chance to escape. Then I noticed the cops' eyes were as wide as everyone else's.

Helen stood next to Murphy and Salt and Pepper near the center. She gave me an infinitesimal shrug. Murphy's eyebrows arched. No one said anything.

Shaking my head and dusting off my hands, I looked from one end of the line to the other before meeting Murphy's eyes again and saying the first thing that came to mind.

"I told you they were big."

CHAPTER TWENTY-TWO

I explained to the gawkers that it had been a close thing, but we had turned the tide and contained the cockroaches. The situation was under control. They bought it. The crowd dispersed, leaving Murphy and his thugs, and Helen and the older woman from their office. I told Murphy that we were on the downside of it now and could be done in as little as an hour. I'd let him know. Returning to Flikklund's office, I breathed a sigh of relief. Francis and Robert slowly returned to something approaching equilibrium. Another fifteen minutes passed, during which we talked about recording with the telegraphone. Francis and Robert had gone back to their usual analytical (Francis) and sweet (Robert) selves. I walked Francis back into the MLA outer office, with a request that he wait thirty seconds and then walk all the way around the perimeter of Murphy's office while speaking in a normal tone.

Closing the doors behind me, I returned to Flikklund's desk and held the receiver to my ear. Other than a hum, I heard nothing. Then a door creaked open. I flipped the recording switch on the telegraphone, and the wire started spooling through the machine.

"Fifteen men on the dead man's che-est, yo-ho-ho and a bottle of rum," Francis sang, extremely off-key, in the receiver. "Drink and the devil had done for the re-est, yo-ho-ho and a bottle of rum." He continued in a like manner for the next thirty seconds or so and then quieted. I'm not sure why, but it felt like the equivalent of an apology, or at least an admission that he understood why I had restrained him. His voice carried well over the loud hum, but I worried about hearing quiet conversation. The door creaked and clicked shut.

He returned to Flikklund's office and waited with me while Robert wound the wire back onto the reel and started it playing. We traded the receiver back and forth. Francis's voice was not as clear as it had originally been through the receiver, but it was still most recognizable.

Now we all were grinning.

"Perfect!" I unwound the reel from the machine and handed it to Francis. "Keep this. A memento of our mission."

He slipped the reel into his coat pocket without a word, and we packed up our remaining supplies and tools. I took one more look through the MLA office to be sure our work wasn't visible. I was hoping no one got the bright idea to move the filing cabinet in the corner to see what had become of the cockroach nest, but I thought it unlikely anyone would. Most people would rather keep themselves in the dark when it comes to nasty things in their environment, and Helen would certainly discourage would-be searchers.

Back in Flikklund's office, I filled our burlap bags nearly to bursting with crumpled-up paper, to simulate our catch. To the top of each I added our cockroaches, the front halves of which peeked out above the knots. We walked from the office with the door key safely in my pocket.

Most of the crowd had dispersed, but Murphy and his men were, as expected, still waiting.

"Lock this door. Now." I pointed back at it. Giving Murphy an accusing glance, I asked, "Did you have the sign made?"

He nodded. While the first thug locked the door, the other held up a sign written out with blue ink: KEEP OUT! POISON! QUARINTINE!

"That's fine. Tape it to the door right away, and make sure the janitors know to stay out. No one, I repeat, no one, can go into that room for three weeks. I'll come back then and get it cleared out. Do you understand?"

"Yes. But . . ." Smoke leaked out the corner of his mouth. "Where is your Electro-Insecto-Annihilator?"

Good point. "It doesn't kill the eggs. And let me tell you, you got eggs—millions of 'em. If I take it out now you're going to end up with a couple million of those little bastards scuttlin' around here." I pointed toward Flikklund's office. "I've got it set up so they'll come out in this office. The machine'll mow 'em down as soon as they do. But like I said, if anybody goes in there at the wrong time . . ." I made a slashing motion across my throat.

"What about the bugs downstairs?"

"Guess they'll have to wait. I can't risk takin' the EIA outta there. The whole damn building will be overrun."

"Ha!" he barked. "Good. Can we get to work now?"

I nodded. "Listen, though. You might see me around here once in a while. I'm gonna be comin' back occasionally over the next few weeks to check on the machine."

We walked down the stairs to the entrance and outside. As a general rule, I try not to touch the boys, but on the way to the truck I slapped them both on the back and gave them a big smile, and I think they enjoyed it. Driving away, I marveled over the incredible work these young men had done.

Sherlock Holmes's Baker Street Irregulars had nothing on the Jefferson Avenue variety.

After I got the boys' exterminator uniforms, gave Francis back his pirate outfit, and swore them both to silence, we climbed in the truck and started out toward the Humes' house. The sun shone overhead, its rays drilling into my brain with a diamond-tipped bit, even through the tinted lenses.

On the way, I wondered how I could ever explain this to Elizabeth, should she deign to continue our relationship. I could only imagine her reaction to hearing that I'd taken Robert and Francis to Eloise Hospital for a late-night burglary, complete with armed guards and policemen, gotten into a vehicular accident with them in the exposed front seat, and told them to lie if anyone asked about their night.

I reckoned I would experience the female version of Mt. Krakatoa's eruption, with all the ensuing destruction the original had caused— although this would be directed entirely at me. I was hoping I could put off that act of God until sometime well into the future.

Fortunately, Elizabeth was working. I escaped with no more than a reminder from her via Alberts that I arrive no later than 8:30 A.M. the next morning to escort them to church.

I left the truck two blocks from their house and took a streetcar back to Campus Martius, so I wouldn't have to deal with the vehicle's condition, the traffic snarls, or the near impossibility of finding parking this time of day. When I hopped off, the clock on city hall's tower showed 2:10. I had perhaps three hours to listen. I rushed behind city hall to the Dime Building and up to the second floor. I loitered until no one was near the MLA offices and then hurried to the door papered with warning signs—skull and bones, KEEP OUT—CYANIDE! QUARANTINE (spelled correctly now). I waited until no one was around, twisted the key in the lock, and slipped inside, locking the door behind me.

Everything was as we'd left it. The faint odor of Old English and bay rum seemed lessened now. The building's memory of Roger Flikklund and David Sanford was fading.

I flipped open the lid of the telegraphone and switched on the power. A quiet hum built over the few seconds it took to warm up. Now I held the receiver to my ear. The hum was much louder, and for a moment I wondered if the machine was working. Then a horn blared on the street below, loud enough for the sound to penetrate the glass of my window. The same sound echoed in the receiver, faint and fuzzy, delayed a fraction of a second.

Hum. Nothing else but the occasional traffic sound. After fifteen minutes, I thought I'd sneak a peek into the office, to ask Helen if Murphy was around. I unlocked the door, walked out like I belonged, and hustled to the MLA office. When I opened the door, I saw the gray-haired woman sitting behind the desk. "So, uh, any cockroaches back yet?"

Her eyes widened, and from the way her stomach seemed to tense, I guessed she lifted her feet from the floor. "No, no, I haven't seen any."

"Good," I said. "Is your boss in?"

"No, he has meetings this afternoon. He'll be in on Monday."

"All right. Just checkin', really. Is, um, the girl that normally works here"—I gestured at the desk—"around?"

"No." She gave me a disapproving look. "She's with Mr. Murphy."

"Okay, thank you."

I hotfooted it out of the building. No sense hanging around with no one to listen to. I realized that, even though we had achieved a tremendous amount, we were far from guaranteed that our efforts would provide a useful result. Murphy didn't seem a circumspect man, but he might be cautious enough to speak of his plans only away from possible prying ears. Regardless, I would not have my answer until at least Monday.

I didn't mind, though. This would give me time to hunt down the other thread—Eli Sanford.

The Wabash offices were steaming hot. I stood in the personnel office, which was manned by a single person—a mousy little man with three-quarter moons of sweat under and around the arms of his white shirt that bled over onto his blue pin-striped vest. He used his forearm to wipe the beads of sweat from his face. "I told you I can't give out that information."

"Be a pal," I said. "Just tell me if Eli Sanford still works for the railroad. Just a yes or a no."

"Listen, buddy, I ain't in a mood. Go away before I call security."

"Where would you call to talk to Eli Sanford?"

Glaring at me, he took a deep breath. "He doesn't work here anymore. Now get lost."

"When did he leave?"

He turned and spoke into the end of the tube that ran up the wall. "Security to personnel. Now."

"I was just going," I said, tipping my derby on the way out. I closed the door behind me and waited in the hall.

A minute later, a rough-looking fellow with a two-day beard and a bottlebrush mustache hurried around the corner. I watched him walk into the personnel office. While the man told him about me, I walked down the hall and waited. A few seconds later, the rough-looking man came back out and closed the door, shaking his head.

"Hey, listen," I said as he approached. "Eli Sanford owes me five bucks. Do you know where he went?"

"Nah. He didn't come in Wednesday morning and hasn't shown up—"

"Wednesday?" My jaw dropped. "Three days ago Wednesday?" *The day after David was killed.*

"Yeah." He eyed me, looking for a threat. "Why?"

"I was told he moved months ago."

"You was told wrong, then. We're splittin' his shift until they hire somebody else. Not that he did a goddamn thing anyway."

I fell in beside him as he walked toward the exit. "Damn. I'm going to have to keep an eye out for him."

We reached the door, and he followed me out. "Why are you really looking for him?" he asked.

I met his eyes. *Could I trust him?*

"Got himself in trouble, didn't he?" the rough-looking man asked.

"I'm not sure. He probably has some answers for me, and I need answers."

"He lives in an apartment over on Church Street, by the ballpark. Don't know the address."

"Why are you telling me this?" I asked.

The man shrugged. "Don't like him. I expect he must really be in trouble for a swell like you to come down here."

"Why don't you like him?"

He shrugged again. "He's just one of those fellas, you know? Cuts corners, always lookin' for an angle. He ain't the guy you want on the other side of the boxcar—'cause he might not be there after all."

"Would you mind answering a few more questions? It's very important."

"Important how?"

How much to tell him? "Eli's brother was murdered Tuesday night. You said Eli didn't show up for work the next day."

The man frowned. "If my brother had been murdered, I wouldn't have shown up at work the next day either."

"Do you know if he contacted the railroad since then to explain?"

"No. Mr. Goop back there"—he nodded toward the personnel office—"said they ain't heard a word. Speaking of him, come on." He started around the building and down the tracks. "If he sees me talkin' to you, management'll shit on me."

We continued past the train sheds while a freight train rumbled down the tracks next to us, the ground vibrating every time the cars passed over a joint in the rails. Just down the line was the Wabash security building, a small rectangular hut with four wooden chairs around a coal stove with a coffeepot perched on top. One man sat near it drinking coffee.

"Pete?" the rough-looking man said. "Can you give us a minute?"

"Sure thing, Al." The other man stood, shrugged on his coat, and walked outside.

The rough-looking man grabbed a coffee cup, held it in front of him, and looked back at me.

I nodded. "Thanks."

He poured two cups, and we sat near the stove.

I took a sip of coffee—scalding hot. "I don't know if you can help, but I'm involved in an investigation that—"

"You ain't a cop," he said with authority.

"No. This is personal. Were you involved at all in the entrapment of the aldermen?"

"Why?" His eyes burned into me. I'd hit a nerve.

"I'm trying to figure out if Eli had something to do with that. This problem I'm dealing with might go back to that bribery. I've got a William Burns man I'm dealing with, and—"

"Who?"

"Warren Brennan."

"What do you think of him?"

I'd take a chance and tell the truth. "I think he's an asshole."

He nodded, just the barest of tips of his chin, and took a big gulp of coffee. "Management kept us in the dark about the investigation. They figured—rightly—that one of us would squeal to his alderman. Somehow Eli found out what was goin' on. Brennan and Sanford had some big blowout. Nobody ever talked about it, but he didn't do shit around here after that, and nobody called him on it."

I held my mug up near my face and blew over the coffee's steaming surface. "You don't think they were working together?"

He grunted out a laugh. "Hell no. The only thing they'da helped the other guy do is kill himself."

I tried a tentative sip. It had cooled to molten lava, scorching, strong, and bitter. "Do you think Brennan is a crook?"

"Mmm." He took another long swallow of coffee, squinted, and

222 | D. E. Johnson

looked off into the distance. "Don't know, but I don't think so. Him and Sanford were at odds, and I'd go with Sanford for bein' on the criminal side."

"Do you have any idea where Eli would have gone?"

"Can't help you there. We weren't buddies."

"Do you think anybody else here would know?"

He shook his head. "Nah. Sanford didn't get along with nobody."

I sipped and swallowed, trying to think of everything I needed to know about Eli Sanford. Most important—"What does he look like?"

"He's a pretty good-sized fella, six foot, I'd say, about two hundred. Smooth face like a woman. Long, pointy nose. Blue eyes."

A chill ran up my spine. "Son of a bitch." *The man at the salt mine.* Eli Sanford had been trying to kill me and steal the ballots.

"What?" he said.

"He took a couple shots at me. I had no idea it was him."

"Hmm." He tipped up his mug, finishing his coffee, and set it on the floor beside him. "Now why would he do that?"

"I had something he wanted to steal, and I saw his face. He kills me, he takes care of both problems. Does he drive a Ford, by any chance?"

He nodded. "A roadster. Got it a couple months ago."

"What color was it?"

"Blue."

Beyond a shadow of a doubt. "Any idea where he got the money?"

"Nah, and he never stopped gripin' about his paychecks."

"So during the alderman investigation, which he shouldn't have even known about, he had a fight with Brennan. Shortly after that, he came into enough money to buy a car and had enough leverage on somebody here that he stopped doing any work."

The rough-looking man nodded. "That's about the size of it. Weren't no coincidence."

I nodded. I still couldn't understand Eli's motivation. "Was he an anarchist, by any chance?"

He snorted. "Eli? All he cared about was finding an angle to make some easy money. He's a capitalist through and through."

I thought about smelling Old English after my apartment had been destroyed. "Did Eli smoke Old English pipe tobacco?"

The rough-looking man shook his head. "'Body's a temple,' he always said. He didn't smoke."

So it was Murphy. I shook my head and stood. "Thanks. I'm Will Anderson." I held out my right hand. He rose and took it. I braced for a manly handshake, but he gripped it normally, causing only a small amount of pain that I was able to keep off my face.

"Al Moore."

"Thanks for your help, Al. I appreciate it." I pulled my wallet from my coat, intending to give him a couple of bucks. I'd forgotten that all I had was Murphy's twenty. It would have been awkward, because I couldn't let that go, but Al waved me off anyway.

"Get him thrown in jail," he said. "That'd be enough thanks."

After checking the load in my Colt, I took a run down Church Street, only three blocks, looking for apartments. The third house on the right looked a likely target, so I knocked. The landlord answered. He said Eli had lived there. He skipped out in the middle of the night on Tuesday, so the man had no idea where he'd gone. Should I see Eli, he said, I should remind him of the thirteen dollars he owed in rent.

Walking back to the streetcar stop, I stared at the sidewalk and tried to put the puzzle together. What did I know?

David Sanford was murdered Tuesday night.

Eli Sanford went to ground the same night.

The next day, he tried to steal the ballots from me at Flikklund's and nearly killed me in the process.

The day after that, he and Murphy destroyed my apartment trying to find the ballots, not knowing they had already been stolen. I supposed I should have been grateful he'd taken a break yesterday from trying to destroy me.

Eli had worked security at the Wabash and had a blowout with Warren Brennan that had to be related to the Burns investigation. Did that mean Brennan wasn't involved in the conspiracy? Either way, on whose behalf was Eli working? Andrew Murphy seemed to drop into place nicely. I was struck by an idea. "Son of a bitch," I mumbled.

"Watch your mouth, young man." Startled, I looked up. An older woman passing on the other side of the walk stared daggers at me.

"Sorry, ma'am," I said automatically, tipping my derby before going back to my thoughts.

Eli Sanford, the man from the salt mine, could have been the man who shot David. He fit the description. The timing worked, but would Eli have killed his own brother? If David was a loose thread, Murphy would have wanted him gone. How much money would one have to be offered to murder a brother? Or perhaps it wasn't money. Perhaps it was personal.

David told me that Eli moved to New Mexico months ago. Had he been lying, or had Eli lied to him? I just couldn't make all the pieces fit.

My eyes were burning. My head was fuzzy. I needed to sleep. After a good night's sleep, I'd be able to think and might be able to puzzle this all together. In the morning, I'd join Elizabeth for church and tell her what I'd discovered.

I reached the stop on Trumball and stood with a dozen other people waiting for a car. A young woman holding a baby stood next to me. Judging from the odor, the baby's diapers hadn't been changed recently, perhaps ever. I took a step back and—

CHAPTER TWENTY-THREE

Monday, October 21, 1912

—white light burned into my brain. The rays snaked in, scorching. I squeezed my eyes shut and pressed the heels of my palms against them. Now the burning faded, but the pounding in my head continued, mallets hammering my brain. I cried out.

"Will?"

I sat bolt upright, but a bomb went off in my head, and I fell back onto a soft surface.

"Here," a man said harshly, pressing something into my hand—my glasses.

I fumbled them onto my face and opened one eye a fraction of an inch. Bright but not so painful. I opened my other eye to a slit and sat up again. A pair of bare lightbulbs beamed from above me. I held my hand at my brow to block the brilliance.

"How long was it this time?"

I turned and looked at the man speaking to me—Detective Riordan. He was unshaven and disheveled, wearing a dirty blue coat over a wrinkled white shirt with no tie. In a room nearby, a man and woman talked, their voices muffled.

"I . . ." My throat was dry and scratchy. "Where am I?" Through a small window, I saw a redbrick building ten feet away. Between the buildings it was dark. I took in the room—fifteen feet square, a radiator, a tiny dresser, three long shelves on the wall, mostly empty, canned food on one end. At a small table, an old man, bent and withered with age, watched me.

"You don't even remember asking for me, do you?" Riordan said. When I didn't answer, he spat, "You're in Little Italy. And you're lucky Mr. Macchione contacted me instead of the Gianollas."

"What . . . what day is this?"

"I knew it," he said. "Another fit. It's Monday morning, Will, and I have to get to work."

"Go. I'll be fine."

"When are you going to listen?" he shouted.

I clapped my hands over my ears. He wrenched away the one nearest him and jerked me over to face him. "You dumb son of a bitch. You . . . are . . . crazy! Listen to Elizabeth. You need to go to a hospital and get some damn rest. Now!" He threw my coat at me and stomped away.

I watched him go through the open door and turn right. His shoes pounded against the plank floor. I was sitting on a single bed. I dropped my legs over the side and tried to stand. My head seemed to keep moving after it had stopped. Vertigo. I sat on the bed again. A minute later, I put on my coat, and, holding onto the bed, I stood. The room swayed right, left.

When I felt I could, I began moving to the door. There I stopped and looked back at the old man. "Thank you."

He replied in Italian, his voice so ravaged by time I don't think I could have understood him had I known the language. I walked out into the hallway. It was empty. Turning right as Riordan had, I stumbled to the end, all the way smelling fried fish and sewage. I reached the stairs and, with my hand never leaving the banister, walked down three flights to a door that led out to a street.

I took a step backward and sat on the second stair, trying to get my bearings.

I'd blacked out again.

I'd left the Union Depot late Saturday afternoon.

Monday morning, Riordan said.

I reached into my coat, pulled out my wallet, and opened it up. A five-dollar bill. I'd had Murphy's twenty and maybe twenty-five cents in coins. I rifled through the pockets of my coat and trousers. My watch was still there—6:42 A.M.—and in my trousers were a crumpled five-dollar bill and a weighty scattering of coins, maybe another three dollars. A day and a half gone, and seven dollars spent.

From the rotten taste in my dry mouth and the sour feeling in my gut, I thought the majority of the seven bucks had gone for bourbon.

Oh, shit. Elizabeth.

I had missed church. I couldn't afford to make her any angrier with me.

A day and a half gone.

I had no idea where I'd been, what I'd done.

They were right. I was crazy.

My mood as black as the truck, I eased to the curb behind the Dime Building. When I left the tenement, I caught a streetcar home to bathe, dress, and drink several strong cups of coffee before driving the truck downtown again. I'd lost a day and a half. I couldn't lose another day.

The sky was a uniform gray, clouds blending with one another as if they were trying to convince me that gray was the color of a clear sky. I couldn't be completely certain that it wasn't.

The truck had barely prowled here at two miles per hour, with ungodly shrieks emitting from the undercarriage. I was afraid to even look at it. I was going to have to exchange it for my Torpedo, which I would undertake while Mel was off killing bugs. No reason for him to pay for my stupidity. At some point I would have to buy the truck, which carried a $1,995 price tag. I didn't have any money, and I owned only two assets. The one with four wheels was going to be indispensible for the foreseeable future. The other sat in a velvet-lined box in my dresser.

I would have to sell both, and I would still be only halfway there.

Elizabeth. I had to talk to her, tell her what happened—but she would shut me out of this investigation, force me to go to a hospital. I couldn't let that happen. I'd tell her . . . something . . . and hope she didn't talk to Riordan anytime soon.

I was swept along the sidewalk by the mass of humanity and followed a dozen older men in long gray overcoats toward the Dime Building. Men of all ages and younger women swarmed the area, heading to work. I wore a gray suit and overcoat with a black derby, though I also had a black scarf wrapped around my neck, which covered the lower portion of my face. For now, the exterminator uniform would stay in the truck.

I had to get my head straight. I couldn't afford to miss anything—anything else. What did I have to do? I thought about my discussion with Al Moore at Wabash. Thank God my fit hadn't happened an hour earlier.

I needed to talk to Helen about the Sanford brothers. Eli had found something out about the alderman bribery and had used it to his advantage. I couldn't figure out how that would tie in here. He'd fought with Brennan. They hadn't cooperated. Would they be cooperating now? If so, how? *Shit.* My head hurt enough without all this useless information swirling around, taking up space.

I walked up the stairs to the MLA office. The door was locked. I rapped on the door with my knuckles. No one answered.

Now what? At some point I would have to throw myself prostrate at Elizabeth's feet. Might as well get that over with. Then perhaps Brennan and I could have a chat about Eli.

I walked down to suffrage headquarters. The man at the door said that neither Elizabeth nor Brennan was in and that he didn't know when they would be, but he would tell them I had stopped by. I had nowhere else to go, so I crossed the street and stood in the shadows at the alley's entrance. Here the wind, channeled through the buildings, roared down the street and bit through my coat.

I was exhausted, and my head hurt, and I was freezing. I was thirty seconds from giving up when a blue Hudson 37 Touring Car pulled to the curb two cars over from where I stood. Warren Brennan sat in the driving seat.

The Hudson was one of the new 1913s with Kettering's damn self-starter. For the 1912 line, all Detroit Electric had to worry about was Cadillac, which wasn't remotely in the same class of workmanship or prestige, but the Hudson, and others in their new model offerings, were very nice automobiles. Kettering's goddamn Delco self-starter seemed to engage every time. It occurred to me that the electric car business was no longer my worry, so it shouldn't matter to me whether the self-starter that was taking the industry by storm might just signal the beginning of the end for electrics. I wanted my mother and father to be comfortable, but I supposed my father's investments would ensure that, regardless of the success of Detroit Electric. No, it wasn't my concern, but they were still my family, and I wanted the best for them. So, if Kettering's self-starters all of a sudden began blowing up, I'd be a happy man.

I was still ruminating when Brennan climbed out of the Hudson and closed and locked the driver's door. He looked around but missed me standing in the shadows. He'd already taken two strides across the street when I stepped out of the alley and shouted, "Hey, Brennan. Give me a minute."

Now halfway across, he gave me a narrow glare, hesitated, and then sauntered back to me. "What?"

"I just need a minute," I said.

"What?" he repeated.

"Tell me about Eli Sanford."

His eyes narrowed to slits. "Who?"

"Eli Sanford. Wabash security. Remember him? They remember the two of you down there."

"It's not your business." He turned and began to walk away.

I grabbed his arm and spun him around. "It's related to this case, so yeah, it is my business."

His face turned dark. "Keep your hands off me."

"Tell me what you know about Eli Sanford."

"I don't know *anything*."

"God damn you, Brennan. You're really in this, aren't you?"

He turned again and began stalking across the street. I followed half a step behind.

"Tell me what's in it for you? Money, right? Who's paying you? Murphy?"

He turned and, before I could react, connected with a right cross to the jaw that knocked me on my backside in the middle of the street.

"I'm not a crook," he growled. "I'm doing my job. Maybe you ought to try that sometime." He stalked across the street and into the building while vehicles honked and veered around me. I worked my jaw up and down to be sure it still functioned, stunned more by his vehement denial than the punch. I had been sure he was involved—at an absolute minimum—and was likely David's killer, but . . . could he be innocent? I was running around in circles, chasing my tail, unsure who was predator and who was prey.

"Will?"

I glanced over to see Elizabeth on the street corner with two women and another Burns man, waiting to cross. Her mouth hung open.

I climbed to my feet and headed toward her, dusting off my trousers and overcoat as I did, and met her on the sidewalk in front of suffrage headquarters. She told the women to go inside and she'd be with them when she could. The man at the door let them in, and Elizabeth turned back to me. "Why were you sitting in the middle of the road?"

"Brennan punched me when I wasn't looking. Ask him if you don't believe me."

Her eyes narrowed. "Why did he hit you?"

"I accused him of doing what he's doing—taking money to defeat the amendment."

"Will . . ."

"I know you don't believe me, Elizabeth, but I'm going to show you. I'm going to find the connection between Andrew Murphy and Brennan and Eli Sanford and whoever else is involved in this."

"How are you going to do that?"

"Among other things, I'm watching Murphy." It wasn't the time to admit I'd led the boys on a three-man crime wave.

"Watching Murphy?" a man behind me repeated. I spun around—Brennan stood just outside the door, looking at me with his head cocked.

"It's none of your business." I turned back to Elizabeth.

She was looking at him over my shoulder. "I'll be right in, Mr. Brennan."

"Yes, Miss." This time I heard the door open and close.

"Elizabeth," I said, "I'm sorry about yesterday. I . . ." What the hell could I tell her? I didn't want to lie. I shrugged and said, "I forgot." That was as true as anything I could say.

"We were late again because we waited for you."

I bit my lip and tried to look chastened. "Sorry. It won't happen again."

"You didn't answer your telephone all day."

"No, I . . . I had a hard day. I'm sorry."

She reached out and touched my arm. "Will, go home. Rest. You need it."

"You haven't found anyone to take your place at the rally, have you?"

She sighed. "Will, I'm going to speak, and I'd prefer not to discuss it again. Is there anything else?"

"Yes. One more thing. On Saturday, I discovered that Eli Sanford, David's brother, is the man who tried to kill me to get the ballots. When I first told you about David, you mentioned that your father had a 'onetime friend' by that name. It sounded like there might have been trouble."

"Hmm." She rubbed her chin. "My father and Mr. Sanford were business partners, but they had a falling-out. I honestly don't know what happened."

"Could you try to find out?" I asked. "I don't know why the Sanford brothers would be involved with Murphy. When we were in school, David was 'Davey.' He might be a junior. If David and Eli Sanford are the sons of the man your father knew, maybe you could find a motive in whatever ruined the friendship."

"You think this is personal?"

"I don't know. The younger David Sanford, the one who was murdered, was a criminal, and his brother is clearly one as well. I'd just appreciate it if you checked into the elder David Sanford for me. It would go a long way toward easing my mind."

"All right," she said. "When I get a chance."

"Soon, please, Lizzie. I don't know how much time we have."

"As soon as I can. Now go home, get some rest."

I tried to smile. "Thanks. Enjoy your day." I shambled down the sidewalk toward the Dime Building and again checked the MLA office. Still nobody home. Well . . . I had to retrieve my car before the truck completely died. It would be unpleasant, to say the least, but this was a day for unpleasant events. It was time to pay the piper.

Or perhaps I could avoid the piper. I slipped into the garage and dropped two uniforms and an envelope into Mel Peterson's mailbox. The envelope contained two five-dollar bills and a note explaining that I'd return the other uniform in a week or two. I skulked over to the Torpedo, staying out of sight, cranked the starter, and jumped onto the driving seat.

From behind me, a man shouted, "Will! Wait!"

I felt my shoulders hunch. It was Mr. Billings, the garage manager. This would probably not be good. Putting a smile on my face, I turned in my seat. "Oh, hi, Mr. Billings. Kind of in a hurry, so if you don't mind . . ."

He pulled up next to me, puffing a bit from the run to my car. He was a hefty man, a perpetual sweater, with a round red face. "Your father"—he took a breath—"needs to speak with you."

"Oh. Well, I'll phone him later. I have an appointment right—"

He clapped his hand onto the top of the door. "He said he needed to speak with you before you took your car. Something about taking the truck."

"No. I have things to do." I was tired of everyone pushing me around. "Tell him I'll call when I get a chance."

"Will, this—"

"I own this automobile. I have every right to take it out of this garage, and that is what I'm going to do." I slipped the car into gear. "The truck is outside." I'd left a note inside a sealed envelope on the driver's seat for my father, telling him I would pay for the truck or for repairs, whichever he preferred, plus interest—as soon as I had the money.

I hit the throttle, squealing the tires on the concrete floor. The noise echoed around me, then abruptly disappeared when I roared out of the building onto Woodward, forcing my way into traffic. The drivers around me laid on their horns, creating an off-key cacophony. I reached up as high as I could to give them all a good view of my one-finger salute.

I spun the wheel hard to the left while opening up the throttle, spinning the car in a tight, smoky U-turn. As I headed uptown, I started laughing. My *father wanted to speak with me?* How would he feel when he heard about the truck?

The Morton Hotel had the cheapest parking lot downtown—still a pricey twenty-five cents a day, a buck for five—and being at the corner of Jefferson and Griswold, it was only a few blocks from the Dime Building, so I gave them a dollar for the week and left the Torpedo there. I walked around behind the Dime looking for the red Abbott, and there it was, parked just down from the entrance. With my face buried in a *Free Press*, I entered the building through the front entrance into the bank's lobby. I wore my long gray overcoat over the exterminator outfit.

So as not to attract attention, I removed my dark glasses but left the derby on my head, pulled down low. I kept my face in the paper as I walked, as casually as I could manage, up the stairs to the second floor. A few people passed me in the hallway, but none seemed to pay me any attention. I sauntered up to the MLA office and turned the knob. This time the door opened. Helen sat at the desk. The older woman sitting by the wall looked up at me.

"So, ladies," I said. "Any bugs?"

They glanced at each other and agreed that none had returned. I looked at Helen and cut my eyes toward the door. Her eyebrows arched. I repeated the gesture, and this time she got it.

"Good afternoon, ladies." I tipped my derby and walked back out into the hall.

A minute later, Helen joined me. "What?" she whispered.

"Could you get away?"

She wrung her hands. "No, Mr. Murphy watches me. I cannot leave."

"How about after work?"

"No. I must go with him."

"What's wrong?"

"If he sees us together, he will ask questions. I do not have answers. He will . . . it will not be good for me." Her words shot out in a stream. She was trying to end this conversation as quickly as possible.

"Tonight? Later?"

"I . . . don't know. I never know what he will do."

"I really need to speak with you."

"If I can, I will come by." She glanced again at the door.

"That's fine. Please come."

She nodded and hurried back inside. I slipped into Flikklund's office and set my briefcase on the desk before switching on the Dictograph and telegraphone. When I picked up the receiver, as before, I heard the hum. Then rustling. A faint sneeze.

I set down the receiver and pulled a pair of stenographic pads and three freshly sharpened pencils from my briefcase. If the telegraphone failed, I'd still be ready. Picking up the receiver again, I settled in to listen.

An hour passed with nothing more interesting happening than Murphy badgering someone over the telephone about a report he was supposed to get the day before. I figured the time was as good as any to give one more test to the recording capability of the telegraphone, so I switched on the recorder. The wire slowly unspooled through the center mechanism and was taken up by a reel on the other side. When the phone call ended, I played it back, listening with the receiver. Even though the sound quality was poor, Murphy had a distinctive voice— high, slightly warbly, almost as if he were standing in front of a rapidly rotating fan. I wouldn't mistake someone else for him.

He spent the better part of the day squabbling with Salt and Pepper, the thugs who, based on their end of the conversation, were clearly on the "before" side of the evolutionary scale. They spent an hour bickering about Ty Cobb's prospects of being traded. (Anyone with half a brain knew that wasn't going to happen. Cobb was the only reason anybody came out to Navin Field.)

It got quiet again. Another hour passed. My arm ached from holding up the receiver. I had gotten over the excitement of playing with a new gadget and realized this wasn't going to be easy. Unless I got lucky and Murphy blurted out something incriminating soon, this was going to be an extremely boring job.

The boredom disappeared around three o'clock. Unfortunately. Murphy sent his minions out for half an hour and called Helen into the office.

The door opened and closed.

"Mr. Murphy?" she said. Her voice was timid, deferential.

"I've been thinking about last night, Sapphira," he said, his voice thick. "Lock the door and come here."

"I have a lot of work to do," she said in a tiny voice.

"Lock the door," he commanded.

No, I thought. *Don't do this, you son of a bitch.*

The lock clicked, and soft footsteps padded across the carpeting, louder, then quieter as she moved to him. His chair rattled, and fabric rustled. A metallic clatter—a belt?

"Mr. Murphy, no, please."

The leather in the chair squeaked, and the wheels rattled again. He was sitting. I was hoping that meant I had misinterpreted the noises.

"On your knees."

"Goddamn him," I muttered and jumped up from the desk.

"Please," I heard her say as I ran around the desk, burst out to the hallway, and ran down to the MLA office. Throwing open the door, I shouted, "Bug check!"

The older woman now sat at the reception desk, which I motored around at full stride.

"No! Sir! You can't—"

"Infestation review! Bug check!" I hurried down the hallway to Murphy's office and pounded on the door. "Mr. Murphy? I gotta check for cockroaches!"

A chair clattered, fabric rustled. I pounded on the door again. Helen opened the door and scurried out, her eyes on the floor. I stepped into the office to see Murphy sitting uncomfortably, legs crossed, behind his desk.

"Seen anything?" I asked. I pictured my fist driving into his nose, over and over, his face nothing more than a bloody mess. But I couldn't. He would pay, but not now. Not this way.

"N-no," he sputtered. "Listen, son, you can't just—"

"Say, I forgot to tell you," I said. "I had to use some powder around your chair and on them chairs and sofa." I gestured behind me, trying to encompass every spot he might use to take advantage of her. "No problem if it gets on your clothing, but it will put a nasty burn on your skin, so be careful."

"I thought you said you—"

"Okay, looks good. Got a job to get to. So long." I hurried out, slamming the door behind me, and practically ran out of the office, calling, "Looks good, ladies. No bugs so far!"

I returned to Flikklund's office and picked up the receiver again, holding it tentatively to my ear. The office stayed quiet until Murphy's thugs returned fifteen minutes later. Thank God. I steamed for the next hour, thinking of the indignities to which that woman had been subjected, simply because she'd been unfortunate enough to be born to a poor Greek family who believed the stories about the Promised Land.

Murphy ignored Salt and Pepper, who continued to babble inanely. It was nearly five when his telephone rang.

"Yeah?" After a few seconds, he said, "I'll take it. You two, get out." The last phrase louder, his mouth away from the phone.

I flipped on the telegraphone. The wire began feeding through the machine. Whatever this was, it was private.

The door slammed shut.

"What?"

A few seconds passed. "Why?" Murphy sounded incredulous. My ears perked up.

Ten seconds later, he asked, "How do you know this?"

A longer pause. "Only visual? . . . You're sure? He couldn't be working around you somehow?"

What? Is this Brennan?

Then, "You'd better be right. Who did you say it is?" Now he laughed. "Right, the Car Killer, or whatever they called him."

Electric Executioner, I thought. *Get it right.*

Murphy listened some more. "At least Addams and Pankhurst didn't get to talk."

The suffrage rally. Son of a bitch! It is *Brennan!*

"What are you going to do if any of them get in *our* way?"

My entire being was focused on Murphy's side of the conversation.

"I don't want to hear about your woes. You're working with her every day. No one is in a better position to keep her under control . . . No! Listen to me. If any of them are going to cause a problem, they need to be dealt with—before they do it."

Five seconds passed while my pulse thundered in my ears. "You'd better be right. If anybody—anybody—costs us this election, I'm going to hold you personally responsible. I think you've got too much to lose."

The receiver clicked onto the hanger.

CHAPTER TWENTY-FOUR

B *rennan!* Just when I thought I might be wrong about him. Now Elizabeth would believe me.

I kept the telegraphone on until Murphy left fifteen minutes later, but he didn't say anything else interesting. I played back the recording twice, trying to imagine Brennan's voice on the other end of the line.

Murphy: "What?"

Brennan: *You're being spied on by Will Anderson. He's watching you.*

Murphy: "Why?"

Brennan: *He's trying to get evidence of a conspiracy against the amendment.*

Murphy: "How do you know this?"

Brennan: *I overheard him talking to Elizabeth Hume about it. Just keep your blinds closed and don't leave the building with anyone you don't want to be seen with.*

Murphy: "Only visual?"

Brennan: *Definitely.*

Murphy: "You're sure? He couldn't be working around you somehow?"

Brennan: *I would know if he was using a Dictograph. He's not.*

Murphy: "You'd better be right. Who did you say it is?"

238 | D. E. Johnson

Brennan: *Will Anderson, the Detroit Electric kid who was on trial for murder.*

Murphy: "Right, the Car Killer, or whatever they called him."

Brennan: *Yeah. He's the one who kept us from killing Jane Addams.*

Murphy: "At least Addams and Pankhurst didn't get to talk."

Brennan: *True. Don't worry. He just gets in his own way.*

Murphy: "What are you going to do if any of them get in *our* way?"

Brennan: *I can't do everything. They'll suspect me if something happens to Miss Hume.*

Murphy: "I don't want to hear about your woes. You're working with her every day. No one is in a better position to keep her under control."

Brennan: *I can't take that—*

Murphy: "No! Listen to me. If any of them are going to cause a problem, they need to be dealt with—before they do it."

Brennan: *They won't be a problem.*

Murphy: "You'd better be right. If anybody—anybody—costs us this election, I'm going to hold you personally responsible. I think you've got too much to lose."

Click.

I listened to it a third time with the same critical ear I thought Elizabeth would.

Is there really anything here that's incriminating?

Murphy insinuated he and the caller were involved in a criminal activity, though he said nothing about what that activity might be. He told Brennan to deal with us and implied that the fix was in on the vote, but nowhere had he admitted to a crime. One thing for certain, though—Elizabeth would have to fire Brennan. I played it once more and copied the text onto one of my pads, tore off the page, and pocketed it.

I waited another fifteen minutes, until the floor had completely quieted, and then tucked the reel into an inside pocket of my overcoat and peeked out to the hall. The MLA's office door was closed, and no one else was in sight, so I slipped out, locked the door behind me, and hurried down the hallway to the stairs. I didn't have enough evidence to get Murphy to break. I had to read this to Elizabeth and ensure she understood the implications. I was just hoping it was enough to get her to listen to me.

The Suffrage Club's headquarters was only three blocks away, so I figured I'd see if Elizabeth was there before going to her house. While I was at it, I'd see if Brennan had been in the vicinity of a telephone lately. Dusk was settling in over the city, the gray sky turning to pewter. Only a hint of light showed in the southwest where the sun kept up its senseless struggle against the inevitability of the looming winter.

A man I didn't recognize stood outside the door to the campaign headquarters, smoking. He was huddled into his duster, his derby pulled down low on his forehead like a tough.

I stopped in front of him. "I need to see Miss Hume."

He asked my name, and I told him. Staring into my eyes, he tried to read my thoughts, then grudgingly turned, unlocked the door, and disappeared inside.

A few minutes later, the man walked out again, followed by Elizabeth, who stood on the doorstep. "Yes, Will?"

"We need to speak—privately."

Her face carefully neutral, she nodded and stepped inside again. We walked past the desks to her office, a large but windowless room. She had done little to decorate. The only adornment was a framed poster on the wall with the text of the suffrage amendment, four long paragraphs. The only furniture was Elizabeth's small oak desk with a chair in front and back and the big table at which I'd seen Robert sitting when I'd been here before. Now half a dozen notepads, a pencil holder full of pencils and crayons, a pair of blunt-edged scissors, and a gluepot were carefully situated atop it.

I thought that might be just a bit boring for the fellows these days.

"It's not enough for a conviction," I said, "but I wanted to show you that Murphy is involved. More importantly, I have conclusive evidence that Brennan is the informer." I pulled the sheet of paper with the transcript and handed it to her, then read it along with the inclusion of Brennan's parts as I imagined them.

"Mmm," she said when I finished.

"Mmm, what?"

"How did you get this?"

"I overheard him on the telephone. It's a long story." One I sincerely hoped she never asked me about.

She walked around to the other side of the table and sat. "Are you sure you got it all right?"

"Word for word." I slipped into the chair across from her and clasped my hands together on the table in front of me.

"You couldn't actually hear the other man?"

"No, but it seems pretty clear to me."

She grimaced. "Well . . . then, we ought to have someone look into it."

"And you need to fire Brennan immediately."

Her forehead furrowed. I studied her. Her expression was just this side of pity. She thought I made this up.

I swallowed my indignation and slid the paper across the table to her. "You can keep that. I have another."

"Wait," Elizabeth said. "When was this telephone call received?"

"Just before five o'clock today."

"Mr. Brennan got on a train at four thirty, and . . ." She thought for a second. "He's still on it."

"Where was he going?"

"Lansing. He's delivering documents to state headquarters."

"He could have gotten off at the first stop. Most stations have pay telephones."

She shook her head. "It was an express. No stops until Lansing."

I stared at her. "An express?"

She nodded.

"You're sure he was on it when it left?"

"No." She bit her lip. "We dropped him at the station. It will be easy enough to find out if he stayed on, though. I can wire a message to Lansing to contact me when he arrives."

"Do that. It had to be him. I'm sure you'll find he took another train. Let me know as soon as you do, all right?"

"All right, but . . . if he was on that train, you need to agree that he isn't part of any conspiracy."

"Fine."

She glanced down. "I don't think it could have been Mr. Brennan." She met my eyes again. "I trust him, Will. His credentials are impeccable. Detective Riordan vouches for him, and he won't do that for many people. Whether you trust Thomas or not, I know he has my best interest at heart. He wouldn't have recommended Mr. Brennan if he thought there was any risk for me." She reached over and squeezed my forearm. "There has to be another explanation."

When I walked out into the cold again, it was night. I stopped outside city hall on the way back to Woodward. The floodlamps bathing the building in their glow lit the statues of famous Detroiters, who seemed to mock me from their lofty positions. I wanted to return to Flikklund's office, to listen to the recording again, to assure myself that it was real, but I had no way in. It would have to wait for the morning. I caught a streetcar to the corner of Woodward and Peterboro. There, I teetered—one drink at the Addison, or straight home?

Home.

I couldn't drink. My life was inches from crumbling around me. Before I could think about it further, I stared straight down at the sidewalk and hurried to my building.

When I unlocked my door, the telephone was ringing. Hoping it was Elizabeth, I ran back to the den and answered, breathless. "Hello?"

"Will?" *My father.*

Quieter now and with much less enthusiasm, I said, "Yes."

"We need to talk. Would it be all right if I stopped by? I'll come alone."

I couldn't have this conversation now. Or anytime soon. "Father, I can't explain this right now. I will, I promise you. Just please, give me the benefit of the doubt for another couple of weeks. I'll make everything right, and you will understand why I'm doing the things I am."

He was quiet for a moment. "All right, Will, but just tell me this. Are you drinking again? Or taking drugs?"

"No, I most definitely am not. I—well, I slipped once, but just once, I swear."

"Edsel came in to see me. He's worried about you, too."

"I appreciate that. I'll be fine, but I have a very important task to perform prior to the election. As I said, you will understand."

"Well . . . all right. I hope you know what you're doing, son."

We wished one another a good night and hung up. Hopefully he would understand. As for my job, I hated it anyway. It was time to strike out on my own, be my own man, stop relying on Mommy and Daddy to take care of me.

I searched for supper and came up empty. My choices being to spend a precious four bits to eat a decent meal at a restaurant—alone—or just make a bowl of plain Cream of Wheat, I chose the latter, a meal not dissimilar to a soggy pile of sawdust, though with slightly less flavor. Still. It was filling. I read the box while I ate.

Chef Rastus grinned out from the front of the box, holding a chalk-board that read in simple block letters, "Maybe Cream of Wheat's got vitamines. I don't know what them things is. If they's bugs, they ain't none in Cream of Wheat but she's sho good to eat and cheap. Cost about one cent fo' a great big dish."

I couldn't imagine anyone being happy to have this as the symbol of their race.

I was reading in the parlor an hour later when my telephone rang. I dashed into the den and answered it. "Hello?"

"Will, it's Elizabeth. You are going to need to realign your conspir-acy theory."

"What do you mean?"

"I just received a telegram back from Mrs. Arthur. Here's exactly what she wrote: 'Brennan arrived on Wolverine Express as scheduled. He will return on overnight. Please advise if you need anything fur-ther. Mrs. Clara Arthur.'"

I fell into my chair and asked her to repeat herself. She did. It sounded no better the second time. "Are you certain it came from her?" I asked.

"I wired her to tell me when and how he arrived. She wouldn't have ignored that or forgotten, and she certainly wouldn't have told Mr. Bren-nan to do it. So, yes, I am reasonably certain the telegram came from Mrs. Arthur, and she saw Mr. Brennan get off the train."

Brennan hadn't made the telephone call? "He must have had a confed-erate phone Murphy," I said.

Elizabeth was silent.

I replayed the call in my head, trying to fit anyone else into the other side. "Murphy said the caller had too much to lose in the election. So who would else would that be?"

"I'm . . . are you sure about what you heard?"

Not this again. "I'm not a lunatic."

"No, that's not what I'm saying. Sometimes we can hear what we want to hear. It's not *crazy*. You think Mr. Brennan is guilty, so perhaps you inferred from what Murphy said that he was the caller. We don't always remember things as they actually occur."

"Trust me," I said. "That transcript is nothing but Murphy's words, verbatim."

"Remember, you said you would forget about Mr. Brennan being a part of the . . . conspiracy . . . if I proved he arrived on schedule."

"You're right. I'll scratch him off the list." Like hell I would. He was on the list until *I* had proof.

A thought occurred to me. "The only people who I know for certain were aware of the surveillance were Brennan, myself . . . and you." As well as Francis and Robert, but they didn't know anyone they could tell, and I still didn't want to discuss with Elizabeth what the boys and I had accomplished.

Elizabeth coughed out an angry laugh. "You're not insinuating that I made that telephone call?"

"No, of course not—but who else knew? Detective Riordan, for example?"

"I didn't . . ." She hesitated. "I didn't intend to tell him."

"Damn it. It is Riordan."

"Will, that's crazy. Listen to yourself."

"What did you tell him?"

"I said . . . I asked him if it might be dangerous for you to spy on Andrew Murphy. He asked why. I had to tell him. He's worried about you, too."

I laughed. "Oh, right. He's awfully worried about me. Elizabeth, he wants me out of the picture. He loves you."

"Will! Stop that! He's a married man, and anyway, he's concerned about you. He—"

"All right, so maybe he loves you like a daughter." I jumped in to cut her off. I was certain he'd told her about this morning. I didn't need to hear another plea to take the rest cure. "But that's beside the point. Please don't tell him anything else. He could be informing Murphy."

"Think about what you're saying."

"He's a man. He's not perfect." I had to get through to her. "Look, Elizabeth, I trust you with my life. I thought I could trust Detective Riordan. But if that wasn't Brennan on the phone, who else could it have been?"

"Assuming the conversation was what you think it was."

"It was."

"I'm sorry, Will. I know you are doing this for me. I just wish you would do as the doctors said and rest."

"I suppose then I'd better get some sleep."

She wished me a good night, and I returned the wish, though without the pity I heard in her tone.

What if it was Riordan? He would die before he would hurt her. Brennan? He'd already had all the chances he needed to kill her. Neither would hurt her, nor, did I think, would either compromise her safety.

Even with Detective Riordan acting so strangely, I couldn't convince myself that it was him. If the caller was neither Riordan nor Brennan, though, I had a very weighty problem—I had never met the person at the other end of the line. It would be like trying to hunt down a wraith.

CHAPTER TWENTY-FIVE

Tuesday, October 22, 1912

No sooner than I lay down, it seemed, my alarm went off. With my eyes more shut than open, I washed and dressed, chewed and swallowed a handful of ground coffee, washing it down with water, and buttoned on the Peterson Exterminating uniform. Then it was off through the gloom of a pitch-black morning to the Dime Building for another day of spying. I took a streetcar downtown and walked past city hall on my way to the Dime. I fell in behind a string of criminals shackled together, heading to court. A pair of cops walked them in, one in front, one behind. The men shuffled along, eyes on the feet of the man in front of them, completely and utterly defeated, shambling toward their judgment. They smelled, were filthy, unshaven, bruised and beaten, and would now be thrown before a judge and jury in the same stinking condition. Who wouldn't convict them? They had to be guilty of something, right?

Except they were *accused* criminals, not criminals. Another easy thought, I realized—that those men we see in such a state are guilty, without a jury of their peers declaring them so, if even that ensured their guilt. It had not been long since I was one of them, but I still harbored the opinions of my youth, the opinions spoon-fed to me. Poor people were unfortunate but generally brought on their own troubles. Any man could raise himself from the dust and become a success.

Ha. What a ridiculous thought. *America—the land of opportunity.* I wondered what these men would think of that concept—what everyone other than the few living in luxury would think of it.

The cops shoved them into the building, and I continued across the street to the Dime. It was half past seven now, and the place was starting to get busy. I was forced to loiter on the second floor for a few minutes to wait for an opportune time to enter the office. However, that moment came, and I got inside, locking the door behind me before any of the MLA people came in.

My shoulder holster was digging into my chest, so I slung my coat onto the chair and hung the holster atop it. The morning passed slowly. Murphy received no one other than Salt and Pepper, who were a complete pair of hyenas. By eleven o'clock, I was in serious need of a toilet. I've never been a fan of chamber pots, particularly for the more objectionable function, so I sneaked a look out into the hall. Seeing no one, I hurried down to the toilet, then, when finished, headed back toward Flikklund's office.

I froze. A man stood in profile just outside the MLA office—a big man in a long tan overcoat. He had a pointy nose. I was too far away to know if his face was smooth or his eyes blue, but I was certain—it was Eli Sanford. He took a few steps away and then back, moving smoothly, like a caged tiger.

I reached up to my chest for my pistol. My hand slapped against nothing but Mel's uniform. My gun was in the office, down the hall, the door ten feet away from him. I was ten times that distance away. I slipped over against the wall, keeping a pillar between us, and edged forward.

The MLA office door opened. Helen walked out. Her head swiveled my way. I ducked completely behind the pillar. A few seconds later, I edged my eyes to the side. She and Eli were walking to the stairway, heads close together, a murmur of conversation trickling out to me. They ducked out of sight.

I crossed the hall and crept along the wall, trying to hear them.

Their voices rose. I could hear sharp edges on their words.

"I do not have any," Helen said.

I reached the corner and leaned toward the stairway. Helen was backed against the wall, Eli in front of her, too close.

Yes. Blue eyes, smooth face. No doubt.

He said something low and deep.

Her hand rose to her breastbone and rested there, as if sampling the damage he had threatened. "Then you must talk with him," she said.

I darted across the hall and unlocked Flikklund's door, rushed inside for my gun, and hurried back toward the stairwell, footfalls from below echoing back up to me. Holding the gun beside my head, pointing straight up, I took it off safety, turned the corner, and ran into Helen, who was hurrying back to her office.

She cried out from the shock. The footfalls below us paused, then accelerated.

"That was Eli?" I demanded.

"Yes, yes."

I ran past her and skipped down the stairs, my eyes darting between the steps and over the rail at the floor below. At the bottom, I turned to the side door. Seeing my gun, an old woman screamed and dropped her poodle. I couldn't see Eli.

What I could see was the bank guards who stood by the doors, both of whom had their pistols pointed at my face.

I thought fast. I couldn't let myself be arrested. The rally was in two days. If I were in jail, I couldn't protect Elizabeth. I kept my gun pointed upward. "Gentlemen, I'm going back upstairs. I'm within my rights to have this gun in the rest of the building."

Both were old men, and neither looked eager to shoot me.

I scanned the hallway in the other direction. No sign of Eli. An idea struck me. "Listen, fellas, I only use it on the really big snakes."

They glanced at each other. "S-snakes?" one of them ventured.

"Had a big one in my sights. Cottonmouth, I think. Damn." I glanced toward the stairway. "Maybe he didn't come down." I looked all around. Eli had slipped away—again.

"You better put that away until you get back up there," one of them said.

"Oh, yeah, right." I flicked on the safety again and stuck the pistol into one of the big pockets in the front of my coveralls.

"Cottonmouth, huh?" the same man said.

"'Course. I wouldn't use the gun on some ol' garter snake." I turned and headed back upstairs, scanning the area in front of me for a nonexistent snake. "You fellas keep your eyes open."

Helen stood at the top of the stairs, looking down as I turned at the landing.

"What did he want?" I asked, glancing behind me. No one had followed.

Half a dozen people passed her and started down the stairs. She watched me wade against the tide as they walked around me. I topped the stairs, took a quick look around, and turned to her.

Taking a step toward me, she said, "He wanted money—to help him get out of town."

"Why?"

Now a dozen boots and shoes pounded against the stairway below us. She glanced down and said, "He is frightened. I do not know why."

Before the men turned the corner from the stairwell, I squatted and examined the base of the wall. They passed, but more were ascending.

"I think he's still working for Murphy," I said.

"What the hell are you two talking about?" a man behind us demanded.

Oh, shit. In the clamor of people passing, neither of us had heard the MLA office door open.

I stood and turned around. "Mr. Murphy, we were just talking about cockroaches."

He pulled his pipe from his mouth and pointed it at me. "Bullshit. What are you up to, Peterson?"

Salt and Pepper stood ten feet back. Now they sauntered toward us, cocky smiles on their faces.

"Don't you have other jobs?" Murphy's eyes were narrowed, his jaw tight. "You seem to spend an awful lot of time checking on us."

"'Course I do. I gotta stay on top of this one. Them bugs are big."

He stepped closer to me and looked up into my face. "We'll call you if we need any more work."

"I'll have to come back to—"

"We'll call you." He drew on the pipe and blew the smoke into my face. It had a heavy flavor like a wood fire. "Gentleman, could you escort Mr. Peterson here out of the building?"

"I'll go," I said. "No problem."

Murphy looked at his men and nodded toward me. I had a decision to make. If I drew my gun, they would let me be, but it would be clear that I was here for a reason other than cockroaches. Not only would that endanger the investigation, Murphy would be certain Helen and I were scheming. I couldn't.

I let the thugs grab me by the biceps. They lifted me off my feet and started down the stairs.

"Fellas," Murphy said.

They stopped and looked back at him.

"Why don't you give Mr. Peterson a bit of foresight as to what will happen if I see him here again."

I didn't think to start shouting until they had me outside. Salt and Pepper pulled me across Fort Street into an alley. I screamed for help at the top of my lungs. Plenty of men filled the sidewalks, but no one intervened—or even seemed to hear me. Without a word, the thugs dragged me around a rear stairwell and threw me against the brick wall.

They were such idiots they still didn't know I had a gun. Unfortunately, I was powerless to pull it unless I wanted to sign Helen's death warrant.

Salt picked me up and drove a hammering right into my stomach. All the air whooshed from my lungs. Pain exploded deep inside me. I couldn't breathe. I fell to the ground, curling up, trying to protect myself. One of them kicked me in the kidney, and the pain arched me backward. Now the other landed a big shoe into my midsection, another to the back, one to my chest, another to the kidney. I writhed on the ground, crying out with each kick, the pain sharp and scalding and deep.

Eventually they paused, panting, and surveyed their work. They must have judged it well done because they stopped. Salt said, "You got some foresight, Peterson? Huh?"

When I didn't respond, Pepper leaned over the top of me and held a gleaming buck knife an inch from my right eye. "Fore*sight*? Next time we'll be cuttin' off your fore*skin* and everything attached to it."

I lay in the mud, resting, for a few minutes. It would have been so easy to pull the Colt and send a bullet into each of them. The next time I saw Helen, I'd have to tell her what I sacrificed. Of course, that was assuming Murphy hadn't heard too much. If he did, it was unlikely I would get the opportunity to speak with her again. The thought of Helen's punishment was what got me to my feet. I carefully felt around the painful areas, wincing as I did. Nothing seemed to be broken or bleeding. I felt as if I would vomit but couldn't imagine the additional pain the spasms would bring.

I thought I had to give Pepper credit for the wordplay. It was likely the wittiest remark he'd ever made.

I would turn the tables. Perhaps I wouldn't get the opportunity to thrash them. I hoped getting them thrown in prison would give me the same warm feeling.

By the time I limped back along Griswold to the Dime, there was no sign of the Abbott, and the lights in the MLA office were out. I went back inside, and sure enough, the office was dark and the door locked. They'd taken Helen away, and I had no idea where. Lunch, I hoped.

I took advantage of the empty office to return to Flikklund's, where I locked the door and—gingerly—sat in the chair. The trauma had set my head to pounding, sending a drill bit through my eyes into my brain. The thugs had been circumspect enough to stay away from my head, but that hurt worse than anywhere else.

I listened to the sounds of the hallway and finally heard the MLA office door open and close, although it was without the normal blustering of Murphy and the yammering of his sluggers. I switched on the machines and listened to hum. After twenty minutes, through the wall I heard a telephone ring in the main office, and a split second later, I heard the faint echo from the receiver. The older woman was speaking. I couldn't make out the words, either through the wall or on the telegraphone. She was clearly the only one in the office. I tossed the receiver on the desk and switched off the machine.

I wondered if there was anywhere close I could get ice for my injuries but decided I couldn't risk a foray out of the office for fear of running into Murphy and his men. If he told them to hurt me again, I would shortly be up on at least two murder charges, because that wasn't going to happen. The only safe approach was to wait.

So I did.

I spent two hours waiting for him, staring out the window, trying to deflect my attention from the pain. I fantasized about what I would do to Salt and Pepper as soon as I had a chance and tried to puzzle out where Eli Sanford would be hiding.

Murphy, his thugs, and Helen did not return. I finally dared to poke my head into the MLA office. The woman glanced up at me. As I had thought, she was alone.

"Will Mr. Murphy be returning today?" I asked.

"He was called out," she said, "for a family emergency."

Family emergency. Bullshit.

I tried to convince myself that there could be plenty of reasons Murphy left with Helen and the thugs. Only one of those would be to get rid of her.

It just seemed the only likely reason.

I was tired, frustrated, and depressed. My head pounded like a jungle drum, striking behind my eyes each time with another blast of pain. I also realized I was starving. I stopped at Smith's Restaurant near city hall and sat at a table in the back corner. I devoured a hamburger sandwich with fried potatoes, fresh brussels sprouts, and a big glass of milk. I topped that off with another glass of milk and a large slab of Dutch apple pie, and then boarded a streetcar home. When I got off at Peterboro, my first glance was at the Addison Hotel, only a block away. A drink or two might take the edge off this pain, a pain that didn't seem to be abating.

No. I couldn't fall into this trap again. Whether or not Elizabeth and I had a future, I had to have a future that didn't involve drinking myself into a stupor every night.

Keeping my eyes on the sidewalk, I returned to my apartment, where I swallowed four grams of aspirin and limped into the bedroom. I lay back, covered myself with the blanket, and slept like the dead wish they could.

CHAPTER TWENTY-SIX

I sat up, startled, and looked around. The windows were black rect-
angles, not even a hint of starlight. I was in my bedroom. I rubbed
my eyes.

The doorbell rang.

Pain shot up my back and throbbed dully in my head. I looked at the
clock—10:45.

The bell rang again.

I stood and walked to the door, realizing most of the pain was gone.
I looked through the peephole. Elizabeth stood outside my door. I unlocked and opened it. Her eyes were red and puffy. Tracks from tears
left dulled lines on her cheeks. She looked small and sad. Defeated.

"What happened?" I looked out in the hall. "Did you come by yourself?"

She just stared back at me, her eyes welling.

"Come in." I reached out and took her arm and gently pulled her toward me. Closing the door behind her, I said, "What's wrong, honey?"

"I . . . could I have some coffee?" She barely had the energy to ask.

"Certainly. Come in. I'll make the coffee in a second."

I guided her to the parlor with a hand in the small of her back. On the way, I noticed she carried a faint odor of liquor—very unusual for Elizabeth. "You sit," I said. "I'll get the coffee started."

She dutifully sat on the sofa. I gave her my handkerchief and got a pot on the stove, then hurried back to the parlor and sat next to her. "Now, what is it, honey? What's wrong?"

"I . . . I don't know if I can do this." Her voice was tiny, pitiful, so unlike Elizabeth. Her navy blue overcoat was buttoned wrong, with one side pushing against her chin, but she didn't seem to notice.

"Here, give me your coat," I said.

She stood and unbuttoned it, still not noticing it hung crookedly. I slung it over the back of the sofa and sat next to her. "Now tell me what's wrong."

Elizabeth pulled an envelope from her handbag and looked up at me. "I'm sorry I haven't believed you. I thought . . . well, you know, I thought it was the radium. Now I see you were right." She thrust the envelope at me, and I took it. "This came in the mail today," she said. "I got it when I came home tonight."

The envelope was letter-sized, white, and of average quality, such as would be sent out in a business solicitation. Elizabeth's name and address were typed. There was no return address. I pulled out the contents—three sheets of paper.

The first page was a typewritten itinerary, dated 17 October 1912:

7:03 AM—walk out of home (BANG), drive automobile to Detroit Suffrage Club HQ.
7:22 AM—Arrive HQ, walk approx. 200 yards from parking lot to HQ (BANG)
10:14 AM—walk to Mueller's Market (BANG) and buy apples
10:53 AM—return with apples to HQ (BANG)

And so on, finishing with a return home at 10:41 P.M. and another (BANG).

Page two was a second itinerary, this one for 18 October, punctuated with the same (BANG) notations.

Dread had been building in me since I first began reading. I looked up at Elizabeth. "Is this *your* itinerary?"

"To the minute." She nodded toward the papers. "Read the next page."

I flipped to the last one. It read:

> *Dearest Elizabeth,*
>
> *I have had 87 opportunities to kill you in the past week, but I will not be satisfied with a private death. You require a public execution. I wonder if you know how close I came to killing you at the last DSC rally. If I were you, I would cancel the Thursday night rally. I say this only because I know you will not, because you believe yourself to be brave. Thursday night a bullet will enter your brain in front of all of your followers, and there is nothing anyone will be able to do about it.*
>
> *I will enjoy the anticipation. Put your affairs in order.*

My hands went cold. "You have to cancel."

"I won't, Will. I'm not going to let him win."

"It's only two nights away. If he's not caught by then, you need to have someone take your place. Anyway, you shouldn't have come here tonight, Lizzie, especially by yourself. There's a maniac out there watching you."

"He said he's waiting until the rally. I'm fine for now."

"Maybe that's just what he wants you to think. You've had a bodyguard with you whenever you've gone out. Now that you're alone, he might try it."

She pulled a pistol from her handbag. "I wish he would. I had this in my hand the entire way here. I'm not helpless."

"I'm not minimizing your skills. It's much more difficult to protect yourself than it is to ambush someone. Besides . . . well, have you been drinking tonight?"

"Two fingers of Scotch. I think you'll agree the letter earned me that."

I nodded and looked at the last page again. "'Dearest Elizabeth.' Do you have any idea who wrote this? Have you seen anyone following you?"

She shrugged. "No, and neither has Mr. Brennan."

"It has to be someone in Murphy's camp," I said. "Did you know anyone there prior to the campaign?"

"No. I just met Murphy the other night, and I don't even know the names of the other men."

"Eli Sanford is definitely working for him," I said, "but it looks like he wants to get out of town now. Maybe Murphy has turned on him. Eli worked for the Wabash Railroad in security and somehow got wind of the Burns investigation there this summer. Somehow that's tied to the election."

"You think he wrote the letter?"

"I don't know. It could just be a ruse by Murphy to scare you into canceling the rally—but it doesn't read like that, does it? It sounds personal. David was just murdered. Perhaps there's some reason Eli believes you're responsible for his brother's death."

"I don't know what that could be," she said. "I didn't know either of them."

"Perhaps viewing the circumstances in a certain light, Eli could believe his brother died because of his work against suffrage—against you."

"I don't think that follows. That's awfully skewed logic."

"He could be a lunatic."

"If we assume the person who wrote the note is insane, it could be anyone." She sighed. "Do you think the coffee is ready?"

The rich aroma tickled at our noses. "Sure. I'll get it." I grabbed a blanket from the bedroom and draped it over her before hurrying to the kitchen for our coffee. I had just opened the icebox to pull out the milk when Elizabeth called, "Will, what happened to your apartment?"

"Just a minute," I called back. I poured milk into Elizabeth's coffee. She preferred cream, but she knew I never had any. I gave her the cup, put mine on the table in front of me, and sat close. "You know about the ballots being stolen from me."

She took a shuddering sip of coffee. "By the whore."

"Actually, no. Now I'm certain it wasn't her, though I have no clue who really took them. The next night, in fact the night I drew my gun on those, uh, men outside?"—she nodded, her face blank. "When I returned to my apartment, I found that someone had torn the place to pieces looking for something—obviously the ballots. That was Andrew Murphy and his men, who include Eli Sanford. He was the man I saw across the street. Clearly there are two different factions involved in this—one that stole the ballots, and Murphy's faction, which came too late."

Her eyes downcast, she nodded slowly. "You disarmed the man at the last rally. Was he the same man who killed David Sanford?"

"That would make things neat, wouldn't it? Unfortunately, no. They were two different men. David's killer was taller and bulkier, built like Brennan, in fact. That's why it seemed—and still seems—clear to me that he killed Sanford. He'd discarded the gun and put on a different coat by the time I caught him, but I would have done the same to throw off a pursuer."

Elizabeth quieted, thinking. I sat close with my arm around her, just letting her be silent. After a few minutes had passed, I said, "Just to be thorough, can you think of any other man you've disappointed?"

"Besides my father?" she asked with a sad smile.

I nodded.

"No one."

"Say, speaking of your father, did you get a chance to look into his situation with the elder David Sanford?"

"No, but I will."

"Right away?"

"After getting this?" She picked up the threatening letter, stuffed it into the envelope, and dropped it into her purse. "Yes. Immediately."

"Will you take more precautions?" I asked.

She nodded and took another sip of coffee. "Yes. I'll be careful."

"What can I do to help?"

She reached up with one hand. Her eyes followed her fingers as they grazed my cheek, then brushed through my hair. "I can hardly stand that I've been so cruel to you." With her hand on the side of my head, she looked into my eyes. "Can you forgive me?"

"I forgive you. It may take a while to forget, but I love you, Lizzie. You know that."

She smiled and hugged me with the fierceness I'd always loved. Elizabeth was a peaceful person, but she was no gentle spirit. She lived a life of passion, and did it on her own terms.

I pulled back and looked into her lovely eyes, green flecked with gold. "Thank you for believing in me again."

She gave me a pained smile. "I don't deserve your thanks. Thank you for giving me the opportunity to make it up to you." Her hands grasped my shoulders. "I didn't want you hurt, Will. We need to get you better. But know this." Her eyes burned into me. "You are the only one for me. I won't betray you. I won't leave you. Ever." She leaned in and kissed me.

Perhaps partly due to sleep deprivation, but perhaps not, tears streamed from my eyes. "I don't know what I'd do if you did," I whispered. "You are my life."

She kissed me again. Her tongue flicked against my teeth, my tongue. She gripped my head, caressing it and pulling me to her, kissing me hard now. Our breathing quickened.

I stood, held my hand out to her, and nodded toward the back hallway. We padded to the bedroom and stood by the bed. I took her into my arms, and we kissed, slowly and tenderly, then with increasing passion. My fingers fumbled with the buttons of her shirtwaist; she stripped off my coat and unbuttoned my shirt. We tore the garments from one another, and I pulled her down onto the bed.

She pulled me to her, into her. Her eyes were fierce, her face intense, fiery, her muscles taut, arms pulling me into her, harder and harder.

It had been so long. I knew it would be over for me in seconds, so I closed my eyes and pulled my mind away. I silently named the Detroit Tigers 1907 pennant-winning lineup and pitching rotation. I had made it through batting averages and won-loss records and was working my way through the reserves when she began to moan, her voice low and sweet. The sound reached inside me, but I pushed it away, trying to stem the tide. Her moans intensified; I struggled to think of relief pitchers. She cried out softly, and again, and finally I could let go, feeling the rush of ecstasy building, welling up, reaching into my body and my mind and my soul, and then exploding and exploding and exploding.

After, she lay back on the bed, and I lay on my side next to her, running my eyes over her perfect form, running my fingers through her hair and down her jawline.

"Mmm," she said, her eyes still closed. "We're doing that again."

I laughed. "You're on. And in the morning, if I have anything to say about it."

By then, I thought, *I might not have to think about baseball.*

Once we'd exhausted ourselves, Elizabeth lay snuggled against me with her arm thrown across my chest, her fingers trailing lightly through the hair.

I thought it was time for some honesty. "Elizabeth," I said, "there are a few things you need to know."

"Oh?" She glanced at me sharply. "What things?"

I prepared myself for Krakatoa and told her the unvarnished truth of my past week, starting with losing my job and running through my adventure with Robert and Francis and the electronic surveillance I was undertaking. When I finished with everything else, I said, "And, as I'm sure you know, I had another fit."

She looked startled. "When?"

"Riordan didn't tell you?"

"No. What happened?"

I shook my head. He hadn't told her. Why? He seemed to spend all his time trying to make my life difficult, but he'd done me a favor this time. I explained to Elizabeth that I had no memory of Saturday night through Monday morning until Riordan woke me in the old man's apartment.

Throughout my monologue, her face had been expressionless. When I finished, she looked at me, waiting for more. "Is that everything?"

"Yes. Everything."

Finally, she sighed and shook her head. "You stole the Dictograph and telegraphone from Eloise Hospital."

Here it comes, I thought.

She burst out laughing. "I can't even imagine," she gasped between guffaws. "The three of you . . ."

Relief flooded through me.

Elizabeth laughed harder, mostly at me, I think, but it was far preferable to the reaction I expected. When she wound down, she wiped her eyes and again shook her head. Serious now, she said, "You could have asked me for the money."

"You're right, but I didn't."

Her brow furrowed, and she looked up at the ceiling, exhaled sharply, and, a moment later, turned to me. "You took two schizophrenic men out with you, one of whom is my brother, to burgle and trespass and commit God knows how many other crimes. My *brother*, Will."

"I did."

She was silent.

"They really had fun," I ventured.

After a long moment, she said, "I was horrid to you."

"No one got hurt," I added.

She sighed and turned to me. "If you need money for anything else?"

"I'll ask you," I said.

Finally, a little smile crept across her face. "Well, a desperate disease . . ." she started.

I finished the saying. ". . . calls for a dangerous remedy."

CHAPTER TWENTY-SEVEN

Wednesday, October 23, 1912

W e woke early. As I had hoped, we were able to linger in bed for a while before getting up to take on the day. Later, while we were sipping coffee side by side on the remains of my sofa, she set her coffee cup on the table and turned to me, meeting my eyes. "Tell me about Sapphira. What has you convinced she's on our side?"

I explained Helen's situation with Murphy, her contact with Eli Sanford, and her efforts to assist me.

"The two of you didn't . . . have any intimate . . . ?"

"Nothing happened between us, Lizzie, back then or now. Never. Nothing ever."

Elizabeth didn't look completely convinced but nodded and dropped the subject. She headed to the back of the apartment to wash and dress, and I started cleaning up.

I wondered if her doubts about Helen and me would forever exist in her memory. Unfortunately, there was no way to prove one had never done something. Back after John Cooper had died, Elizabeth was disgusted with me for having been attracted to "the whore." However, Elizabeth had also realized that my relationship with Sapphira, such as it was, took place long after Elizabeth and I stopped seeing one another. I had the impression she had believed me when I said nothing had happened between us.

Now I wasn't so certain. All those memories had been picked from Elizabeth's stockpile of history and become relevant again. Should she and I continue to climb the slopes necessary to remain together, this could show itself again and again in far-off looks, pauses in conversation, sharp words when none were needed. I thought she might always wonder—had I lied? Had I engaged in sexual intercourse with Sapphira/Helen, the whore and trickster?

All I could do was to live the best life I knew how. Perhaps one day the memory would return to the stockpile where it belonged. Elizabeth was a woman, and women were complicated and challenging and difficult.

And I wouldn't change one thing about her.

She needed to go home to dress, and I was already late for my surveillance. Still I said, "Let me go back with you. I'd feel a lot better."

She amazed me by not arguing. I excused myself and got my Colt and shoulder holster, then helped her into her coat again before donning my duster. We walked out to her car without a word, my eyes scanning the street and sidewalks, looking for movement.

The Baker sat against the curb on the other side of the street. We climbed in, and Elizabeth drove home. I kept my eyes peeled but saw nothing of a threat from any quarter.

I walked her up to her front door. "Why don't I come for you tonight? I should be done by five, six at the latest. Will you be at the office?"

She said she would.

"Will you wait for me?"

Smiling, she nodded. "So long as you don't hold me up too long."

I moved in close and kissed her. "I'd rather hold you down."

"Pervert," she whispered.

"Thank you." I kissed her again. "I'll take that as a compliment."

I glanced down the hall while unlocking Flikklund's door. Murphy's office was lit but quiet. I got set up at the desk, flipped on the

Dictograph, and listened to the hum, smiling all the while. I couldn't believe my luck with Elizabeth.

The nightmare—at least that nightmare—was finally over.

I wondered about Helen's nightmare. She had risked a lot to help me. I'd get her alone at some point today, make sure she was all right. If I could just get an incriminating recording, I could get her out of here altogether. Perhaps she would be able to have a normal life, or at least one approaching normal. She had the skills to hold down a regular job. If she wanted, she could find an apartment, a job, maybe someday find a husband.

Murphy and his thugs tromped into the office only a few minutes after I'd gotten set up. All morning, the normal buzz of conversation through the wall was missing. When Murphy left for lunch, I peeked out the door. Murphy, Salt, and Pepper marched down the hall, all chugging away at their respective tobacco vices like a trio of steam locomotives.

I waited a few minutes, then walked into the MLA office. The older woman sat at the desk. She glanced up at me, then down at her work, then up again as she recognized me without my uniform. "No bugs," she said. "You did a good job."

"Good. Thanks." I made a point of looking around. "Say, is Helen here today?"

She busied herself with a sheet of paper. "She doesn't work here anymore."

"What? Why, I spoke with her just yesterday, and she didn't say anything about it."

"No, it was sudden. Her mother took ill, and Helen had to move to Peoria to help her."

"Peoria?"

She nodded.

I leaned down over the desk. "Did she tell you this?"

Shaking her head, she said, "No, she told Mr. Murphy last night. It was all very sudden," she repeated.

"Do you believe she moved to Peoria?"

Her hand rose to her throat. "Why wouldn't I? Do you—no, of course I believe it. She was trouble anyway, always trying to get Mr. Murphy to pay attention to her."

I swallowed the response that came to mind. I still needed her to believe I was the bug man. Trying to smile, I slapped the desk. "All right. Say, if you don't want those cockroaches to return"—I backed to the door—"make sure to pick up all food scraps every night."

I retreated to Flikklund's office and sat with the receiver to my ear, thinking. Helen's mother—if she was even alive—didn't live in Peoria. Helen wouldn't have lied to me about that, and she would have gotten word to me somehow if she had to leave town between late last night and this morning. No, Murphy had done something to her—gotten her out of the picture.

He and his thugs returned at about half past one. Not half an hour later, the MLA office door opened and closed, and, through the telegraphone, I heard Murphy's telephone ring. "Yeah?" he said.

A second later, "Sanford? Shit!" Murphy exclaimed, his voice a dinghy in an ocean of hum.

Eli Sanford? Could I be so lucky again? I switched on the telegraphone, and the wire began spooling through the machine.

"Goddamn it," Murphy mumbled. "Yeah, send him in." Louder, "You two get out of here."

The door creaked open, and Murphy's thugs traded greetings with a man they called "sir."

The door closed again. "Goddamn it," Murphy said, "I thought we agreed we would only talk on the telephone."

"I think our agreement ended when you killed my brother."

"Your brother? He's dead?"

"I'd think you'd be a better liar, Andrew, as much practice as you get."

"I know nothing of it," Murphy replied.

"You owe me," Eli said. "Anything I want. You owe me."

"Just wait until after the election," Murphy said. "You can do whatever you want then. We can still win this, but not if we give them a martyr."

Elizabeth!

"I provided the leverage you needed, Andrew."

Something thumped against wood—a fist on the desk. "And I paid you for it! Goddamn it, we have an agreement!"

"We need a new agreement," Eli said. "Look, Andrew. It doesn't matter how anybody votes. The ballots are being printed right now, and the ward bosses will torpedo the lot of them, if need be. The saloon owners are mobilized. They'll be bringing in the drunks—two or three times apiece." He laughed, but I heard no mirth. "We've got sluggers contracted to roam the streets in the Protestant wards making it difficult to get to the polls. Even if all that fails and the vote comes in for the amendment, our ward bosses will burn the yeses and get the misprints thrown out. There's nothing to worry about."

Silence, a long ten seconds. *Say his name, Murphy!* If I had Eli's name on this, the evidence would be impenetrable.

"No loose ends?" Murphy asked.

"No."

"Everyone is still doing their jobs?"

"Of course."

Say his fucking name!

"If your actions cost me this vote, you'll regret it."

"Nothing could cost you the vote. It's done. Look at it this way—would I risk my money? I'm getting out of town as soon as the vote comes in, and I can't do that with the pocket change I've gotten from you so far."

A long silence ensued. I could picture Eli glaring into Murphy's eyes.

Murphy finally said quietly, "All right. Do what you want. Just so you understand that if this turns the election, I will hold you personally responsible."

"Thank you, Andrew," Eli said. "You just remember the rest of my money. Fifty thousand dollars—payable the minute the amendment defeat is announced."

"Yeah, I have the dough. You're clear that I can have nothing to do with . . . what you're doing?"

"Of course."

Upholstery creaked again as the men stood.

"I think we can both go our own ways in a couple of weeks." Eli's voice rose as he moved toward the sound collector, then quieted again. "I don't think we'll need to talk before then." The door opened and closed.

"Goddamn pup," Murphy muttered. "Treats me like a . . ." He trailed off in dark-tinged curses. The door opened and closed again.

———

A dead calm washed over me. I would kill him. Now. I'd follow him out of here to someplace I could put a bullet in him and have some chance of escape. If it came to it, I'd shoot him in public and hope I could talk my way out of prison. With Eli out of the picture, Elizabeth would be safe. Murphy didn't want her killed. It was only Eli, with his depraved vision of revenge for his brother.

I left the reel on the telegraphone and crept to the door. The wire could wait. Outside, a door opened and closed. Eli leaving. He crossed the hallway to the stairs. I had to let him leave the building, get the bank guards and police behind us.

I had started to open the door when the MLA office door opened again, and Murphy and Pepper stalked out, turning right to go up the hall rather than left to go down the stairs. I pressed the door closed and stood quietly, waiting for their footsteps to recede. As soon as they did, I burst out the door and hurried downstairs to the closest entrance. I ducked my head into the bank but saw no sign of the big man with a smooth face, pointy nose, and bright blue eyes, nor anywhere did I see a tan duster.

I ran out to the street and looked up and down, through the automobiles, trucks, wagons, carriages, streetcars, and bicycles, each moving past the other in a riot of noise and color and motion. I ran fifty yards west and doubled back nearly to Woodward.

He had gotten what? A ten-second head start?

He should be right here. Any big man? There—with a black derby—but balding, no; there—fedora, opera coat—gray hair, too old. I looked all the way up and down the street, in and around the vehicles parked at the curb, then ran to the other side and did the same. No one. Couples walked down the street, into and out of businesses; individual men and women moved at varied paces; a man in a gray overcoat and derby, another in a gray overcoat and black derby, yet another in matching gray.

Damn it! I slammed my palm against the granite wall of a building. *I had him! He was here! . . . Then he wasn't.*

Anger burning behind my eyes, I ran back to the Dime, searched the rest of the second floor, and walked around the first level, trying for a sense of composure so as not to be harassed by the authorities.

No sign anywhere.

I had to slow down, think. I returned to Flikklund's office, rewound the reel and pocketed it, and walked out the door. I wouldn't be coming back.

I had what I set out for—Murphy's head on a platter—but now the stakes had been raised.

Eli Sanford was out there somewhere. Now all doubt had been eliminated.

He planned to murder Elizabeth.

Tomorrow.

An older man stood at the doorway of suffrage headquarters. He didn't have the look of a Burnsy, and he seemed kind, which pretty well ruled out the possibility. Elizabeth was out, and he couldn't say where, but he assured me that she was well guarded. Given the state of affairs, I understood that they couldn't give out her whereabouts, but that didn't make it any less irritating.

I crossed the street to Schultz's Bakery, one of the few downtown bakeries open past noon, with half a dozen little two-seat tables in the front window, two of which were occupied by pairs of men I didn't recognize. A line of muddy footprints stained the plank floor between the front door and the counter, behind which stood a red-faced old man in an apron. He looked none too happy to see another wet-footed customer. The sweet, yeasty odor of a bakery is probably my second-favorite smell, yet it barely registered. I ordered a hard roll with butter and a cup of coffee and sat at the window, watching for Elizabeth. It was hard to contain myself. I had the evidence necessary to have Murphy arrested and the conspiracy blown wide open—and I needed Elizabeth to hear it before I handed it off to the authorities.

Even then, what should I do with it?

I had to coerce Murphy into turning over Eli, but on my own the MLA could still beat me. I couldn't bring the recording to Detective Riordan, which was surely what Elizabeth would want to do. The rest of the Detroit police were out of the question, as were the Burns men. The state police? Federal marshals? I didn't know if they were any less crooked than the locals.

The red-faced man gave me a dark look, and I saw I was now the only customer in the place. I glanced at the clock behind the counter—a quarter to three. He wanted me gone so he could start cleaning. I made a point of sipping my coffee while he was looking. The sign said 5:00 A.M.–3:00 P.M. I had fifteen minutes.

Unfortunately, those fifteen minutes passed without Elizabeth walking into suffrage headquarters, but I decided to check to see if somehow I'd missed her. I crossed the street and asked the man if she had returned.

"No, sir, she hasn't," he said with a nervous look at my black-gloved hands.

Brennan stuck his head out the door, looking at me. "Mr. Anderson, did you need something?"

"Just Elizabeth."

"Would you give me five minutes of your time?" He pushed open the door and held it for me. He was polite and professional, which made me nervous.

"Why?"

"Please." He said the word carefully, not begging, not authoritarian, just a single word said in as neutral a fashion as can be.

I decided to give him a few minutes. I wouldn't have to wait in the cold, and where was I going to go anyway? I walked past Brennan into the building, asking, "How was your trip to Lansing?"

"Uneventful."

"No stops on the way?"

"It was an express, Mr. Anderson. In case you're not familiar with the concept, 'express' means they don't stop."

"Convenient," I said. "Deniability."

He just shook his head and brushed by me, heading for the back. He stopped at Elizabeth's office, opened the door, and walked inside. "What in the world?" he bellowed.

I followed him in. Francis, in full pirate garb, and Robert sat hunched over the table on the left, which was loaded with three wooden consoles, two of which looked to have exploded. Wiring and tubes, gears and magnets, coils and transformers—most everything that made up modern electrical equipment—lay out on the table. A large horn lay next to one, which made it clear that it was, or had been, a Victrola.

Robert buried his face in his hands. Francis shot to his feet. "This is not your office, William J. Burns!"

"No, but that telegraphone is mine." Brennan pointed to the third console, which looked intact.

"We did not touch it!" Francis shouted.

"It's all right . . . Edward." I looked at Brennan. "And Warren. If the other two machines are for the boys, it's not your problem. I'm sure they know what they're doing."

Shaking his head, Brennan sighed and looked at Francis. "Could we please borrow this office for a few minutes?"

"This is not your office, William J. Burns," Francis repeated.

"There's somewhere else we can talk, isn't there?" I asked.

"Yeah," he said, "but nowhere else I can listen to your wires."

CHAPTER TWENTY-EIGHT

I stared back at Brennan. "My what?"

"You've been recording Murphy. I want to hear what you've got."

"I don't know what you're talking about."

"Look, Mr. Anderson." He nodded toward the door, and we walked out into the hall. "I'm going to put my cards on the table here. You've been looking for Eli Sanford, right?"

"How do you know that?"

Biting the inside of his cheek, he glanced away, then met my eyes again. "Let's set that aside for a moment. Would you like to know what I know about him?"

I suppressed the urge to punch him in the face and simply said, "Yes."

His tongue worried the part of his cheek he'd been biting. "I could lose my job for telling you this . . . but I'm going to. Take that into account when you decide if you can trust me."

"Fair enough," I said. "What do you know?"

"Let's find some privacy." He walked to the end of the hall, ducked his head into the conference room, and walked in. I followed him into the empty room and shut the door. Leaning on the edge of the table, he said, "I managed the aldermen operation in the fake Wabash office.

None of their security people were supposed to know about it until after we finished. Eli Sanford had been seen on at least one occasion walking out of the adjoining office, the one with the telegraphone, and at the end of the operation, we were missing three of the blank wire reels. We couldn't prove he took them, and when we brought it to Wabash's attention, they told us to drop it."

"You think he made some recordings of his own?"

"It makes sense."

"Any idea what was on them?"

He shrugged. "None."

I thought about it. "One of the Wabash security men said Eli didn't do any work after that, and they let him get away with it. Some good blackmail against the railway would make sense."

"There were only a few of the brass who knew what was going on. It's possible he got something on the railway, but I'll be damned if I know what it was."

"Who else might have gotten recorded?"

"Some of the aldermen brought along their underlings, and a few don't go anywhere without their sluggers. As far as I know, no one with any power or influence was there except the aldermen."

"So how could he and Murphy be using these recordings as leverage in the election?"

He shrugged again. "None of the aldermen have been forced to step down, and most are wets. Half of them—all of them, for all I know—could be helping Murphy. All I heard at the Wabash office was business—how much money they wanted to approve the land grab."

"Why would Eli Sanford want to kill Elizabeth?"

"Kill her? Is that what you have on the wire?"

"Let's set that aside for a moment," I said dryly. "Why would Eli want to kill her?"

Brennan shook his head. "I don't know him well, but Eli Sanford didn't strike me as a killer. Some of the men I've come up against just have that feel, almost a smell, you know?"

He paused and glanced at me, and though not entirely sure what he meant, I nodded.

"Something was done to them that ate into their souls, rotted it out so it stunk when they opened their mouths." He shook his head, not satisfied with his explanation. "It's not a smell, but it's like a smell; it's this rot that just leaks from them. I don't know if everybody feels it, but I'd be dead now if I didn't. Anyway." He shook his head again, as if clearing it. "Near as I can tell, Eli Sanford isn't one of them. He's a pissant. Forget about him, and protect Miss Hume."

"All I can say to that is your instincts let you down this time."

"Yeah?" He cocked his head at me.

"Going back to your 'set-aside,' how do you know I've been looking for Eli?"

"The same way I know you didn't write the letter Miss Hume got yesterday."

"Which is?"

"I had you followed."

"What?"

"I had to determine whether you were a threat to Miss Hume."

My face was getting hot. "Did she ask you to do that?"

"No. Until the campaign is over, I have control over the DSC security and do what I believe necessary."

I was burning.

Brennan took my lack of response as understanding. "Now I'd like to get back to the topic of your set-aside. On at least three different occasions you spent hours inside the Dime Bank Building in the office adjoining the MLA office. That pretty girl in their office says you're the exterminator, which obviously isn't true. A lock pick was all it took to find your telegraphone. You're here now, and you tell me Eli Sanford is a killer. He's never been prosecuted for a violent crime, and my men say he's not a threat. I'm betting you have a wire that says otherwise."

I certainly couldn't argue with his logic. Why was I so sure Brennan had killed David? "When did you have me followed?" I asked.

"Last week, on and off."

"When did you find the telegraphone?"

"Friday."

Friday. Three days before Murphy's telephone call.

Brennan hadn't been the one on the telephone with Murphy, and he wasn't at Wayne Pavilion to kill David. Elizabeth had sent him there to protect me. So he was an abrasive son of a bitch. It was probably his nature.

"Let's wait for Elizabeth," I said.

Brennan asked the man at the door to alert him the minute Elizabeth arrived, and we sat in the conference room to wait.

"Say, Brennan," I said, "did you have me followed last weekend?"

He shook his head. "No. Friday was the last."

Saturday night and Sunday would remain a mystery. I hadn't broken out in any rashes or received any blackmail notes, so I hoped that, whatever I'd done, I'd behaved myself.

The noise from the lobby rose. I opened the door and ducked my head out into the hall. Elizabeth was picking her way through the volunteers, offering words of thanks and patting shoulders. Two large men walked before her and another pair after her. She saw me and made a beeline toward us. When she'd cleared the volunteers, her face changed, and, just as last night, she looked frightened and exhausted. Outside, she stopped and asked her escorts to give us some privacy before she hurried to me and gripped my bicep.

"It *is* Eli Sanford!" she and I said simultaneously.

"What did you discover?" she asked, breathless. She sounded genuinely frightened, and I wondered at how she had managed to stay so strong in spite of all the troubles she'd had to confront.

"I have a very disturbing recording I made this afternoon," I said into her ear. "You need to hear this." I stood back and let her come into the room with us, then closed the door behind her. "What did *you* discover?"

Elizabeth glanced at Brennan and looked back at me. "Let's . . . let's listen to your wire first." Looking at Brennan again, she said, "Have the two of you reached some accommodation?"

He nodded.

"I believe he's trying to protect you, honey," I said.

"All right, then." She forced a smile. "Please."

We walked back to her office, and she shooed the boys out after giving them an assignment to write a speech for her and promising they could return shortly. Francis was insistent that we not touch their equipment and forced us all to swear we would keep our hands off it. Once they were gone, I took the reel from my coat pocket and handed it to Brennan, who began winding the wire into the machine. Elizabeth slipped into a chair and sat, slumped.

"The boys seem to be having fun," I said, pointing at the machines that had undergone major surgery.

She nodded distractedly. "I thought it would be good for them to have something to do here, and they so love the electrical gadgetry."

"Thank goodness they didn't destroy mine," Brennan said. Holding the receiver to his ear with one hand, he switched the telegraphone to play and used a small screwdriver to adjust the mechanism in the center.

"Yes, Mr. Brennan requested one of these," Elizabeth said to me. "For this reason, I would guess?"

He nodded, wound the reel back, and handed the receiver to Elizabeth. "I can't get the hum out of it, but it's clear enough to understand." He glanced at me. "I can see why Mr. Anderson wanted you to hear it."

Elizabeth held the receiver to her ear, and Brennan switched the machine to play. Her face darkened, and she muttered a quiet curse. Her eyes began to widen, and her mouth opened in surprise. Finally she handed the receiver back to Brennan, moving slowly as if her arm were pushing through molasses. "Unbelievable. I recognized Andrew Murphy's voice. Of course, Eli Sanford is the other."

I nodded. "Now what did you find?"

Elizabeth turned to the Burns man. "Mr. Brennan, I am going to have to ask you to leave us for a few minutes. We need to discuss a family matter."

He looked confused and disappointed, but he left the room without protest, closing the door behind him.

Elizabeth fixed me in her gaze. In this light, her eyes looked brown rather than green, and dull, like dead leaves. "I discovered what happened between my father and David Sanford Sr."

"Oh?"

"This morning, my mother was having a good spell, so I asked her about it. She told me that they had partnered on a number of real estate purchases and sales, and had both done very well. She recalled Mr. Sanford as having two handsome sons—Davey and another. She couldn't remember the name of the other, but that is clear enough."

"Of course."

She sat back and sighed before continuing. "Mr. Sanford and my father were part of a consortium building a new skyscraper downtown. They and three other men had already invested fifty thousand dollars each, and many more were lining up. Mother said that Mr. Sanford had taken a lead position and was the secretary and treasurer of the corporation. He worked directly with the building companies and paid them deposits and material costs—nearly all of the money they had raised." Her eyes fell to the table in front of her. She shook her head and fell silent.

"What had he done?"

"According to my mother, not only had Mr. Sanford not paid in his fifty thousand dollars, he also had falsified all the invoices from the contractors and cashed the checks himself. My father discovered his treachery and alerted the police. Her recollection is that they caught up with Mr. Sanford as he was boarding a ship to Belgium. The money was never found."

"What happened to him?"

"Life in prison, though, as it turned out, it wasn't a long sentence. Last year he was knifed to death in an altercation."

"My God!" I exclaimed. "We need not look farther for motive. Eli thinks your father was responsible for the death of his father."

"I wish it were that simple, Will."

"Why? What haven't you told me?"

"I'm certain Mr. Sanford had done nothing wrong." Shaking her head in astonishment, she said, "It was all my father."

She needed a moment to compose herself, so I left to get her a cup of coffee. When I returned, she looked better, but still I pushed a chair around the table and sat next to her, grasping her hand in mine.

She took a drink of coffee and scrunched up her face. "I'll never get used to bad coffee." A laugh burst from her the way a sob might. "This is worse than yours."

Smiling, I nodded and waited for her to continue.

She took a deep breath. "You know all those papers I found in my father's hidden room?"

"Yes," I said. "You destroyed them."

"I . . . didn't. When I found them and realized what they were, I stuffed them into boxes and hid them in the attic. There they sat until this morning. After I spoke with my mother, I wondered if there might be a record of this project. I dug through two boxes before I came across the Hume Building file."

"The Hume Building?"

She grimaced. "My father's legacy. The file included bank records for an account in the corporation's name. Mr. Sanford, as treasurer, would have had access to it. The records show deposits of $200,000 and checks cashed against this account totaling $197,500. Bank examiners traced those checks. All were deposited at various banks in St. Louis, and when they had cleared, the money was withdrawn. The checks were all cashed by one man using three different identities and false identification. Bank tellers identified Mr. Sanford as being that man."

"Then what did your father have to do with it?"

"You should know first of all that Mr. Sanford and my father shared many physical characteristics. They both were big men, and portly. My father was bald, and Mr. Sanford still had his hair, which of course could be imitated with a wig."

"Okay," I said. "They looked similar. That doesn't mean anything."

"My first thought was that I had never heard my father say anything about traveling to St. Louis, so I looked through our old calendars—fortunately, Mother saves them—to compare the dates of the withdrawals against the dates of his travel. Each time a withdrawal was made, he was traveling. Of course, the calendar never showed his destination as St. Louis."

"Elizabeth, that's circumstantial at best."

"I'm not finished. I also have his personal ledgers—the ones no one knew about. He was maniacal about records. Those ledgers show cash receipts in the amounts of the withdrawals—to the penny, all within days of the withdrawals. With a simple disguise and the false identification that had been provided to the banks, my father cashed those checks. "

"Oh, Lord," I muttered. "He set up Sanford to be the fall guy."

CHAPTER TWENTY-NINE

We brought Brennan back into the room. Elizabeth told him that we were one hundred percent certain that Eli Sanford was the threat, and that his motive stemmed from a family grudge.

I'd been thinking about David and Eli. "David was in jail when his father was murdered. As soon as he was released, he came to Detroit and got the job with the MLA. Eli was already working surreptitiously for Murphy. I don't think they give two hoots about suffrage or the MLA agenda. They both wanted to destroy your dream. Maybe when we catch Eli, he can tell us if they were planning all along to kill you or if he decided to do it after David's death."

"Why would Murphy have killed him?" Elizabeth asked.

I shrugged, and Brennan cut in excitedly. "David must have told him he was going to kill you. We know that Murphy thought you being murdered would help the amendment to pass. He couldn't let that happen."

I was nodding. "Right. As far as Murphy knew, David and Eli came on board to help him defeat the amendment. He didn't know about the grudge against Elizabeth. He eliminated David when he couldn't trust him to wait."

"Why would he agree, then, when Eli told him the same thing?" Brennan asked.

"Eli provided the leverage," I said. "Perhaps he's got something on Murphy, too."

"Or perhaps Murphy was just getting him out of the office," Elizabeth said, "so he could kill him before he could do any harm."

"Wouldn't that be a treat?" I said. "Let the criminals kill the other criminals."

Elizabeth grimaced. "At least now the motive makes sense."

I kept thinking it through. "Murphy was already working with Eli when David started at the MLA. Eli sold Murphy the recording they're using as leverage." I told them about Eli getting David the job.

"Leverage against whom?" Elizabeth asked.

Brennan and I traded a glance. "I've got no idea," I said. "It's clearly someone they believe can help them beat the amendment, but I've heard nothing."

"Neither have I," Brennan said.

"Mr. Brennan," Elizabeth said, "outside of the person or persons being blackmailed, is there anything we're missing?"

Pursing his lips, he arched his eyebrows and tilted his head to the side. "I don't see any holes. I think you have it in full."

"This is great news," Elizabeth said. "We can destroy Murphy and the antisuffrage movement, and now all your men have to do, Mr. Brennan, is keep an eye out for Eli Sanford."

"I should be able to get a photograph from Wabash," he said. "I've got contacts."

"Good," she said. "If you distribute that to your men before the rally, we'll be fine."

"Hold on, Elizabeth," I said. "I'm sure Brennan will agree with me—if we can't locate and control Eli Sanford, you shouldn't get anywhere near that rally."

She waved the idea away. "Unthinkable."

"Elizabeth—" I started.

"No. End of discussion." Her tone was iron. The word was final. Nodding toward the telegraphone, she said, "The knockout blow hinges on that recording." She shifted her attention to me. "Will, let's take it to Detective Riordan. He'll know what to do with it."

"I'm not giving it to him," I said. If I eliminated Brennan as

Murphy's informer, I knew no one other than Detective Riordan who fit the bill. Hardly damning evidence, but I couldn't go along with it.

"Please, Will. You're not being rational. You know him. He's an honest man."

"There's something he's not telling me. Something to do with this conspiracy. I'm not giving it to him."

"This might be a bit dicey," Brennan said tentatively, "but I think Mr. Burns would be willing to get behind this." He gave us a wry smile. "He doesn't exactly run away from publicity, and this wire would bring it. Even though the sound isn't the best, it's solid evidence"—he glanced at me, acknowledging my work—"and I could tell him I've been involved in the investigation. I think he'd see it as the frosting on the cake for his work against corruption in this city."

"He's an honest man?" I asked.

"You don't have to take my word," Brennan said. "Think about how much this would benefit him. It's great publicity."

"How quickly could you find out?" I asked.

Brennan pulled his watch from his vest. "He's in the office this week—likely an hour, tops."

Elizabeth reached out and gently laid her fingers on my forearm. "Will, let's see if Mr. Burns will help."

I thought for a moment. "Yeah, all right. It makes sense." I have to admit the thought took a bit of the starch out of me. I was in line to be the hero here, but now Burns would come in, trumpeting that he had solved another case, and I would be nothing more than a footnote, if that. It didn't matter, I told myself. Protecting Elizabeth and ensuring that this wire was made public could be my only priorities.

"I'm going to transcribe the wire onto a pad," Brennan said, sitting at the table, "so I've got all the details for Mr. Burns. I can take it from here."

"I need to do the same," I said, "and I'll be taking the wire with me." I still didn't know how far I could trust him.

"Oh, for Pete's sake," Brennan snapped.

"Mr. Brennan," Elizabeth said quietly, "Will made the recording. It's his property."

"Yes, miss," Brennan said, again the professional. He gave me a level gaze. "Where are you going to be tonight? I have to be able to connect you and Mr. Burns."

I looked at Elizabeth.

"I have meetings that start in ten minutes and run until at least nine o'clock," Elizabeth said, intertwining her fingers with mine. "I can't stay with you."

I thought again of Helen. "I've got a few things to do, but wire me at home."

"Maybe you ought to spend the night here," Brennan said. "Both of you. I think this will be the safest spot for everyone."

He wasn't pleased I would be taking the wire elsewhere. It was probably genuine concern for the recording, but what if it wasn't? "Sorry, no. Wire me."

Elizabeth waited while Brennan played the recording, and he and I wrote down its content. When we finished, he handed the reel back to me and left to wire his boss.

I kissed Elizabeth, and she returned it warmly.

"I think we're almost there," I said. "Who are you meeting with tonight?"

"We're having a final planning meeting for the rally. It will be all friends."

"Here?"

"Yes."

"You'll have your guards?"

"Yes, I'll have my guards. What are you going to do with the wire?"

"For now I'm going to lock it up in your father's safe, if that's all right with you."

She nodded. "Good idea." Little vertical wrinkles appeared between her eyebrows. "Are you going right there?"

I nodded.

"Could you take the boys home? They need their supper."

"Sure."

We rounded up Francis and Robert and prepared to leave. Fortunately, Francis was "starving to death," so he didn't put up a fuss.

Elizabeth walked us to the door and gave me another kiss. "Don't worry about me. You just get that wire to Mr. Burns. Tomorrow this is going to explode."

We marched out of the office and into the gray October cold. I felt like I had a target on my back. With the wire reel in my pocket and one hand on the butt of the pistol in my shoulder holster, I retrieved the Torpedo from the parking lot. It took ten minutes to start, though Francis's continual commentary on my ignorance made it seem much longer. After I'd tinkered with everything I could think of, the engine caught. When we reached the Humes' home, the boys hurried to the kitchen. Alberts opened the safe in Elizabeth's father's office, and I placed the recording in it for safekeeping.

Then I sped to Helen's apartment, hoping to find her there so that I could get her out of town. Harold the pimp was nowhere in sight when I threw open the door, pistol unholstered. I climbed the stairs to her room and knocked. Then knocked again.

Boots clattered on the stairs behind me. A man. I turned toward the stairway as Harold's head cleared the top of the landing, followed by his hands, empty, fingers pointing to the ceiling.

His hound-dog face was nervous, not belligerent. "She ain't been here for two days. I think somethin' happened to her."

I searched his face. "Why are you being nice to me?"

"She tol' me you were a friend. 'Some friend,' I says to her, but she says you two were helpin' each other out."

"What do you think happened?" I asked.

"Dunno," he said. "She plays her cards close, you know?"

"Murphy's telling people she's gone to Peoria. Does she have people in Peoria?"

He scowled. "Unless they just got off a boat, her people are all in Greece."

"I hate to leave it at this. Do you have any idea where she could be?"

He shrugged. "Wish I did."

I nodded. "Well, listen." I searched my pockets for paper and fished out an old laundry ticket, on which I wrote my name, address, and telephone number. "If you hear from her, let me know as soon as possible."

He nodded, and I handed him the ticket. On the way back to my building, I wondered about Harold the pimp. He seemed to care about Helen, not the income he might derive from her. Perhaps she only lived here. He'd said before she wasn't working.

I returned to my building without incident and asked the day man,

William, if I had received a telegram. None had arrived. I climbed the stairs to my apartment, switched on the lights, and picked up *Huckleberry Finn* again. After five pages, I realized I had absolutely no idea what I had been reading. I set the book down and wandered around the apartment, straightening up.

It was after five o'clock when I heard a knock on the door. *Finally,* I thought. *The telegram.* I headed for the door and put my eye to the peephole.

Shit. I stood at the door, frozen. It was Riordan.

"I heard you, Anderson. Open the door. I'm coming in either way."

The wire reel was locked in the Humes' safe, and I had a gun. I exhaled loudly and opened the door. "What?"

He stepped into the apartment and closed the door behind him. His face was grim. "You don't know what you've gotten yourself into. Give it to me."

"Give what to you?"

"The wire. They're going to kill you, you know."

"They? Who are they? Who's going to kill me?"

"Who specifically? I don't know, but it will be on Murphy's orders."

"At this point I don't particularly care. Those men are going to pay for what they've done. Who told you I had the wire?"

"It doesn't matter."

"It matters a great deal to me, Detective."

He thought hard before answering. "Elizabeth asked me to protect you."

Elizabeth.

"She doesn't want you to get hurt," he said. "Listen. Give it to me. I can keep you safe."

"So—assuming I had a wire—what would you do with it?"

"I'll take it to a man I can trust. A prosecutor." His eyes bored into me, as if he were consciously making eye contact—like a man who was lying and desperately trying to look like he wasn't. "He will bring these men to justice. I can keep you—and Elizabeth—out of it."

"No. It's too late anyway."

He took a step closer to me. I stepped back, keeping him farther than arm's length.

"Will, you have to think about Elizabeth here."

"I already took it to the U.S. Marshals."

He stopped, glaring at me with those cold blue eyes, like a wolf sizing up its prey. Then he surged forward, grabbing me by the lapels. I tried to reach my pistol, but he got it before I could and threw it to the floor. He forced me backward and slammed me into the wall as easily as I would have a child. "You dumb son of a bitch!" He pulled me forward and slammed me back again. Waves of pain radiated from the back of my skull, the way a rock thrown into water hits with a splash and ripples outward. Pinpoints of white light flashed before my eyes.

I threw my right elbow into his jaw, stunning him, and tried to bring my knee up between his legs, but he blocked it, lifted me off my feet, and slammed me to the floor. He landed on top of me, his fists still on my lapels, digging into my throat. His face was contorted with rage. The pressure on my throat was incredible. I couldn't breathe. I struggled with him, but he was strong and insane with fury. Then, suddenly, he rocked back. I threw him off and scrambled to my feet.

Riordan sat on the floor, his face in his hands . . . and he wept. His body was racked with sobs.

I scooped up my gun from the floor and aimed it at his face. "You son of a bitch! You've got ten seconds to tell me why I shouldn't blow off your goddamn head."

After a moment he looked up at me, silent, pleading with tear-filled eyes.

CHAPTER THIRTY

Riordan slumped on the sofa, utterly defeated. I brought him a glass of water and sat across from him, massaging my throat.

"There were more wires," he said, his eyes staring sightlessly out the window. "Glinnan and his bunch were just a part of it. They got me."

"You? What did you have to do with it?"

"With the railroad? Nothing. But Tom—Glinnan—and I go way back. He faked the paperwork for Anna—my wife—to live here."

"Explain."

"She came to the U.S. illegally. Glinnan got me fake paperwork for her. If it's exposed, she'll be sent back to St. Kitts and hanged."

His words sent a shock through me. "What?"

"Her parents lived on a sugar plantation. When Anna was thirteen, the plantation owner brought her to his bed and raped her. The first chance she got—about three months later—she slit his throat. Her parents were barely able to smuggle her off the island before they were both lynched. If she goes back there, she hangs."

"What's the connection between this conspiracy and your wife?"

"Tom brought me to the fake Wabash office for some unofficial protection." He shrugged. "I was just doing him a favor. We got there an hour early—some sort of scheduling error, and they left us there to wait. He asked after Anna; we talked about the old days. I didn't know anything about the bribes. I waited for him in the outer office while he did the business." Riordan sighed. "A week after the aldermen were arrested, I received a transcript of my conversation with Tom along with a note telling me they would be expecting a few favors should I want my wife to live."

"Who sent it?"

He shrugged. "At first I thought it had to be Brennan, but I'm sure he doesn't know anything about it. He'd have let me know somehow. Somebody else must have sold it to Murphy."

One of Eli's wires. "Ah," I said to myself.

"What?"

"I'll tell you later."

That put me in mind of my other recording—the one with Murphy on the telephone. It hadn't been Brennan. No doubt at all. *That means . . . oh, shit.* I fixed Riordan with a glare, but his revelation had tamped my anger down to a sputtering flame. "I made another recording. On Tuesday. Someone on the telephone with Murphy."

I waited for him.

Finally he sighed and said, "Yeah. It was me."

"You told him that I was watching him?" I was astonished. It was true.

Riordan said nothing.

Suddenly the picture became clear. My viewpoint had been an inch away from the canvas. As with an Impressionist painting, now that I stood back, the dabs and dashes of paint formed a clear picture. In this case, I just didn't like what I was looking at. Two different people had tried to steal the ballots from me. Murphy and Eli Sanford were controlling the main group of conspirators, which was the obvious choice for one of the thieves.

The other . . . "You stole the ballots from me, didn't you? You got the message that I'd found them, and you stole them."

After a moment, he nodded. "I burned them."

"So you kept them from being made public. But you didn't give them to Murphy, which is why his men destroyed this place trying to find them."

"Right."

"Why didn't you just ask me? Do you think I would have let them hang your wife? Do you give me no credit at all for being a human being?"

He shrugged. "One thing led to another . . ."

I blew out a hot breath of frustration. "Why were the ballots important?"

"I don't know, but Murphy was frantic about them."

"What about my hundred bucks?"

Nodding, he gave me a wry smile. "I had to make it seem at least a little like a burglary. I saw Sapphira leave, and thought you would buy her taking both."

"When do you plan on giving it back?"

"I've got it at home. I'll give it to you."

"So what's your job exactly? To deliver the election to the wets?"

He barked out an angry laugh. "If only I had that kind of power. No. Murphy's got me directing the friendly ward bosses and muscling the unfriendly ones. I'm also supposed to keep Elizabeth and her people out of the mix. Election day I have more duties, but that's it for now."

"Bringing in the sluggers to suppress the vote in Protestant areas? That sort of thing?"

He took a deep breath and nodded.

"Murphy's going to expose your wife if they run into any snags with the election."

He nodded again. "If the amendment wins a majority vote in the city, or anyone in Elizabeth's camp causes a problem, we'll have to disappear—fast."

"So you ruin my life and do your best to make me seem crazy." I looked out the window and thought. He couldn't be lying. Riordan didn't have it in him. To fake crying? Never. I leaned forward, clasped my hands together, and looked up at him again. "I might be able to help you."

Shaking his head, he said, "It's too late. You can't help."

"Let's say I could."

He looked over at me, meeting my eyes for the first time since we'd entered the parlor.

I sipped my coffee and set it down on the dining room table. "Assuming you're telling the truth now, what do you know about Eli Sanford?"

Riordan sat across from me, warming his hands with his cup. He shrugged. "Nothing more than I told you before."

I told him about Eli being seen in the fake Wabash office and stealing the wires from the Burnsies. "I have Eli on the recording I made today. It confirms he's the one who's coming after Elizabeth. It's a—"

"Whoa," Riordan said. "Slow down. What do you mean, 'coming after Elizabeth'?"

"Well, the letter, of course."

That made him sit up straight. "What letter?"

"She didn't tell you."

He shook his head.

"Elizabeth received a death threat for the rally tomorrow, accompanied by a detailed itinerary of everywhere she'd gone over the course of two days, with insertions of the dozens of times the man claimed he could have killed her. It was completely credible."

"Why wouldn't . . . Why wouldn't she have told me?"

"You would have forced her to cancel the rally. She's going to go there to speak if it's the last thing she does."

"No." He gazed at me from hollowed eyes. "I wouldn't have asked her to cancel, and I support her going. We can't let them win—ever—even if Elizabeth is risking her life. We just have to minimize that risk."

"Then I guess she didn't want you to worry."

I had no decision to make. I couldn't let Riordan's wife hang. My recording implicated Murphy and an unnamed other man I couldn't prove was Eli Sanford. The revelation of Murphy's dirty dealings would create a political firestorm that would end in his arrest and possibly cinch the election for the suffragists, but it would get Anna killed and put me no closer to stopping Eli Sanford.

Surely Murphy wouldn't sacrifice himself for Eli, and he was who I wanted.

And what of Helen? Murphy had to know where she was.

What . . . what if we bargained with him? We give him my recording, which keeps him from spending a very long time in jail; he gives us Riordan's recording and delivers Eli Sanford and Helen to us. Good for us. Good for him.

I smiled at Detective Riordan. "You probably didn't know this, but it's your lucky day."

Once Detective Riordan had read the transcript of my new recording, we walked outside to the Torpedo and began our drive. I splashed along the rain-washed streets, faster than I should, given the invisibility of missing cobbles in the mud puddles. Traffic was light, those with better sense staying home tonight. The streetlamps made their feeble attempts to stave off the darkness, but the steel gray sky felt like a soggy blanket. Raindrops ricocheted off the tops of the doors and into the car. I pulled my duster tighter around me, wishing I had bought a coupé rather than a roadster. The lights became brighter as we neared downtown.

Glancing over at Riordan, I said, "What are you going to tell Elizabeth? She'll have to know what we're doing."

He stared straight out the windscreen. Rain hung on to the bottom of his fedora's brim and slipped along to the side, the lowest point, coalescing there to form new droplets that released one by one onto the seat between us. "I'm going to tell her the truth," he said. "She deserves to know." He turned to me. "I'm sorry, Will. I never should have put you in this position."

I glanced over at him again. "I can't argue with your motive. I just wish you would have trusted me."

"The doctors said you were out of your mind. I didn't think I could."

I thought of all that Thomas Riordan had paid for. His eyes burned with a fever in hollow sockets; his scar threw a ragged black shadow in the light of the streetlamps.

"Your wire is good," he said, "but don't get cocky. We need Murphy to deal. Juries don't trust these newfangled inventions. You don't have the solid proof that this was recorded at Murphy's office like they did in the alderman case, and even then, as carefully as the Burnsies managed the recordings, I'd be surprised if any of the aldermen do time."

"It sounds like Murphy," I said, "and he says plenty to incriminate himself."

Riordan cleared his throat. "It's not that simple. If it goes to trial, the defense will find half a dozen men who will sound exactly like him on the wire. It's going to come down to your word against theirs." He glanced at me. "With your history, the defense will blow your credibility to smithereens."

"Brennan said Burns would step in to take credit."

"That's almost as bad as you. Nobody trusts a private detective, and a couple of Burns men have already been convicted of perjury in other places. No home runs here."

"Yeah, fine," I said. "If this gets to trial, we're all in a lot of trouble."

I stopped outside the Dime and looked up through the streaks of rain at the MLA office windows. All were dark. Riordan directed me toward Murphy's home address, with which he was already familiar. We headed west to Trumbull, into Corktown, no surprise for an Irishman's address. We passed the redbrick Catholic high school and turned left at the next street, Baker. Most of the area was comprised of neighborhoods of row houses built in the middle of the last century, but this section was lined with newer, and fine, if not huge, Victorian homes, the majority of them built of red brick with the occasional plaster Italianate.

We drove once around the block, to get a look at the place. The street was jammed with automobiles and carriages, and Murphy's home, one of the brick three-stories with a white porch and trim, was lit like a beacon, with spotlights blazing on two six-foot-wide American flags hanging from the porch rail, and a pair of smaller flags paralleling them below two of the second-story windows. Very patriotic.

Riordan leaned over in front of me, looking up at Murphy's home. All three floors were lit. People's shadows played against the curtains in a front room—the parlor. I couldn't say how many were there, but it appeared to be a party.

I pulled to the curb at the only open spot on Baker Street, a hundred feet from Murphy's house, facing a pair of horses that stood in front of a black carriage. The horses whinnied and stamped in the puddled water, but the driver settled them quickly. I felt for the man, sitting as he did, hunched atop the carriage against the steady rain, so I called out an apology to him. He waved it off in a congenial manner.

I ducked my head toward Riordan. "We can't confront him publicly. That defeats the purpose. Does it make any sense for us to be seen here?"

"It's fine," Riordan said. "I'll pull him aside. He can explain the visit to his guests however he wants to." Turning up his collar, he said, "Stay here. It'll be better if he doesn't know you're involved."

I grabbed his arm. "No. I'm going in. And listen. Part of this deal is that he turns over Helen—Sapphira—to us unharmed. I don't know what he's done with her, but it can't be good."

He stared into my eyes, wondering, I'm sure, what was wrong with me, before giving me a tight nod and stepping out into the rain. We trotted across the street to the sidewalk, down the block, and up to the door. Inside, a piano player banged out "In My Merry Oldsmobile," again reminding me of Wesley McRae. I remembered the first time I allowed him to be my friend. He'd played this song at the Crowley-Milner department store, substituting "Detroit Electric" for "Oldsmobile."

Inside the house, men and women talked and laughed, the sound muted as though underwater. Standing under the porch light, Riordan glanced at me. "Let me take the lead. Our position is he delivers Eli, Sapphira, and my wire to us before dawn. For that he gets your wire."

I nodded, flipped my derby from my head, and slicked back my hair. He rang the bell, and a moment later an older Negro man in a starched tuxedo opened the door. The piano and crowd noise trebled. "Yes, sirs?"

"We need to speak with Mr. Murphy," Riordan said.

"Do you have an invitation?"

I stepped forward. "Sir, I don't mean to be rude, but this is a matter of utmost importance for Mr. Murphy. He'll see us."

The man glanced from me to Riordan. "Your names?"

Riordan glared into the man's eyes. "Tell him Detective Riordan of the Detroit Police Department is here to see him."

He appraised me a moment longer, but when no answer was forthcoming, he said, "Please wait," and closed the door.

We waited in the cold, fortunately at least out of the rain while the drops tapped against the porch roof above us. "Do me a favor," Riordan said. "Head around back. Make sure he doesn't run on us."

I slapped my derby back onto my head and bolted down the steps and around the drive at the side of the house, pulling my pistol, the metal whispering against smooth leather. Holding the gun to my side,

I looked around the corner to see a small lawn of brown grass crowded by looming trees with bare branches that reached up into the darkness. I edged toward the door, my back against the house, and waited.

A minute passed. Another. I was thinking about going up front to see where Riordan was when the door next to me burst open, and he stuck his head out to look for me. "Inside. Now."

I grabbed the handle and hopped up the two steps to the kitchen.

Riordan strode into the central hallway toward the front of the house, pushing past half a dozen young men and women in gay attire. "Come over here by the staircase. Watch both doors for Murphy."

I hurried along behind him, noticing that his gun was still holstered. I decided to do the same before I frightened too many people. "Is he here?"

He glanced over his shoulder at me. "The butler says he's not, but I'm not taking his word for it. Wait here." He turned the corner at the staircase and took the steps two at a time, heading upstairs.

I stood awkwardly where he'd left me, next to a narrow shelf covered with statues and busts. The hallway walls were festooned with paintings and mirrors and photographs in gilded frames, so much so that it was difficult to see the fuzzy burgundy wallpaper. Every piece of furniture was dark wood, ornately carved. The house was gaudy, a poor man's image of a rich man's house.

At least fifty young people, perhaps my age, moved through the interior, drinking some sort of red punch from a bowl in the dining room to my left. Many were congregated in the parlor, listening to the piano, now to the ever-present "Alexander's Ragtime Band." It was a toe-tapper, but I was wearying of it already.

Mrs. Murphy, wearing an emerald green dress that fit like a sausage casing, charged down the stairs toward me. "What is the meaning of this? You get that other man and leave this house immediately." She stopped on the last step so as to see eye to eye with me and held a quivering finger an inch from my nose.

"Good evening, Mrs. Murphy." I smiled and doffed my derby.

"You get that man and leave my home immediately!" The finger still quivered in my face.

The house had gone silent. She leaned over to see into the parlor and gestured to the piano player, who started into a rag. At least the distraction had gotten her finger out of my face.

"That man, ma'am, is a Detroit police detective," I said. "I can't tell him what to do. If your husband would speak with us for a moment, this can all be avoided."

By now, we were drawing a crowd, and a few of the men appeared ready to intervene. I pulled my pistol again as she screeched, "He's not here."

The appearance of the gun had its desired effect. Everyone backed off a few steps.

"This is my daughter's birthday party!" Her tone was moving dangerously up toward hysteria.

I had noted by now that Murphy would have seemed out of place here tonight, so her words rang true for me.

"We have friends in the mayor's office!" The finger appeared again, same place. "If you are not out of—"

I gently pushed her finger aside and kept my tone genial. "Listen. If your husband isn't home, you need to tell us where he is. If we are not able to speak with him tonight, he is looking at the possibility of a very long prison sentence—probably the rest of his life."

Riordan thundered down the stairs behind her, his heavy leather heels slamming into the wooden steps, slowing just enough to guide her to the side so he could pass. She sputtered while he did and then unleashed a furious harangue at his back.

Ignoring her, he hurried around me toward the kitchen again. "I'm looking in the cellar."

She gave up yelling when he turned the corner out of sight. People had moved back when Riordan ran down the stairs but were edging toward me again. On my right, a bull of a young man in a green cardigan had a glint in his eye that said he wanted to hurt me. I watched him, my pistol rising from my side. A brawny ginger-haired youth slid toward me from the left.

"No! No!" Mrs. Murphy shouted, holding her hands out to her sides. "Get back, Sean! Peter! There'll be no fighting." They stopped, stymied by the matron. Turning back to me, she spat, "He's working. He's at work." Now she just sounded exasperated.

"He's not at his office."

"Well, then, he must be out to supper."

Riordan ducked back into the hall and met us at the staircase. "Where is he?" he demanded.

"I already told this simpleton." She pointed at me.

I glanced at Riordan. "Working, she says."

He flipped a card out of his coat pocket and handed it to her. "Then the minute he gets in, or you speak with him, have him telephone the number on this card and ask for me. If I don't hear from him by sunup, his life will become very unpleasant—and very short."

"How dare you threaten—"

"By sunup," Riordan repeated. He turned for the door just as it was flung open.

With one hand on the crown of his derby and the other holding a furled umbrella, Andrew Murphy stepped inside. Salt was directly behind; Pepper stood on the porch, a cigar in his mouth, trying to peer over the two men.

Murphy froze, the derby six inches off his head, and stared at Detective Riordan. "Riordan? What the hell do you think . . ." His voice trailed off as he took me in. "Peterson?" His eyes flickered back and forth between us as he desperately tried to make sense of seeing Riordan and me together. I'm not sure how much he figured out in those few seconds, but to judge from his face, he had a pretty good idea.

The house was dead silent. Now Salt threw open his coat and drew a revolver. Before it cleared the holster, Riordan, barely seeming to move, bent back Salt's hand, knocking the gun to the floor. Salt dove on him. Pepper threw his cigar on the porch, shoved Murphy aside, and drew a pistol, murder in his eyes.

"Stop!" Mrs. Murphy shouted. "Stop!"

I raised my gun and tried to aim at Pepper, but Riordan and Salt were between us. Riordan chopped Salt in the throat, and he dropped to the floor like a bag of flour.

"My God," Mrs. Murphy shouted, "there are children here!"

Andrew Murphy slipped his hand into the side pocket of his overcoat, and the young men on the sides jumped me simultaneously. One landed a heavy fist to my face while the other grabbed for my gun. I backhanded him across the face with the pistol. The butt landed with a crack on his forehead and raked a long furrow across his cheek. He went down. The other was behind me now, with his forearm crushing my throat. He choked me with one arm while clawing for my gun with the other.

A gunshot exploded, deafening in this close place, shocking everyone into a moment's hesitation. The house was silent, other than the echo of the report.

"Stop!" Andrew Murphy shouted. "The next one to start it's gonna get a bullet!"

The pressure eased on my windpipe. I glanced at Murphy. He stood in the doorway with a six-shooter in front of him, which moved left to right and back again, daring anyone to disregard his order.

The young man let go of me. Riordan's face was red. Pepper sat on the wood floor, leaning against the wall, chest rapidly rising and falling, his unfocused eyes taking in nothing. Salt still lay at Riordan's feet. The youth I'd hit moaned on the floor, blood pumping from the cut on his face. The one behind me stepped out and slipped into the parlor.

Murphy gestured toward me with his gun. "Put the gun on the floor."

"You shoot him, I shoot you," Riordan said, his voice low and flat.

"Let's put them all away," I said, "and talk. That's what we came here for. To talk."

Murphy glanced at Riordan, then back to me. He'd never get the gun back on Riordan before he got shot. His eyes out between us. "What do you want?" he growled.

"You don't want to do this here," I said. "Outside."

He again glanced between Riordan and me. I held open my coat and holstered my gun.

Someone had to do it.

CHAPTER THIRTY-ONE

Andrew Murphy read the transcript and then eyed me from across the porch, apparently seeing me as a bigger concern, or perhaps a bigger mystery, than Riordan. I felt my head tilt just an inch to the side as I met his gaze with a level stare. I wanted to reach out and take him by the throat, but I did nothing. The buzz in the house rose to nearly a conversational level again.

All this time, Riordan said nothing, just stared at Murphy with that wolf stare, his breathing slow and measured. Now he spoke, his voice dull against the ringing of my ears. "I need my wire. Along with Eli Sanford, in any condition, and Sapphira Xanakis—" He turned to me. "Helen, you said?"

I nodded.

"Helen," he continued, "returned to us in perfect health."

"And free from you for good," I added.

I watched Murphy's face, judging it for surprise or concern, but I saw only careful neutrality. He hadn't gotten where he was by showing his cards.

"I don't know what you're talking about," he said.

"That's fine," I replied. "We have operatives ready to deliver the results of our investigation to the governor, the prosecuting attorney, and the three major Detroit newspapers this evening."

His eyes burned into me. His desire to take me by the throat was at least as strong as mine had been. He turned and opened the front door, but instead of going inside, he plucked his derby and umbrella from the floor and slapped the hat against his leg, trying to dry it. "Let's have a stroll, gentlemen." He buttoned his overcoat, unfurled the umbrella, and ducked out into the rain, down the steps to the sidewalk. He walked briskly past the next house and down the alley that cut between streets. We followed just behind.

Murphy turned left at the sidewalk in front of Eldred Street and headed toward the school. The heels of his polished black boots clicked against the concrete. He began taking longer, slower breaths, steam swirling into the yellow light of the streetlamps.

I began glancing left and right and behind us. Murphy remained at the lead, quiet. I didn't think we had to worry about an ambush, but he was unpredictable. When we reached the lawn of Holy Redeemer High School, he stepped up on the grass, and we followed him into the shadow of the building, a blocky, prisonlike structure.

Finally, Murphy stopped and whirled toward Riordan. "Tom, don't try to strong-arm me. You've got more to lose than I do."

Riordan bit the end off a cigar and spit it to the side. "Andy, you'll be going to prison for the rest of your miserable life. Our wire proves you're involved in a conspiracy to commit murder." He lit a match and started puffing on the cigar while the match flared.

"What makes you think I know where Eli Sanford and Sapph—Helen—are?" He turned, and the umbrella scraped against the wall, sending a shower of water down the side of the building. Murphy glanced back at it and then quickly returned his gaze to Riordan. He was jumpy. That was good. We were getting to him.

Riordan pulled the cigar from his mouth, holding it between his thumb and forefinger, and used it to point at Murphy. "Eli Sanford—any condition; Helen—alive and well; the wire you've got on me."

"I'd have to have proof this is on a wire," Murphy said.

"We can meet at the Detroit Suffrage Club at 9:00 A.M. tomorrow,"

Riordan said. "There's a telegraphone we can play the wires on. Bring Helen to that meeting. I need Eli before then."

"No—a neutral location, and I don't think I can come up with either of them that quickly, if at all. I don't know where they are."

"Bullshit," I said. "You know where Helen is, and it's not Peoria. I'd guess if Eli can find you so easily, you can find him if you want to."

"Nine o'clock," Riordan said. "Where?"

"Noon," Murphy said. "I'll be lucky to find either of them by then."

Riordan glanced at me, and I nodded. Elizabeth's rally wouldn't begin until 7:00 P.M.

"All right, then, Union Depot," Murphy said. "We'll take an office there."

Riordan took a long draw on the cigar. "I pick the office."

"We can't get it until morning anyway. We can agree on one when we get there."

"Fair enough."

"You bring the Dictograph," Murphy said.

I nodded.

"This is the only chance you get, Andy," Riordan said. "After this, all the weight I can bring is coming down on you."

Murphy gave him a sly smile. "I think I see how much weight you've got behind you these days, Tom. Don't worry. If goddamn Peterson there actually has the wire, you'll get what you want."

Detective Riordan wanted to contact a few policemen he knew to be loyal to him to start a search for Eli Sanford, so I drove him to the Bethune Street station. We agreed that I would phone him at the station in the morning to finalize our plan.

Ralphie had a telegram for me. I brought it up to my apartment. When I tried my door and found it both closed and locked, I thought I ought to be delighted, after finding it unlocked or open so many times recently. Once inside, I ripped open the envelope. Below my name and address, the telegram read:

Dear Mr. Anderson:
I would be happy to take over the investigation you have
capably begun. Please wire particulars soonest.
　　　　Yours,
　　　　William J. Burns
　　　　William J. Burns International Detective Agency

No longer did I have mixed emotions on this topic. If we hoped to allow Detective Riordan to escape his predicament, we couldn't let William Burns or his men get involved in any way. I would decline with apologies to Brennan and deal with the ramifications later.

My head throbbed. It seemed so long since I had felt rested. I desperately needed at least a few hours' sleep tonight. Our plan seemed a sound one. Nothing I did before tomorrow morning would move us any closer to safety.

I phoned suffrage headquarters, asked them to give Brennan my message regarding William Burns's offer, and told them I would contact Elizabeth in the morning. That done, I climbed into bed fully clothed and lay there, looking up at the ceiling. What had I forgotten? We had no margin for error if we were to ensure Elizabeth's safety.

My telephone rang. I jumped up and ran to the den.

It was Riordan. "Are you still dressed?"

"Yes."

"I'll pick you up in ten minutes. Be down at the street."

"I was thinking about getting some sleep."

"You'll want to see this." The receiver clicked onto the hook.

The face was familiar—the smooth skin with no trace of whiskers, still wet from the river, the bright blue eyes, duller now, long nose that ended in a point, wavy black hair matted to the side of his head. Now, however, his skin color reminded me of industrial zinc, blue-white, cold, dead.

We'd just arrived at the pier north of Michigan Alkali in Ford City, ten miles or so downriver of Detroit. Eli's throat gaped open two inches from top to bottom. The cut ran nearly ear to ear. The blood had washed away, marbling the wound in pale whites and pinks. Tubes, tendons, muscle, slashed by a very sharp knife.

We stood on the pier, Riordan, me, and a uniformed policeman from Ford City, watching a doctor finish his examination of the body. Rain fell through the arc of a floodlight above us in extended white streaks, looking like it was raining harder than it felt.

Riordan squatted down next to Eli and pivoted to look up at me. "Well, 'Goddamn Peterson,' it looks like we put a scare into Mr. Murphy."

The policeman cocked his head at Detective Riordan. "Is it Sanford?"

"Yep," Riordan said. "When did he turn up?"

"About an hour ago," the cop said.

Riordan leaned in toward Eli. "Looks pretty fresh to me."

The doctor, a gangly man in a green rain slicker, glanced over at Riordan but didn't say anything.

"You got an opinion, Doc?" Riordan asked. "How long it's been since he got that necktie?"

He shrugged, picked up his bag, and stood. "I'd need to get him on a table to make anything more than an educated guess."

"A guess'll do," Riordan said.

"He was bled out before he got dumped in the water—I'd say probably yesterday."

"How about early this afternoon?" I asked. "I know he was alive until then."

The doctor squinted at me. "You see him?"

"Something like that."

"Well, like I said, it wasn't anything more than an educated guess. There are a lot of variables. I'd have to run some tests."

Riordan poked around at Eli's throat with a pencil, then squinted up at the policeman. "How long's it take a body to float here from the city?"

The cop threw a glance out at the water. "River's up. Hour, maybe two, if he didn't snag on nothin' before."

"How long ago was it we left Murphy's?" Riordan asked me.

I pulled out my watch—11:49. I remembered the clock gonging eight while we were still inside the house. "Three and a half hours."

"Plenty long enough for one of his henchmen to slice up old Eli here and start him on his trip to Lake Erie."

"I'll have the report over in the morning," the doctor told the policeman before starting up the pier. "Good night, gentlemen."

"Doc?" Riordan said.

The doctor stopped and turned around.

"Are you saying he couldn't have been killed in the last four hours?"

"No." The doctor turned and walked out of the light. "I'm saying I'd need tests."

"It doesn't matter," I said. "Maybe Murphy followed him and had him killed right after he left the office." I thought about chasing after Eli. He had turned into smoke. "No! I know what happened. I assumed. Shit, that's got to be it!"

"What?" Riordan asked.

"Shortly after Eli concluded their conversation, the MLA door opened and closed. Maybe ten seconds later, Murphy and one of his men left. I assumed the first person whose steps I heard leaving the office was Eli, but when I ran after him, he had vanished into thin air. So change the assumption. There was only one clerical worker in the office. They make her leave first and then incapacitate Eli. Murphy and one of his men leave while his other slits Eli's throat. After the building closed at five, he could have gotten the body out of there a dozen ways and then dumped it in the drink." I looked at Riordan. "Right? That would work."

"Sounds plausible to me," the other policeman said.

"Yeah, seems to work," Riordan agreed. "That would explain the doc thinking he's been dead longer. That would mean Murphy didn't do this because we scared him tonight. He did it to keep Eli from killing Elizabeth."

"Frankly, I'm just glad the son of a bitch is dead," I said. "No matter how or when, the fact is, we don't need to worry about Eli anymore." A load of concrete seemed to fall off my back. The stakes had just been lowered to a manageable level. Elizabeth was safe. Now we just needed to get Helen from Murphy's clutches and get Riordan's wire back.

Just.

I'd already filled Riordan in on the telegram from William Burns and my response to Brennan. On the drive back to Detroit, he was quiet, occasionally flipping the wiper blade across the windscreen, otherwise pulling on the cigar and sticking out his jaw to let the smoke drift up past his eyes. When the lights of the city were in sight, he said, "Don't forget, we've pushed a rat into a corner. He could do anything. We can't let our guard down on him or on Elizabeth just because the Sanford brothers are out of the picture. There are still plenty of lunatics who would like to see their names in the newspapers."

"Understood."

"I think she's safe for tomorrow, anyway, or as safe as anyone in politics can be in these times. I know I'll sleep better, and now it's looking like I'll get a couple hours tonight."

He stopped the car outside suffrage headquarters. The lobby lights were still on, though no one was in sight or standing at the door. I wondered at that, but when I knocked, Warren Brennan answered the door and asked us in before locking up again.

"You know, Anderson," he said, "you dropped a big monkey wrench on my career. Was it payback?"

"No. The circumstances changed, that's all."

"I'll put in a word for you if that would help," Riordan said to him.

Brennan looked surprised. "Yeah, maybe, Detective. That might help." He excused himself to get Elizabeth.

She met us in the deserted lobby, and Riordan and I filled her in on recent developments. The news of Eli's death disturbed her, though I read a stronger sense of relief on her face. When we were done, Riordan stood stiffly, hesitating, his fedora twisted in his fists. "Elizabeth?" he mumbled.

"Yes, Thomas?"

"I'm sorry. I've betrayed your trust."

"Nonsense." She saw his face and stopped, then glanced at me. I looked away. Reaching out to touch his arm, she said quietly, "What, Thomas? What did you do?"

He stared at the floor in front of him. "First, I want you to know that Will's a good man, better than me." A sound that might have been a laugh forced its way out of his throat. "A whole lot better. I can't ever make up for what I've done to him, or to you."

Elizabeth stared at me, dumbfounded, her eyes wide and questioning. I gave her a short shake of the head and looked back at Riordan.

"He's done everything I should have been doing." He met Elizabeth's gaze, and tears shone in his eyes. "I'll make it up to you some-how." Now his eyes took me in as well. "Both of you. Somehow."

"The two of you should talk," I said.

Elizabeth nodded. "That's fine. Will, I hate to ask again, but could you see the boys home?"

"They came back?"

She shrugged. "It's hard to keep them away. It's far past their bed-times and they're getting cranky."

"You mean Francis is getting cranky."

"Francis is always cranky," she said with a smile.

"All right. I'll come back for you."

"Mr. Brennan and his men are going to escort me. Why don't you find an empty bedroom at my house, and we can talk in the morning."

Brennan's men were competent, and the only identified threat had been eliminated, not to mention that I could barely keep my eyes propped open. "A bed sounds awfully nice."

"The boys are in my office," she said, nodding toward the hallway. She turned back to Riordan. "Let's find a place to talk, Thomas."

Not meeting her eyes, he nodded.

I walked down the hall to Elizabeth's office and knocked. "Closing time!" I called. "Time to go home!"

Chairs scraped, metal clanged, people scrambled.

I tried the door. It was locked. "Francis! Robert! Come on, we've got to go."

"We are nearly ready, John Doe!" Francis shouted. The scrambling continued unabated.

"What are you doing in there?" I asked.

"I said we are nearly ready, you nincompoop!" Francis shouted.

Finally the door opened. Francis—wearing regular clothing—and Robert marched out. I glanced into the room. One of the consoles that had been torn apart, the second telegraphone, had been reassembled in some bizarre configuration with pieces from the Victrola sticking from it like they'd built some sort of electronic Frankenstein, stuck together with baling wire and string. Wires and unused parts were strewn across the table and the floor.

Bad idea to take two machines apart at once, I thought, chuckling to myself, *when you don't have schematics.* Perhaps I could give them a hand setting it right before Elizabeth had to return them. I managed a straight face by the time I met up with the boys at the door.

"Ready?" I asked.

"Yes," Francis said. "We need to leave now."

"That's good," I said. "Let's go catch a streetcar."

Brennan let us out, and the three of us waited at the stop silently, the rain, softer now, pattering against the cobbles and tapping against our hats. When the car came, we climbed on. It was late enough that only two other men were on board. The boys waited until I sat near the back to walk up the aisle and sit in the front row. I didn't mind. I just needed to keep an eye on them. They talked in fits and starts along the way. I heard bits and pieces—talk of pickup magnets, wiring, take-up reels. I thought it a good sign that they were so concerned about fixing the machines. A conscience was a sometimes necessary evil.

It was nearly 2:00 A.M. when we got to the Humes' house. Alberts, dressed in a nightshirt and cap, wearing a blue bathrobe and slippers, answered the door, his eyes barely open. He looked more tired than I felt. He locked the door behind us and walked away without a word. Francis and Robert had lent an entirely new dimension to the household—and probably doubled his workload.

"Off to bed with you two," I whispered.

"We will be going up soon, John Doe," Francis said, his left eyebrow rising half an inch.

"Okay, well, I'm going to bed."

They both stared back at me, Francis stonily, Robert with his twitchy little smile. I walked to the staircase and started up the steps, glancing back at them. They still stood where they had, watching me.

Well, the Humes knew by now what they had gotten into. Francis and Robert had their own minds. Since they hadn't burned the house down by now, I didn't think it would happen tonight.

The bedroom door creaked open. "Will?" Elizabeth whispered. "Are you still awake?"

"Oh, uh, yes, sure." I'd fallen asleep the second I climbed into bed.

"Is everything okay?" The room lit only by a far-off hallway light, she padded in and sat on the edge of the bed.

I wondered. "Are Francis and Robert still up?"

"No, everyone's asleep."

"Then I think it's okay."

She reached out and rubbed the backs of her fingers against my cheek. "I'll never doubt you again."

"Honey, I need you to keep doubting me. Okay, not all the time like it's been lately, but I've learned I have very bad instincts. I think I'm getting control of them, but you are the levelheaded one. I'll tell you what—just don't doubt my sanity again."

"Deal," she said and leaned down and kissed my forehead. I pulled her to me, and she wriggled around to lie on the bed. "Will you be able to get back Thomas's wire?"

"I think so. Murphy would be a fool not to make the trade. You don't have doubts about us going through with this, do you?"

"Why would I?" She laid her arm across my chest and snuggled closer.

"We have a wire that would destroy the Michigan antisuffrage movement in about two minutes. It would also get Murphy sent to prison."

"And let Murphy have Thomas's wife sent to her death? No. I have no doubts."

I kissed her forehead. "Are you excited for the rally tomorrow night?"

"I am."

"How many days now until the election?"

"Thirteen."

"I knew you wouldn't have to think about it. Lizzie, I hope you win. I really do."

Her breathing slowed and deepened.

"Honey?" I said.

"Mm."

"You've got to go to your room. What would your mother say?"

She laughed, just a little one that showed itself by a chuff of air from her nose. She pushed herself to her feet.

"I think we can sleep late," I said. "We should be ready."

"Okay." She turned for the door. "G'night."

I wished her a good night and watched her leave, closing the door behind her. I clasped my hands behind my head, eyes open now, telling myself that we had everything under control. Murphy would give up Helen and Riordan's wire, and then I could join Elizabeth for the rally.

She and I were completely back to normal. In thirteen days, the amendment would pass, and women would finally have their say in Michigan elections.

In one day, it seemed, my life and prospects had turned one hundred eighty degrees.

I'd never had a day like this, and I had no reason to worry. Still, somehow, I knew.

It was all too simple.

CHAPTER THIRTY-TWO

Thursday, October 24, 1912

The red sandstone of Union Depot sharply defined its silhouette against a brilliant blue sky. The offices were located in the narrow six-story tower at the corner of Fort and Third, which was flanked by attached three-story covered platforms that blocked the rail yard from the cross streets, and finally the shorter train sheds that ran another hundred yards down Fort Street.

"It's a pretty good spot for a meet," Riordan said. "There's only one set of stairs up to the offices, and lots of people around to keep him honest."

"Yeah, seems that way to me, too. My stomach doesn't seem to believe it, though."

I glanced up at the central clock tower. Nearly ten. Two hours to the meeting. Riordan shut off the Chalmers, and we climbed out. It was a balmy day for mid-October, with the temperature already well into the sixties and the sun shining to beat the band. He locked the doors, something I had thought unnecessary for a police car, but then again, this was Detroit.

"We'd better assume he's got people here already," Riordan said. "So be on your guard."

I gave him a tight nod.

"We'll get the telegraphone when we have an office," Riordan said, pointing at the boxy machine in the backseat—Brennan's telegraphone.

"Fine. I'm hanging on to the reel, though."

He nodded, and we walked the short distance into the station, where we stood for a moment in the lobby, then headed through the small crowd in the waiting room and along the platforms, looking for any sign of an ambush. After a look through the tower, peeking into every room, we walked down to the business office and asked to rent a conference room on the lowest floor available that had a good view of both Fort and Third streets. A small conference room on the corner of the third floor was available, and we took it for two hours. I had forgotten to bring any cash, so Riordan coughed up the two dollars. While I waited there, watching him through the window, Riordan returned to the Chalmers and carried in the telegraphone.

Satisfied, we waited, watching both the Fort and Third Street entrances for Murphy or any of his cohorts. Teamsters came and went, businessmen walked in and out, a few families disappeared inside. The tower shuddered every few minutes with a train coming in or out, and the wood floor vibrated with energy from the powerful locomotives.

I glanced over at Riordan. "Detective, what are we going to do if Murphy already killed Helen? Let's say he'll exchange the wire but says he can't locate her."

"Yeah," Riordan said. "That wouldn't surprise me. This is your operation. What do you want to do?"

"We need to get your wire, but the minute we hand over ours we lose all our leverage."

"For what it's worth," Riordan said, "I think he'll deal square. He's not going to take the chance of creating a national scandal and, more importantly, spending the rest of his life in prison."

"He may want to, but if he dispatched Eli that quickly, I don't doubt he'd have done the same to Helen. She was helping me."

"Think about it," he said. "I'm going to take another stroll through the building, see what's what. We'll talk when I get back. Lock the door behind me, and keep your pistol ready."

I followed him to the door and locked it, then returned to the window. Helen was no more than a pawn, the same role she'd played all her life. Riordan didn't care whether we got her from Murphy. He wanted the wire that could hang his wife, which was completely understandable. To Murphy, she was a pretty girl on his arm, a pliable, if not enthusiastic, mistress. He'd replace her without a thought.

How far would I go to save her? Was her life worth Anna Riordan's? Mrs. Riordan had killed a man who had raped her. Helen had been a prostitute and an accessory to murder, but she'd been kidnapped by white slavers, raped and forced to become addicted to drugs and sell herself.

What was this universal suffrage movement all about, anyway? The struggle for equality. Equality. With men. We were a long way from that. Men ruled the country, the state, the city, the home. Women ruled . . . the table? The bed? Even those were if, and only if, the man allowed it. In the eyes of the law, men ruled those as well. To think that Elizabeth, by far more intelligent and sensible than me, was not allowed to vote made the United States seem backward, colonial.

Helen never had a chance. Men had controlled her every movement since she got on that ship for America. I would not let her down. With Eli dead, the immediate threat to Elizabeth was gone. If this took a day, or longer, it wouldn't matter.

Riordan made additional forays through the building every twenty minutes, to look for signs of a double-cross. He saw none. At five minutes after noon, I got Detective Riordan's attention and pointed out the window. A red 1913 Abbott-Detroit limousine pulled to the curb on Fort. All the curtains in the rear were drawn. From the window, all I could see was a driver decked out in black livery. "If this is him," I said, "it's a different driver. Usually it's Pepper."

"Pepper?"

"The dark thug."

The driver left the automobile at the curb, looked nervously down both streets, and marched inside, a folded piece of paper in his hand.

"Stay here. Lock it behind me." Riordan jumped up and hurried out the door.

I did as he asked and had to wait only a few minutes before he returned with the paper in hand. With a sour look on his face, he handed it to me. I flipped it open and read:

Mr. Riordan and Peterson,
I am doing everything within my power to meet your demands.
Demand 1 is in my possession, and I am prepared to give it to you.
Demand 2, the man, is no longer anyone's concern, which Mr. Riordan
ought to be able to confirm.
Which brings me to Demand 3. The woman has been delayed on her
trip from Illinois. The railroad estimates her train will arrive around
five o'clock this afternoon. I had planned on being able to meet all your
demands by noon, but I have been done in by what they say is a faulty
oil cup.
I throw myself on your mercy. Assuming you are willing to wait so that
I might complete my end of the bargain, please tell the man bearing this
note where you would like me to contact you with a new meeting time.
A.M.

Riordan had fallen into one of the chairs at the table. He looked up at me, defeat writ on his face.

"Shit," I said. "He's lying. She never went to Peoria."

"I'll do what you want, Will. If you want to give your wire to Burns, just give me a couple of hours to clear out of town."

"We'll wait," I said.

"What do you want me to tell him?"

"I'm not keen on sitting here for five more hours. What do you think?"

His eyes narrowed. "We need to stay away from Elizabeth and our families. It's possible they'll tail us and try to snatch the wire."

"How about my apartment? You bring an arsenal, and we'll mow 'em down as they come in."

He shrugged. "If that's what you want."

"Tell him to phone us at this number." I scrawled my telephone number on the bottom on the page and ripped off that section. "We'll just have to stay on our toes. It won't take him five minutes to put an address to that number."

Riordan and I sat in the parlor. I had my Colt .32, four daggers, and a sawed-off shotgun he'd lent me. He had a pair of Colt .45s, which he said would be enough unless Murphy brought an army. We'd been sitting there for three hours now. Both of us had made numerous forays downstairs to look around, and one of us always sat near the window over the fire escape, both to watch the back of the building and ensure no one snuck up on us from there.

At four forty-five my telephone rang. I ran to the den and snatched it up. "Hello?"

"Mr. Anderson, I presume?" Murphy. He knew who I was now.

"Have you got her?" I asked.

"The train will be pulling in any minute. She's being picked up by one of my men."

"Where and when?"

"There's a little house on Dumfries I believe you're familiar with," he said. "We'll be there at six."

"That's not acceptable. We want a public place."

"This is not a public matter. I will bring my wire and Miss Xanakis. You bring your telegraphone and your wire. We'll trade, and everyone will be happy. Do you follow?"

"Of course I follow, but—"

"If you're not there, my wire will be turned over to the authorities— and I'll think of something to do with Sapphira; don't you worry about that." Click.

I stood with the receiver in hand, staring at the telephone.

"What did he say?" Riordan called from the parlor.

I walked down the hall and explained what Murphy wanted.

"How do you want to play it?" Riordan asked.

I was shocked he was asking me. I shrugged. "I say we do it. We need to get your wire, and I need to get Helen away from him."

He stood and walked over to me. Putting his hand on my shoulder, he said, "It's his place and his terms. We're going to be on foreign ground. If at any time you want to call it off, say the word. There's no shame, no judgment. I know you're doing this for me and Anna."

"And Elizabeth . . . and Helen, too."

"All right," he said. "Let's saddle up."

The house was empty when we arrived at a quarter past five. Outside, the conveyor clanked and creaked, and the salt blocks boomed. We searched the house with painstaking detail before I lugged in the telegraphone and set it on the kitchen table. Nothing had changed since my last trip here other than a pile of bird bones, from small chickens perhaps, or more likely pigeons, that had been tossed into a corner of the kitchen. Someone had been camping out here, but there was no sign of any inhabitants now.

Riordan hoisted himself up on the counter and popped the magazine out of one of his pistols. "I imagine they're going to ask us to give up our weapons, and in return they will do the same. I don't trust Murphy enough to give up my guns. If it comes to it, I'll just shoot them all."

"Hopefully it won't come to it."

Shortly before six, a car pulled up in front. I walked into the parlor and looked out the window. The red Abbott-Detroit limousine sat at the curb. The driver who'd come to the train station jumped out and opened one of the rear doors. Murphy climbed out, and Salt hurried out the other side. Murphy said something to the driver before he and Salt walked toward the house, crunching over the hard white crust. The car stayed put.

Even though he hadn't made a sound, I could feel Riordan's presence behind me. "No Helen," I said, "and no Pepper."

In back, the conveyor slowed and stopped.

"She could be in the car, but you can't expect he brought her." Riordan unbuttoned his suit coat, pushed it back to expose the big pistols he wore on his hips, and walked to the front door. "He wants to see our hand first." He opened the door and looked back at me. "Be ready to shoot. Aim for the chest, not the head. You'll hit your man twice as often."

I nodded and pulled my Colt from the shoulder holster, holding it at my side.

Andrew Murphy and Salt walked through the door. Murphy drew on his pipe. "Well, gentleman, shall we?"

Riordan and I shared a glance before he nodded toward the kitchen. Murphy showed a bit of courage by going first, and Riordan followed him. Salt and I waited for the other until finally I said, "Get in there. Now."

He glared at me and then smiled a crooked smile. Slowly he pushed himself off the wall and sauntered in behind Riordan, and I followed him.

No demands to drop our weapons. It seemed too easy.

When I walked into the kitchen, Murphy was standing over the telegraphone. "Electro-Insecto-Annihilator," he muttered. "How could I have been so stupid?"

"Where's Helen?" I asked.

"Let's get to the evidence first." Murphy knocked his pipe against his heel, clearing the ash, and set to refill it from a red and blue tobacco tin.

"You've got one chance at this, Andy," Riordan said. "We trade reel for reel, but you have to produce Helen Xanakis before you leave with our wire."

"Once I signal my driver, he'll bring her here," Murphy said. "She's close by. If your wire is what you say it is, we'll do this just like you wanted."

"You don't get our wire without delivering her," I said.

Murphy looked at Riordan. "What'd I just say? Has he got a hearing problem?"

Riordan glanced at me, holding his hand at his side, pressing his palm down. *Cool off. I have this under control.* "Let's hear yours first," he said.

Murphy shrugged, waved at Salt, and went back to chugging on his pipe. The smoke filtered through the room, filling it with the woodsy odor I'd smelled at the Dime. Salt threaded their wire through the machine, handed the receiver to Detective Riordan, and played their recording. He was satisfied, but Murphy insisted I listen, too. I admit I was curious. Salt wound the wire back and turned the switch. The recording started playing through the receiver. It was Riordan and another man, apparently Thomas Glinnan, shooting the breeze. The electronic hum was nearly inaudible. It helped to have a professional setup.

After about two minutes of insignificant conversation, Glinnan said, "No word from St. Kitts?"

"No. The warrant's still out there, but nobody's come looking for her."

"That's good, Tommy," Glinnan said. "She's a sweet girl, your Anna." They were quiet a moment before he asked, "What would you do if they came for her?"

"We'd run. Out west, Mexico, Canada, somewhere. I'd find a job.

She can teach or sew or a half dozen other things. I'm not letting her hang."

"What about Katie?"

"She's got her own life now. We'd give her the option, but I think she'd stay. It's her last year at Michigan State Normal College. Next year she can teach."

"That's fine, just fine, Tommy. You've got to be a proud papa. You know, it's hard to imagine that sweet Anna of yours cuttin' a throat."

Riordan laughed. "Only because you've never seen her mad, Tom. She'd dig him up and kill him again if she could."

And there we had it.

I hung the receiver on the hook.

"Satisfied?" Murphy demanded. "Both of you?"

We agreed that we were. Now I loaded our wire onto the telegraphone. Murphy ambled over to the table, puffing on his pipe. Once he had the receiver to his ear, I switched the machine to play.

He listened, his face first impassive, then becoming puzzled. Finally he threw the receiver at me, though the wire caught it before it hit me. Instead, the receiver fell short and swung back and forth under the table. "What the hell are you trying to pull?"

"What do you mean?" I asked.

"Some moron singing, and a coupla idiots talking? I'm supposed to trade you for that?"

"What are you talking about?" I asked.

"Listen to it. Sounds to me like Mrs. Riordan's gonna be movin' back to a warm climate." He leaned against the counter next to his man.

Riordan's eyes were wide. I started the reel winding back and said, "This is the right reel. I put it in the safe myself."

It reached the beginning. I started it playing and put the receiver to my ear.

"Fifteen men on the dead man's che-est," Francis sang, "yo-ho-ho and a bottle of rum. Drink and the devil had done for the re-est, yo-ho-ho and a bottle of rum."

What the hell? The load of concrete that had fallen off my back with the news of Eli's death now dropped to the bottom of my stomach. *This . . . makes no sense.*

He sang for another thirty seconds. All the while I was searching my memory. I gave this reel to Francis. Had he put it in the safe for some reason? Had there been two reels? No. I was positive. There had been only one.

What are we going to do? I wracked my brain for an idea.

A loud click popped in my ear. Robert said, "Is the horn right?"

"How many times do I have to tell you, Robert Hume, that you have to wind the wire counterclockwise?" Francis.

"It doesn't matter which way," Robert said meekly.

"If I have to come over there and do it myself," Francis barked, "I am going to smash you to smithereens!"

"Oh," Robert said. "Wait." Another loud click.

Hum. Another click and louder hum.

"Goddamn it," Murphy mumbled on the wire, barely audible underneath the noise. "Yeah, send him in." Louder, "You two get out of here." It sounded terrible, much worse than I remembered.

A door opened. Voices said something quiet that was garbled in the noise on the wire.

Slam. "Goddamn it," Murphy said, "I thought we agreed we would only talk on the telephone." *Good. I could hear him.*

"I think our agreement ended when you killed my brother."

"Your brother? He's dead?"

"I'd think you'd be a better liar, Andrew, as much practice as you get."

The sound was awful, but I could hear it all. I listened to the end, then wound the reel back a dozen turns, listened and adjusted it to the beginning of Murphy's conversation with Eli. Switching it off, I looked up at Murphy. "We just weren't to that spot on the wire." I held the receiver toward him. "Listen."

After making a point of dramatically pushing himself from the counter with a big exhale, he sauntered over and ripped the receiver from my hand. "Play the goddamn thing."

I did.

He listened, his face carefully neutral. When it was over, he threw the receiver down on the table and looked at Salt. "Have him pick her up."

CHAPTER THIRTY-THREE

Salt walked into the parlor. I shadowed him. He stopped at the window and signaled the driver, who started up the limousine and drove off. Even under the circumstances, I realized how odd it was to see a gasoline automobile start moving without the driver climbing out and cranking the starter. It was hard to get used to.

Salt walked back to the kitchen, and again I followed him, watching his hands, which remained at his side.

"Any recommendations, Thomas, on a replacement for you?" Murphy asked.

Riordan just gave him a sour look.

"No less than I expected." Murphy turned to me. "And you, Mr. Electric Executioner, what are you going to do with Sapphira? Is she your sweetheart?"

"I'm going to let her start over. You and your kind are why we need suffrage. I'm ashamed to be of the same species."

He laughed. "The arrogance of youth, eh, Tommy? We've seen a bit more of life. I daresay you have a different take on the young lady; am I right?"

Again, Riordan didn't answer.

"A child like you wouldn't understand, Mr. Anderson, particularly given your upbringing. By the time you reach my age, or even the age of the detective here, you'll be singing a different tune. Your idealism is a lovely thing to see, but I'm happier knowing that in twenty years it won't even be a memory. I'm sure you're familiar with the phrase 'The ends justify the means.'"

"Of course. I don't believe it applies."

Smiling, he said, "Women voting would be the worst thing that could happen to this country. The U.S. of A is on the brink of greatness. To get there, we need strong leadership, a willingness to join a fight, to start one if necessary. If the weaker sex is allowed to choose our leaders, we'll end up with namby-pambies who want nothing more than to make sure all the momma's boys don't get hurt. This country will retreat, rather than charge. Do you really want that?"

My face had been getting hot through his monologue, and I wanted to knock a few of his teeth down his throat to shut him up. Instead I said, "I'm happy for you that you find yourself so superior. Delusions of grandeur aren't unusual in criminals."

He laughed again. "You think me a criminal, yet you are undertaking this little enterprise to get a murderer and a whore off the hook. You're not a criminal?"

"It's a matter of honor, which I don't expect you to understand."

"Honor." He smiled. "Let me tell you about honor, Sunny Jim. The people of my old country have been trying to throw off the yoke of the Brits since they discovered our little island. Last year, an eight-year-old Irish boy gave his life to kill two of the Tommys. An eight-year-old, can you imagine? Now that's honor."

"Tommys?" I asked.

"Redcoats, you called 'em. Listen, Anderson, you think you're on the side of the just, which, if you don't mind me sayin', is what's wrong with your bloody country. You all believe God shines his blessings down on America, that this is the ultimate society. Onward Christian Soldiers and all that. But you're just lookin' at one side. I don't expect you'd see any different if you looked at another side, but there's a lot of 'em. There's a lot of ways to be right, young Mr. Anderson. One of these days, you'll learn that."

Riordan rested a hand on the butt of one of his pistols. "You're giving me a headache, Andy. Why don't you shut it?"

The rumble of a gasoline engine got louder and then silenced. All of our eyes went to the front of the house. Salt and I returned to the window in the parlor. Murphy and Riordan stayed behind.

The limousine had returned. Pepper climbed out and pulled Helen from the car. She wore no coat, just a white shirtwaist, a gray skirt, and a pair of button-top shoes. She was unsteady, wobbly. Pepper held her up by the arm as she stumbled toward the house, her head lolling forward. "Murphy?" I called. "What did you do to her?"

"Nothing she wouldn'ta done to herself," he said.

Her legs gave out underneath her, and she collapsed, held up only by Pepper, who dragged her forward. Salt opened the front door. When Pepper reached it, he wrapped an arm around Helen's waist, hoisted her up sideways, and squeezed through the door.

They carried her to the kitchen and dumped her on the floor. I knelt down next to her. Her eyes had rolled up in her head. Her mouth was flecked with white spittle. I shook her, and she didn't respond in any way.

I jumped up and spun toward Murphy. "What did you do to her, you son of a bitch?"

"Gentlemen," he said, "I don't think the bargain you proposed was entirely fair. You wanted three things from me and were only going to give me one. I've already taken care of one of them, which ought to be enough for a fair trade, but just to show good faith, I'm going to give you another. You can have the detective's wire, or you can have Miss Xanakis here, who is, what?" He looked at Pepper. "Thirty minutes, an hour, tops, from death by way of an opium overdose?"

Pepper nodded. I noticed now that both he and Salt had cleared their coats from their holsters in case there was gunfire.

"Still time to get her to the hospital," Murphy said, "and get her stomach pumped. She ate a ball of the stuff, so most of it's still there."

"You son of a—"

"What happens to the wire if we take her?" Riordan asked.

I stared at him, astonished.

"Our deal stays as is, Tom. You help me until the election's over and then I give it to you."

"If she dies, you're next," I said.

Murphy laughed. "Such bluster!" He made a point of looking at his watch. "You're wasting precious time. What'll it be?"

"We'll take her," Riordan said.

"Are you sure?" I asked.

He shrugged. "We can't let her die."

Murphy began reloading his pipe again from the red and blue tin. The wood-fire smell. A thought began to niggle at me. I looked carefully at the tin.

Par Excellence Tobacco—not Old English. "Wait. Don't you smoke Old English?"

"Not unless there's nothin' else available," he said.

I rushed up to him, grabbed his lapels, and pinned him against the wall. His pipe and the tobacco tin clattered to the floor. "Tell me the truth!" I shouted. "Did you break into my apartment?"

His men grabbed my arms and wrestled me off of Murphy.

I fought against them. "Tell me! Was it you?"

Riordan stepped in front of me, his palm flat against my chest. "Will! Give him the wire and let's get out of here while she's breathing."

"Tell me!" I shouted.

Murphy jerked down the lapels of his coat. "If you think I do my own field work, then you understand even less than I thought."

Dread began to fill my mind. "It wasn't Eli in your office yesterday, was it? David Sanford's alive, isn't he?"

Murphy hesitated a split second, just long enough for me to realize he was going to lie to me. "You saw him get killed, didn't you?" he asked.

"I thought I did." I threw the wire reel at him, then bent down and picked up Helen under the arms. Dragging her toward the door, I shouted, "Come on, Riordan! She's not the only one we need to save."

I carried Helen toward the car while Riordan backed down the yard with his hands on the butts of his guns, watching the house. "What are you doing?" he asked.

"I'll tell you in the car. We've got to hurry!"

I pulled Helen into the backseat and propped her head on my lap. She was barely breathing now. Riordan ran around the front and cranked the starter. Nothing. Again. Nothing.

"Come on!" I shouted.

On the third try, the engine caught, and he jumped in. "What the hell was that?" He threw the car into gear and started down the road.

"I need you to drop me at Wayne Gardens on the way to the hospital," I said.

"Why? What do you know about Sanford? You're the one who convinced me he was dead."

I filled him in on my epiphany. First I told him about smelling Old English in my apartment—after David had been killed. Murphy's operatives didn't smoke pipes. Salt smoked cigarettes, and Pepper smoked cigars. Even if Murphy had lied about "field work," I believed that he wasn't an Old English tobacco smoker. The only time I saw him smoking it was that first night at the party. He stopped David on his way out and could easily have given him back the tin that David used later. The two were identical. My only assumption was that they were the same tin.

"Why couldn't it have been Eli?" Riordan asked. "You don't know if he smoked, do you?"

"I have it on good authority that he didn't."

Perhaps it was coincidence. Perhaps I had only imagined the smell of Old English in my apartment. Perhaps David really had been killed that night by the river.

No. It was too convenient. David Sanford must have killed Roger Flikklund, and Murphy needed him out of the picture—but couldn't kill him because of Eli. Eli pretended to shoot him—with me as a witness—and David had fallen backward, into one of the boats, perhaps, and covered himself with a tarpaulin. It was someone else with his identification who had been shot in the face and dumped into the river. I hadn't really thought about it at the time, but there had been a delay between David tumbling over the edge and the splash.

What Brennan said about smelling a killer had stuck with me. David Sanford had always made me uneasy. Maybe I had that same sense Brennan did.

Anyway, with Murphy it was purely business. David's motivation had nothing to do with business or the amendment.

With David, it was a matter of family honor.

I set my weapons on the seat beside me. I'd never get in with them, and I couldn't afford the delay. As soon as Riordan slowed the car, I was off and running across the wide expanse of concrete in front of the convention center. Already I could hear the swell of the crowd, a buzzing, moaning creature, over which a woman's voice shouted.

David would shoot Elizabeth at the first opportunity.

I threw open one of the doors and ran inside.

"—is the end of men's rule!" Elizabeth's voice boomed out of the single open pair of doors, in front of which stood two uniformed policemen. "We have the power to throw off the chains of slavery, the yoke that has been forced upon us!" The crowd roared.

Both policemen stepped in front of the doors. One drew his sidearm. I pulled up short in front of them and raised my hands. "I'm unarmed. Just came to listen."

One of the men searched me. I stared inside as he did, my eyes scanning the huge room, looking desperately for Sanford. He was here. I could feel it. Finally, the cop finished and waved me in. I ran inside and plunged into the crowd, forcing my way in, shoving through the men and women.

Elizabeth continued, but her words were lost to me. My full concentration was on my search—every raised arm, every man moving toward the stage. I pushed and shoved, bulling my way through the crowded hall.

Now, as if I had been transported back in time, I saw a man in a gray suit slipping behind a marble pillar. He appeared on the other side, his face shaded by the brim of his fedora. But different, though—his eyes never left Elizabeth, who continued with her speech. Her fist slammed against the podium, but I couldn't make out her words. I was underwater, sounds dull and distorted, motion sluggish—or was it the crowd, too tight to move? I elbowed people aside, driving toward the front. The man in the gray suit was furtive, nervous. Blood roared in my ears. A hammer pounded inside my head, against the front of my skull.

Elizabeth exclaimed something, words emphatic. The crowd shouted its approval.

The man was gone, lost in the sea of hats. I zigzagged through the crowd toward the other side of the stage, my neck craned. There he was—fifty feet from the stairway that led up to the stage.

No . . . no . . . the steps were unguarded.

All the while, Elizabeth spoke, her voice soft and soothing, then strong and powerful, the words always just out of my grasp. The audience applauded, whistled.

The man in the gray suit reached the stairway and bolted up into the darkness without once looking back. I hurled myself through the mass of people, pushing and shoving. Finally, I reached the front and ran up the steps two at a time.

The voice was different, new words, new sounds, underwater, dull, indistinct.

Without thinking about any other location, I ran around the back of the stage, ignoring the few men I passed, knowing they would not be the one for whom I was looking. Each step took an eternity, until all at once I burst out from the darkness.

There he was, just as before, staring at the women on the stage, a narrow beam of light angling across his chest. I ran toward him, but he was so far away, fifty feet or more. A glint flashed through the beam of light.

"Elizabeth!" I screamed.

Startled, the man turned and looked at me. The pistol had already cleared his belt, and he raised it, turning his body toward me, the barrel rising, flattening, the black hollow at the end pointed at my feet, then my thighs, now my midsection.

I was too far away to stop him. I ducked, my hands in front of me, as the gun flashed. My right hand tugged backward, hit. The report boomed, echoed.

David Sanford stared down the barrel at me as I clawed toward him, running through molasses, though I knew I was moving at top speed. Pain arced in lightning bolts from my hand, my already destroyed hand. Time slowed to nothing. The corners of David's mouth turned up, his thoughts passing through me.

Will, he thought, *it's about time you figured this out.*

I was still five strides away. His finger tensed, tightening on the trigger. I stared into the barrel, getting larger and larger, now pointed at my eyes, big enough to swallow me. No one could miss from this distance.

"Elizabeth!" I shouted, thinking to warn her with my last breath.

David's head jerked to the left as his gun flashed again. *Crack!* A cannon blast shocked my ears. In that split second of doubt, I wondered if I would feel the bullet, if I would know I was dying. David staggered left half a step, caught his balance. The barrel of his gun flashed yet again, jumped, but now it was pointed at the ceiling. The report blasted my ears, echoing.

I dove for him, clawing for the gun, but I met only empty space. I fell hard to the boards, pandemonium in my ears, people screaming and shouting.

I rolled and looked up at a face framed in the lights, nearly a silhouette.

Brennan.

He leaned down toward me, speaking. A pistol hung from his hand, smoke rising from the barrel.

"Get Elizabeth out of here!" I shouted.

Another face appeared above me. My angel.

Elizabeth knelt on the floor next to me. Her hands caressed my face. Her tears fell into my eyes, onto my cheeks.

"Elizabeth!" I shouted, wrestling her to the floor to cover her. "David has a gun!"

She made noises, said something, hugged me to her. "Shh," she said now, cradling me like a baby. "He's gone, honey. He's gone."

CHAPTER THIRTY-FOUR

Friday, October 25, 1912

Andrew Murphy, please," I said.

"Your name, sir?" A different woman on the telephone than I'd heard before in the MLA office.

"Will Anderson. Tell him I've got something he needs to hear."

She asked me to wait. I raised my bandaged right hand in front of me, stretching out my fingers, feeling a sharp pain beneath the red dot in the center of the bandage where David's first bullet hit me.

Not half a minute later Andrew Murphy came on the line. "I owe you a big thank-you, Anderson. Not only do I have the leverage I need for the election, you cleaned up the one mess I'd made. My men found the wire his brother had that gave them . . . certain leverage over me."

When he finally shut up, I said, "Listen to this, you son of a bitch." I handed the receiver to Francis. He took the candlestick from the table in front of me and held the mouthpiece in the center of the horn of their bastardized telegraphone. I nodded to Robert, and he switched the machine to play.

Elizabeth and Detective Riordan stood in front of us, surveying the proceedings with worried looks on their faces.

A loud hum emanated from the horn. Now Murphy mumbled,

"Goddamn it," just audible over the noise on the wire. "Yeah," he said, "send him in. You two get out of here," the last part much clearer.

A door creaked. Murphy's thugs traded greetings with David Sanford.

The door closed again. "Goddamn it," Murphy said, "I thought we agreed we would only talk on the telephone."

"I think our agreement ended when you killed my brother," David Sanford said.

I couldn't help but smile listening to the recording spill out the horn of the machine Francis and Robert had modified to play out loud, rather than through a telephone receiver. From there it was simple enough for them to hold the sound collector from the Dictograph in front of the horn and create a reproduction of the recording on another machine. After I put the recording of Murphy into the Humes' safe, the boys had taken it back to suffrage headquarters and made a reproduction over the reel with Francis singing, and that was what I brought to the meet with Murphy. They'd hidden the original for safekeeping.

I let it play through the important parts before I asked Robert to switch it off. Francis gave me back the receiver and slid the candlestick onto the table in front of me. I leaned in and said, "How do you like those apples, asshole?"

"Asshole is a bad word," Robert muttered, as Murphy said, "How . . ."

"We've got the wire, Andrew," I said. "And I think we're going to leave it this way. Are you familiar with the word 'détente'?"

"W-what . . ." he sputtered. "No."

"How about 'mutual destruction'?"

"I think I understand that."

"If Riordan's wire is ever exposed, yours will be immediately released. It will destroy the MLA, and, as you are well aware, get you thrown in prison until you die. As much as we all would like to see that, we will be satisfied by you accepting this bargain."

"I'll have to think about—"

"This is a onetime offer, asshole. Accept it and hide that wire away somewhere very safe, and we'll do the same. We both own the means to destroy the other. Will you accept?"

He hesitated. "Ye-yes, I accept."

"Detective Riordan will no longer be doing your bidding. You are not to contact him for any reason. Do you follow?"

"Yes." Now he sounded sullen. At least I'd upset him. At least I got that.

"We are going to alert the authorities to an 'anonymous group's' plan to disrupt the polls in the city and warn the ward bosses that they will be monitored. You and your minions are to stay away from the election. Do you follow?"

"Yes."

I hung up the telephone and looked from Elizabeth to Detective Riordan. "Was that okay?"

"It's as good as we're going to get." Riordan looked at Elizabeth but didn't quite meet her eyes. "I'm sorry I kept you from being able to expose him."

"Will would never have gotten that recording had you not been involved, Thomas. We would have relied on you. That wouldn't have worked out for any of us. By the way, Dr. Miller called me. Helen is going to be okay."

Biting his lip, he nodded. "Good. If we're done here, I'm going home to give Anna a big hug."

"Go," Elizabeth said, and Riordan opened the door.

"Detective?" I said.

He stopped and turned toward me.

"What are you going to do? Are you staying in town?"

"I don't know. Anna and I will discuss it. It might be time for a change."

Elizabeth reached out and touched his arm. "Let us know what you decide."

He nodded and ducked out the door.

I looked at the boys. "All right, geniuses. Is it time for an Avenue dessert?"

Francis's left eyebrow raised half an inch, his eyes turned sleepy, and his mouth twitched. Pulling the tricorner hat onto his head, he said, "If you mean, is it time for *a number* of the Avenue Servself desserts each, then the answer is yes."

Robert just grinned.

EPILOGUE

November 25, 1912

I raised my handkerchief up to Elizabeth and gently wiped a tear from her cheek before sitting back again with my arm around her, sinking into the soft cushions of my new sofa.

We were both stunned. The amendment—the certain-to-win amendment—had been defeated by less than a thousand votes. Not even a day had passed since the announcement, and it seemed half the state was clamoring for answers, a recount, some sort of satisfaction. The newspapers trumpeted the accusations of treachery; Governor-elect Ferris had already put out a call for a recount. The suffragists weren't giving up, but it had been an unexpected blow, perhaps the final nail in the coffin.

"I'm done with this." Elizabeth leaned her shoulder in and rested her head against mine. "Can we go somewhere far away? Get away from everything for a long time? Perhaps I could show you Paris."

Paris. I pictured the avenues, the cafés, art, music, dancing. Another world.

The picture cracked, shattered into a million tiny pieces.

That world wasn't real. Elizabeth's Paris was an illusion built in my mind, an illusion built on fantasy, conjecture . . . hope.

The real Paris was no more or less stark and brutal and unforgiving than this city, the "Paris of the West," the city in which my friend David Sanford, who had tried to kill me, lay six feet underground, his eyes staring up into oblivion.

The city in which the man I thought most honorable was guilty of heinous crimes.

The city in which the woman I loved had been convinced beyond a shadow that I was mad.

The city that had torn my limbs, seared my mind, and nearly stolen my soul.

Paris. Was it different enough that I would be able to start anew, shed the memories that tied me to this city, become a different, a better person?

I looked at Elizabeth, my Elizabeth. I so wanted to please her.

"Lizzie?" I blew out a breath. "I'm not ready."

I wasn't finished with Detroit, nor, I was sure, was it finished with me.

AUTHOR'S NOTES

Ah, corruption! For a novelist, it's the stuff of dreams. Somehow, it's comforting to me that Detroit's problems with crooked politicians aren't the result of the collapse of the city's finances. No, the city was known a hundred years ago as one of the crookedest places in America.

In 1912, Detroit had its own scandal, that of the aldermen demanding bribes from the Wabash Railroad. This scandal played out as I've outlined it in this book, with a Mr. Brennan of the William J. Burns International Detective Agency sniffing out the demands for bribes via a Dictograph in a phony Wabash office. Burns was known as "America's Sherlock Holmes" for solving seemingly unsolvable cases, including the bombing of the Los Angeles Times Building, but in 1912 his trick—the use of Dictographs—became well known. Still, it was so rare and such cutting-edge technology that few criminals gave it a thought.

Many of the aldermen tried to move their meetings to safer places, but Brennan would only meet them at the office, for obvious reasons. Seventeen aldermen were arrested (although the cases against eight were so weak that the prosecution decided to go forward with only nine) including "Honest Tom" Glinnan, the secretary of the city council—and mayoral candidate—whose (alleged) demand was $1,000, more than any other.

Fittingly, it appears that the investigation was completely politically motivated. Glinnan was running for mayor. Andrew Green, a Democratic supporter, was encouraged by William Thompson, the incumbent Democratic mayor, to finance the Burns investigation and ended up spending $10,000 before it was over. The requests for bribes appear to have been entrapment—the Burns men and Green completely fabricated the story of the Wabash expansion. Of course, (allegedly) demanding bribes, entrapment or not, seems wrong, doesn't it?

The postscript to this investigation is that Glinnan was the only alderman whose case even went to trial. After two years of delays by the defense, he was tried in 1914. Mr. Brennan (actually Walter, not Warren, Brennan, but I thought readers' memories of actor Walter Brennan might make that distracting) and William J. Burns were repeatedly grilled by the defense. It seems that not all Burns operatives were beyond the occasional falsehood, and a few had been convicted of perjury prior to 1914, though neither Brennan nor Burns ever was. (Burns went on to become the director of the United States Bureau of Investigation, the predecessor of the FBI.) Even though the prosecution's evidence included Glinnan making the bribery demand, it took only forty-five minutes for the technophobic jury to find him not guilty.

The larger scandal, that of the fix in the vote for the universal suffrage amendment, was a statewide issue, though of course Detroit played its part. Nothing was ever proved, but the common wisdom was that liquor interests were behind what was clearly a fixed election. By this time, suffrage and prohibition had become almost one and the same in people's minds, and the brewers and distillers potentially had a lot to lose if women were allowed the vote.

In 1912, suffrage was on the ballot in six states (three of which passed their amendments). Michigan was a battleground, with many prominent suffrage supporters, including Jane Addams and Sylvia Pankhurst, stumping for the vote. By election day, full women's suffrage looked like a sure thing. After nearly a month of tallying ballots, during which time suffragists were assured they had won by 10,000, and later 5,000, votes, the amendment lost by 594 votes. Governor Osborn and Governor-elect Ferris demanded a recount, which revealed that tens of thousands of ballots, largely from Detroit, Saginaw, and Kalamazoo, had either been lost or burned, or had to be disallowed because the verbiage on the ballot was a summary, rather than the actual language of the amendment. Allegations of fraud at the polling places was another common theme, with diverse accusations including not initialing suffrage-amendment "yes" ballots and putting "yes" ballots into the wrong box, both of which would cause them to be disallowed, and the ever-popular bullying of likely "yes" voters to keep them away from the polls. The results of the recount showed the amendment lost by 760 votes.

The issue returned to the ballot in 1913 and lost again. Michigan women were unable to vote in all elections until 1918.

On October 14, 1912, Teddy Roosevelt, known to most Americans as TR or "the Colonel," was shot in the chest point-blank by John Schrank, a Bavarian-born anarchist, while stumping in Milwaukee. TR's folded fifty-page speech and steel spectacle case saved him by slowing down the bullet enough to keep him from being mortally wounded. He decided to go on with his planned speech after determining that his lung hadn't been punctured since he wasn't coughing up blood. He started his speech this way:

"Friends, I shall ask you to be as quiet as possible. I don't know whether you fully understand that I have just been shot; but it takes more than that to kill a Bull Moose. But fortunately I had my manuscript, so you see I was going to make a long speech, and there is a bullet—there is where the bullet went through—and it probably saved me from it going into my heart. The bullet is in me now, so that I cannot make a very long speech, but I will try my best."

The bullet remained lodged in his rib for the rest of his life. Schrank was committed to a Wisconsin asylum in 1914 after doctors determined him to be insane. (He claimed the ghost of President McKinley had ordered him to kill Roosevelt.) He remained there until his death twenty-nine years later. Upon TR's death in 1919, Schrank admitted that Roosevelt was a great American and said he was sorry to hear of the Colonel's death.

Finally, "white slavery" was a subject very much on the minds of Americans during the early twentieth century. Single women, native and immigrant, were moving to the big cities for jobs, and thousands of them were never heard from again. Many were kidnapped and sold into a life of prostitution and drug addiction; others were victims of violent criminals. The story of Sapphira Xanakis, while fictional, is representative of the lives of many of these poor women whose futures were hijacked from them.

Corruption I can make sense of, and I admit it's a fun topic to write about. Murder, oftentimes, is at least understandable. Trafficking in human beings, however, is so far beyond my comprehension as to seem outside the capability of our species.

If only it were so.